THE
PARDONER'S
TALE

THE PARDONER'S TALE

JOHN WAIN

THE VIKING PRESS   NEW YORK

Copyright © John Wain, 1978
All rights reserved
Published in 1979 by The Viking Press
625 Madison Avenue, New York, N.Y. 10022

LIBRARY OF CONGRESS CATALOGING IN PUBLICATION DATA
Wain, John.
The pardoner's tale.
I. Title.
pz4.w14Par   [pr6045.a249]   823'.9'14   78-24114
isbn 0-670-53825-6

Printed in the United States of America
Set in Photo Electra

Gloria's

THE PARDONER'S TALE

1

I STOPPED THE CAR AND GOT OUT AND EXAMINED THE vegetation. It looked all right. I wanted to be sure the sea didn't come in this far.

It didn't, I decided. The grass looked as if it were never under salt water, and there were some of those flowers, I don't know their names, that have rather dry, bushy, pink heads, like miniature chrysanthemums, and long droughty stems. They don't grow where the sea covers them. Otherwise, I would never have left the car anywhere but on the road. It's very hard to tell, on this jagged bit of the Gwynedd coast, what particular shape the sea has fretted into the land. It comes through all sorts of channels and inlets, very silently and suddenly. And salt-marsh grass can look like ordinary grass from fifty yards away.

I took out the two big green bags, and the heavy airship-grey skin. Then I locked the car and put the keys carefully away in the zip-up pouch of my anorak. Ready. Except for the little matter of assembling the canoe and getting it on the water.

They don't make folding canoes any more. It's all fibre-glass now. So I'm glad I got a folding one while you still could. It's a sweat, of course, putting it together and taking it apart, but if I didn't have a canoe that folds up and stows away I'd just have to give up canoeing. In a flat in town, there's no room for things like boats. And I haven't even got a garage. I rent a few feet of space in a multi-storey horror down the road. Not an inch of room to spare there either.

I looked round. The tide seemed to be still going out, but according to the tide-table in the *Caernarvon and Denbigh Herald* it would soon be on the turn. The nearest steel-grey glint of sea water looked about a quarter of a mile away. I stood on a rock, to see if I could spot an inlet any nearer, but I couldn't. If I assembled the boat here, it would be very heavy to drag to the water. If I took the two bags and the skin separately, it would mean two journeys. I'd have walked a mile before I got started.

I wondered, aloud, why I go on canoeing. There are always so many snags. But all the time, I knew. You get this marvellous feeling of freedom on the water. Having a fluid medium under you makes all your movements and rhythms different from what they are on land. I started canoeing when I was about fourteen, and now at forty-odd I still get the same release from it. With one difference – that when I was fourteen people weren't always trying to get me on the telephone, or corner me in the office and bore me with some squalid fuss over details. I run a press-cuttings agency. That's just as horrible as it sounds.

It was a dull, warm September afternoon. I'd spent a long lunch-time in a pub and was feeling drowsy. It almost seemed too much trouble to put the damned boat up. Two gulls drifted overhead, riding lazily on some air-current that wasn't perceptible at ground level. Everything was very quiet. The sun was away somewhere behind high white clouds, but you could feel its warmth in the air. For a moment I thought of just driving back to the cottage and having a good sleep. I was paying a fortune for the place, so I might as well get some rest there. Then I could go out to a restaurant tonight and perhaps see a film. It was a pretty un-eventful holiday, but that was what I wanted. Events had been a bit too thick on the ground with me of late.

Then I saw a channel of fresh water, not many yards off, making its way among the sand flats. I went over and looked. Yes, it was deep enough to float on. That decided me. I set to work like a madman. I tipped the rods out on to the grass – the longitudinal ones from the long bag, the stretchers and back-rests from the round bag – and laid out the skin. It was always a curious experience: like bringing a dead thing to life. You had to assemble the stern and the bow separately, and thrust them hard into the skin, and then lean heavily down on them to force them out flat. The assembly itself was partly a matter of using the brass fittings at the end of the rods, poking innumerable male bits into female bits, and partly of using the flexibility of the wood. It's beautiful wood. That's another reason I'm glad I got one of these canoes. Fibre-glass is just another dead substance, made by mixing chemicals in some factory. This wood grew out of the earth, and was lovingly cut and measured and polished.

My face was streaked with sweat by the time I had the boat assembled, and I'd given my fingers a hell of a pinch at one stage, bringing up a blood blister. Still, there I was. The boat was ready, the car was all right, I had the bags stowed under the deck, and we were ready for off.

I dragged the canoe over to the stream, put the two halves of the paddle together, and got in. It was difficult because the stream didn't have regular solid banks. It had just carved itself a channel through muddy sand. The bank caved in a couple of times as I was trying to hold the canoe still and get in. Each time it did that, I lost my balance and pushed the canoe out into midstream with the foot I had planted in it. I let off a few curses, choosing my words carefully so as to combine the worst obscenities I could think of, with a top-dressing of the names of people I disliked. That made me feel better. Finally I managed it. The bank held firm for just long enough, and though I took a fair amount of mud and sand into the canoe with me, I was water-borne at last and grasping the paddle firmly. All systems go.

There was a light, salty breeze on the water, just enough to make the spear-grass nod rhythmically, as if saluting me as I went past. When I reached the point where the fresh water emptied itself into the salt, there was that old twitch of excitement. Though this was no more than a finger of sea obtruding itself deep into the land, it was sea-water all the same, that magical, deadly substance. I was afloat, in my funny little rubber-skinned contraption, on the amniotic sea. Theoretically, though of course nothing would induce me to do so, I could paddle on till I got clear of Anglesey, out across the open sea, till I got to Ireland – or, for that matter, to Narragansett or New Orleans or Panama. If I lived that long.

Tiny waves slapped the bottom of the canoe, rocking it gently fore and aft. Having no keel, she pancaked gently on the water, and every ripple ran down her length like a caress. I began to relax. I could feel my neck muscles loosening up, my shoulders moving easily, the tensions of months of boring work and personal frustrations melting away.

I looked at my watch. Nearly half-past four. It had taken me longer than I realised to put the boat up. Or the pub session had gone on longer than I thought. Or both. Well, never mind. There were hours of September daylight left.

The tide had just about made up its mind, and turned. It was beginning now to pour in, silently yet with utter relentlessness, thousands of tons of water coming smoothly in to the straits, lapping over the weedy rocks and refreshing their green coating that had begun to parch, making the mussels open their shells, disturbing bait-diggers and a few late picnickers. Within a quarter of an hour, I found I was having to put more energy into paddling. Soon, the tide would become too fast to push against, and I would turn and go with it, into the estuary. I was content with that. The sun came out and made the mountains a soft, luminous green against the hazy sky.

Then I saw the car.

It was a little red Mini. Some crazy fool had driven it the whole way along a narrow spit of raised land, and parked it about fifty yards from the water's edge. The water's edge at low tide, that is. Already the sea had gained twenty or thirty of those yards and was pushing in all the time.

I hadn't seen the car before because a sandbank hid that particular spur. When I came in sight of it, I was already near enough to see that there was somebody sitting in it. A girl, with a fringe of black hair, sitting behind the wheel and staring straight ahead of her.

I paddled nearer. Somebody had to tell the little fool to get that thing into reverse and drive back to safety. I headed towards the car and came in close.

'Hey,' I called. 'Hey, Miss!'

It sounded silly, like someone trying to attract the attention of a waitress. But I couldn't stop to choose my style of address.

She turned and looked at me through the side window, not even winding it down. She gave no sign of having heard me, apart from looking towards me with that rather blank expression. She had a pale, oval face. Her dress was dark red, and she wore no coat. Her arms were bare: I could see them lying pensively across the steering wheel.

'The tide!' I shouted. 'Go back!'

For a moment I wondered if she had been taking drugs. She gave me what seemed an uncomprehending look, and she still didn't open the window.

Leave it to me, I thought. Only the third day of my holiday – I had driven up on the Monday, settled in and rested on the Tuesday, and this was my first outing – and already I get mixed up with some fool kid who's been tampering with her nervous system and is too stoned to save herself from drowning. Of course, I reasoned, she won't necessarily drown. She can get up on the roof of the car and wave a scarf or something until someone comes out with a boat. It would do her good, I thought. Teach her to have a bit of sense.

Then I saw that she had opened the car door and was getting out. Slowly. Like a very old person.

'What's the matter?' I called to her. 'Aren't you well?'

I didn't have to shout now, because she was standing on the sand beside the car, looking straight ahead. Even now she wasn't looking at the water that was moving in towards her feet. She was looking across at the Anglesey coast-line, as if trying to memorise it.

'*Please*, pay attention,' I said. 'If you want to go swimming, you should have brought a costume.'

She turned and looked at me.

'Swimming?' she said. 'Does the tide come in this far?' Her voice was not high but very clear. If she sang within her speaking range, it would be mezzo-soprano. Of course, most women sing higher than they talk.

'Does it come in this far?' I said. 'Why else would I be bothering you?'

She looked as if she didn't know the answer to that one. She just stood there, beside her little car. It was grimy and the paint looked old. She didn't seem irresolute or hesitant. She just stood there as if she were watching it all happen to someone else.

'Look, do as I say,' I told her. 'Start your engine and go backwards. There's not much time.'

I felt a fool sitting there, paddling slowly to stay in the same place against the push of the tide. But I couldn't leave her to it. The water was coming in faster than I had thought possible: the first ripples were almost nibbling at her front tyres.

'I thought it would be all right here,' she said. 'I saw wheel tracks.'

'You saw wheel tracks because somebody had driven a Land-Rover out here at low tide, getting shellfish or towing a boat,' I said. 'Whoever it was took care to be somewhere else by now.'

She nodded her head and said, 'Thanks.' Then she got into the car and sat still a moment before putting her head out through the

— 11 —

window. 'I'm sorry you had the bother.'

'I'm not,' I said. 'I'm just glad I was here.'

She nodded again and started the engine. Then, looking back over her left shoulder, she began steering the car backwards along the narrow spit.

I watched her get started, then dug the paddle into the water – left, right, left, right – and began to move against the tide again.

I thought I would go in a wide circle, rounding the orange buoy I could see out in the middle of the water, and then come back on the tide.

It was hard work and for a moment I gave all my attention to punching the tide. I was glad to. There was something stirring underneath that effort which I had no wish to define: some tiny little crumb of regret, of wishing-in-vain. That pale oval face, those dark brown eyes and black hair, had come into my life and gone out again, all in five minutes. I braced my muscles and paddled hard, putting that feeling behind me as I drove the water back on either side, facing the two tasks at once.

The tide was really racing now: clean and salty and challenging. A big fish leapt out just ahead of me, another one over to the left. I felt they were all round me, rejoicing in the salt and their own streamlined energy. It was such a still afternoon that I could hear the sound of the little car's engine, coming across the water unevenly as the girl lifted her foot from the accelerator and then dropped it again. Suddenly it changed its tone. It became high and irritable, then choked almost into silence, then rose high again.

I pulled hard on the right-hand blade, keeping the left out of the water. As I came round I saw that the car had halted. The engine note kept rising and falling, and blue smoke was coming from the exhaust in small, irregular clouds.

I paddled towards the scene, suddenly going fast now that I was riding the weight of the water. The canoe bobbed like a swan. As I got near, I saw what was happening. She had hit a patch of soft ground and the wheels were spinning. There was a swirl of tide at that point, reaching in behind her, and it had soaked the sand. The front wheels, the ones driven by the engine, were spinning and sinking in. Soon, they would not go round at all.

I shouted, to draw the girl's attention, and it seemed to me that she looked straight at me through the smeared windscreen. But still her face had no expression.

'Get out!' I called, motioning with my arm. 'Get out and walk!'

It crossed my mind, then, that she may have been trying to commit suicide and had given it up when I came and pestered her. Absurdly, a twin thought came to me in the same second: A girl like that shouldn't throw herself away.

Then I thought – and all these thoughts came so quickly that one pull of the paddle contained them all – No, she couldn't be trying to commit suicide. Not in that long-winded way. She'd just throw herself off a jetty.

She got out, now. The engine was still running. She looked at the wheels, embedded in that muddy sand, and then at the way she would have to go on foot. There was water on either side of her now, and a long, shining puddle of it between her and safety. The puddle was becoming a pool, and broadening before her eyes.

Some big, dark-grey birds flew past me, low over the water, seeming like an ill omen. Mist was coming down over the mountains: I could see it streaming down, as fast as milk boiling over out of a saucepan. Nature suddenly seemed enigmatic, as if wondering whether to turn hostile and throw all her weight against these two foolish human creatures, destroying them like a couple of toys she had grown tired of.

The girl took off her shoes and started to walk, splashing ankle-deep through the pool. I paddled along, keeping level with her. Then she stopped again, and looked back towards the car.

'My handbag,' she said.

'Go *on*, for God's sake,' I said. 'It can't be that important.'

'I need it,' she said, as if that explained everything. She turned and splashed back through the pool. Already, in those few seconds, it had deepened; now it came up to her calves.

She got to the car and opened the door. The engine was still turning over smoothly, but soon the water would rise and begin to choke it. As if to spare it this humiliation, she switched it off. I liked that. It was one of those small, random acts that show a sensitive nature. Then it struck me that she may have needed to take the key out of the ignition because it was on a ring that contained other keys she needed. Never mind, she could still have a sensitive nature.

I waited while she took another look round the interior of the car to see if she had forgotten anything. She was bending down to get her head inside the little door. I could see her through the glass, that pale face intent and yet registering nothing. I wondered again if she were on drugs. But how could she have driven a car if she was stoned? Still, how would anyone who wasn't stoned have driven a car where it would be covered by the tide?

She shut the door at last. The water was right up to the front bumpers now. I shipped the paddle and sat still, rocking gently up and down, and watched her straighten up and look along the causeway that led back to dry land. It was disappearing fast. She held the handbag lightly in one hand, swinging it from its strap as if it didn't matter much. Yet she had gone back for it as if it had contained the Crown Jewels, serum for a sick child, and a bundle of love letters in rose-pink ribbon. I knew now that I should have to take her in the canoe, and with that I relaxed, because there was no hurry, as long as I got her aboard before the water reached her mouth.

'That handbag must be worth something,' I said, pitching my voice sarcastically over the ten or twelve feet of water that separated us.

'I haven't any luggage,' she said. I waited for her to add something more, but she just left the statement lying there, like a stick of wood floating on the water.

I brought the canoe in close to where she was standing. Since it is impossible to move a boat sideways through the water, I had to do it by clawing round in a tight half-circle, which brought me up facing out to sea. I leaned forward and picked up the front painter and threw it over to her.

'Hold that, would you?' I said.

She bent down and picked it up, just as if she were doing somebody a trivial favour. Nothing seemed to be getting through to her. I did the same thing with the rear painter and she picked that up too.

'Just hold them steady,' I said. 'I'm coming ashore.' There were uneven, weed-covered rocks that made it impossible to paddle the canoe near enough for her to step in, so I had to get out and hold the boat and make sure she got in properly. I had decided to treat her like a drugs case even if she wasn't one.

'You can let go,' I said and she dropped both the painters. We were standing together now and she came just about up to my shoulder. I'm not very tall.

'I'll hold the boat and you get in,' I said. 'At the front.'

— 14 —

'Get in?' she said, as if the idea came as a complete novelty. 'Can't I walk?'

'If you haven't any luggage,' I said, 'you haven't a change of clothes. And you'd be wet, pretty well up to the waist, by the time you got back. Why get wet when you can sit in a nice dry boat?'

Actually it wasn't a nice dry boat by the time we were both in. I held it steady for her, and she got in with light, quick movements but even so she brought a fair amount of water in. And I somehow managed to get wetter than she did. I got in behind her, clumsily, lurching on the weed-slippery rocks and shipping a ton of water in my soaking trousers.

Still, she was in and I could get her to dry land and say goodbye to her and let her take her thick, soft-looking black hair and brown eyes and bare slender arms out of my life. Oh, goody, goody.

I dug the paddle in and we began to swing round. The boat rode the water differently with her weight in front of me. It was better.

When two people sit in a canoe – at any rate, of the kayak type – the legs of the one behind have to go on either side of the one in front, from about knee-level down. It was just this area of my legs that was soaking wet. I paused in my paddling and slipped off my shoes and socks, put them under the deck behind me, and rolled up my trousers to the knees. It would be more comfortable for her to be in contact with wet feet and ankles than with wet trousers. Besides, I liked it better. My naked feet felt clean and salty and they nestled along the sleek shape of her dark-red dress where it enclosed her thighs and her neat little rear end. If this makes me seem like a middle-aged character with his mind on all the wrong things, that's about accurate.

A light breeze had come up, blowing in from the Irish Sea. It didn't disarrange her hair much. She had the kind of hair that lies in a solid shape, giving an effect of sculpture. The breeze stirred it a little, like the surface of a field of corn, but it lay so compact that there weren't any stray tendrils to blow about. You have to remember I was sitting about three feet behind her and when I faced directly forward the chief object in my field of vision was her head. And the nape of her neck, of course. That was all right too.

She sat quite still, not turning her head to either side. Once or twice I made a meaningless remark, just so that we didn't wallow along in complete silence, but she either said 'Yes' or 'No' or seemed not to hear me. She certainly was withdrawn inside herself. Of course she had problems; after all, the car would pretty well be a write-off after six hours in the sea, even if the tide didn't rise high enough to cover it completely, and she seemed to have made no provision for being suddenly dumped on the coast of North Wales. No luggage, no overcoat. Presumably she had been on the way somewhere, and expected to find all necessities when she arrived. But if she had been on the way somewhere, why had she turned off to drive along a spit of raised land into the mouth of the incoming tide? And what had held her there, day-dreaming while the water came in?

I wished I could see her face. But I could only see the back of her head, and it told me nothing. Or almost nothing. The stillness, the way she never turned to look about her, told me that something inside her was switched off.

So I speculated, with no possibility of coming up with an answer. But my bewilderment didn't have to last long, because the trip was a short one and we were there. The little freshet on which I had launched the canoe had disappeared now, though its track could still be seen as a snake of smooth water amid the roughness of the sea, a streak where the river and the tide were pushing against each other and neither was winning. And there was my car, waiting. Waiting for what?

I paddled over, looking for a place to disembark. It wasn't easy. The tide had not yet come in far enough to fill its channel, so that it was a matter of getting out on to oozy rocks or into marshy sand that was quickly getting more and more completely waterlogged. I could see there was no way of doing it neatly, so I went ahead and did it messily, bringing us in near a couple of big rocks that we could at any rate lean up against and splashing straight out into the water. One of my bare feet rasped on a starfish or a rough stone. I groaned softly and shifted position. Then I was holding the boat against the pitch of the water.

'You'd better get out now,' I said. 'It's the best I can do.'

Wordlessly, she got out. Once again I noticed how supple she was, and how she moved quickly and lightly. She still had her shoes in hand, although I suddenly noticed that she hadn't even tried to do the same for her stockings. Doubtless she was wearing tights and it would have been too much of a struggle to try to get them off. She waded up to the flatter of the two rocks and sat on it, holding the shoes in one hand and that precious handbag in the other.

— 16 —

I hauled the boat on to dry land, once again consulting the vegetation to make sure it was going to stay dry. Then I turned and looked at the girl. She was still sitting on the rock, gazing straight in front of her.

'Do you want me to take you to a doctor?' I asked abruptly.

At that, she turned and looked at me. 'A doctor? Why?'

'Well,' I said, 'something isn't right.'

She thought a bit and then said, 'I suppose not.'

'Would a doctor help you?'

'No,' she said.

At that, I knew what was going to happen. She was coming back with me, to the place I had rented for my holiday, and I was going to see what she needed and give it to her if I could.

'Would you mind picking up one end of the canoe?' I asked her. 'I don't want to make you wait while I take it to pieces, so I'll put it up on the roof-rack.'

We lifted an end each. She lifted hers quite easily, and even when we had to hoist it to shoulder-height to get it on the roof-rack, she did it without any effort. There was nothing wrong with her physically, at any rate. But she still had that withdrawn, inward-looking gaze. Almost like an autistic child.

I unlocked the car, took out a length of rope, and made the canoe fast to the roof-rack. Then I opened the door for her on the passenger's side. I deliberately did so without speaking. I wanted to see if she would do what was obviously expected of her, without discussing it. Words seemed to trouble her. Perhaps we could avoid the necessity of putting anything into speech.

I was right. She just got in, as calmly as if it had been agreed beforehand.

I got in beside her and reversed the car along the bumpy track to the road. Then, still without any explanation, I got into forward gear and moved off, with the canoe rocking gently up and down on the roof-rack.

The cottage I had rented was half-way down a wild valley that opened off the main coast road. It was a journey of about ten miles. For the first three or four, I drove without speaking and without looking at her except for a side-glance or two. She sat quite still, looking ahead of her through the windscreen as she had done when her own little car was waiting to be drowned by the tide. Her hands were folded loosely in her lap, and under them were her shoes and handbag. Her stockinged feet were drying in the warm air that the car's heater was circulating at floor-level. I had put my shoes back on so as to drive better. We halted at a road intersection, to let other traffic go by, and it was then that I saw she was shivering.

'Here,' I said. 'Put this on.' I leaned into the back of the car and pulled towards her an old anorak with a fur-lined hood, one of those high-altitude jobs. It had long since had its day, the zip was broken and the lining torn in several places, but I carried it in the car as a general-purpose oddment. Sometimes it was useful as a travelling-rug, at others it stopped bottles from clinking, that kind of thing. She put it on and said 'Thanks.' Neither of us spoke again until I stopped the car at the end of the track leading to the cottage and said, 'We're there.'

'Yes,' she said in the same uninvolved, accepting voice. It was beginning to seem like a dream. For a moment I wondered if it was my grip on reality that was slackening. Then I reached up and touched the canoe. The rubber lining of the skin had dried in the wind as we went along, but the dark-blue canvas of the top deck was still damp in streaks, and grains of sand clung to the damp parts and brushed roughly against my fingers. That touch of physical reality, the stubborn unchangeable nature of small things, made me realise that I was awake and as sane as I ever am.

'You have to get over this stile,' I said, showing her the way. She came along as if she were some acquaintance who had accepted an invitation to tea.

The cottage stood at the foot of a hillside with bracken and rocks. Up on the shoulder of the hill, the tip of an abandoned quarry could be seen through a screen of trees. It made a long, grey stain on the green of the hillside. There were one or two isolated small houses dotted about near the quarry: probably people connected with its working, men of the overseer and clerical type, had lived there. The actual work-force, the quarrymen themselves, must have walked over the mountains to their work and back again; there were no signs of any houses for them. The cottage I was renting had doubtless been the home of some sheep-farmer, scratching a living along the valley. It had been taken over and prettified by the astute person who was renting it to me for two weeks, but he had been too clever to gut it and rebuild it as a modern suburban house. The old pastoral charm had been preserved in the big oak beams and the split-level effect, so common in these Welsh cottages, whereby the main living area reached right up into the rafters, but the kitchen and bedroom were one above the other. So that to go upstairs to bed you climbed up a ladder, and there you found, so to speak, half an upper storey. Someone lying in bed could talk to someone sitting by the parlour fireside, though not see them.

I led the way along the path to the house, skirting rocks and clumps of gorse. The girl followed me. The house was bathed in warm sunlight, though the late-afternoon shadow had already crept down the other side of the valley as far as the little river that ran along its floor.

I opened up and went in. She came too, still wearing my torn old anorak, and sat down on a straight-backed wooden chair by the table. Neither of us spoke. There seemed to be nothing much to say. I went out to the shed for firewood, brought it in and set to work to make a fire. Fortunately the astute landlord had been just sophisticated enough to leave the fireplace and chimney open instead of sealing them off and putting an imitation-log fire in. There was electric heating, if I had cared to switch it on, but I wasn't going to waste that wonderful fireplace. I got newspaper and sticks, and the smallest and driest of the logs, and soon the fire made a magnet of warmth and light to which she and I turned our faces instinctively. It also released us from the need to talk. If you sit with somebody in a centrally heated room, you either talk or stare helplessly into each other's faces; in a room with a fire, you can just look at the fire.

After a while, when the fire was burning securely enough not to need watching, I went and put the kettle on and made tea. There was running water in the kitchen, and a little electric stove. All mod cons. Well there might be, at the rent they were charging.

I came back with two cups of tea. Then I saw that she was still shivering.

'Go nearer to the fire,' I said.

'I'm not cold,' she said and tried to stop shivering. But she couldn't.

'Something's the matter, isn't it?' I asked.

'I've had a shock,' she said.

I waited in case she was going to tell me anything more. When she didn't, I went over to the cupboard and got out the whisky bottle and poured in a big slosh into her tea. And another into mine, just to be fair.

— 19 —

She drank hers as if enjoying it, sipping slowly and — I would have said thoughtfully, but there seemed to be no thinking behind those unchanging eyes. She was looking into the fire, but I could not tell whether her eyes were focusing or not. Her face was entirely still, and, as the firelight threw a wash of colour across its pallor, it was beautiful. Her hair, which in the daylight had seemed almost blue-black, now shone with the colour of the darkest chocolate.

It was her shoulders that trembled most. She had taken off the anorak now, and the waves of shivering seemed to start at the base of her neck and go down through her body.

She had finished her tea. I poured another two fingers of whisky into her cup, where a few tea-leaves floated in it like tiny boats trying to go somewhere, then got to my feet and said, 'Food is emotionally calming.'

'Yes?' she said, as if I had brought up some abstract question that couldn't possibly concern her.

'Yes,' I said. 'If you can force down a big meal, you always feel more tranquil afterwards. Some of your interior energy gets taken up with your metabolism, and you haven't so much left for suffering.'

She said nothing to that, but I had finished my speech anyway. I went into the kitchen and looked at the stock of food I had laid in. It wasn't much; I had planned to eat out, mostly. But there was bread and butter and tomatoes and two tins of Irish stew. What impulse had made me buy two tins I didn't remember, but I blessed it now.

I opened the tins, chucked the stew into a saucepan, sliced some tomatoes into it, and started it heating. Then I cut some good solid slices of bread and plastered butter on them. As I worked I stole a glance or two at her through the doorway. She was sitting quite still; but at one point I saw her lower her head very slowly into her cupped hands. I felt an impulse to go in and put a hand on her shoulder, but then I thought that it would be silly to act like a kindly uncle. I didn't *feel* like a kindly uncle. What did I feel like? Oh, nothing, nothing. Just a canoeist who ran a press-cutting agency and was taking a late summer holiday. I turned back to the stew and gave it a stir.

It was ready. That kind of tinned stew is pretty horrible, glutinous and anonymous, but it was hot and there was plenty of it and the slices of half-cooked tomato gave it some character. I got two plates and slapped a good helping on each. I took the bread-and-butter in on a separate plate, then went and fetched the helpings of stew.

'Eat,' I commanded, putting her helping down beside her. I watched as she slowly turned towards it. Her eyes seemed to be focusing now.

'I haven't got anything to eat with,' she said. Just about her longest sentence so far, and a good sign.

Of course. I had forgotten the eating-irons. They say absent-mindedness is a sign that repressed material is becoming active. I went and fetched knives, forks, and spoons. While I was at it I got two glasses and gave each of us a good shot of whisky and water, about half and half.

After that there was nothing to do but eat. She seemed hungry enough. When she had finished her stew, and a couple of slices of bread-and-butter, she sat back, looking more animated, and took a drink from her glass.

'It works, doesn't it?' she said.

I nodded. She had stopped shivering. Then I saw that her eyes were brimming with tears. I opened my mouth to speak, but closed it again. Let her cry, I thought, let it come out, don't pester her.

Outside, the sky was bright but the ground was shadowed. The colours were deep and very defined. A rowan tree that grew just outside the window held its leaves and berries so still that it looked like a painting. I remembered that the canoe was still on top of the car. Perhaps I ought to bring it to the house. I'd be lost if it got stolen. They don't make them any more.

'I shan't be long,' I said to the girl. She didn't seem to hear me. I went out and down the path to the road. The canoe had dried by now and the ropes had tightened. I unfastened them and slid the canoe down to the ground. Then I picked it up, amidships, and carried it back a few yards at a time. Every twenty or thirty paces it became unbearably heavy and I had to put it down, rest with my arms hanging loosely by my sides, and then pick it up again. Finally I got it to the cottage, leaned it against the wall by the door, and went in. The girl was sitting just as she had been, holding an empty glass. She had at least drunk her whisky, then. But the tears were rolling down now. She was crying silently and helplessly, making no attempt to hide it. I couldn't tell whether she knew I was there or not.

I knelt down beside her chair and put my hand on her arm: very gently, so as not to scare her.

'What is it?' I asked. 'Can I help?'

'I couldn't take it,' she said. 'Not four of them. Not all four of them in there.'

I didn't know whether I was supposed to understand this, so I just said, 'There's a limit to what a person can take.'

She turned and looked at me then. 'I can't go back,' she said.

'Of course not.'

'But I don't know where to go. I don't know what to do. If I had the car I could just drive on.'

'There'd be no point in that. Sooner or later you'd fall off the island.'

'The car was a kind of home. A place to be. Something with walls round me. Now it's gone.'

'It's gone all right,' I agreed. 'No car survives a night in the sea.'

'I can't just get on trains and things. I've got to stop running some time.'

'Stay here,' I said. The idea wasn't a new one. I'd been hoping all along that I could get her to stay, and this seemed the moment to put it into words.

'I don't want to trouble you,' she said.

'You wouldn't.'

I put some more whisky in her glass, and she drank it and looked at me again and said, 'Why are you here by yourself?'

'I'm getting away from my wife.'

She gave a little ghostly smile. 'Funny. I'm getting away from my husband.'

He must be the one who'd done whatever it was she couldn't take. But I decided against trying to get her to talk about it.

She got up, and stood holding on to the back of her chair. 'I must lie down,' she said. 'I think I'm drunk.'

'You're just terribly tired. No wonder, after driving all the way from London.'

'How d'you know it was London,' she said in a softly weary voice, not caring much how I knew.

'Your car had a London number-plate.'

'Oh,' she said. Then she swayed slightly and said, 'I don't feel well.'

'Rest,' I said. 'That's all you need. And there's plenty of it.'

'Where d'you wash?' she asked.

I showed her. Then I came back and stood by the fire. I heard her splashing about.

'I haven't got a toothbrush.'

'Use mine,' I called.

'Thanks. I'll give it a good wash on the soap afterwards.'

'Don't bother.' I couldn't imagine her having any offensive germs.

She went on running the tap and splashing for a bit. I was glad she wasn't so knocked over by her sufferings, whatever they were, as to let herself go. As long as a woman can get herself together enough to wash her face, she isn't going to go to pieces. I poured out the last of the whisky (had we really drunk a *bottle*?) and downed it as I coined this piece of folk-wisdom.

Then she appeared in the doorway. Her arms looked beautifully sculptured against the dark red of her dress. She had washed the tears off her face, and she looked tired but composed.

'Is it up there?' she asked, looking at the ladder.

'Yes,' I said.

She went over to the ladder and climbed up it. I was glad I had made the bed that morning. I waited till she had gone out of sight and then went up after her. She was lying on her back on the further side of the bed, looking up at the roof-beams. I didn't blame her: they were beautiful.

'Why don't you get into bed? You'll be cold,' I said.

'I want to go to sleep,' she said, as if it were some kind of answer. Then she closed her eyes and rolled over on to her right side, facing me, with her head burrowing down into the pillow. She closed her eyes and seemed to be willing herself into sleep.

I went down the ladder again and got my overcoat: the good one, not the ragged old anorak. It was leather with a fleece lining. I climbed up again and put it over her. Her breathing became regular and deep, and I decided she was not just pretending to be asleep.

I went back down the ladder. (All this exercise was good for me.) There seemed nothing to do but make up the fire with some more logs and sit by it. Don't get the impression that I'm a Sir Galahad, vowed to chastity. Normally I'd think it a crime to miss any chance that came along. But this didn't look to me like a chance of that kind.

I sat there for a long time, watching the fire and wishing there were some whisky left. For something to do, I even went and washed the dishes. Then I went back to the fireside and began to think of bunking down on anything soft I could find. I was just beginning to work on the problem when I heard her crying again. It sounded as if she were sobbing in her sleep. I went to the ladder, put my hand on it and stood still, undecided. Her sobbing ceased, she seemed about to settle back into normal sleep, and then suddenly she said, in a very clear voice and distinct utterance, 'Why here?'

Why indeed? I thought.

'Why did you bring them here?' she said. 'You can't tell me that, can you? You can't tell me that!' Then the springs creaked and I could tell she was sitting up.

I went up the ladder very quickly. She was sitting up in the pale light; holding her arms out in front of her as if reaching for someone. Her eyes were open.

'I want to help you,' I said. They were the first words that came into my head.

She turned and looked at me, though whether she was really seeing me I couldn't tell. Then, slowly, she swivelled her body towards me, still with her arms held out. I sat down on the bed close to her and her arms reached round my neck. I put mine round her and we lay down together. For a long time we were silent and motionless. I could feel her heart beating.

At last she said, in that soft clear voice, 'Was I having a nightmare?'

'You were talking to somebody,' I said. 'Somebody who'd hurt you.'

'Oh, yes,' she said, 'him.'

As if this thought had reminded her of something she had been meaning to get round to, she unwound her arms from me and got out of bed. As I watched, she took off her clothes calmly and methodically, as if she were alone, and hung them over a chair. All of them. Then she folded back the counterpane and got in between the sheets.

I lay still for a moment, thinking. For some foolish reason the thought possessed me: if she goes to sleep I'll leave her alone. I listened to her breathing. But then she said, in that quiet clear voice, 'It's all right. You're expected.'

I wriggled out of my clothes and dropped them on the floor, then got in with her. And then? What happened, that hasn't been described a million times before? But each time is a little different, and this was good, deeply good, warm and close and satisfying. I could just see her face in the diffused firelight, and as we went on it lost its dead-pan expressionlessness, and became soft and eager. Her mouth seemed to grow fuller and her eyes larger. In their brown depths I read something I couldn't quite decode. It may have been my destiny.

Afterwards we lay quietly and talked a little, before going to it again.

'Why are you getting away from your wife?' she asked.

'I bored her, so she started a relationship with another chap. When I found out about it, I left her. Not that I minded much, but since she was technically in the wrong, it gave me a chance to leave her.'

'And that was what you wanted to do?'

'Yes. I hadn't admitted it to myself, but when she cuckolded me my chief feeling was of relief. So that showed me I must have wanted to get rid of her.'

We were silent for a time. I stroked her hair and kissed her forehead. Then I said, 'Why are you getting away from your husband?'

'Because he's a murderer.'

'Who has he murdered?'

'Not who. What. Our love.'

I pondered this for a moment. Then, as she turned and kissed me close, I lost interest in conversation.

I must have fallen asleep then. I don't remember when or how I drifted to sleep, though I remember many other things too good and too personal and too sacred to describe in words for everybody to read. One of the last things I remember is the flickering of the firelight on the wall; it had that irregular, leaping quality that a fire sometimes has just before it goes out; so I could, if I wanted to, work out roughly how long we lay awake together. But I don't want to.

When I next woke, it wasn't the firelight that shone on the wall, but a clear September light filtering in through the uncurtained windows downstairs, and softly flooding the whole cottage. I sat

— 25 —

up, wide awake at once. She had gone. I looked across at the chair. Her clothes had gone.

Quickly I went down the ladder. The place was empty; it had the unanswering silence of a house where there is nobody but you. A foolish thought struck me: I wanted to call her, but I didn't know her name. Not even that. In my memories of her, and memories were all I had now, she would just be the girl with the helmet of black hair.

I stood by the dead fire, looking round the room and out of the window. The rowan-tree was as still as ever, as much like a painting. Nothing had changed except that night had passed over the earth and day had come. Nothing had changed, except my life.

Then I realised that I was stark naked. I went to the back kitchen and washed and then I slowly climbed the ladder to the half-bedroom. My clothes were on the floor. How eagerly, how quickly I had shed them, and how slowly and painfully I put them on now.

I straightened the bed. Those creases and rumples were suddenly painful to look at. It wasn't that I didn't want to remember. It was just that I didn't want to remember *now*, amid the smart of finding her gone. I wanted to look back on it one day, after a safe and healing lapse of time, as a beautiful memory. At the moment, all I could think of was that when I went to sleep she was here, and when I woke up she was gone, and that she had left nothing, not even her name, just a rumpled bed and a memory.

Then I remembered the car. If the tide had reached its highest point about six the previous evening, it would have been high again at about six this morning. That was so, wasn't it? The tide rose every twelve hours, didn't it? I realised, of course, that it wouldn't be as regular as that, otherwise there would be no variation. But I thought it might be roughly true. She might have gone back to see what had happened to her poor little car, stealing away as I lay snoring. (A woman once told me that men always snore after making love. And brother, she should have known.) I could picture her waking up full of worries, all her problems coming back to her like unwelcome homing pigeons, now that the firelight and the love-making were over, now that even the sleeping had stopped: wondering what would be best to do, then thinking she might at least have a look at the car, dressing and going out quietly and walking along the road and getting a lift on some early-morning lorry or with a farmer going off in good time for a cattle market.

Suddenly I saw it all, as clearly as if I were sitting watching it on a cinema screen, saw the fixed, intent look on her face, all the softness gone now, and the hurried jerky movements as she dressed.

I was tugging my own clothes on while all this was moving in my head, and when they were on I couldn't wait to be on my way, snatching up a crust of bread from the table and chewing it as I walked rapidly to the car, just so as not to have an empty stomach. I wanted to get to the swilled-out ruin of the little red Mini as fast as she did, or not long after her, though of course I had no idea how much of a start she had. Damn it, why had I slept so deeply? But it had been a sleep born of bliss, bliss.

I got to the car and was already fishing in my pocket for the ignition key when I saw the folded piece of paper stuck in the windscreen-wiper. Even before I took it out and unfolded it I knew intuitively it was from her.

I was right. *Thank you. Really thank you. It was rescue, and warmth, when I needed them. Forgive me for running away—but it's best that I should come and go like a ghost, which is pretty much what I am.*

That was all. No name. Well, Mrs No-name, you haven't quite finished with me. Your need to get away and be by yourself is one that I'm not going to respect, not unless you try much harder to shake me off.

I got into the car and started the engine, and then I asked myself, Why? She doesn't want to go on, she has chosen not to let any kind of relationship develop, why not respect that? You had a magical experience last night, why not let it go at that? A self-enclosed, magical experience, like a soap-bubble that floats a little while and then bursts; why not leave it alone? Surely you don't want to turn into the kind of person who never knows how to let go, who clings on to what he's had?

'Yes, I do,' I said aloud as I backed the car out in a series of jerks, and turned it round and pointed it towards the coast road. 'That's exactly the kind of person I do want to turn into. A person who clings on with teeth and toe-nails.' So I gave up arguing with myself and just drove.

It was a perfect day. The light was soft and dreamy and the mist had cleared away from the mountains. The trees were still as green as in high summer, except that here and there they hung out a lemon-coloured leaf as if they were doing it just for fun, to try the effect. My confidence came back as I drove. Surely this would be a day for something good to happen. I began to keep a sharp eye on the grass verges of the road in case she was there, walking along, looking over her shoulder at the sound of an engine. Would she be wearing her red dress with no overcoat? Or had she had the sense to take the old anorak against the morning chill? Come to think of it, I hadn't noticed the anorak in the cottage. I hoped she was wearing it.

I didn't see her, and then the sea came in sight, and then I was driving down the little road that led to my canoe-launching point. I was near, I was almost there, I was there, and I stopped. The tide had ebbed sufficiently to leave the causeway along which she had driven. The little red car was there, looking even at this distance very sodden and forlorn. And she was not there.

She was not there. She had taken her rich dark hair, and her big brown eyes, and her lovely pale arms and her red dress, away.

I got out of the car and walked along the causeway to the wrecked Mini. The windows were caked with salt and there was a deep well of water under the dashboard. The upholstery was ruined and the engine would obviously be a write-off. The weight of the water had caused the car to lurch heavily to one side and now, stranded, it looked ready to topple over.

I tried the doors. One side was immovable; salt in the lock? Or just locked? I went round and tried the other side. It opened. I got in, putting my weight where it would tend to level the car rather than tip it over, and gave it the kind of going-over that the local inhabitants traditionally give to wrecks. I wanted it to yield up some secrets; as its last act on earth before being dragged away to a scrap-yard, I wanted it to tell me something.

'Come on,' I said to it, 'talk. Tell me who she is. She drove you all this way, you must know something.'

Obediently, it offered up what I needed. In one of the door-pockets there was a thick plastic envelope. Somebody must have been quite a careful and methodical motorist. Inside the envelope, considerably damaged but not entirely spoilt by the hours of salt water, were the car's log-book, a certificate of membership of the A.A., and an M.O.T. test certificate. I put the whole bundle in my pocket.

After that, there was nothing I could do but move away as fast as possible from the scene of the crime. If anyone saw me removing things from an abandoned car that didn't belong to me, the result would be, at best, hours of time-wasting explanations and waiting about while policemen made entries in ledgers. And I wanted none of that. What did I want? I wasn't sure. Just to get away by myself and think, and put together such information as these documents would give me and think some more.

As I went back to my car I looked round. Nobody was watching me. A sailing dinghy with a gaily striped spinnaker was trying hard to pull itself along in the sluggish air; the two men aboard were too busy encouraging it to bother about a solitary figure poking about in a car on the shore-line. A big herring-gull circled overhead, watching me. But he couldn't tell the police he had seen me steal a plastic wallet.

I got into the car and drove – aimlessly, just anywhere. I crossed over the main coast road and went a mile or two up a winding mountain road. When I felt I was a long way from anywhere, I stopped, got out, sat down on a large rock and opened the wallet.

The car was registered in her name, and so was the A.A. membership. None of your joint husband-and-wife package deals. But she was married all right. The writing in the log-book had smeared into illegibility, but the A.A. certificate had fared better. her number was 27MX1-967-804JC. Her name was Mrs L. J. Delmore. And her address was 12 Windermere Gardens, S.W.3.

I sat staring down at it. Windermere Gardens? The name meant nothing, though 'S.W.3' meant it was somewhere smart, somewhere expensive, not the sort of place I ever got asked to. There are plenty of well-off people on the books of my little agency, but they never seem to ask me to drop round for a sherry before dinner.

The sun was getting up now and the day was warm and hazy. I felt listlessness and indecision seeping into my bones. I had blasted over here with the foolish fancy that I might see her. But people who lived in S.W.3 addresses didn't need to grieve over losing a low-priced car that was obviously past its best days. Probably it was one she just kept for shopping and running about town. She was rich, that was it, rich. Having a tantrum and running away from her husband for forty-eight hours, just to scare him a bit. Upset over something he'd done, as what wife isn't sometimes? And, because she came from among people who did what they liked and took what they wanted, she'd amused herself and soothed her irritation with the first chap who happened along. Viz and to wit, me.

Then I remembered her face. I remembered the deep shock and withdrawal in her eyes. And I remembered other things I will not tell about.

I crumpled the A.A. certificate into a ball and tossed it down among the bracken. Then I went and got into the car and started the engine. Then I got out, leaving the engine still running, and looked for the screwed-up bit of paper and found it, and straightened it out carefully, and put it in my wallet. The log-book I just left beside the rock. It was litter, but some things deserve to be litter.

I drove to the nearest town and parked the car. The car-park was beside the harbour, and I walked along looking at the boats for a bit, till I realised that I wasn't really seeing them. I went and sat in the car and looked at the A.A. certificate again. Then I went and had a cup of coffee. By that time the pubs were open and I went and sat in one and had a few drinks. There was a man in a raincoat sitting near me and I noticed that he kept eyeing me. I tried to see myself as he must see me, and then it came to me that I had taken the A.A. certificate out of my wallet about twelve separate times and read it carefully, number and all, and then put it back and put my wallet away. I looked up and caught the raincoat-man's eyes, and realised that he thought I was having a mental breakdown and was feeling sorry for me. He looked a nice man and I was sorry I had made him feel sorry. I nearly spoke to him and told him I was all right, but I could not do that because I wasn't all right.

I went to another pub and had some more drinks and ate a pie. Afterwards I couldn't remember eating the pie, but it had been in a little dish made of tinfoil or something like that, and the empty dish and a few crumbs were in front of me, so I assumed I had eaten the pie. I went and got the car and drove back to the cottage, telling myself to get on with my holiday. But there was nothing much I wanted to do. Standing in the doorway, looking across at the hills on the other side of the valley, I decided that if I wasn't going to enjoy myself and get some relaxation I might as well use the time to have a good constructive think about personal problems. I had enough of them to sort out, that was certain. I stood there with my hands in my pockets and tried to fix my mind on definite questions. What ought I to do about my wife, for instance? Or about my daughter, who was a student nurse somewhere, stuck in the endless corridors of an enormous hospital in a big anonymous city?

I didn't know, so to change the subject I started trying to worry about the business. But it all seemed light-years away. I knew my assistant, Miss Sarson, would be getting on with it, myopically peering at columns of newsprint and running her soft, manicured fingers over a card-index, hour after hour. And dictating letters to Daisy, our dizzy secretary. If the business was going down, so be it. We had a good reputation and a solid clientele, and if I lost my grip altogether and started making consistently wrong decisions, it would still take us ten years to go broke. And who knew what might happen in ten years? If it came to that, who the hell wanted to be still running a press-cutting agency ten years from now? Ten more years of ministering to people's vanity, pumping up their wilting little egos.

It was four o'clock, then half-past. Just the hour of the day when I had first seen her, sitting in that stranded little car and staring palely at the Anglesey coast, her body in danger while her mind was hidden away in some private country of suffering. I turned abruptly and went into the house. I supposed I ought to make a fire. But for some reason I climbed the ladder up to the half-bedroom. Sometimes, looking back, I try to remember why I did it, but I never can. It was just an impulse that never explained itself to me. I went up, anyway. And in the golden but already dimming sunlight I saw the bed where, only a few hours before, it had all happened, and a great wash of longing went through my mind and body.

I went down the ladder, quite calmly. It wouldn't be true to say that I had made a decision: a decision had made itself and I was the container in which it happened, that was all. Coolly, methodically, I got my toothbrush and shaving gear and some underwear and socks and two shirts, put them in a small bag, locked up the cottage and moved off down the path to the car. There was not much petrol in the tank, I noticed as I switched on the ignition, so I drove straight to the nearest pump and got her filled to capacity. Then there was nothing to do but drive.

Darkness fell when I was somewhere in the south midlands. The ugly sodium lamps came on and I went past endless housing estates. I was glad of the nothingness, glad of having no thoughts in my head, not even any desires in my body. I felt no hunger, no thirst, no need for anything but motion, so long as it was motion towards where she was. Or where I could find out where she was. Or where I could find out that it was not possible for me to find out where she was. Or where I could find out why I could not find it out, and who was stopping me, and what I could do to persuade them. Or, if I could not persuade them, to do something hostile to them, to inflict damage of some kind on the people who stopped me seeing her and talking to her, to fight the whole world if the whole world stood in the way of that.

And I didn't even know her first name.

After about eleven p.m. there was nothing on the road but huge articulated lorries, roaring onward remorselessly, shifting hundreds of tons of goods. I thought of all those cramped, red-eyed men staring into the beams of the headlamps, working out in their heads distance run and money earned. They had no choice. I had no choice. We were all chasing our needs.

It was still night when I hit the outskirts of London. Thousands of dark, sleeping rooms. Everyone recharging their batteries for another day. Only fools like me, or hard-headed night-workers like the lorry drivers, were awake. I must have been getting drowsy, with these and other platitudes jogging through my mind, because I suddenly discovered, when it was too late, that I was driving along Western Aproaches Avenue. I had meant to avoid that road. It was where my wife and I lived for fourteen years.

Western Approaches Avenue is one of those immensely long, totally featureless roads that lead from the outer suburbs of London to the inner suburbs. They may, though I doubt it, have a certain amount of character to the people who live in them, but to the outside eye they seem so entirely without flavour that you feel somebody must have been doing it for a bet. Hundreds upon hundreds of semi-detached houses, neither very small nor very large, with little privet hedges and pre-cast garages and neat half-moons of lawn. Every now and then a clump of shops or some amenity building like a public library or a swimming-pool; at other points, a Town Hall or some immense, barn-like cinema, built forty years ago when it seemed that the silver screen would rule people's lives for ever, and now ratty and Bingo-infested.

The house where my married life had taken place – well, most of it: the first five years we had been nomad flat-dwellers – was one of these, whipping by on my left-hand side in the cold light cast by the concrete lamp-standards. It had one of those enormous numbers, eight-hundred-and-fifty-something, and God knows it needed a number because there was nothing else to tell it apart from the houses for a mile on either side. The local pub, a monstrosity with a green roof, was six hundred yards in one direction; the local Underground station – except, of course that in those regions the trains are out in the open and looking rather surprised about it – was six hundred yards in the other. Everything was clean, quiet and dead. Except for the endless traffic on the Avenue, which was dirty, noisy and alive in a clean, quiet and dead way.

It must be one of these, I thought. Ah, yes, I recognised a silver birch that grew, leaning slightly outwards, in the garden of the next house but three. That was it – one, two, three – and it was past. Like the marriage-sentence I had served in it. Daphne wasn't a bad sort. She had started with high hopes, just as I had. I supposed it was nothing we did wrong, just the deadness of mid-twentieth-century suburban life that drove us both mad with boredom. Or was that just a get-out? If we hadn't been bored with our marriage, bored totally stiff with each other, wouldn't it have been quite possible for us to weather the deadliness of a suburban life and still be interested and vital?

What exactly (I mused, steering beside the concrete lamp-standards and over the crossings) had gone wrong? To take it right back to its roots, I could never remember what my motives had been for getting married in the first place. It seemed to be something I had done absent-mindedly. Daphne's motives were presumably plainer: in those days, back in the fifties, the emanicpation of women and the sexual revolution just hadn't happened, and an unmarried woman, unless she was very strong and independent, was at a decided disadvantage. I don't think it occurred to most girls, then, not to get married if they got half a chance. So I got in with Daphne, she was keen to get married, and I suppose I went along with it more or less automatically, in a might-as-well frame of mind. The first few years were all right – just about; at any rate they contained one absorbing and fascinating experience, the birth of our daughter April.

I thought of April. Born two days into May, but Daphne had so nursed the thought of a child called April, born in a mist of spring blossom and spring hope, that we had disregarded the calendar, when she turned out a bit unpunctual, and gone ahead with the name. Dear little April. She had always treated Daphne and me as a couple of fractious children, which is just about what we were. When we bickered, she soothed us and put us in order just like a nanny. That was right too. Only love gives parents any authority. Parents who love each other can build something that children haven't had time to build, and the children see that and respect it. But when love fades and wears away into nothing, as ours had, the parents are just like two ageing children, as petulant and unreasonable but without the high spirits of children. So of course a girl like April was bound to think of her parents as naturally below her, naturally her inferiors, needing to be helped and kept in order.

Not that we bickered much. The real problem was our absolutely numbing boredom. It used to settle down on me, like a ton weight of wet feathers, the moment I entered the house. Even now I can't sort out whether it was because (i) Daphne was a boring person, (ii) I was so bored with her that I became a boring person and drove her into being even more boring, or (iii) whether I was the original bore and then she became one and then I became a worse one. There were two other possibilities, I realised; (iv) that the institution of marriage is a perpetual, never-exhausted well of boredom anyway, and (v) that the institution of marriage is all right in itself but that I wasn't cut out for it.

The possibility that it was Daphne who wasn't cut out for it never seriously entered my thoughts. All women are cut out for marriage, at least early on (she married me when she was twenty-three); admittedly, by the time they get up towards thirty and find that being alone suits them, they sometimes become impossible to break in.

But that boredom! It was suffocating, palsying, paralysing. We used to face each other at meal-times and have nothing, absolutely nothing, to say to each other. The fact is, your brain only quickens itself into motion if there is some motive for trying to involve and engage, and perhaps impress, the person you are with. People who are sexually attracted to each other, for instance, are always more vivacious and quick-witted in each other's company than they would be otherwise, because in the back of their minds – and it doesn't matter how far back – there is always the wish to impress and perhaps to dominate. When you come right down to it, you can't talk interestingly to someone unless you need to have the impulse to show off to them. And the very idea of Daphne and me showing off to one another was enough to bring a lop-sided smile even to my grim face at that moment.

But boredom on its own isn't a dynamic enough motive for breaking up a marriage. Millions of people endure boredom with each other, year after year, a boredom so unruffled and unplumbed that except in rare moments of revelation they don't even know they're enduring it. I suppose I would have gone on living with Daphne, going to work and coming home and being bored, going on holiday and being bored, staying in or going out in the evenings and being bored, going to bed and getting up and being bored – if she hadn't suddenly, surprisingly, given me the jolt that made me swerve off that straight, flat highway into the ditch labelled 'divorce.'

Briefly, she had started an affair with someone she met at work, at that part-time job which she did because she was bored. (Always *that!*) This fellow was a prissy type with a bow-tie; he had translated Baudelaire and brought out the volume at his own expense, and was always thrusting it in your face. 'My translation of the FLAHS OF EVIL.' Not that I objected to him. I hardly noticed him, the two or three times we met. With his limp handshake and his natty little bow, and his Flahs of Evil, I assumed he was a harmless queer, in so far as I thought about him at all. But Daphne must have found him less boring than she found me, or his line of bullshit must have worked with her, or something, because she took to going to his neat little flat, first for a drink on the way home and a nice talk about Théophile Gautier or something equally exciting, but before long, so help me God, she was snatching a crafty fuck before coming home to give me my dinner. Even then I would never have known about it, so utterly remote was any such thing from my thoughts, if she hadn't gone away with him for a mid-week conference (so-called). I might have remained the tranquil (i.e. bored) cuckold and she might be still at it with him, getting her sniff at the good old f. of e.

Anyway it came out, never mind exactly how, but it did, and once I had the definite evidence and she had, in fact, tearfully confessed it all to me, I heaved myself out of my mental armchair and took an axe to our domestic life. I rented a flat, moved into it, and Daphne went to stay with her sister Hilda because she couldn't bear to be alone in the house. (April had left home by then.) This was another chance, and once again I acted with unaccustomed speed and decision. As soon as Daphne left the house I put it up for sale, and in a few weeks managed to flog it, not at a very good price but I was happy so long as I was rid of it. I did it all so precipitately because I knew that if I hung about, letting the situation drift into stalemate, I should find it harder and harder to stick to my resolution and presently I'd be back in my boredom-cage.

Poor Daphne! I knew, of course, that I was catching her out on a technicality. She didn't want to break up our marriage, didn't want to be left alone to make a new life for herself at the age of forty-three. It was I, not she (I discovered, when I examined my feelings) who wanted to break it up. I felt I would rather be bored on my own than bored with her, and besides there was always the little glint of hope that perhaps life would offer me a second chance at happiness – either with another woman, or in a re-planned, re-organised life that might prove pleasant and varied.

So I caught her out at silly mid-off, so to speak. She was the one who made the mistake; I detected her in a technical infringement of the rules, and appealed to the umpire. That's another of the unfair things about marriage. It's the one who commits the action that can be shown up in public – who goes to bed with someone else, or leaves the domicile – who gets done over, while the real blame may lie with the other who just sat there and waited.

So I had scrambled, and got rid of her and of the house, and here I was. Not, in fact, much better off. The life I was living now was just as dull and habit-ridden, and the physical surroundings were much less pleasant. But the fact was, inertia had descended again. Having once made the effort to escape from marriage and put myself into single life, I just couldn't face the fresh effort to undo it all and go back. I had nothing against Daphne; I didn't resent her going off with the Flahs man, though I admit I was surprised that she couldn't find somebody a bit better. (He, needless to say, scuttled into the woodwork as soon as the whole thing came out, and wanted no more to do with her.) I knew she had done it because she found our life together so boring that it drove her to any folly, any misjudgement, that might bring a little variety. I had never, as it happens, taken the same step myself, though I had idly thought of doing so, often enough; I suppose my inertia saved me from that too.

The fact is, I was as boring as hell. I had driven Daphne mad with sheer ennui; she had finally been goaded into making one false step; I had seized on that false step as a pretext for getting rid of her. And where, after the whole pitiful little game of musical chairs, were we all sitting now?

Well, but I was free. Free to do what? To rent cottages in North Wales and save the lives of beautiful girls who then went to bed with me. And free to wake up and find the said beautiful girls gone. And free to drive all the way down to London on wild goose-chases. Free to find a few hours of happiness, and free to lose it again. Free to be a great lover for one night, and a bloody fool for the rest of my life.

At any rate, that was Western Approaches Avenue, and that was the house where we had been married. I had sold it to a couple called Wrongbottom, or something like that, from some ashpit town in the North-East, very thrilled to be moving to the big city. I spared them a brief thought as I drove along, hoping they weren't making all the mistakes Daphne and I had made, setting life up in the same dreary way; but I expected they were.

It was still pitch dark when I drew up at the place I nowadays laughingly called 'home'. A grotty flat in a grotty nineteen-thirties building with a grotty flat roof that flooded in wet weather. Cracked concrete paths, unswept stone stairs. And I had had to buy it, of course, squandering a huge portion of the money I had netted by selling the house, so that I now hadn't enough to give Daphne to set her up when she gave up living with Hilda, which of course she soon would because she didn't like Hilda any better than I did. Round and round we go. The break-up had been six months ago and I knew she wouldn't be able to stick it at Hilda's longer than about Christmas. At that thought, the thought of Christmas, my stomach turned over and came to rest on its back, flopping like a new landed flatfish.

Oh, God, I thought, what a mess, and I left the car in the street and went into the building. What to do now? Well, the A.A. certificate was in my pocket. Mrs L. J. Delmore, L. J.: Louisa Jane? Liza Joanna? Lily Jacqueline? Lois Joplin? I went up the cold concrete stairs and unlocked the door of my pad. It was just as I had left it – cold, tidy, lonely. As there were about six hours of the night left, I lay down on the bed, without bothering to take my clothes off, and tried to rest. I had my coat over me and the electric fire on, but I was still cold; not because it was a cold night but because my mind was chilled with loneliness and discouragement and that made my body cold too. I lost consciousness once or twice during those six hours, but I can't say I really slept. When I heard my neighbours, through the paper-thin walls, bumping about and putting their radios on, I got off the bed, washed and shaved and drank some sugarless milkless coffee – the only sustenance the den afforded – and by nine o'clock I was out again and sitting in the car. Ready to go. Ready to go to Windermere Gardens. Ready to talk to somebody. About something. Ready to find out. Ready.

I got into the morning traffic, of course, and inched my way along. All round me were men doing the same thing: driving a few feet, stopping, idling the engine, listening to the radio, driving another few feet. Their faces slid past, or stayed still, quite close to me and I could tell the kind of thoughts they were thinking; I could even guess, or thought I could, which of them were listening to news and talk on Radio 4 and which were listening to sport and pop music on Radios 1 and 2. We were all together and yet all separate, in our little moving boxes of glass and steel, being fed with centralised, predigested, processed pap. Everybody off to do another day's work, keeping the system going. What system?

But I wasn't going to work, I was chasing a private obsession that had come to me on a tide-threatened sandbank and stayed with me in a double bed beside a fire-flickered wall. I was looking for life, in what form I didn't quite know, but any form that was the opposite of death and was called L. J. Delmore.

Windermere Gardens was a block of flats standing in a land-scaped site that was conspicuous waste in itself, considering that the grass and shrubs were taking up space that could have been sold for millions of pounds. But it was all for a reason. Obviously rich people lived there, and rich people like a little clear space round their dwelling-places. It makes for peace and quiet, which are the most expensive commodities in the world, and it helps to pin-point anybody who is coming at you with a gun and a stocking mask over his face.

The building itself was warm and spacious. Its lobby had acres of clean marble floor. Most of the flats I went to in London, if they weren't simply walk-up jobs like mine, were the kind where you have a list of residents on a brass plate outside, with little brass pimples that you pressed and got a buzz to push the door open. But none of that here. You walked up to the magic-eye doors, they opened, and instantly a commissionaire in a blue uniform –

with epaulets, yet! – dodged out from behind a potted palm and wanted to know your business.

'Can I help you?' this one said to me. That's one notch up from 'Get out,' but it's a small notch.

'Mrs Delmore,' I said, looking confident.

'She's not at home,' he said smartly.

'Mr Delmore will do,' I said.

He gave me a come-off-it look. 'Mr Delmore isn't available,' he said. I had decided by now that I didn't like him. He was a long, thin chap with a downward-curving nose that looked as if it ought to have had a permanent dewdrop on its tip. Out of doors, it probably did, but the central heating inside this place dried it up.

'I have an appointment,' I said. I was beginning to have the strange, unreal sensation of playing an elaborate game in a dream. Your move, my move, edging round some complicated board and with no end in sight except clearing away the board and packing up the pieces.

'Mr Delmore doesn't make appointments,' said Epaulets. (Why? Is he a deaf-mute or something?) 'His secretary does that.'

I reached into my breast pocket and took out one of my trade cards. Making it clear that I ran a press-cutting agency. That usually opens a door, and it did this time.

'I'll see if Mr Delmore's secretary has got in yet,' Epaulets said, and went over to a telephone in the corner. He kept his voice down so that I couldn't hear him, but when he came back the satisfaction in his face showed that he had bad news for me.

'Mr Delmore's secretary has no record of any appointment,' he stated.

I looked at him coldly. 'This is getting ridiculous. I'm a busy man.' Busy making a fool of myself. 'Please tell Mr Delmore's secretary that I made an appointment for nine-thirty this morning and I'm on my way up to jog her memory.'

I turned towards the lift, but he put out a hand to restrain me. 'We have to be careful,' he said.

'All right, be careful,' I said. 'Search me for weapons, check on my identity, telephone my bank manager to see if I'm solvent, take a specimen of my urine, and then let me get into that lift. I want to see either Mr Delmore or his secretary and I'm going to see them before I go. I'm not a criminal or an assassin and I don't choose to be treated like one.'

As I said this I was aware, out of the corner of my eye, that the magic-eye doors were opening, and a man was coming in. Evidently it was someone Epaulets was used to, because he took no notice of whoever it was and kept his eyes on me. The newcomer himself, though, seemed to take an interest. He stopped beside me as we glowered at each other.

'Any problems, Dennis?' said this chap to Epaulets.

'No. Everything's in order.'

'Does he want to see Jake?'

'I think I said, everything's in order.' Dennis's tone conveyed pretty plainly that he didn't trust this snout-poker any more than he trusted me.

I thought there was a chance that the two of us might gang up on Epaulets-Dennis and get some action, so I turned to the chap and said, 'My business is with Mrs Delmore, but she isn't here, so I'd like to speak to Mr Delmore.'

'You claimed to have a business appointment,' Dennis put in.

'I don't take back that claim,' I said.

'What kind of business is it?' the new arrival asked me.

I had been taking no notice of him, up to then. No, it was more than that, I had been making a conscious effort to take no notice of him. I had my hands full already, I needed every atom of my concentrated attention for getting past Epaulets and bearding this Delmore character, and I was determined not to waste mental energy on any stray oddment of humanity who happened along. But at this barefaced piece of impertinence, I turned and looked at him carefully. He seemed to me worth studying. The all-time Nosey Parker.

He was a small man, about thirty-five, compact and neat. His suit was grey, his shoes black and well-polished, his shirt blue and freshly laundered. He held himself taut and upright, as a small man has to do if he isn't going to be overlooked. His face was strange, somehow: the jaw-line was strong, but there was something wrong with the upper part of the face. The eyes, was it? They seemed like eyes I had seen somewhere before, but they were wrong. They were too far apart, and they were restless, wandering.

The whole was topped off by a receding hairline which actually improved the man's appearance, making a low-to-average forehead look slightly higher. His hair was dark, cut short and well plastered down.

This was the character who had taken it upon himself to ask me my business. He stood looking at me – not steadily, not staring me down, but glancing to and fro, now at me, now away, very attentive and bird-like; on the balls of his feet; his right hand held a rolled newspaper which he tapped lightly against his leg. Physically, alert and in good condition. Mentally – I sensed it – confused, lost somewhere in a series of wrong turnings.

'What kind of business is it?' I gave him back his own words. 'What kind of business man would I be if I told all the details to everyone who happened to ask me? It's something between me and Mr Delmore, surely that's enough.' I made it sound like a breach of promise case, or something equally personal and shady, I realised as I spoke the words.

'Why do you call him Delmore?' this bloke asked me. Did his face really seem familiar? Surely I had never seen him before?

I was just about to tell him to mind his own business, when the lift doors opened. Somebody had just come down. The somebody was a girl, and she came up to us without hesitation as if that had been her purpose in taking the lift.

'Is this the gentleman, Dennis?' she asked Epaulets.

I was already pretty banjaxed by the rapid succession of events and new people, but this bird really threw me. I called her 'a girl', but that description doesn't begin to get her. She was very, very beautiful, to start with, and over the top of that she was lacquered and finished and bandboxed and manicured and styled and packaged and, for all I knew, depilated and deodorised. She looked as if she had been poured into her clothes. And she had orange hair. Yes, it actually was orange, and in contrast to everything else about her it looked as if it might be natural.

Altogether, she wasn't the sort of girl who could possibly have anything to do with the likes of me. She had been born, reared, groomed, trained and equipped to function in some Empyrean where I would never dream of poking my nose. Nevertheless, she addressed me: distantly, but with a kind of impersonal sweetness: a sweetness not really meant for me, just sprayed out on the surrounding air.

'Could you tell me what you wanted to see Mr Driver about?'

'Not Mr Driver,' I said. 'Mr Delmore. I want to see Mr Delmore.' Once again I had that sensation of being in a dream.

'Look, shall we just go up to the flat and sort it out there?' said the

— 41 —

orange-haired girl to me. 'You won't be able to see Jake, but I can probably handle whatever it is.'

Jake. I didn't want to see Jake. Unless his name was Jake Delmore. 'All right,' I said.

'I'll be in a bit later,' said the chap who had come in with the newspaper.

'Jake said you weren't to trouble,' she told him.

'It's no trouble. You make good coffee.'

He grinned and watched us walk over to the lift. Dennis watched us too, but without grinning.

The lift swished smoothly upwards. I saw from the indicator that the building had eight floors. Not a skyscraper: that wouldn't be exclusive enough: on the other hand, a mere five or six floors wouldn't add up to an impressive enough building. Everything was just so, and very, very expensive.

That made me think of the orange-haired girl again. Who the hell was she? Delmore's secretary. Was his flat an office, then? Did he run some kind of business from here? If so, what business?

I looked at the girl. Her orange hair was quite short and very bright. In the lighting of the lift, her eyes looked pale-blue, but I could well imagine that in certain lights they might look almost green. Well, turquoise. She had on a white dress with a simple gold belt, and white shoes.

She took no notice of me, but not offensively. She just stood there, balanced on her heels, looking calmly at the opposite wall of the lift. I suddenly realised that I was tired. The last sleep I had had, all those hours ago, had been the sleep from which the black-haired girl had stolen gently away. Why hadn't she stayed a little longer? Why?

All at once I decided not to be pushed around any more by any of this mob. I was there to find out where I might start looking for Mrs L. J. Delmore (Lingering Jasmine? Lilith Jacquetta?) and I was going to get a lead before I went away from here.

'Here we are,' said the orange-haired girl with impersonal brightness, as the lift subsided to a halt. We got out on to a polished wood landing. There were two doors: she opened one with a key. As she did so, the lift sighed away downwards, answering another summons. I followed the girl into the flat. It seemed to have about ten rooms; but she led me straight to what seemed the main one. Big windows, a black leather sofa, a staring white wall dominated by a single large painting: one of those enigmatic jobs they sell in Vigo Street galleries. So far, it was exactly like any trendy, rich pad. There was a smaller room opening on to this big one; I looked through the open door and saw a desk in the corner with a typewriter and a dictaphone on it. Evidently that was where Miss Orange-hair did her work, whatever it was.

She turned to me now, the sun flashing on her gold belt as she did so, and without inviting me to sit down she asked me what she could do to help me.

'I have a query,' I said. 'It isn't business, it's personal.'

'I handle most things for Jake. You'd better tell me what it is.'

'Certainly,' I said. 'Two nights ago I ran across his wife.'

Her expression changed, very slightly, though I couldn't really say from what to what. Just from non-committal to more non-committal. She said, 'Yes?'

'Her life was in danger. I saved it. There was nothing heroic involved. She seemed to be in a state of shock, and if I'd left her to herself she might have drowned.'

'Yes?' the girl said again.

'Don't you want to know where all this happened?' I said.

'It's you who came here to ask questions.'

That was fair enough, so I said, 'She was driving. But the car's wrecked now. It spent the night under salt water. It was in North Wales. And she's moved on, I don't know where.'

'What is it you want to ask?' the girl said, crisply now, as if I were getting to the end of the time she could spare me.

'I'm worried about her,' I said. 'I don't think she's in a fit state to be wandering about on her own. So when I looked at her car, what's left of it, and found out her name and address, I thought I'd come down and see if she'd got home and if she was all right.'

'That was good of you,' she said, not meaning it.

Meaning it, I said, 'I couldn't do anything else.'

'Let me get this straight. You came across her in North Wales, on the sea-shore or something, and saved her from drowning but you left the car under water, and then you lost sight of her again.'

'More or less, yes,' I said. I didn't feel obliged to give this chick a blow-by-blow account of the whole episode.

'And you came straight down here to see if she'd come back to this address?'

'I was worried about her. I still am.'

'You came all the way from North Wales?'

'It's not far,' I said foolishly.

'You didn't think of telephoning?'

It may sound incredible, but till she said those words I hadn't even thought of telephoning.

Such dealings as I had had with the black-haired girl had been expressed in physical terms: I had taken her into my boat and paddled her away out of reach of the tide, I had put food into her, I had given her shelter and made love to her, and suddenly to switch to an abstract plane, to look up numbers, to speak into a bakelite mouthpiece across hundreds of miles – it hadn't occurred to me.

I couldn't explain all this to Miss Goldbelt-Whiteshoes, so I opened my mouth to say something trivial, I don't remember what. But it turned out that there was no need for me to speak anyway, because a man's voice suddenly called from an adjoining room.

'Have you got somebody with you, Penny?'

'Yes.'

'What's he want?'

I seemed to have heard the voice before. It was penetrating and authoritative. Damn it, everybody I saw or heard this morning seemed to remind me of someone or something I couldn't place. It must be softening of the brain, I thought.

'He's asking about Julia,' she called back.

Julia!

There was a pause and then this man's voice said, 'What does he want to know about her?'

'He wants to know where she is.'

'Wait a minute,' said the voice. 'I'll get dressed.'

We waited a minute. Then he came padding in, a thick-set man with a mop of hair, wearing a white shirt-cum-pullover with a roll-neck, dark-grey slacks, sandals on bare feet. As soon as he appeared I recognised him. Jake Driver! The name hadn't registered, pre-occupied as I had been with other thoughts; I had heard 'Jake' and 'Driver' but hadn't put them together. Now I saw him, the name and the face merged. One of those actors whose face television has brought into every living-room. Even I, who have no television set, couldn't avoid knowing about Jake Driver. He had only been a star for about eighteen months, but he was big business. One of those breezy, bouncy actors who have no subtlety but make an impact with 'dynamism'. His presence on the small screen was somehow noisy even with the sound turned off.

In the flesh, he was a bit more puffy than they made him look on the set. Strong, though, with wide shoulders and a bull neck. His eyes were prominent: slightly hyperthyroid, in fact. He needed a shave, which was understandable if I had arrived just as he was getting out of bed. It was pretty early, after all.

He now fixed those prominent eyes on me, in no very friendly fashion, and spoke.

'Are you a friend of Julia's?'

'Strictly speaking, I don't know her.'

'But you're trying to find where she is.'

'So would you be if you'd seen her on Wednesday afternoon,' I said. I was in no mood to be treated as a pathetic Nosey Parker. 'She's wandering about somewhere and she's in no state to be.'

'Are you a doctor?'

'I run a press-cutting agency. But what business I'm in doesn't come into this. It's like being first on the scene after an accident. You do what you can.'

'So you did what you could,' Jake Driver said, looking at me thoughtfully.

'I put her up at the cottage I'm renting for my holidays. When I woke up in the morning she'd gone.'

'Any idea where?'

'If I had, I shouldn't be here.'

'You're beginning to sound like a detective,' he said.

'I've never met a detective and I don't know what they're supposed to sound like. It's just that chance threw her into my way, a woman who seemed' – I hesitated – 'not to be in proper control of what she was doing or thinking, and then chance took her away again.'

'Why not leave it at that?' he said smoothly. 'You can pretty well take it for granted that she'll be all right.'

'And if she isn't all right, that still doesn't make it my business, is that it?'

Jake Driver's answer was wordless: a long, meditative stare that was doubtless intended to unnerve me. It succeeded. Standing there, my muscles fluttering with fatigue, I felt once again that it was a long time since I had had food or sleep, and that I was among people who couldn't be expected to like me much.

'Do you mind if I sit down?' I asked him. It was a confession of weakness, but I didn't want to *fall* down.

He nodded, then turned to the orange-haired girl and said, 'Penny, get us some coffee, there's a darling.'

She went out. A voice in my head said, 'You make good coffee.' Where had I heard those words? Was it a few minutes ago or many years?

I sank down on the black leather sofa and Jake Driver sat on it too. As it was about ten feet long, that didn't put us very close together, but it made for a more relaxed atmosphere. And, actor-fashion, he used the change of physical position to signal a change of style. His blank, stony stare disappeared; he looked at me now with a softer, more meditative expression, though I could sense no warmth behind it.

'How did Julia seem when you saw her?'

'In shock,' I said.

'Did she . . . say much?'

'Very little.' I couldn't tell him what she had said. Though he was her husband, and must at one time have been close to her, he seemed to me not to deserve to know intimate things about her, things I knew. How her shoulders had trembled. How she had said, 'Not all four of them in there.' And other things I will not put down.

'Anyway, you found her wandering about?'

'No. Standing still.'

'Oh, dear. We are being literal, aren't we. Standing still having wandered about, would that get it?'

'I suppose so. She'd driven two hundred and fifty miles and she didn't seem to have any clear notion of why she'd done it.'

'Perhaps she just wanted to,' he said.

'Have you ever driven two hundred and fifty miles just on an impulse?'

'I might have,' he said calmly.

The orange-haired girl came back with a tray. On it were two cups of coffee and a small, slender glass full of colourless liquid.

'Black or white?' she asked me.

We went through all the details and then I was holding a cup of coffee and Jake Driver was holding a cup of coffee and what I supposed was a shot of *fine* or *marc* or something. The glass, anyway, was the kind you see French workmen drinking from at eight o'clock in the morning, having a slug of alcohol before they start work. She didn't bring one for me, and suddenly I thought that it was what I needed more than anything else in the world. But to offer me a drink would have been something like a gesture of welcome, and I wasn't welcome there.

'Good health,' I said as he downed it.

'Would you like one?' he asked.

'No, thanks,' I said.

He finished his drink, chased it with a swig of coffee, then suddenly said, 'What's your name?'

'Gus Howkins.'

'Well, Gus,' he said, settling his haunches more comfortably on the black leather – change of gear! Here we go into more personal contact! – close up! – 'it doesn't look as if we can help each other much. I don't know where my wife is. Neither do you but you're interested in finding out. What your motives are I don't know. It could be just pure kind-heartedness. You were worried about her because she seemed upset.'

'No,' I said. 'Not upset. In shock.'

'When people are in shock', he said smoothly, 'they go very cold and have to lie down and be covered with blankets. They can't do anything. But she was driving a car.'

'Not when I saw her. She was just sitting in it, staring through the windscreen. And the sea was coming up all round her.'

'So you saved her. You got into the car and drove it out of danger, with her sitting beside you.'

'No. I told her to back away from the tide. She started to but the car got stuck. Then I picked her up in a boat.'

'A boat?'

'A canoe.'

He thought for a moment. 'So she was fit enough to scramble in and out of a canoe? She wasn't ill or anything?'

'If she hadn't been able to get into the canoe,' I said, 'she might quite possibly be dead by now. It would have been a swimming job, and if she hadn't been able to get into the canoe . . . '

'She wouldn't have been able to swim. Precisely.'

'You know,' I said, 'you're making me feel as if I were on trial.'

'That's funny,' Jake Driver said calmly. 'I could have sworn that was what you were trying to make me feel like.'

'Without wanting to be rude, I'm not interested enough in you to want to make you feel anything. I'm just worried about your – about Mrs Delmore—' The name clogged my tongue and I stopped.

Jake Driver sat still for a while. he was very good at sitting still. His thick strong body was like a dolmen; his eyes were brooding. You could see it was all a performance, but it was a pretty professional job. Study of a man sitting patiently thinking how to deal with an unbalanced intruder.

He let this sink in and then turned away from me and asked the girl, 'Did Janice ring, Penny?'

'No,' she answered.

'That's strange.'

'Yes.'

'She got my message, didn't she? She did know I was expecting her round here last night?'

'I gave her the message all right.'

'Will you give her a ring?'

'Now? Or a bit later? It's rather early—'

'Ring her now,' he said decisively. 'And keep trying till you get her.'

Penny went into the other room and started dialling. Jake Driver turned back to me.

'So my wife went off in her car yesterday. She drove to North Wales and you met her. That may seem a bit strange to you, but people don't all live in the same way. Julia doesn't have anything much to hold her here. She hasn't any household duties, unless she takes it into her head to cook or choose fabrics or something, and we haven't any children. I'm out a lot of the time. My work isn't the kind that can be done at home. So she spends a fair amount of time on her own. And when a woman has a lot of time she sometimes does things that seem odd, just to be doing something. I've never run barbed-wire round her. If she wants to go away for a few days, she takes her car and goes.'

I stood up. There didn't seem to be any point in staying there and letting him snow me under.

'In other words, it's the most natural thing in the world for your wife to be sitting in a car all by herself, watching the tide coming in and doing nothing about it. And I'm poking my nose where I don't belong. I can quite see how it must look to you.'

'How does it look to *you*?'

'She needs help,' I said.

'She got help from you. And she'll get it from the next person she meets. A lot of people help a pretty girl in distress.'

'Don't you want to be one of those people?'

'She'll come back to me when she's ready to,' he said easily. 'Then I'll help her. But I'm not going to report her as a missing person and start a big search, after only twenty-four hours. As I said, Julia's a free person. She goes where she likes, and she comes back here when it suits her.'

'Well,' I said, 'I'm sorry I troubled you.'

'Don't be. I'm sure you meant well.'

Miss Orange-hair came in and said, 'I'm not getting any answer.'

'Show Gus out and try again, darling. And if there's still no answer you might see if she's at Val's.'

Something about the casual way he called me 'Gus' made it more insulting than if he had said 'Show Mr Howkins out.' He made it sound like the name of an animal. Yet I knew all the time that he wasn't really trying to insult me. I wasn't important enough to ruffle his good humour. And he had far more important things to do than worry about his poor bloody wife. Such as getting after this babe Janice.

Miss Orange-hair saw me out. She too was not interested in me enough to be rude. She just took me to the door and gave me an impersonal smile as she saw me through it. As if I had been a reporter on some village newspaper, interviewing Jake Driver after he had opened the garden fête.

So there I was, out on the landing. Wide as the building was, there were only two flats per floor, and the front door of the opposite number of Jake Driver's flat was across the hallway at a distance of about thirty feet. It was open, and standing in front of it, as if waiting for somebody, was the chap who had come in with his newspaper. The one who had invited himself to go in later and have some of Penny's good coffee. And who had poked his nose into my business.

All at once I knew he was waiting for somebody, and the somebody was me. He greeted me with a question, one of those questions that are meaningless in themselves but are designed with a hook to draw the other person into talk.

'How d'you find Jake this morning?'

'I'm not the doctor,' I said.

'I know that.' He jerked his head and grinned. 'I mean what kind of a mood is he in?'

'Oh, so-so,' I said and pressed the button for the lift. I wanted none of this chap. I wanted none of anybody in this building, come to that.

'Don't be in such a hurry,' he said. 'Come in and have a cup of coffee.'

'I've just had one,' I said.

'Well, have another. I'm sure we've got things to talk about.'

All of a sudden I felt terribly tired. The floor seemed unsteady under my feet, and since it was unlikely that in an expensive place like this the floor actually would be unsteady, I knew my legs must be buckling. A feeling of shivery cold surged up my back; I felt I wanted to hold on to something. The lift sighed up and stood waiting for me to go down, but I didn't want to. I wanted to lie down, right there on the floor, and go to sleep.

'I'll come in and sit down for a while,' I said to the chap. 'I could do with a rest. I didn't get to bed last night.'

'You look like it,' he said, and held the door wider open for me to go through.

I went in and made straight for a comfortable-looking armchair. It was the only one he had – the place seemed very sparsely furnished – but I didn't wait to be invited to sit down. I felt I was going to black out. As it was, when I lowered myself into the chair and leaned back everything went misty for a moment and I wondered if I were going to faint.

My dizzy spell can't have lasted more than a second or two, because he didn't notice anything. He followed me through the door, turned and closed it, and then came and stood on the hearthrug, looking down at me. Not that there was a hearth, in that centrally heated paradise. But there was a hearthrug.

He was so small and spry and fit-looking. And I was so saggy and flabby and tired out. I had made love – God, how many lifetimes ago had that happened? – and I had driven here and there and sat in pubs and thought and worried and then driven all night and then hunted up Delmore . . . no, Jake Driver . . . and confronted Epaulets and Orange-Poll and . . . and . . . I was falling asleep, and I brought my head up with a jerk.

'Jake doesn't usually do business before lunch,' he said. 'He comes to rather slowly in the morning. Yours must have been urgent.'

'You're trying very hard, aren't you?' I said.

'It's my job,' he said easily.

'Your job? Are you his bodyguard or something?'

'Bodyguard? That's good. He doesn't need a bodyguard. He's not *that* important, for God's sake.'

'Well, you're not his secretary,' I said, 'because I've seen her and she's got orange hair and her name's Penny.'

'Right,' he said, nodding.

'And you're not his bodyguard because he doesn't need one. And you're not his agent.'

'How d'you know that?' He was suddenly narrow-eyed.

'Because agents have plushy offices and they keep you waiting a long time, usually on stairways that smell of cheese, and then they let you into the office and it's got thick carpets and beautiful secretaries and filing-cabinets. You're not anybody's agent.'

'I am,' he said. 'I'm my own agent. I work for myself. Nobody owns me. I come and go as I like.'

'But you seem pretty dependent on Jake Driver,' I said at a venture.

A second later I wished I hadn't. He came dancing across the rug to my chair and bent down with his face very close to mine. He was a lot fitter than I was and some years younger, but that wasn't what frightened me most. What frightened me most was his face. It was both weak and dangerous, a nasty combination. All of a sudden I felt he might murder me and feed my body into the dispose-all. I tried to push my chair back, but it was too heavy.

He drew back without actually hitting me, and since I was able to muster the nerve to hold his eyes pretty steadily, he became uncomfortable and drew back, just as an animal does when you look it in the eyes.

'Don't tell me that kind of thing,' he said. 'Jake doesn't own me. Nobody owns me, mister.'

'All right,' I said. 'I don't see what makes it my business anyway. But you invited me in here. You must have wanted to talk about something. And surely I wasn't wrong in thinking that the something was to do with Jake Driver.'

'Let's put it this way. I have more than one iron in the fire. Jake Driver is one of them.'

'Yes?' I said.

'He has a lot of business, of one kind and another. He's a busy actor. A star. He has more work than he can handle. So I take some of it off him.'

'Yes?' I said. It seemed the best feed line to keep his words tumbling out. And if they tumbled out enough, I might get some clue to this strange set-up. And behind the set-up, there might be something that would lead me to those brown eyes, that pallor, that gentleness they called Julia.

'Penny's his secretary,' he said. 'O.K. She makes good coffee and she answers the telephone.'

'She's ringing Janice now,' I said on an impulse.

'What's Janice to you?' he snapped, suspicious again.

'What's any of it to me?' I said. 'Look, did you mean it about coffee?'

'You must think you have business here,' he said, 'or why did you come busting in here at nine o'clock in the morning?'

'Half-past,' I said.

'I didn't come out into the street and drag you in. You came. Now tell me what you came for.'

'I've already told Mr Delmore,' I said primly.

'Don't give me that Mr Delmore crap,' he said. 'The only time Jake ever gets called Mr Delmore is in the bank. Or if he were to go into a lawyer's office.'

'He might, at that,' I said. 'I've an idea he'll be talking to a divorce lawyer soon.'

Damn it, why did I say that? I could have got up out of my chair and kicked myself round the room. But fatigue plays funny tricks with one's mind. To box clever, I ought to have concealed what I was thinking, and above all to have concealed the gnawing, burning red-hot wire that was threading its way through my emotions, that longing, that sense of loss, of hunger and thirst . . . . Oh, God, I thought, mating ought to be a simple, happy activity; every time a male animal gets his penis into a female animal it ought just to be a light-hearted thing like singing a song or making a joke, and it would perpetuate the species just as well, but when has it ever been like that, ever, ever? And I knew I was falling asleep again with that question ringing in my ears. Oh, I was in a bad state, no mistake.

Of course he had me on toast then. 'Oh, I see,' he said.

'You see what?'

'Everything. You're a lawyer, acting for Julia.'

I had just enough sense to keep my mouth shut.

'That makes it more important than ever for you to work in with me.'

'Yes?' I had gone back to my formula.

'Well, damn it, of course,' he said irritably. 'I'm the only person she trusts.'

You? She trusts *you*? But all I said was, 'Yes?'

'Well, of course,' he said. 'That's one of the troubles between her and Jake.'

'Yes?'

'Jake's a very stubborn man. He doesn't see what's under his nose. He could serve his own best interests but he gets funny ideas, digs his heels in. His attitude to me isn't the only cause of that. He's funny about a lot of things. Let's put it this way. If Jake would relax, turn over the ordinary day-to-day running of his career to me – the thousand and one things that crop up and call for decision-making – well, he'd have more energy to put into his work. He lets things worry him, you know. He's not as calm as he seems on the outside. And yet when he has the answer, when he has the perfect management aid built into his own family, he starts to shy away, he says yes, then he says no, he wobbles and dithers.'

Built into his own family? The perfect what? Built into what?

All of a sudden I saw it. Saw why his face had seemed to remind me of someone's. The eyes were the same deep brown, though they were somehow wrongly placed in the head: the jaw-line was just as cleanly rounded, like the heel of a shoe; the set of the head on the shoulders was similar, though she kept hers still with that beautiful repose and he was always giving that nervous, evasive jerk. 'You're related to Julia,' I said.

'Related? I'd better be. She's my little sister.' He looked sharply across at me as if checking whether I took his word for it. 'That's how I come to be in contact with Jake. The good old in-laws. Everybody has 'em, the way everybody has Income Tax and the dentist.' He grinned mechanically at what was evidently the accustomed point in a set speech. 'But this was one in-law that Fate sent as a blessing. If he'd only been wide-awake enough to recognise it. His trouble is, he thinks he's clever. Actually he's a babe in arms. Anybody could get the better of him on any deal. He can't buy a packet of cigarettes without being short-changed. But he doesn't see it. He thinks because he's a star and he makes a lot of money, that shows he's clever. Going over big has damaged him. He wasn't so big-headed when he and Julia were just bit players, working in rep., taking anything they could find and glad of it. And he needs good advice now, more than he ever did then, to save him from being taken to the cleaners. Because let's face it, there's a hell of a lot of sharks about.'

None of this meant anything to me. He seemed to be airing some familiar grievance in words he had used many times before. In any case, I was in no mood to take it all in. While he was talking, I was thinking. This strange creature, who seemed closer to a jerking mechanical toy than to anything fully human, was obviously – on his own statement, and more certainly on the testimony of his appearance – related to the girl I was searching for: her brother, in fact. So, although I was no nearer to finding her, I had located her husband and her brother. Not a bad haul for one morning. But to what use could I put this haul? The husband was blankly unhelpful, and as for the brother, he was putting out such a smoke-screen of words that it was going to be very difficult to ask him anything. Obviously, a dodgy character. But not successful, not smooth. As he clacked on I looked unobtrusively round the flat. It was large, like all the flats here, and there were gaping empty spaces between the pieces of furniture. The hearthrug he was standing on was the only piece of carpeting on the floor, which didn't matter because the wood of the floor was polished and beautiful, but you could tell that wasn't a deliberately sought-for aesthetic effect: it was simply that he had no carpet. The door into an adjoining room was open; on the pretext of shifting my position in the chair, I leaned forward and took a look through the doorway into the room. I saw a narrow bed, unmade but not squalid – obviously, he was quite neat in his habits – and, near it on the floor, something I couldn't identify for a second or two, it was so long since I'd seen one and I so little expected to see one there. But yes, it was. A rowing-machine.

He was rattling on. 'Actually, Jake's got a very peculiar make-up. Let's put it this way; he hides from himself the extent to which he depends on me. Deep down he knows he needs me, but he'll do anything rather than admit it and he even keeps it a secret from himself. He wasn't always like that. When he first married Julia he used to ask my advice about things. He knew I'd knocked about in the world and I'd got a head on my shoulders. He used to say, "How does it look to you, Cliff?" before he did anything that meant taking a decision. That's my name, Cliff Sanders.'

So her name used to be Julia Sanders. Now it's Julia Delmore. Julia Sanders, Julia Delmore, I love you. Stupid, unteachable fool that I am.

'But it all changed when he suddenly made it into being a star. It was the box that changed it all, of course. From one day to the next and everybody knew his face. And of course it wasn't just me that started having trouble with him then. Everybody did. Julia too, of course. In a way you can't blame him, all those little hot pants about the place. Flocking to the scent of a star. Thinking he could make their careers for them. He'd have had to be very level-headed and he never was that, poor old Jake, oh dear no.'

'Did you mean it about that cup of coffee?'

'I haven't got any coffee,' he said smoothly, 'sorry. I ran out a week ago and I keep meaning to get some. But there's a joint just down in the street that always seems to be open when I want it. And it's easier to go down and get a cup there than sit up here by myself. It's more sociable. You make contacts.'

'All right,' I said. 'You've made a contact now. Me. Without even going down to the coffee bar. So why not use it? Is there something you want to tell me?'

He stood quite still and looked at me for a second, before glancing away in the fashion I had come to expect. 'Other way round,' he said. 'I thought you might want to know something.'

'No,' I lied.

'But you went to see Jake.'

'Yes, I went to see Jake.'

'What about?'

'You've just told me he won't let you act as his manager. So what makes his business yours?'

'I've told you a lot more than that. I've told you he needs me to look out for him. He pays the rent of this place, why d'you think he does that? He needs me near him, even if he gets cussed now and then and digs his heels in. I have to work twice as hard, once to get possession of the facts and once to put them in order. Let's put it this way. If you've got business with Jake you'll find it goes through a lot more smoothly if you work with me. Never mind what he tells you in his stubborn moods. I'm the only person who can keep him on the rails and deep down he knows it.'

I had an idea. 'You're very sure I must have business with Jake,' I said. 'But Julia's an actress in her own right. What if my business was with her? If I wanted to get her back to work?'

'Are you booking for a theatre?'

I stood up. 'Thanks for the coffee,' I said, 'but I must be going now. I went to the Delmores' flat because I'm trying to contact Mrs Delmore. I'm glad to meet her brother and it's interesting to know that you're the indispensable kingpin of Jake's business life. All that's fine but it doesn't really concern me. I have business with Mrs Delmore, and since I haven't found her here I'll be moving on.'

'No, you won't,' he said. 'You'll stay here and talk to me.'

'Why should I do that?' I asked.

Hands in pockets, he did a little shuffle along the hearthrug, then abruptly stopped and swivelled his head round to look at me.

'Because I know where she is,' he said.

Giles Hermitage laid down his ball-point writing implement. It needed a new refill. In any case, he had done his stint for the day. Before writing another day's-worth of concocted biography he would have to go to the stationery shop again and ask again if they were still 'out of', or 'waiting for', the refills that fitted the only kind of ball-point he could use. It was chunky and rather heavy in the hand, like a small pistol, ready to fire the words out with accuracy. He did not feel confident of writing well with any other kind of pen, though he had tried many, from the cheapest to the most expensive, and had even experimented, disastrously, with dictating his fictions into a recording machine, miserably improvising sentence after sentence into the indifferent eardrum that stored it all without reacting and without forgiving. He had abandoned the method, and the money he had forced himself to spend on the tape-recorder had to be written off as simply wasted. Then it was back to the stubby, metallic ball-point. Novel-writing was such a tediously *subjective* process: no doubt any kind of pen, or any kind of dictaphone, would serve as well as another to write a report saying whether somebody was a good insurance risk, or offering a chance to acquire space in a prestige office building: all those jobs that were done by neat men with well-trimmed moustaches and shiny cars and freshly painted suburban homes with shaven lawns and underfloor heating.

Giles Hermitage, novelist, did not have a well-trimmed moustache. He did not own a freshly painted suburban house or any kind of house. He was a thick-set, clumsy man of fifty with a thatch of greying hair, wearing a pullover down which he had several times spilt food and failed to clean it off properly. For reading, and desk work generally, he wore glasses with heavy black frames. He lived by himself in a four-roomed flat in a cathedral town; he had originally gone there for no better reason than that it had been his mother's flat, during the years of her widowhood, and when she died it had seemed to him that he might as well move into it himself. Previously he had rented a house in London with two other men, one of whom bred Yorkshire terriers and kept them in a wire-netting enclosure in the back garden. Giles had now lived in this town, in this flat, for seven years, spending most of his hours in working. His novels were civilised and responsible, neither condescending to nor affronting the reader, and commanded a small but not fickle public. Surveys of contemporary literature always mentioned him.

Having decided to stop work for the day, Giles felt at a loss. He gathered up the sheets he had written, and put them away in the box-file that contained his work-in-progress. This was another sacred habit. He always used the same box-file, though it was now twenty years old and the hinge of the lid had given way. He had repaired it with plastic tape, but it was always on the point of coming off. Also, one corner was broken, the result of his knocking the file off a high shelf on to the floor about fifteen years previously. He had been drunk at the time. He quite often got drunk, sitting in the flat by himself, listening to the radio and thinking up the most perfect descriptions of the horribleness of people he disliked. Some of these people were his personal acquaintances, others were known to him only by some tenuous contact such as having seen their faces on television. He had no television set and when he watched it at friends' houses he only did so in order to fuel his hatred. Irascibility, he found, started his adrenalin going and helped him to write.

Giles looked at his watch. Twenty minutes to one. Rather early to eat lunch, too late to start on any meaningful task. He felt restless. Outside, the cold rain of early spring fell on the dingy square of grass in front of Sunderland Court. No one knew why the block of flats was so called; the town was nowhere near Sunderland. It was simply a meaningless, pretentious name, and as such it was perfectly adapted to the building it designated, which had been designed just before World War II by an architect whose mind had clearly been on something else.

And now, as he closed the lid of the box-file and moved away from his desk, Giles Hermitage abandoned his pathetic attempt at self-hypnosis and admitted that what he felt was much worse than restlessness. It was pain, compounded of grief and loss and disappointment and the long, trailing after-effects of severe emotional shock. He had been writing with peculiar intensity, living as completely as possible in the story of Gus Howkins, because it was the only way of escape from the anguish and alarm that flooded every cell of his being as soon as he took his head out of the creative sand.

Today was the day Harriet was going to Australia, for ever. If her aircraft had taken off on time, she had already been in the air for eighty minutes. He tried, miserably, to calculate how far a plane travelling at five hundred miles an hour would move in eighty minutes, to form some notion of where on the earth's surface, or rather up above it, Harriet was now. But his mind would not perform the task; it was sodden with misery. To make it more sodden still, in the hope of dulling some of his pain, Giles broke open the cap of a new bottle of whisky and took his first drink of the day.

The postponing of his first drink until now was in itself an achievement. Since Harriet had ended their relationship – steadily refusing to discuss matters or to have any contact with him at all, returning his gifts, sending back his letters unopened, putting down the telephone immediately at the sound of his beseeching voice – Giles had taken a great lurch towards alcoholism. He was conscious of the desire to start drinking as soon as he got up in the morning: unhappiness of this intensity was a very physical sensation, located mainly in the pit of the stomach, and his mind whispered to him that only a shot of alcohol, dumped straight on to the central point of the agony, would ease the gnawing. So far, he had resisted that early-morning temptation, being a man of some stubbornness and self-respect. After a hastily swallowed breakfast (for food was as unwelcome to his fluttering stomach as drink was welcome), he had picked up his ball-point pen and gone straight into the world of his imagination, seeking refuge among characters whose problems were not his problems, though they were recognisably akin, and whose names and faces he could conjure out of the air instead of from the pain-ridden catacomb of his memory. He had several times read, and heard in conversation, the statement that suffering was not so bad for an artist as for other people; at least the artist could capitalise on it, could exploit and canalise and transmute it into art. Now that intense suffering had, for the first time in his life, fallen to his lot he was inclined to be sceptical. How could numb, corroding, paralysing pain help any man to do anything? Would there come a time when he could surmount it and begin to use it for an access of fresh and deep vision? He would have to wait and see, but how long?

Giles's fifty years had of course not been without their distresses, frustrations and disappointments. But nothing that had hit him yet had been as bad as what he was going through now. Harriet had been at the centre of his life; she had suddenly removed herself, and now his life was without a centre. He did not know how to begin picking himself up. His grief had not, thank God, destroyed his capacity to work, but it had destroyed everything else: laughter, health, joy in nature, art, the company of his friends.

Harriet was flying in the sky. She was going to Australia with Frank Bodkin, or Fred Bodenheim, or whatever his blasted name was. She was going to be the man's wife – perhaps, since he had no direct source of news about her, had already become so. Mrs Bankhouse. Mrs Breadbasket. Giles knew the man's name perfectly well, but was trying to scribble it out of his mind. The awful, stonily glaring fact remained – that Harriet was no longer his. She had pulled away, suddenly, and half his guts had come away with her, and now he was walking around with a huge hole where his guts used to be, a hole full of blood, and pain, and pus. The question was, what could he do?

Harriet had been Giles's mistress for seven years. During that time they had been, or so he had confidently supposed, steadily happy. Except that their partnership lacked the final seal of legitimacy, it had been very like an idyllic marriage. And Harriet had never wanted to get married. He had several times told her that if she wanted to be Mrs Hermitage he would see to the matter, but each time she had smilingly refused. 'It's just perfect as it is, darling. I've no wish to settle down as a housewife and I don't want children. So I'd do my job anyway. And I like the freedom of not actually *living* with you. I suppose if we moved in together we'd save expense, but we'd need a bigger place and that would cost more. And you need solitude for your work. No, it all suits me as we have it now.' And she would squeeze his hand, or kiss him, giving that little physical touch of reassurance that she was happy, that he was secure of her. And since Giles was terrified of marriage, having been forced to watch at close quarters the writhings of people related to him who had made unhappy marriages, he had felt relieved, and serene.

So things had stood, or rather moved on in peace and happiness all through those seven years. Harriet, aged thirty-three when they first met and somewhat breathless and battered from a succession of lovers who had treated her with casual cruelty, had been employed as a teacher of art at the local College of Further Education. She was deeply interested in art, worked at tapestries, spent her holidays going to see paintings in all the famous collections. He had been with her a number of times; she had walked him through the Prado, the Uffizi, the Louvre, explaining things or just pointing to them, breaking down his wordsmith's obtuseness to the arrangement of colour and line.

Standing sadly there, whisky-glass in hand, Giles tried to fight down the memories, though he knew it was hopeless: the memories would win, there were so many of them and they were so much stronger than he, they would march over him, shatteringly, for years, perhaps for ever, leaving great grooves and trenches of pain. He and she had spent most Saturdays and Sundays together. They had prepared food and argued and laughed and wrangled and made love. Sometimes he had slept at her flat, a mile away; sometimes she had slept at his; sometimes they had spent the day together and gone back to their respective dens at night; often a day went by without their meeting, but in that case they always spoke on the telephone. As the years went by Harriet had plumped slightly, but Giles had been happy about this too, taking it for a sign of contentment; and her large fine eyes and breathless laugh always excited him. Her body was smooth and buxom, she was all woman, and now she belonged to someone else and it had all been so cruelly sudden.

Giles's knuckles whitened as he unknowingly squeezed the glass in his hand as if to force the truth out of it. Why, why had he never insisted that they got married? Overcome first his own fear of wedlock, then hers, and dragged her to a register office? (It could not have been a church, since she had absent-mindedly got married to one of her early lovers, who had shortly deserted and divorced her.) If they had been settled down together, as man and wife, the temptation for her to change her mind, to drop him so suddenly and so hard, would have been much less, and if he had seen signs of unrest he could at least have talked to her, calmly, soothingly, protectingly, making her feel safe in his love, till the counter-attraction died away into calm.

Well, he hadn't. He had accepted her assurances that she was happy with him, that she liked things the way they were, and all the time this smooth bastard of a vice-principal, or whatever he was, at her place of work, had been undermining and corrupting her. And now, he was going to some fat job in Australia, he had persuaded her to go with him and to be his wife, and Giles's life was left without its core. Out of the blue, Harriet had written him a letter – a letter! – saying that their relationship was over and that he was not to try to get in touch with her. Dazed, he had stumbled to the telephone, but her voice over the wire was even cooler than her words on the page. 'I shan't change, so don't hope.' It had happened a month ago, and so far he had made no progress at all towards healing.

For the ten thousandth time, Giles wondered why she had done this to him. It was the abruptness, the utter unpreparedness, of the change that had shattered him. If she had shown signs of discontent at not being his wife, or had begun to criticise details of his behaviour and attitudes, he would have read the warning and done something about it – done anything, anything to keep her. But she had matured the terrible deed behind a completely placid front. She must have been thinking anti-Giles thoughts during the whole of their last few weeks, must have been preparing her escape and his destruction even while eating and sleeping with him, even while talking and making jokes and reminiscing – how could she, *how could she?*

Giles downed his whisky and poured another. She had done it, that fact had to be faced, and somehow his pain had to be coped with. He knew that getting drunk would be, at best, a short-term solution. While he was actually in a state of drunkenness, there would be some relief, if only because his mind would be too confused to retain one thing consistently, even suffering. But then he would fall into a heavy afternoon sleep, and during that sleep his guard would go down, and he would have one of those horrible, horrible awakenings, when the pain came first and the recollection of what the pain was caused by came afterwards. He doubted, seriously, whether his mental balance would stand any more of those agonies. Better to keep some sort of grip on himself, even at the price of uninterrupted suffering, than submit to a treacherous anaesthetic which would leave him naked to the next instalment of the flogging.

Food, then. It was one of the days when Mrs Pimlott, his cleaning lady, came and dusted out the flat. On these days she also prepared a simple lunch and left it on a tray. He went into the kitchen. Yes, cold ham, bread and butter, tomatoes, a bottle of beer and a glass, with the opener ready beside them. A frugal lunch for a frugal man. Suddenly, Giles saw himself clearly as what he was: middle-aged, entering the last twenty years of his life, wedged immovably beyond all hope of change. Harriet had been his last throw at happiness, and after seven years she had vanished like a puff of smoke.

He opened the beer and poured some out, took a draught, half-heartedly champed ham and bread. Mrs Pimlott. A worthy soul. Too garrulous, so that he was forced to avoid her; in fact, she had contributed largely to the formation of his regular working habits, since if he was at his desk, behind a firmly shut door, when she arrived, he could avoid contact with her except on the day each week when he paid her and listened to a statutory half-hour's cascade of information about her domestic life. On days when he was absent from home, she cleaned his study. It all worked perfectly, just as the arrangement with Har— No! Back, down, with that thought!

Besides, Mrs Pimlott had been, quite possibly, the means of saving Giles's life. During that first few days, dazed with shock and with the taste of grief perpetually in his mouth, he had faced the fact that existence held no more attraction for him and that he wished he were dead. Never having thought of suicide before, he had no idea how one set about it, except that most people seemed to do it by means of an overdose of narcotics. Well, nothing would be simpler than to ask his doctor for a bottle of sleeping-pills (a middle-aged writer with nervous problems) and then swallow the lot at once and be done with it. On the third night of his agony he had decided to go to the doctor in the morning and take the pills as soon as he got back. But suddenly it came into his mind that people who kill themselves in this way, he had read somewhere, always soil their clothing in the last moments of life, when the body relinquishes control. And for some reason, although he did not want to live, Giles could not face the thought of Mrs Pimlott letting herself in and finding him dead in a mess of excrement. It was so *undignified*: the thought was absurd, but undeniable. Was Harriet going to roll him in shit as well as break his heart? No, no, he would go on living, with however little zest, rather than be so humiliated.

Then he remembered something else he had read: that Jean-Paul Sartre had said of Flaubert, 'He used writing as an alternative to suicide.' He had no idea what Sartre had meant to convey about Flaubert, was not interested in the truth or falsity of the statement, but the words came back to his mind like a thin shaft of light. Writing as an alternative to suicide! Or, for that matter, to death in any form! Yes, yes, it might work. Because to be a writer, at any rate of fiction, is very much the same thing as being a ghost. During the writing of a story, all life ceases except what goes on inside the skull. He would be out of life and yet observing it, moving restlessly among the scenes in which he had lived, re-calling reality and re-shaping it. A ghost comes and goes as it pleases, has no experience of its own, feeds on that of others; it cannot act, but it can speak.

Very well, he would speak.

But for the time being, the energy that enabled him to speak was used up, and he had the rest of the day, and the evening, still to get through. He quailed in fear, knowing what was waiting for him, especially as darkness closed in on the rainy spring evening. What could he clutch at? The cinema? He had seen all the films that were on locally, except for the inevitable pornographic offerings, which he avoided if only because sexual arousal, in his present deprived state, would only add another layer to his misery. Books? He knew he could not keep still for long enough to read a page, perhaps never would again. Friends? He had tried, but his misery made him inattentive; it was as if their voices came from an immense distance, saying things in which he could not feign an interest: what did anything matter now?

Well, he must do something. Now that lunch, or as much of lunch as he could face, was over, the afternoon stretched ahead. Don't drink: do something useful, some chore. Something you don't like doing. If you're going to be unhappy, you won't notice the boredom of some piece of unwelcome drudgery, so get that much mileage out of it.

This last piece of self-advice left Giles with only one possible course of action. Moodily, he approached a brown cardboard box which stood in a corner of his workroom. This box – it had originally contained a dozen bottles of cheap wine – was his depot, or halting point, or Sargasso Sea (the nomenclature varied with the level of his impatience and pessimism) for incoming mail. Wearily putting down his glass, he opened the flaps and peered now into the carton's shadowy depths.

Letters were for Giles a problem permanently insoluble. When, to the distant accompaniment of Mrs Pimlott's thumping and clattering, he approached his work in the morning, he never opened the day's mail, knowing that it would start trains of thought that would ram headlong into whatever hesitant imaginative caravan was just setting out across the dunes of his mind. And when, after the hours of dusty effort, he laid down his pen, the thought of staying at his desk to read, and ultimately answer, letters was one that made his stomach churn. So that the envelopes – square white ones, brown oblong ones, cellophane-windowed ones, duck-egg-green tinted ones, slobberingly sealed ones addressed in backward-sloping script – stayed for weeks on end, unopened, in their cardboard waiting-room, their Ellis Island where Giles could interrogate them at his leisure.

But now, the box was almost completely full. The accusing tide had risen to within an inch of spill-over point. If the next morning's delivery were to contain a couple of fat circulars, a seed catalogue not recognisable as such through its thick white envelope, and a third-carbon copy of the volcanic boilings of some adolescent versifier, there would be nowhere to stack further instalments and Nemesis would be upon him.

He glanced out of the window. More needles of cold rain. It was a miserable day anyway, why not waste a little of it? Grimly, he turned back to the carton. Six letters. He would open and answer, or at least consider answering, the first six letters he pulled out. With any luck, at least three of them would be self-answering, in the sense that if he simply ignored them the senders would go away.

At first, his luck held. In succession, his fingers closed over a brown envelope containing some meaningless piece of rigmarole from a government office: a request to judge the literary competition at a local school: and a demand for information by the compilers of a biographical dictionary, confident of being able to make a profit on a stout volume whose every word had been written for them, free of charge and with obsessional attention to detail, by the chosen subjects. Each of these, with a muttered imprecation, he dropped into the waste-paper basket. Three more to go. Giles drove his hand far down into the heap, so as to give a fair chance to some of the letters that had been there longest, and, tugging hard, brought up a creamy envelope of good quality addressed in a large, decided but unmistakably feminine hand. He weighed it doubtfully. Its thickness indicated a longish letter; or, if not long, on thick paper. People who wrote on thick paper did so to establish that they were important and must have an answer. Rapidly Giles went back over the resolution he had just formed and modified it. Circumstances alter cases. He had made a pact with himself to open six letters: but if this turned out to be the pest it seemed likely to be, he would count it as two. That would leave only one more, and he would take care that that one should be an obvious piece of junk mail.

Strengthened by these thoughts, he clawed open the envelope. It was of a kind that asked to be slit open neatly with a paper-knife, but Giles's paper-knife had a knack of hiding and turning up only when all danger of work was past. The thick outer paper tore in one pattern, the delicate damson-coloured lining in another. Feeling despite himself a faint tingle of anticipation, he unfolded the thick (yes!) paper and began to read the long (yes!) message in its large, clear, feminine (yes!) hand.

2 Princess Terrace
10 April

Dear Mr Hermitage,

It will not surprise you to receive a letter from a complete stranger. A writer of your reputation, necessarily a public figure, must receive many such. Perhaps the only circumstance that makes this letter at all different, that gives it a momentary claim on your attention, is that it is written by a hand that will soon cease to hold a pen.

In a word, Mr Hermitage, this is a letter from an old woman who will soon be dead. That statement is not intended to be melodramatic. My sole excuse for troubling you with a letter, for obtruding on your attention the fact that I exist at all, is that I am bedridden with an illness which I know to be terminal. My doctors have told me so, and in any case I feel it in my bones, and in all the fibres of my body.

You are a man of imagination, Mr Hermitage. I suppose you must have meditated, sometimes, on what the foreknowledge of

— 66 —

death does to the human mind. Dare I say that I am in a position to tell you? To speak with authority in *that* domain at least? At any rate I can say this much: the knowledge that one is soon to die closes up some avenues and opens others. There is no need of introspection and thought. It is as if one's illness did the thinking and decision-making on one's behalf, ruthlessly discarding some velleities one has nursed perhaps through half a lifetime, causing others to blossom and take on an aura of practicability. It is as if it knew, one's illness, this all-claiming and all-knowing enemy that has singled one out, which were the genuine needs and which were the fads.

After this long preamble, let me come straight to the point. Of course by this time you will have realised that I want something from you. Practised and seasoned in life as you are – for your birth-date, Mr Hermitage, appears on the dust-jackets of your books, and I know you have weathered five decades of our human experience – you will have learnt long ago that people do not write letters out of the blue unless they are seeking to satisfy some need of their own, even if it is no more than a need to communicate. In my case, it is that, but also something more. I have a favour to ask you; more than a favour, a kindness; more than a kindness even – an act of mercy and benediction towards a dying woman.

For years, I have admired your work. I possess most of your books – only those published in paperback, alas, for I have little money to spare from daily necessities; but my daughter, Diana, who lives with me and runs our home, is so kind as to go to the library very often, to fetch and carry those books of yours which I do not own but constantly re-read. Notably, if I may single out a favourite, that wonderful book of stories, *Adventure Playground*. I can honestly say that I treasure every page of every one of those stories. Surely even you have never written better! Why was that book never issued in paperback? But even as I write that question I know that it is not the kind of book on which a commercial publisher could take a risk. It is written for the judging eye and the understanding heart.

Now, winding up my courage to the point of no retreat, I come at last within sight of my request. I know you, Mr Hermitage, very well by sight. You will have seen the address at the head of this letter, and will recognise it as a house you regularly pass on your meditative walk in the direction of the Cathedral. Now here at last is my request. Will you break your routine one day, and instead of walking past the house will you open the gate, walk the few steps to the front door, and ring the bell? My daughter will let you in, and, recognising you at once – for she knows you as well as I do – will bring you into the room where the last scene of my little play is being acted out. And I shall ask you to talk to me for a little while: not mere empty conversation about this and that, but real talk about your thoughts, about the book you are writing. For surely you must be writing a book, and must indeed be some distance on with it. Two years, all but a month, have gone by since you brought one out; all that time I have scanned the publishers' advertisements to see if there was another deep and rewarding experience on the way, and during the second of those two years I have been scanning them with increasing anxiety and finally with something like desperation, as it has become more and more clear that my own life-span was shortening. Finally, I have decided not to wait any longer but to ask you, as point-blank as this, if you will make me happy before I die, by sharing with me some of the thoughts and perceptions that are destined for your next book, a book I may not live to read. Will you grant me that happiness? Or am I, even when all claims of privilege have been allowed, trespassing too far?

I can only await your answer, dear Mr Hermitage, but whether you answer or not, please accept my gratitude for all the joy and illumination your books have brought me through the years. Do come if you can. I am terminally ill – I have already told you that – but I am not a disgusting sight and I have no symptoms that are likely to cause distress in other people. Diana keeps me clean and neat. Look at the handwriting of this letter. It is firm and clear, is it not? You would not guess, would you, that it was written by someone who counts the days she has yet to see, and finds the number inexorably dwindling?

Yours with every good wish and grateful thought,
Helen Chichester-Redfern

Giles's first reaction on reading this letter was to wonder whether it was a hoax. Why should anyone want so much to see *him*, especially someone who was not feeling well? He was not famous enough to be lionised; making his acquaintance could not minister to any imaginable vanity. On the other hand, who would want to play a practical joke on him by luring him into this house with some cock-and-bull fable of a dying woman who admired his books? He was not rich and had no rich relatives, so it was unlikely that any criminal organisation had decided to kidnap him. He thought over the roster of his friends, but they were mostly as stolid as he was. Not a practical joker among them. Perhaps it was true after all. He turned back to the address. Princess Terrace? A row of solidly built Edwardian houses, semi-detached, gabled and timbered with a touch of pretentiousness not unpleasingly redolent of their epoch. The epitome of everything respectable, conservative; if this dying woman were a widow, she might well be finishing her life, on the savings of some respectable husband, in just such a house. And the daughter, Diana, who looked after her . . . Giles had a momentary vision of spectacles and scraped-back hair, a tired, patient girl who had laid aside a docile career in nursing or the social services, or perhaps school-teaching, to be the equally docile roadstead of her mother's passage towards the eternal. Why did he think of her as docile? Because the mother was so obviously a strong character. This, whatever else it might be, was not the letter of a weak or scatterbrained woman. And she was educated, too. He had seen that immediately from her handwriting, but the content of her letter confirmed it beyond doubt. She used words like 'velleities'. She constructed her sentences like a person who has read Henry James.

He looked down at the letter, turning it over in his hands as if it might yield some clue. This brought to his attention a postscript, on the back of the last sheet, which gave the telephone number of 2 Princess Terrace and suggested a call ahead of his visit. For some reason that small item of practical advice broke the log-jam in Giles's mind. He walked straight over to the telephone and dialled the number. Listening to the ringing tone, he imagined the two women responding each in her own way to its jangling signal: the young one putting aside whatever task at that moment lay before her, the old one lying upstairs listening eagerly to know whether the ringing heralded his visit. The clean, drab interior formed itself with unusual clarity on his mind's eye: he saw the daughter in her plain, neat clothes walking with quiet, methodical steps from the sink or the washing-machine, or the bureau stacked with letters and bills, to the impatiently shrilling despot, while. . . .

The ringing stopped and a voice said 'Hello?', uttering the word as a question, with an enquiring upward inflection. Something about the voice caught Giles's attention. Quick, light, interested, it was not the kind of voice he associated with his mental picture of the docile, uncomplaining girl.

'Miss Chichester-Redfern?'

'Yes,' lightly and decisively.

'This is Giles Hermitage.'

'Oh, yes. Thank you for ringing. Mother wrote to you some time ago, didn't she?'

Guilt. The letter had lain in his cardboard box for anything up to a month. And the woman's time was short.

'Well, yes, I'm afraid I . . . '

'You must be very busy. And it's nice of you to be in touch.'

'Well,' said Giles, 'since it took me so long to get round to answering the letter, let me say now that it will be a pleasure to come and visit your mother and talk with her, if she's well enough.'

'Oh, she's well enough. She has good days and days that aren't so good. Today's quite a good one.'

'I'll come today.'

'Well, she'll be delighted. That is good of you. I hope it's not an imposition.'

'Not at all.'

'The doctor's coming at three o'clock, but it's just a routine visit: he should be finished with her by half-past.'

'I'll come then.'

'Thank you. She'll be so pleased. You know where we live, I expect?'

'Yes, I do. I've often been past the house.'

'Well, thank you again. Mother'll be looking forward to half-past three.'

He murmured something polite and rang off. Don't thank me, young lady. If you only knew what you're saving me from. The long, empty, aching afternoon. One of those afternoons that are like walking down an endless dingy street between high ugly buildings, with a harsh hot wind blowing gustily, whirling scraps of rubbish and paper continually into my face. The street is my life, the ugly buildings are meaningless tasks, the hot wind is my unhappy love, the scraps of paper are memories of Harriet.

— 70 —

Memories never still, never ending, always flying into my face, always taking me by horrible surprise.

His meal was eaten, his telephone call made, and three-thirty was still ninety minutes away. Giles stood irresolute, staring out of the window. There were numerous small tasks he ought to be doing, mostly paying bills or writing letters. But he could not settle down indoors. The rain had stopped; he would go for a walk till it was time to call on the woman.

Mrs Chichester-Redfern had been correct in noting that his daily walk usually took him in the direction of the Cathedral, not because he responded much to its ecclesiastical statement but because the Close, and the quiet streets that lay about it, were pleasant to walk in, and his way led him past some old-fashioned shops that supplied his few wants. Everything here was quiet and orderly. Even the parked cars had a well-bred look, as if their owners never raced their engines bad-temperedly or took risks at road junctions; as if they were taken from their brick-built garages only on useful and respectable journeys, and then only after deliberation. This town was out of touch with the grimy, anxious and feverish modern world. To live here was to hide one's face from the nature of contemporary reality. These important advantages, Giles reflected, were enough to outweigh the considerable drawbacks of the place.

Now, however, walking rapidly along with lowered head, he threaded his way through side-streets and back alleys to avoid going past certain familiar shops, because he had been into them so often with Harriet. In particular, he knew himself unable to stand the pain of seeing a certain grocer's where they had often bought their food for the weekend, pricing this and arguing about that, enjoying the small pleasures of a domesticity that had no stifling element. Oh, curses on that decision to keep it so free! Curses on his inability to bind her!

'Harriet, go away, darling,' he said out loud. 'You've gone to Australia, remember? You're not here any more. For God's sake go away and take this pain with you.'

She did not hear him. The pain continued. It was like cold, hard stones grinding against each other in his stomach.

Ought he to leave this place? Would the tumult of London drown his sorrow? Or a deep, somnolent country peace? But a small grain of stubbornness in him rejected the thought. He liked this town. It was urban, and yet one could meditate in it as in the country. He glanced round, appraising it. Quiet, middle-aged women with sensible clothes walked past on shopping errands. A cat jumped from a fence.

Approaching Princess Terrace, he made another detour; for some reason he was reluctant to walk past the house so long before time. If the daughter saw him (he assumed that the mother would be too ill to sit looking out of the window) she would probably guess that he was just killing time until he could make his visit. Whereas a busy and successful man would be about some piece of work right up to the moment when he glanced at his watch and rose purposefully from his desk to fulfil this human duty.

Why did he wish to project the image of a busy and successful man? Whom was he trying to impress? Himself, surely. The two females he was to visit were, he was sure, nothing that needed to be lived up to. The old woman would want half-an-hour's polite conversation and his signature in a book. The young one? He had envisaged her as dowdy, over-disciplined, resigned, perhaps moustached. But the voice had not matched such a dispiriting picture. Perhaps she had some liveliness in her, perhaps could give him some feminine vibrations that would act, however momentarily, as a poultice for his anguish.

In any case, he thought, walking briskly along towards the Cathedral, I *am* a busy and successful man, or at any rate I am not unsuccessful and I am busy enough. There are lots of things I ought to be thinking about, instead of this self-pity and groaning. I ought to be thinking about the story I am writing.

Dutifully, he thought. Gus Howkins, middle-aged press-cutting-agency operator, as seen by Giles Hermitage, middle-aged novelist. G.H. sees G.H. And what does he see him doing? Compensating, of course. Dealing with life, finding happiness with a beautiful brown-eyed girl, combating horrible TV stars, escaping from an unhappy marriage – something much more positive than merely avoiding marriage, as his author had done, and smugly congratulating oneself on not getting into the net. Better to get into the net and tear one's way out of it if one had to. Besides, it had left the man with something tangible: a daughter, April. How did he, Hermitage, imagine Howkins's relationship with April? At the moment, only in shadowy outline. But surely he, flesh and blood Hermitage, would give a great deal now to have a flesh and blood April. A girl, fresh and vibrant in the morning of life, who loved him as her father and would help him to smother this dull ache that he carried everywhere. . . . Sentimentality! A lot of girls were nothing like fresh and vibrant, they were lethargic and sullen, and they disliked their fathers when they thought of them at all. And then, whose daughter would she be? Harriet's? Well, but if he had had a child by Harriet the child would only be six years old now, and surely Harriet would never have left a six-year-old daughter as well as a husband. Round and round we go. It was like standing on a rock surrounded by a whirlpool. Push out in any direction and after a few giddy revolutions you were back at the rock again. No escape, no escape, ever. Except to be sucked down, to drown, to cease to live. As he rounded the corner into the Cathedral close, Giles faced once more the fact that he genuinely wished to die. Writing as a substitute for suicide! Could he honestly say that it was working?

Well, if he managed to write another book he would make a little money, to enable him to continue this existence that he had no wish to continue. His publisher would make a modest profit too. Perhaps that was what publishers did: scoop up the profit from substitute suicides. All those suffering writers, dying into books because they could not face the pain of their lives, and the publisher sitting on top of the heap, with expense-account lunches and an elegant house in some place like Egham or Maidenhead.

You're babbling, he told himself. A lot of writers enjoy their lives. You used to enjoy yours when you had Harriet. Harriet Harriet Harriet Harriet Harriet. The rock again, back at the rock.

Baffled, he looked at his watch. Almost three-thirty. At least for the next hour or so he could contemplate someone else's suffering, and perhaps do a little to alleviate it. He bent his steps to Princess Terrace. Yes, here it was. About a dozen houses. Semi-detached: why, in that case, had the architect called it a terrace? Some attempt at grandeur, some memory of Nash? The houses were solidly respectable: a low garden wall, a wrought-iron gate, a clouded glass front door. Archetypal suburbia. Built strongly and on fairly generous lines. Old-fashioned middle-income. He stooped, and activated the iron knocker at the foot of the door.

Straightening up, he saw through the glass the uncertain shape of someone approaching. Bulky, rapid-moving. The daughter? A rhinoceros-woman?

Then the door was open and a ginger-haired man, youngish, tall and fleshy, was looking at him. Watchful, but tolerant. Enquiring, but with a trace of professional *bonhomie*.

'Good afternoon?' phrased as a question.

'I'm Giles Hermitage. I believe Mrs Chichester-Redfern is expecting—'

'Oh, yes. You're exactly on time. She's ready for a visit.'

The ginger-haired man held the door fully open. Giles stepped into a parquet-floored hallway. In front of him, a stairway; to the left, two doorways into the downstairs rooms; beyond them and facing him what was evidently the kitchen.

'Is it . . . ?'

'Straight up. The room facing you at the top.'

A voice, *the* voice, the telephone voice now suddenly in high definition, came through the six-inch-open door of the first room on the left.

'Is that Mr Hermitage? Do send him up. I'll bring tea.'

Come out, he willed her. I want to look at you.

The ginger man, smiling a contained welcome, an uninvolved permission, indicated the staircase.

There was nothing to do but climb. He climbed.

In the fifteen seconds it took him to get up the stairs, Giles considered the ginger-haired man. He was evidently in his thirties; well-conditioned; looked after his health, was pink and scrubbed; the slight overplus of flesh indicated only that if he had not taken such good care of himself, kept himself so trim and exercised, he would have been unhealthily fat. He exuded professional confidence. Ah! The doctor! Why was he still there at three-thirty? Answering the door downstairs? Acting like one of the family?

In the household of a dying person, he told himself, the doctor *is* one of the family.

On the landing, he stood for a moment, collecting himself. But the top stair had creaked, and the door of the room facing him was half open. An alert voice, with no trace of feebleness or fretfulness, a mature woman's voice, called, 'Is that Mr Hermitage?'

'Yes.'

'Do come in, please.'

He entered. Helen Chichester-Redfern was sitting up in bed. She was holding herself erect and did not seem very feeble, so that in the first fraction of a second that his eyes rested on her the

— 74 —

thought formed in Giles's mind: she is not like a dying woman. But then he looked at her face and saw that her eyes were hollow behind rimless glasses, and the skin was tight over her cheekbones. Yes, he thought, she could be on her way to death.

'How good of you to come,' she said, 'and so soon.' Her voice was firm, and her eyes steadily held his. Illness might be eating away her body, but her will and intelligence were still what they had been, and evidently they had been formidable.

She stretched out her hand to him, and he took it in a brief clasp of greeting. It was fleshless, but its stringy grip was still firm.

'This is an event in my life,' she said. 'Strange, isn't it, to be still having events in one's life, even at this late stage?'

'Oh.' So they were to speak of death already, he thought.

'Don't worry.' She smiled. 'Our talk isn't all going to be about . . . that. In fact none of it is. We have so many things to talk of that concern life.'

'Yes,' he assented, sitting down in the Windsor chair she indicated was ready for him. 'Life has to be attended to. Otherwise it creeps up on us from behind.'

'I've always felt it in your work,' she said. 'That wonderfully alert sense of possibilities. The possibilities there are even in an ordinary, impoverished life.'

'Thank you.'

'That sense you convey of the richness of choice that we all have – even if our experience is immutable, we can exercise a choice of attitudes towards it – I've been helped by it. It's helped me to live my life.'

'I'm glad.'

She pointed to a small wooden structure within reach of her bed, which was, he now saw, a revolving bookcase.

'There they are, stored where I can get at them any time – your thoughts and imaginings.'

He looked. They were there, most of the books he had written: three in the dark-red binding of the public library, the rest in paperback.

He smiled. 'You must have been amassing these for some time. Several of the ones you've got here are out of print.'

'Oh, yes. I started with your first one. *Icicle Towers.*'

Giles wrinkled his forehead. 'I think you're missing one out. *Icicle Towers* wasn't my first.'

'Really? I could have sworn . . . . '

'A writer never forgets his first book, even if he lives to be ashamed of it. That first publication – it's the biggest hurdle of all, and it comes right at the beginning. So of course I remember. It was *The Honey Marsh*.'

'Ah,' she breathed out, expressing relief. 'I was afraid there was some early book I hadn't known about and was unobtainable. I've got *The Honey Marsh*. I knew it was an early one but I hadn't realised it was your first. I don't read the dates on title-pages carefully enough.'

'Why should you?'

'Oh, but I should . . . . I want to have an *accurate* sense of your work, how it's developed and got to where it is today. The peak it's on now.' She looked towards the bookcase. 'Would you mind giving that a turn? I think *The Honey Marsh* is on the other side.'

He spun the device gently on its axis, and identified the book. The sight of its shiny cover sent his mind wheeling backwards twenty years to his dead, youthful self: that thin, untidy figure hunched over a typewriter, seething with frustration, burning with eagerness for life. Well, life had been granted. What would that young man have thought, if he could look forward to the sad disaster that was Giles's life now? Would he have welcomed the whole mixture, happiness and grief together? Or would he have shrunk back, not daring to grow up?

But if he had not dared, what then? Time goes on in any case, and we go on with it, prisoners, prisoners.

Just before he could form in his consciousness the name 'Harriet,' his attention was recalled by the voice of the woman in the bed.

'I may be beginning to run your books together in my mind, into one big book that's as real to me as my own experience.' She lay back on her pillows for a moment. 'I read a good deal, but I find now that I can't read a whole book consecutively. The effort of sustained concentration . . . . I can very rarely manage it. So I pick them out of the case almost at random, and read a few pages. An episode perhaps, or a description. Reading them in fragments like that – they tend to form one big canvas in my mind.'

'I hope it's a canvas you enjoy.'

'Enjoy? It's the only unalloyed pleasure left to me.'

He did not know what to answer.

She leaned forward, as if with a new access of energy. 'But there's one book of yours I shall have a connected experience of. I shall know it coherently, in its logical development.'

He was puzzled. 'Which one is that?'

'The one you have not yet finished.'

'Oh, yes. That's the reason you asked me round. To tell you—'

'It's not the only reason. But it's one of them. I can't tell you how eager I am to know what your creative spirit is busy with at present. That sounds gushing, doesn't it? Women who say to artists things like "your creative spirit" – they've had so much fun made of them. But all that doesn't matter any more when you get to my stage. Those are the natural words that suggest themselves and so I use them.'

'Quite right. Well, I—'

Hesitant, creaking into action, Giles was surprised but not sorry to be halted by a voice behind him.

'I thought you might both like some tea.'

He had not heard the door open. Turning, he saw Diana Chichester-Redfern, the daughter he had been faintly curious about, moving with a tray of tea-things towards the table on the other side of the bed.

'Thank you,' he said, and the woman in the bed echoed his thanks with a patient inclination of the head.

'I'll pour it out for you,' said Diana, 'and then if you want any more you can come round this side and get it.'

As she spoke she set down the tray and began with swift, accurate movements to pour out two cups. Evidently she was not joining them. The usual questions about milk and sugar were asked and answered. Giles took advantage of the short hiatus to sit back and take notice of the girl.

She was of medium height, slender in figure to the point of boyishness, wearing a plain dark-brown dress that would have been almost too severe but for a V-shape of bright checker pattern that started between her breasts and fanned out to the neckline. Shiny black shoes. Her way of dressing was obviously aimed at a neatness and restraint in deliberate contrast to the restless vitality that flowed through her limbs and issued in her quick, precise movements. Her legs, as slender as the rest of her, were unmistakably feminine in their elegance.

What else? Hair: brown, glossy as if with frequent washing and brushing, in a fringe coming down over her forehead, and framing her face: straight, with just the ends curling inwards.

Eyes: parsley-coloured; lively, enquiring, darting interested looks at the world.

Features: generally good; high forehead; mobile, sensitive lips; pale skin; the nose delicate and rather long, sweeping down her face and coming out into a pert, inquisitive curve at the tip.

She was handing him his tea, leaning across the bed. Taking the cup and murmuring his thanks, Giles saw the litheness of her body and the narrowness of her hips. Then, as he took the cup and saucer from her hand, there was an instant in which their eyes met.

'I'll be downstairs, Mother.'

'Has Dr Bowen gone yet?'

'He's just leaving. I'm going to practise.'

'Very well, dear,' said the dying woman, manipulating her cup with scrupulous carefulness, giving her serious attention to the small task. She drank, Giles noticed, very light tea with a slice of lemon palely floating on its surface.

'All right now?' Diana asked her mother, as she straightened up and turned to go. Receiving an affirmative, she looked across at Giles. This time, being on the look-out for it, he noticed the flash of interest and responsiveness in her green eyes.

'I can see Mother's having a wonderful time. It must be nice to get a famous author all to oneself.'

Gravely, he said. 'I'm not tiring her, I hope.'

'She'll go to sleep when you are. It's as simple as that. You'll be in mid-sentence and you'll suddenly notice that she's asleep.'

'It sounds disconcerting.'

Helen Chichester-Redfern put her cup down in the saucer and said, 'But you won't be disconcerted, Mr Hermitage. Already I feel that you're a good friend and that you understand how it is with me.'

'Well, if you hear me practising,' said the daughter, moving with light steps towards the door, 'you'll know that I'm not listening at the keyhole, much as I'm tempted to.'

The neatness of her little shiny black shoes. It was the last detail he noticed as she went out, except for the smile she threw back into the room as she turned in the doorway.

Then she had gone, and the withdrawal of her quick, contained energy left the room suddenly lifeless, as if the dying woman and the heartsore, bewildered man were not enough to fill it, as indeed they were not.

Giles knew that he must turn back to the dying mother and away from the living daughter, knew that his merciful errand was to the one whose effortful heart-beats were rationed, but before relinquishing the thought of that slender and vibrant presence he could not resist asking one question.

'Your daughter speaks of practising. Does she perhaps play the piano?'

Helen Chichester-Redfern closed her eyes in a momentary weariness, but at once opened them and said, 'Diana is a professional musician. Her instrument is the guitar.'

'Oh.'

'She has accepted this interruption in her career to come and help me to die. Before that, I had seen very little of her for ten years.'

'Oh,' he said again, feeling that he should have made some intelligent remark but with no idea what it might have been. Wrenching his thoughts back to the immediate situation, he looked about for something to comment on. The room itself contained nothing remarkable; one bunch of flowers – she must be fond of flowers to have them at this time of year, when they would be expensive. He glanced out of the window: a nondescript square of lawn, one unremarkable tree, perhaps a sycamore; beyond, a quiet tangle of back lanes. Soon, the whole area would be urgent with bird-song, and she could have the window ajar in the milder air, and listen to it.

'You'll be hearing a lot of bird-song soon,' he said, setting down his empty cup.

'Bird-song, yes,' she said.

He waited to see if she would explore the subject, but her face was closed and tense. She too had put down her teacup, and her fingers fidgeted on the counterpane: which, he now saw, was not an ordinary bedspread but a duvet, Continental-style.

'I see you have a duvet,' he said. 'Are they comfortable?'

'Mr Hermitage,' she said abruptly, 'I haven't enough time.'

'Enough time for what?'

'For anything. But especially not for small-talk.'

Giles looked down, unable to meet her eyes. He knew he had been guilty of an offence against her.

'I'm sorry,' he said.

'You mustn't waste my dying hours with trivialities.'

'I understand and I'm sorry. It would be better not to come here at all than to do that.'

'I have so little time left. I want to discuss the deepest issues that my life has brought me face to face with.'

'What are they?' he asked, settling back in his chair, glad now that their talk could begin in earnest.

She looked at him with those deep, shadowed eyes. 'Some of them resist definition, even now. They lie just outside the reach of my mind. But others are very clear. Relationships, mostly. Does it seem strange to you that I should still find them important? Still try to understand them?'

'Why should it be strange?'

'Some people would find it so. People who deal with life only as a series of contingencies. They never trouble themselves with a situation that isn't actually facing *them*, concretely.' She was speaking quickly and with animation, leaning forward eagerly. Giles wondered if this sudden expenditure of energy, from a dying organism, would bring on a pendulum-swing of exhaustion. 'My relationships, after all, are over. Apart from my daughter, who has temporarily come home to be with me, I have no relationships and therefore no problems of relationship. Yet I still ponder them. I want, before the end, to understand as much and as fully as I can. That's why it's so important to talk to someone like you, someone with wisdom and imagination, about human beings and the nature of their dealings with each other.'

'I'll be glad to talk. But I don't know if—'

'I'll tell you one thing I wanted to ask you. Why are there in your work so many portraits of broken marriages?'

He considered. 'I suppose there are.'

'It's a theme that comes up again and again.'

'More than in most novelists?'

'I haven't read most novelists. I've read you and I want to know why failure of love, separation, divorce, are such matters of concern to you.'

'Well,' he ruminated, 'to write about people is to write about their most important relationships. That means, in nine cases out of ten, the love of man and woman. And one doesn't find oneself making stories out of happy, successful love because there tends to be nothing to say about it. No news is good news, and good news is no news. A successful marriage is often very uneventful, seen from outside.'

'But what if it's seen from inside?'

He frowned, thinking. 'It ought to be within one's skill to do that. But . . . well, it's true that I seem to have found trouble easier to write about than serenity.' He hesitated. 'There may be personal reasons, I suppose.'

'You're not married yourself, are you?'

'No.'

Helen Chichester-Redfern seemed to be sinking into the predictable exhaustion. Her long-boned face was grey; she sank back on her pillows. But she evidently wanted to speak, and was hunting for the right words.

'I . . .,' she began. Her voice breathed into hesitation.

'What is it you want to say? Take all the time you need.'

'It isn't time,' she said, so quietly that he scarcely heard her. 'It's . . . not knowing.'

'Not knowing what?'

She rallied a little. 'How far I dare venture. Into the personal.'

'Don't speak of venturing,' he said. 'Venturing implies danger. At least, if there *is* any danger of being hurt, it must come from within you. Not from me.'

'You see,' she breathed, 'I want to ask things that are bound to . . . seem intrusive.'

'Please,' he said. 'Please, banish the thought.' He remarked inwardly, as he spoke, on his own complete sincerity. He had, without consciously thinking about it, crossed a certain bridge. If this woman needed contact with him, he would give it to her without reservation. I'm being unselfish, the thought flashed. Then came its companion thought within the same second: No; for a writer this is the kind of bread that always comes back on the waters.

Then she shot at him the question: 'What is it about a permanent relationship between man and woman that frightens you?'

'Frightens me?' For a moment his mind went numb, refused to take in her words: he was afraid of the territory they were entering. He had come here on an easy errand of mercy, to impart comfort to someone who needed it, and at no cost to himself – and now, without warning, she was making him tread through the red-hot ashes of his life with Harriet: the smouldering, searing embers that were all he had left.

'Forgive me,' she said faintly. 'I see I've overstepped the mark. I'm interfering in your inviolable personal life, and it's the last thing I—'

'No.' He had meant never to interrupt her, but the word burst from his mouth from the pressure of what was behind it. 'It's not that. I don't mind . . . being personal.'

'But you still find the question difficult to deal with?'

'Oh, God knows I've thought about it enough times. Of all questions you could ask me it's the least unexpected. But now, this afternoon, I find it difficult to talk about. Because . . . well . . . life doesn't stand still. One's own perspective alters.'

She was waiting in silence for him to say something meaningful, and suddenly he felt ashamed of these vague generalities. If he could only explain his bafflement by opening his heart and showing her the crawling maggots of pain inside it, well, why not? In talking to the dying, one does not trouble to be discreet: what is it but to write one's confession on a piece of paper that will shortly be thrown on the fire?

He looked straight into her face. 'All right, I'll say it. You happen to have caught me at a sad time. Sad and unstrung. A month ago if you'd asked me why I wrote so much about broken relationships, divorces, emotional shipwrecks, I'd have given you the easy, surface answer. I have a brother and a sister and they've both made unhappy marriages. Neither of them is going to get a divorce and pull apart, not only because there are children but because their unhappiness has never reached the point of total agony at which one feels ready to do *anything*, however fiendish and desperate, to get out of it. They're just negatively not-happy with, as far as I can see, occasional excursions into actively tormenting misery – but the excursions don't go on long enough to force them into action. All of us are the same, in our family – we prefer to stay where we are rather than make a move, we're slothful and perhaps a little bit good-natured, reluctant to hurt other people and reluctant to hurt ourselves. So we tend to live with misery rather than stand up and fight it. There must be a lot of people like that.'

'Most people,' she nodded.

'That's what I would have told you a month ago. But it wouldn't have been the whole truth. There'd have been a thin mist of disingenuousness over my statement, and that mist was in fact where my happiness was located. Am I speaking in riddles?'

'Not in riddles. But so figuratively that I can't altogether—'

'It's all right, I'm going to spell it out. Until the age of forty-three I fought very shy of marriage, and not only marriage but of any relationship that threatened to impose the burden of commitment to a person, commitment through all the unpredictable changes that come over people. When I was excited and interested by a girl I used to think, yes, I like you, I even love you, but how can I speak for the me of ten years hence *vis-à-vis* the you of ten years hence?'

'Of course,' she breathed. She was very still among her pillows, listening, listening.

'And then, seven years ago . . . .' Giles's voice trailed into silence as the presence of Harriet came suddenly upon him. Her rich auburn hair, the warm, fragrant scent of her body, the ripe globes of her breasts – the images trampled over him like the hoofs of a raging war-horse. He felt breathless, clobbered, stunned. Harriet, why did you do it? Harriet! *Harriet!* Panic flooded his being.

'Please don't go on,' she said. 'Something's upsetting you. I shouldn't have asked.'

'I must go on,' he said, 'now that I've started. It's all right. This is something I've got to live with.' Amazingly, he saw the flash of a pair of eyes quite different from Harriet's, parsley-green eyes in a pale, alert face, and for a micro-second the pain lifted. When it came down again, he still felt able to go on. 'Seven years ago I met a young woman here, in this town . . . . I'd only just come to live here and I was, well, looking round. I was lucky – I met her almost at once, in my first week or so. We attracted each other, and we started a love-affair that I very soon saw was going to be different from anything before.'

'Different, how?' Faintly.

'Richer. Warmer. More intense, but also more tranquil. We'd both had a history of unstable relationships – she'd been married and divorced, which might have tended to reinforce me in my general view of sexual alliances, that the short-term ones were the best. But with' – he wanted to say 'Harriet,' but the name would not be uttered; he had not been able to utter it since she left him, and now only the 'h' came out like a sigh – 'her, with her, I knew from the very beginning that we were playing a different game with different rules. I knew nothing would ever stop me loving her. I knew she could grow old, and get fat or haggard, or be maimed and disfigured in an accident, or paralysed, or anything, but she would always be the person I loved most in the world and the one I wanted to be with.'

He had stopped again. The pain caught hold of his throat and shook him. Helen Chichester-Redfern lay back as if the last flicker of energy had died in her: but those deep-set, searching eyes were open.

'We never married. Partly that was a residue from my fear of marriage all those years. But mostly it was her doing. I suppose, looking back now, she can't have been as certain of her love for me as I was of mine for her. She *seemed* to be. For years, she insisted that there was no need for us to marry because our love didn't need any riveting or institutionalising. "You're boringly secure with me," she used to say. Perhaps the boredom was on her side, not mine. But I accepted it all. I let her tell me she loved me and always would, that I was the man she had been waiting for, all that over and over again for seven years.'

'And then?'

'And then, a month ago, she left me. Just like that. Wrote me a letter saying she didn't feel able to go on, and that she was going out to Australia with some man she had been working with, and was going to marry him. She didn't even tell me face to face. She wrote me a letter. On the typewriter, yet. With paragraphs and indentations. And she sent it to me in a lined envelope.'

As he said the words, Giles remembered that Helen Chichester-Redfern had also sent him a letter in a lined envelope. It must be a woman's way of marking a letter 'Important'. Was there some comfort in that? Did Harriet at least recognise that breaking his heart was an action that came into a serious category? Not just something one did casually?

The afternoon sun, now sinking towards the horizontal, shone into the room and picked out every detail in colour: the vase of flowers, the pattern on the counterpane, the candle-wax of the dying woman's face. In the hushed, exhausted peace of the room, they both sank into their own thoughts. Finally she said, 'Will it affect your writing?'

'It's bound to. But the full effects are going to take time. They'll have to sink into my life and come up again. That is, if I have any life. I'm not being histrionic, but in the last month I've wondered many times whether there's any point in going on. The happiness I've lost won't come again, and I don't know whether I can face the next twenty years without it. Perhaps the tidiest thing would be an overdose or something.'

Her wasted body heaved in the bed. She was trying to sit up.

'Don't, don't, please,' he said. 'I have the feeling that you're very tired. It's nearly time for me to leave you to rest. You mustn't try to react.'

'Yes, I must. What you've just said . . . . I must react. Don't try to spare my energy. What use have I for it?'

Well, he thought, that's true.

She had struggled into an upright position. Her eyes were blazing straight into his. Suddenly he saw that they were parsley-green. Ah, where was all that? In another galaxy?

'Mr Hermitage . . . .'

'Giles.'

'Giles. You must live. No matter what the pain.'

'Why?' he asked flatly.

'The body is so tragically short-lived. It fails us just when we begin to break through into wisdom.'

'Wisdom? A clear-sighted view of our condition? Who wants that?'

'I want it,' she said fiercely. 'I'm still struggling for it although night is coming down on me.'

'I respect that, Helen. But you must have a courage that's lacking in me. If my intuition is right, the rest of my life is a radio-active desert in which no self-respecting creature would bother to live for an hour. Even the rats would get out. Why should I keep my body alive, when it's no longer an instrument of happiness?'

'It makes me very sad to hear you talk in that vein. Your body carries your brain about, feeds it and protects it. And your brain will go on, triumphing over loss and grief. It will achieve, achieve, achieve.'

She fell back among the pillows. This time he was really frightened.

'I'm going, Helen,' he said, leaning forward to bring his face

— 85 —

close to hers. 'I've tired you too much. I'll come back soon and we'll go on talking. Soon.'

The eyes behind those rimless glasses remained shut, the faint breathing remained just as faint, but the pale lips uttered one word. 'When?'

'Tomorrow, if you like,' he said. 'I'll come tomorrow.'

The fleshless head on the pillow managed a small nod. He stood up, looked down for a moment at the almost dead body which a few minutes ago had mustered such intensity and will: then he turned and went out of the room, keeping his footfall on the carpet.

Outside, he closed the door gently behind him, and stood pondering. Not that he had anything in particular that needed to be thought about; it was rather that he needed time to recover from the tense, effortful experience he had been through. Strange, that she, a woman spent with age and sickness, an organism clinging to the edge of life, should have such authority over a man still not past the prime of his strength! In their talk, she had been from the first the dominant partner: out of the room, he had felt a release from bondage, like a boy leaving the headmaster's study. Was she a naturally forceful woman? Would she have controlled and dominated him in the same way if he had known her in the days of her health? Or was it the approach of death that lent her a touch of majesty? There was, he decided, no way of telling.

Giles began to walk down the stairs, and at once the movement of his body brought him back into contact with mundane reality. The daughter! In the intensity of his spiritual wrestle with the mother, he had forgotten her. Nor, for that matter, did he recall hearing any sound of a guitar being played.

Well, there was nothing to hear now. If she had, unheard by him, been practising, she must be resting. The door of the empty kitchen was open – looking back from the foot of the stairs, he saw how neat and clean it was, with everything put away and the drying-cloth hanging tidily on a rail – but the living-room door was firmly closed and no sound came from behind it.

For a moment, Giles felt an impulse to knock on that closed door, to tell Diana Chichester-Redfern that he was leaving and intended to come back tomorrow. But the door was too uninviting, the message too trivial, for his courage to rise high enough. After all, the mother would tell her of their arrangement, and to announce that he was going was perfectly unnecessary. He picked up the mackintosh he had slung over the foot of the banisters on entering, opened the front door and let himself out. For some reason he found himself turning the knob not just quietly but stealthily: not just with the natural deliberation of a considerate man in a house that contained an invalid, but with something like the furtiveness of a burglar, or at least of an intruder hoping to get out before he was discovered. Why? What was it that made him feel out of place, unwelcome? He had entered the house as an invited, even an honoured, guest.

The door clicked shut behind him, he was out in the late-afternoon light and the familiar street, and whatever strange mood had come upon him was no more than one of those small, unfathomable mysteries with which life abounds. What now? It would be some six hours before he could decently go to bed, there was nothing he wanted to read, no friend he much wanted to call on, nothing he wanted to see at cinema or theatre. Some orchestra, he had noticed, was giving a concert in the Town Hall, but he was not musical enough to concentrate on pure sound for a whole evening; if he settled down to listen to the concert, within a few minutes he would start thinking about Harriet, and the pain would begin twisting and scalding his guts.

Harriet would be in Australia now. No, hardly. How many hours was the flight? He did not know, and had no wish to find out, to imagine in any detail where she was and what she was doing. He wanted to dismiss the subject before it could fairly present itself. But here it came, nevertheless, as inexorable as all his suffering over Harriet had been. Oh, curse it! He was so *bored* with suffering: why wouldn't the pain go away and let him get on with life? Was she, at that moment, sitting in an aircraft seat, or was she waiting at an airport? Was she travelling alone or with her accursed man, the clever smiling thief who had taken her from him, her rightful lover? Obviously they would travel together if they could. They would be sitting side by side, whiling away the long journey, chatting sometimes, dozing sometimes, holding hands sometimes. Was he making a joke, and being rewarded with that rich, gasping chuckle that had always fallen so excitingly on his, Giles's, ears? Or were they talking soberly, planning the shape of their new life together? If they were at an airport, was he buying her a drink? Were they moving from one level to another, pausing at bookstall and souvenir shop, scanning notices and television screens for information?

They would be sharing every detail of the journey; the excitement and interest, and the worry and inconvenience, would all bring them closer to each other hour by hour. And then journey's end, their destination, an hotel room, bath and bed and blissful tiredness in each other's arms . . . . hate flooded Giles's being: he had never been a violent man, but at that moment he could imagine no greater joy than to have a gun in his hand, and the man who had stolen Harriet in front of him, and to fire at point-blank range again and again and again.

Oh, hell, this would never do. He must get a grip on himself before the core of his personality broke apart and he went mad in earnest. Then an idea struck him. Since he was in such pain, why not throw away all anodynes and make it an evening of sheer, blinding agony in which, at least, something was accomplished?

Why not, in short, make this the night of the Harriet Pyre?

This was the name Giles had already attached to an ordeal he knew he would sooner or later have to go through. The years with Harriet had left his life strewn with sharp, painful mementoes of things they had done together. In his pockets, in the drawers of his desk, in corners here and there, was the crowd of small torturers that could leap on him at any moment and throw the acid of memory in his face. It was not the big things that did the damage; Harriet had come shopping with him to buy curtains and an armchair for his flat, and advised him on the choice of a new gas stove, and sometimes written letters on his typewriter. These solid objects were part of his life, and now that Harriet had gone they did not particularly accuse him, except insofar as the whole of life accused him. It was the trivial things – the bus tickets, the odd foreign coin lingering in a pocket, the cheque stub for a Christmas present he had bought her – that kept ambushing him. In the month since the blow fell, he had known that the only remedy was a thorough search-and-destroy operation, ransacking desk and wardrobe, hunting down all the little things she had seen and touched and that now burnt and stabbed him so mercilessly. But he had lacked the courage to do it. Even the continual small shocks of agony had seemed preferable to the blood-bath of gathering all the fragments together and taking them down to the dustbin. But this evening, as he stood on the pavement outside Princess

Terrace, Giles suddenly felt that the courage was there, in his blood and bones. He *would* do it, he *would* touch and look at all those last, pitiful reminders of his happiness, and when he had got rid of them the flat would be free of Harriet's ghost. And what then? Would it be a worse desperation than ever, without even her ghost for company? That was a risk that had to be faced. He could not live for ever in Limbo.

His thoughts had so preoccupied him that his bodily movement had passed unnoticed; he had, in fact, moved with slow, vague steps some fifty yards down the road from Princess Terrace. Now, taking a grip on the situation, he halted and turned round. Wine. An evening like the one he was facing called for a bottle of some good vintage. It was unthinkable to face the ordeal cold turkey, and no other drink would give him the right kind of resilience: beer would make him sodden and self-pitying, and if he drank spirits he would pass through aggressiveness to abject depression.

Come, Hermitage. Courage, positiveness, and a sound grip on practical realities. Tonight, the detritus of your life with Harriet must go out to the dustbin; all those little clinging burrs that try to remind you of the world you have lost, they must go out, without pity or ceremony, and when they are out in the rainy night and you are warm and vacant in your lonely bed, that will be the end of one road even if it is not the beginning of another. You must not loiter among fragments and loose ends: better a conclusion, and darkness, than a twilight among curled-up, dead leaves.

So admonishing himself, Giles began to walk briskly back the way he had come. The best wine-merchant in town was further towards the centre, on the other side of Princess Terrace. Engrossed in his new resolutions, he spared scarcely a glance, scarcely a thought, for the Chichester-Redfern house as he approached it. But his attention was caught for a moment by the fact that, as he was about to draw level with the house, the front door opened and the ginger-haired doctor came out. Looking neither to right nor left, the doctor moved down the short garden path to the pavement, opened the door of a car that was parked by the gate and had in fact, as Giles now realised, been there when he first arrived, and got in. It was now four-thirty: if Dr Bowen (that was the name the woman had mentioned, wasn't it?) had been there since three, he must have had something important to inculcate. But then, helping a person to die was a serious matter: Diana, young as she was, would need a good deal of instruction and help, for all her evident capability and confidence.

These thoughts had barely time to form themselves before Giles's rapid tread had brought him level with the car. The doctor's large, fleshy frame had just settled in the driving seat; as Giles passed, he started the engine and the car began to move away. For an instant, Giles was close to the doctor, separated only by six feet of space and the glass of the car window, a man standing looking down at a man sitting. Unaware of being watched, Dr Bowen was facing straight ahead; and on his face was a small, contained smile, as if he had some secret reason for being very, very pleased with himself.

The car glided forward, the pavement outside Princess Terrace was silent and deserted, the early spring sunset was almost over, and Giles Hermitage walked on towards the wine shop.

3

A S CLIFF SPOKE HE FIXED ME WITH HIS UNPLEASANT WIDE-APART eyes. For an instant, my exhausted body came alive with a surge of angry vitality. I wanted to seize hold of this horrible little man and shake him till his teeth rattled and any information he had came spilling out of his mouth in painful jerks.

I didn't, of course. With one part of my mind I remained very aware that he was fitter and stronger than I, and that anything he had to tell me would have to be coaxed out of him; and, when it came, carefully unpicked from the skein of lies in which it would doubtless be entangled.

'You know where she is,' I said, keeping my voice as casual as I could. (But how my pulse was hammering. *He knows where she is! He knows where she is!*) 'Well, that'll save me a lot of trouble.'

'It depends,' he said and gave me a slanting look.

'Depends?' I asked.

He nodded. 'On how badly you want the information. Nothing comes free, you know.'

'You mean,' I said, speaking carefully, 'that you need to be paid before you tell me Mrs Delmore's whereabouts?'

Suddenly my whacked-out mind came up with a childhood joke. Mrs So-and-so's wearabouts. Hanging on a line in the back yard.

'Her whereabouts,' I said firmly. And in a vivid flash I thought of her little white knickers, lying on the chair in that rented cottage, a million miles away: in another country, another world, another time-scheme, another dimension of the universe.

'Why do you need money before you'll say where she is?' I asked him, point-blank.

He took a few quick, pivoting steps on the polished wood with his neat, spry little feet, just like a wound-up clockwork toy.

'It must be worth something to you to know,' he said. 'You won't tell me who you're working for, but whoever it is they must want to get hold of Julia for a reason and that reason must be something to do with cash. So the money might as well start changing hands right away, at the first link in the chain.'

'And if it was just personal?' I said.

He grinned. 'That would cost twice as much.'

How I wished, at that moment, that I had the strength in my muscles, and the quick co-ordination in my nervous system, and the hardness in my fists, to knock him about till he told me where Julia was, and then go on knocking him about a bit for luck, and leave him out cold on the floor. But of course I hadn't. So, like everyone who doesn't feel confident enough to fight, I talked.

'How can I trust you? If there's money in it, you might just make up some phony information.'

He looked at me as coldly as a shark. 'That's a pretty unpleasant thing to say.'

I shrugged. 'Don't you agree that pleasantness goes out of the window when money comes in?'

'It may do. But trust doesn't. Let's put it this way. There'd be no business done if people didn't trust each other up to a point.'

Yes, I thought. And that's what crooks like you rely on. But I didn't say it aloud. He would probably have gone for me.

'Well,' I said, 'I suppose I can trust you, because if you gave me the wrong information, and I went there and found you gave me a phony address and she wasn't there, I could always come straight back to you.' And what I'd do when I got there, of course, I didn't say, because it was nothing. And he knew it.

He took a few more of those clockwork paces, then suddenly whirled to face me and said, 'Her present address will cost you a hundred pounds.'

I got up and started buttoning my coat to go out.

'Thanks all the same. But I haven't got that much. Sorry I wasted your time.'

'The people you're working for have got it.'

'No, they haven't,' I said wearily. I began walking towards the door.

'Fifty,' he said quickly.

I stopped. 'You mean fifty buys me an address where I can find Julia? Now? Today?'

He nodded, watching me with those empty, alert eyes. I got my cheque-book out and unfolded it.

'Cash,' he said.

I stood there, feeling a fool, with the cheque-book flapping uselessly in my hand. 'It has to be a cheque. I've no cash.'

'No,' he said, 'but you can get it.'

I put the cheque-book away. 'I suppose so,' I said.

'Where's your bank?'

'Finchley,' I said. At the thought of the immense, dragging distance that separated me from Finchley, it seemed to me that I might just as well have said Labrador.

'Well, we'll go there.'

'We?'

'I might as well come with you,' he said easily, 'as wait about here.'

There didn't seem to be much left to say. We went down in the lift together and got into my car.

The drive to Finchley seemed phantasmagoric. Everything was normal and humdrum, the buses and the people and the traffic and the horrible shop-fronts. But I was separated from it by plate glass. I was so close to ordinary dailiness, close enough to reach out and touch it. Yet I wasn't living in it. I was living in a strange dream.

At one point we went past the building where my office was. The Howkins Press-Cutting Agency. No fancy title, no come-on. An air of quiet reliability. I felt a short-lived but intense hankering to pull the car off the road, stop, and go up in the old-fashioned cage-like lift to our three poky little rooms. Miss Sarson in one, Daisy in the other, and the third one empty, waiting for me, with the old green-topped desk and the filing cabinets. I could have done with a shot of that quiet reliability. But of course I couldn't have done it. This was my holiday, bang in the middle of same, in fact, and for me suddenly to show up would have thrown Miss Sarson. (Nothing threw Daisy.) Miss Sarson liked everything to go along predictably. That's why I enjoyed working with her. Her quietness and reserve were assets too. Although I knew she had a first name, Delia, I never called her by it. Delia Sarson! I often got pleasure from just saying it over to myself, quietly, but I never used it. Even when talking about her to other people I always called her Miss Sarson. Yet Daisy called her Delia, right out to her face. They had a bond, those two. Daisy used to tell Miss Sarson about the things men did to her and Miss Sarson used to sympathise and feel glad she had no man in her life to ill-treat her. There was only about twelve years between them but they were like mother and daughter. A sad but indulgent mother and a wayward but loving daughter. They were both a-but-b people. Miss Sarson was shy but firm. Daisy was promiscuous but sentimental, the one-hundred-per-cent contemporary chick but old-fashioned underneath it all. I sighed as I thought that I was neither cosily at work in the office, nor miles away from it all walking up a mountain in North Wales, but driving this nasty, twisted little man through the unreal streets of a dream.

At the bank, he stood right at my elbow while I drew seventy-five pounds in cash. I had the the feeling that his mind was working all the time, trying to stay one jump ahead of life, weighing up the next chance. I half turned my back on him in a pathetic attempt to keep some privacy; he was probably trying to size up how solvent I was, thinking whether he should up the ante for his information. So I wasted no time. Before his mind could change, I turned to him, there in the bank, and peeled off five ten-pound notes into his hand.

'Now,' I said. 'Where is she?'

I could feel the cashier looking at me from behind his window. On the other side of the bank was a long desk where the investment manager lurked, and I could see him looking at me too, over his frosted glass fence. They must have thought I was being black-mailed. Well, I didn't care. It was true, wasn't it?

Cliff Sanders took the money and folded it away into an inside pocket. 'Don't let's be in a hurry,' he said.

'You were in a hurry to get the money,' I said with quiet fury.

'Oh, I'll give you the information,' he said. 'I'll tell you where she is, don't worry.'

'I'm ready,' I said.

'Let's go and have a cup of coffee. I'm sorry I couldn't offer you one at home. And you look as if you could do with it.'

'I don't need coffee. I don't need anything except Julia's address.'

'Well,' he said, 'there's a story attached to it.'

'What kind of story?'

'You'd much better come and have that coffee.' He smiled.

Curse him, he had me in the hollow of his hand. If he chose not to tell me where Julia was, or if he turned out not to know at all, there was nothing I could do about it. My only hope, and that was beginning to seem pretty slender, was just to go along with him and humour him.

'All right,' I said, 'I know a place.'

We went to a joint with a name like Luigi's Espresso Lounge, where they give you thimble-sized cups of thick, black, radio-active sludge that brings your liver out in studs. I had been there once by accident and vowed never to return. But it was the nearest.

We sat facing one another and he turned on a sulky look. 'You made a bad mistake there,' he said.

'You mean giving you the fifty pounds?' I asked.

'No,' he said, scowling. 'I mean the way you handed it over there and then, in the bank. Everybody watching.'

'If you've nothing to hide, what does it matter if people saw me giving you money?'

He took a sip at his espresso, then set the cup down carefully in its little saucer and looked up at me from under his eyebrows.

'Who says I've got nothing to hide?' he asked.

I didn't say anything.

'I know where Julia is, right,' he said. 'I'm prepared to tell you for fifty pounds, right. I've got the fifty pounds, right. But that doesn't mean I want every Tom, Dick and Harry to know that I figure in the business at all.'

I waited. There seemed to be nothing else I could do.

'It's like this,' he said. 'She's been kidnapped.'

At that, I knew for certain that I was living in a dream. One minute I don't know of the girl's existence, the next I'm watching her sitting in a state of shock with the tide creeping in round her, the next I'm in bed with her, the next I'm sleuthing round London after her, and the next I hear that she's been kidnapped. I must be asleep in that half-bedroom, restless after drinking whisky and eating toasted cheese. I must wake up, and take a stomach tablet, and empty my bladder, and then go back to sleep and try to get some real rest. Otherwise my holiday would do me no good. As for Luigi's Espresso Lounge, and this degenerate who sat staring into my face, and Jake Driver in his sandals, and Penny with her orange hair – obviously none of them existed or ever had.

But wait! That would mean that she, Julia, didn't exist either! She belonged to the same order of reality as they did, and I knew for a fact that she existed. That pulled them back from the world of illusion to the world of hard actuality that had to be dealt with.

'What do you mean?' I said roughly. 'Come on, talk. Plenty of witnesses saw you take fifty pounds from me. I could take you straight to a police station now, with my money in your pocket. The bank probably even know the serial numbers. If you know something you're trying to hide, they'll soon get it out of you.'

'Dear me.' He grinned. 'We're sharp, aren't we?'

'Never mind the jokes. What's this load of horse-shit you're trying to tell me?'

'Your fifty pounds,' he said smoothly, 'didn't buy you the right to be rude.'

'They didn't buy me anything, as far as I can see.'

'That's the same thing as calling me a crook.' He let that sink in, then added, 'I'm in the confidence of some people who would probably answer to that description, if they had to. But myself, I'm straight.'

'Well, for God's sake be straight with me and tell me where Julia is and who, if anyone, is holding her.'

He swirled his coffee round in his cup two or three times, looked at it as if he might almost be going to drink some, then thought better of it and set the cup down in its saucer. I waited. After pausing a bit more, he said, 'Have you ever heard of the Crystal Palace Organisation?'

'The what?' It sounded so absurd, just like something in a dream.

'You heard. I'm not going to say it again and I'm not even going to ask you if you know the name of the man who controls it because I know you won't have heard of him. His name is kept very, very deep in the background. But I'm in touch with him.'

'So,' I said softly, 'you're a member of this gang of criminals who call themselves the Crystal Palace Organisation.'

'A member, no,' he said. 'That would mean working for somebody and taking orders all the time. Cliff Sanders is his own boss.'

I made a despairing gesture. 'It's all too much for me. I wanted to trace Julia and now I find I'm deep into some kind of cops-and-robbers story about a South London Mafia.'

'Keep your voice down,' he scowled.

I wanted to stand up and overturn the table and bawl as loudly as I could, 'Cliff Sanders is involved with the Crystal Palace Organisation!' And I honestly think the only thing that restrained me was the thought of what a bloody fool I'd look.

'Are these political extremists?' I asked him, just for something to say.

He shook his head. 'They work for profit. Nothing else. Just profit.'

'And they're holding Julia for profit? It seems a big risk. There's always a lot of publicity for a kidnap, and a police hunt. Is it worth it for the ransom they'd get out of Jake? Assuming he was interested to pay out at all?'

'That's where you're wrong. There isn't always a lot of publicity for a small snatch job. The relatives pay up and nobody ever gets to hear about it. Look, supposing you're a business man in Golders Green or somewhere. Probably a Jew – they go for Jews because one, they're very fond of their families and two, if they get into a hole they can always borrow money from other Jews. Right. They cruise around and pick up the man's wife or his old mother. Not kids very often because kids talk. Afterwards, when it's all over, they boast about it to other kids at school, stuff like that. The grown-up people can always be frightened so much that they keep their mouths shut. The money's paid, the kidnapped person gets back home, rejoicing all round, and nobody opens their yap. They know the police can't protect them for ever. They could be watched and guarded until it all seems to have died down, and then late one night they'll get into the lift and find a man there with a razor who'll carve them up like a turkey and be out into the night in fifteen seconds. A professional.'

'Oh,' I said.

'These little snatch jobs go on all the time. Mostly, nobody gets hurt. And it turns in a nice little profit for the Palace.'

I looked at him, trying to hide the despair that was flooding my mind. 'How do you know all this?' I asked.

'My contacts are very good,' he said in a voice that hardly reached my ears.

'They must be.'

'That's one of the many reasons why Jake's a fool not to take me on. I get around. I'm here, there and everywhere. Never in one place long enough for the grass to grow under my feet. One of the people I know is. . . .' He grinned and swilled his coffee around a bit more. 'No names.'

'You must know him pretty well if he doesn't mind letting you know where his mob are holding Julia. Which, by the way, I have paid fifty pounds to know and you have not yet told me.'

His response to this genuinely surprised me. He reached into his inside pocket and took out my five ten-pound notes and handed them back.

'What. . . ?' I stammered.

'Go on, count them,' he said.

'I can see they're all here. But what the hell is this all about?'

'I can't tell you where she is. Not right away.'

'Well, if you don't know where she is why the hell did you. . . .'

His horrible eyes were full of amusement and superiority. 'I didn't say I don't know. I said I can't tell you. That's why I've given you your money back.'

'But. . . .' I was choking. 'Why go through all this blasted rigmarole at all?'

'Look,' he said, 'relax. Calm down and drink your coffee, or at least sit still. I got that fifty pounds from your hand into mine just to see if you were serious. People don't part with money unless it's for something they really want, not just say they do. You really want to know where Julia is. You've proved that now. All right, it's all I wanted, so you can have the notes back.'

I sank back. 'Go ahead. You've got all the cards. I suppose there's nothing I can do but sit here till it pleases you to tell me something that makes sense of the situation.'

'It seems to me to make pretty good sense already. Look, let's put it this way. The Palace are holding Julia. Jake doesn't know yet. And I'm the one who's going to tell him.'

'Why you?'

'The man wants it that way. I'm on the spot, I live just across the hall, I'm outside any suspicion because I'm Julia's brother. I feed him the information, feed him the directions for payment, watch his reactions at close quarters, and report back. I'm in a position to make the whole operation smoother.'

'And you get a retainer for it, I suppose,' I said bitterly. 'Conniving at this dreadful— Standing by and seeing your own sister put through hell.'

'They've got her anyway. That was none of my doing. As for a retainer, let's put it like this. I get a retainer already. I have a Barclaycard and a cheque-book. Neither of them are in my name and address. I can go all over town and get what I want. Every few weeks, I turn them in and get new ones. Not from Barclays Bank. From the man.'

'You're sitting there telling me,' I said, 'that you live on the proceeds of crime and violence?'

'I've got to live on something. In this particular case let's put it like this, Julia's a lot safer with me in the middle. I can guide Jake towards being sensible, I can keep the man in a patient frame of mind if Jake's a bit slow. They're asking twenty thousand. Jake can get it all right. She could be back with him inside three days.'

All of a sudden, it came to me. *He must be lying.* The whole thing was a fantasy. If my mind hadn't been so caved-in with lack of sleep, I'd have seen through this pitiful nonsense from the beginning.

He knew that Julia had disappeared, leaving no word with Jake as to where she'd gone. I didn't know how he knew that, but he knew. Then I come along, wanting to know where she is, and at once his little twisted mind sees an advantage. If I don't know where she is, then perhaps no one knows. So make out she's been kidnapped, deliver ransom notes, scoop up twenty thousand of Jake's money. And all the time there's no Crystal Palace Organisation, no far-back wily character called 'the man', nothing but this crazy little fool with his grey suit and his polished black shoes. And if he thinks that being Julia's brother puts him outside suspicion, he's even dafter than he looks.

This all swept through me in a second. Then cold panic. Could I be *sure*? If there was just a faint possibility that it was all horribly true, that she had been kidnapped, that she was in danger. . . . This chap was obviously a psychopath. But wasn't every criminal? He might be really in touch with underworld characters and still be as off-centre and schizoid as he seemed. I should have to go carefully. The first thing was to play the only card I had: the fact that I knew, and he didn't, that Julia had been in North Wales the night before last. In my bed. But don't think about that now. She was in North Wales. He doesn't know that. Work, exhausted brain, work. But nothing came.

'How long has she been gone?' I asked him.

He looked stony. 'That's none of your business. I've given you your fifty pounds back and you've no right to any information.'

'Considering that, you've given me plenty already. You've told

— 99 —

me that Julia's being held to ransom, and how much for, and what mob are doing it. That's pretty good to get for nothing. What's the idea of bringing me into it at all? And then suddenly getting cagey?'

'Look,' he said. 'I'll get cagey when and where I like. If it suits me to get cagey I'll get cagey.'

I stood up. 'Oh, to hell with it,' I said. 'I'm sick of you playing cat-and-mouse with me. Amusing yourself. I don't know whether there's a word of truth in it all, but what I do know is that it isn't getting me any closer to Julia.'

'Yes, it is,' he said. His eyes had taken on the same watchful anxiety as they had when my patience snapped earlier on, and I was ready to walk out of his flat. For some reason, he didn't want to lose me. I began to feel that perhaps I had some leverage too, though I couldn't be sure what it consisted of.

'It is, how?' I was signalling for the bill.

'Bit by bit you're getting quite a lot nearer to her. Like you say, you know a hell of a lot that you didn't know half an hour ago. Stay tuned in. There may be more. At least you can keep in touch with developments.'

Luigi, or one of his minions, came over with the inflationary bill. I paid it. Both Cliff Sanders and I tried to look normal until we were left alone again.

'How long has she been gone?' I said again.

'Classified information.'

'Did you first hear of it from this Crystal Palace mob?'

He thought for a moment. 'There doesn't seem to be any harm in telling you that. Yes, I did.'

'And they told you to act for them and you agreed.'

'I do the man little favours. That's how I earn my Barclaycard. This is one.'

'Did they give you the job of telling Jake that they're holding her?'

'Yes.'

'Why haven't you done it, then?'

'Because I only got the word last night. These things have to be done carefully.'

'But they won't want you to hang about. Presumably you're going to communicate their demands to him very soon.'

'This morning,' he said. 'And that's exactly why I drew you into it.'

'Me?'

'You're going to help me,' he said. 'You can make things a lot easier.'

Some other people were standing by impatiently waiting for our table. We went outside and sat in my car. I started the engine, and only then did I break the silence between us.

'Tell me one good reason why I don't take you straight to a police station. Or possibly a mental hospital.'

'And tell them what?'

'All the things you've told me.'

He laughed softly. 'If we turned up at a nut-house they'd all think you were the patient and I was looking after you. Have you seen yourself in a mirror?'

'Not for some hours,' I said.

'You don't look normal, mate.'

I believed him.

'And as for going to the police,' he went on placidly, 'they'd either take no notice or put out a routine missing persons enquiry. And the minute they did that, the Crystal mob'd cut Julia's throat and leave her body on a rubbish tip before this time tomorrow.'

I knew he was lying. Making it all up. Or *almost* knew. What clutched at my gizzard was that *almost*.

'Where are we going?' he asked.

'I don't know,' I said truthfully. I felt in any case that I'd soon be too tired to drive. Another few notches down into fatigue and I'd be running head-on into something coming the other way. Well, perhaps that would solve all our problems.

But no! Julia! Snap awake! Force yourself on a bit further . . . just in case, just in case it's true, that she really is in danger, that you really could help.

I saw a place where I could stop, pulled in, and turned to face Cliff Sanders, with the engine still running and the car vibrating gently all round us.

'I'm tired,' I said flatly. 'I drove all night and I can't do anything more till I get some rest. You don't need me. If it's true that you're working for this mob and they want you to deliver a ransom note to Jake Driver, you'll do it without me. And if it's not true, you can run along and con someone else.'

'Don't talk to me like that,' he said, looking ugly in the confined space of the car.

'If you attack me,' I said, 'you'll be seen by scores of witnesses.' I nodded towards the crowded pavements, with people going past only inches away. 'We might as well stay peaceful.' A great wave of longing for sleep was washing through my bones. I took out a pocket notebook, tore off a page and wrote my telephone number on it. 'There you are. If you want to be in touch, I'll be at that number.'

He thought for a moment. 'Drop me off at Windermere Gardens,' he said at last. 'I was hoping you'd be some use to me. But you look all in.'

We drove in silence to Windermere Gardens, and he got out without saying anything more. Then I went back to the pad and let myself in. It was as cold and unwelcoming as ever. But there was a bed.

I suppose it was about midday when I blacked out. When I opened my eyes it was between five and six. I didn't feel completely rested yet, but I did feel that I had had the first instalment of the gigantic sleep I needed, and I was prepared to be human.

I rooted round and made some tea. I hadn't any milk, and it seemed too much trouble to go to the milk-vending machine, which was a couple of streets away, so I drank it black. At least, I started to. I was about half-way through the first cup when the telephone rang. My mind snapped awake and jangled with apprehension. Was it that desperate little character getting after me already? Another step deeper into the *roman policier* that my life seemed to have become? I lifted the receiver with absurd caution, as if it might go off in my face, and let the other person speak first.

'Gus?'

I froze. It was my wife, Daphne.

'What do you want?' I asked.

I heard her make a little sound that was half-way between a snuffle and a sob. I guessed she had been crying for some time before deciding to ring me. Then she said, 'You know what I want.'

I did, too. She wanted to go back to the old life, the semi-detached on the surburban main road, the car in the garage, the cornflakes and boiled eggs and the evening paper and the television and hanging the washing out in the back garden. And there was a part of me that wanted to say, 'Well, why not?'

'Can't I come round and see you?' she went on. 'I could put it all right, I'm sure I could.'

I wanted to say, 'All right, do,' but something stopped me. I could hardly, then or later, have said what the something was. Cussedness, obstinacy, coldness: a little hard nugget of selfishness: a cool voice in my head that said quietly, 'Tell her to go away and stop bothering you.' There was an ingredient of casual cruelty; and also of deep, deep tiredness.

'Gus, *please*. I haven't even *seen* you for four months.'

'What is there to see me about?'

'Oh, come on. There are hundreds of things to talk about, darling. And one thing most of all – how soon we're going to drop this silly game and come back together.'

'We can't,' I said.

'What d'you mean, can't? It's just a matter of wanting to. And I want to already, you know that, so all we're waiting for is you, honey.'

'Yes,' I said. 'We're waiting for me.'

There was a silence and then Daphne said, 'April's coming down next weekend.'

'Oh?' I said. 'Will she come and see me?'

'I thought we might both come together. Talk everything over. After all, what we do concerns her. She's very upset at what we've done.'

Somehow I couldn't imagine April being very upset at anything we did. Irritated, yes, like a young nanny with children who deserved a good spanking with a hair-brush, only her employers would never let her do it. But upset? And *very* upset? She had her own life, a long way from us both physically and mentally, and if we made a mess of things it would be no more than she expected. Daphne was just trying to use April as a lever to move me in the required direction. She must be desperate, and I didn't blame her.

I took a deep breath. 'Look, Daphne,' I said. 'You're only upsetting yourself. It's all over and you know it. I've sold the house—'

'I was always against that. Always, from the start—'

'And I've settled myself into a new shape of life and you'll just have to do the same.'

'I can't. I can't get along without you.'

'You should have thought of that.' As I spoke the words I was aware, right down to the depths of my cold, reptile heart, of their cheap cruelty. My God, I thought, why am I behaving like this to a fellow human being? What leprosy of soul has affected me?

'I *did* think about it.' She was beginning to cry now, and the words came thickly. 'I never meant our marriage to end. What I did was just a . . . oh, just a foolishness, something that was never meant to last, you know that. . . . I've told you all that. . . .'

'Yes, you've told me. And I believe you. But the fact is, the shock you gave me was enough to make me break up our marriage, and now it's done, I'm on the other side of the wall, and I just don't feel like climbing back all over again.'

She sobbed for a bit and then said, 'I never thought you were a *cold* man, Gus. All the years we were together, I thought you were quite gentle and loving . . . capable of loving, anyway. . . .'

'I am capable of loving,' I said and with the words I saw Julia's face, smiling and then suddenly going serious. 'I even have a certain amount of love for you. It's just not strong enough to make me go through all that upheaval again, that's all.'

'What upheaval? All we've got to do is kiss and make up.'

'That's just it. Make up what? Look, I'll be quite frank. The life I'm living now is meaningless, and the life I lived with you was meaningless. And having made a hell of an effort to throw out one meaningless life and set up another, I just don't feel like making the effort to do it again the other way round.'

'But I *love* you, Gus. I want to make you happy.'

'You can't make me happy, Daphne. If we came together again and bought a new house and settled down, you'd be happy enough and you'd pretty soon convince yourself that I was too. But to me it wouldn't make that much difference. My life would be just about the same as it is now – pretty much of a nothing. So why bother?'

'I'm bothering because our life together is important.' She had stopped crying now and was coming back more crisply. That's it, my girl, show some spirit, because you're going to need it.

'Yes, it's important to you, but not to me,' I said. 'I'd just as soon be on my own. You're only forty-three, you're still young enough to get another man—'

'I don't *want* another man.'

'Perhaps not, but you're going to have to find one. Unless you want to stay with Hilda.'

I heard her draw in her breath, sharply, and it occurred to me to wonder whether she was telephoning from Hilda's house and if so whether Hilda was lurking in the background, listening.

'Gus, you're just being cruel now. It's so unlike you. You know I can't stay at Hilda's. She's fed up with having me and I'm absolutely totally fed up with being here.'

Hilda must be out.

'Well, my advice to you is to look round for a job and a flat. You'll be happier when you get things settled.'

'Is that really what you think?'

'Yes.'

'Is it really all you've got to say to me? After all the years I've been your wife?'

'Yes.'

Her voice had become cold now, and lifeless. I could imagine her face. Normally she had a high colour, going with her reddish hair and strong, energetic body, but now it would have drained away and her eyes would be swollen, with no sparkle. I felt sorry for her, but only as I felt sorry for all human beings, caught in the web of sex, the endless plotting of relationships, the needs, the frustrations, the terrible unsatisfied hungers that we are all left with.

'Gus, don't ring off.'

'I'm not going to, till you've finished.'

'I'm not going to accept this from you. I'm going to give you time to think it all over again. I think you must be in a very cold, hard state of mind.'

'I am, but it's not going to change.'

'If it doesn't, it's me that'll change. I'll get very tough with you, Gus. I'll have my rights out of you.'

'What are your rights?'

'You sold that house and put the money in your pocket. I want half of it, for a start. I put years of my life into running the place. And I'm not going to go out and scramble for a job. If I have to work, I'll take my time and get trained for something I really feel like doing. And you can support me.'

'Why not go back to what you used to do?' She had been secretary to a pathologist.

'Don't be silly. I haven't done secretarial work for years. I've lost my skills. And in any case I'm not going back to taking orders and writing things down. I'm going to have a decent, responsible job for a mature person. And if it takes training and costs money, let it. You can take care of that side of things, it's the least you owe me.'

'All right.'

Then she was crying again. 'Oh, Gus, Gus, why are we talking like this? What dreadful thing has happened to us? Surely I'm going to wake up and find it was all a terrible nightmare and you're beside me?'

'I'm not beside you,' I said, 'but I'm a well-wisher. I'll give you all the help I can.' And with that I rang off. My hand was trembling as I replaced the receiver. I hated myself, but even more than that I hated my life. It had got itself into such a grotesque, dreary tangle; nothing I did or could envisage doing seemed to be the right way to happiness, for myself or for anyone else. Because I knew that if I did what Daphne wanted me to do and went back to her, the boredom would only start again, till I started screaming and had to be led away by men in white coats.

Standing in the shadowy flat, I faced the hideous fact that my life was empty. There was nothing in it; only this bloody awful flat, and the office with Miss Sarson and Daisy, and behind those realities there was a hinterland of empty dreams. Julia Delmore came into the category of empty dreams. I smiled thinly as I thought of the fever that had gripped me for a few hours. Of course a night with an attractive girl would go to any middle-aged man's head – fill him with crazy notions that wouldn't disperse until his blood cooled again. That was what had happened to me, nothing more. Jake Delmore! Penny! Dennis with his epaulets! I nearly laughed aloud, except that I was so damned depressed I felt I'd probably never laugh aloud again. As for that silly little play-acting misfit who called himself Cliff Sanders, how the hell had I been induced to listen to him even for five minutes?

It was all dead, dead. I was getting old, my joints were stiffening, my hair was receding, it wasn't for the likes of me to go chasing after pretty young actresses who were married to rich TV stars. Even if the marriage was a mess and made them suffer, even if they ran away from it, they wouldn't be running in *my* direction. If they gave that appearance it was just for a moment, and by accident.

Reality was certainly coming back at a cracking pace. I supposed I ought to be grateful for that. It was moving in just like the tide on the Caernarvonshire coast, surrounding me as it had surrounded that lonely little motor-car with the pale, withdrawn girl in it. But when that happened I had been on hand to rescue her. Was anyone going to rescue me?

Rescue me from reality? Don't be silly. Who needed that? Reality was something you had to *welcome*.

I welcomed it. The light was beginning to drain away outside. I crossed the room and switched on the electric light. That made the sky, as I stared at it through the window, dusk-blue. The sudden flood of light brought me back to the present moment, and I realised all at once that Daphne knew the address of this place and was quite likely to follow up her telephone call by coming round to throw herself on me in person. In fact, the more I thought about it the more certain I became that she would be at that very moment racing towards me, purposefully driving through the traffic in Hilda's car. I couldn't face her. I knew I had to go out. But where? To the cinema, to a pub (they would be open now), to a restaurant?

I didn't want to see a film, I didn't feel thirsty or hungry. If I went out just so as not to be in, Daphne was capable of lurking in the neighbourhood and swooping again when I got back, however late. I had a wild thought of going to the office and locking myself in. But the thought of the office reminded me that this was my holiday, the only one I should have this year. The cottage, all those light-years away, was still rented. The logs for the fire were still there, the bed was ready to be slept in. Why not? Why the hell not? It meant a long drive, but I might as well be driving as doing anything else, and this time it would be a drive towards a rest, not towards a mess of problems.

I picked up the bag I had brought with me. It was still packed. I had taken my shaving things and toothbrush out of it, so I put them back. That was all the preparation I needed. I felt in my pocket to make sure I had the cottage key and the ignition key of the car. And of course I had seventy-five pounds, now that Sanders had given me back that fifty. A tight grin spread across my face: that was one tiny little silver lining, anyway.

I went to the meter and turned out the electricity. Then I walked through the shadowy flat to the front door. As I did so the telephone started ringing. I hesitated, but only for an instant. It would either be Daphne, or something meaningless, or just possibly it was that sick little man in his grey suit, trying to involve me some more. I went straight on through the front door and shut it behind me. As I went down the stairs I could hear the telephone still ringing.

4

Tranquil in the knowledge that this was not one of the days on which he had to fear an invasion by the conversation-hungry Mrs Pimlott, Giles Hermitage sat down at his writing-desk on the morning after his visit to Helen Chichester-Redfern. In front of him was a stack of clean paper, in his hand the stubby ball-point pen, his word-pistol. Ready for invention.

But invention would not come. Giles found his mind enormously, draggingly reluctant to engage with the story of Gus Howkins and his love for Julia. Yet the story was interesting enough, surely? It was, at the very least, a channel through which meaningful thoughts and impulses could be made to flow? But he could not get on with it.

Long experience suggested several reasons for this. If he found a story deeply repugnant, so much so as to be forced to lay it aside, the explanation often lay in a breaking of contact. The story had simply wandered too far from his, Giles's, own concerns, had become a mechanical exercise in moving counters across a board. Sometimes, on the other hand, the opposite had happened. The contact had become too close; the invented story had thrown a bear-hug round his own actual situation, and the combined weight of the two of them was simply too much to move.

Well, which was it? Surely he, Giles Hermitage, novelist, bachelor, cathedral-town-inhabiter, was not in any way close to Gus Howkins, press-cutting-agency operator, separated husband, outer-suburb-inhabiter? He closed his eyes. How did he imagine Gus Howkins? A stocky, untidy man. But damn it, he himself was a stocky, untidy man. Well, but why should not one stocky, untidy man write about another, if they were sufficiently distinct as characters? Did Gus Howkins really live as an independent being, or was Giles simply projecting himself?

He thought carefully. Julia must be the key. *Cherchez la femme.*
Whatever else they did, men certainly defined themselves in
relation to the women they found attractive. Was he, Giles, really
expressing his own feelings through the puppet-figure of Gus
Howkins? If so, he would discover, if he searched hard enough,
that he was in love with Julia.

Sitting back, wrinkling his brow, Giles summoned from the
recesses of his mind the image of Julia – her pale, oval face, rich,
dark hair, deep brown eyes, that stillness, that expression which
somehow combined brooding attentiveness with a detachment, a
withdrawal, as if part of her being was somewhere else. Her body,
strong; well-shaped, yet delicately structured. Her graceful movements, her quickness in sitting or standing. Her sudden irradiating
smile.

He studied the image. Delectable, certainly. But in love? An
image to be in love with? Clearly no man writes a love-story
without imagining, in the woman's role, one of his own possible
ideals. He could get close enough to loving Julia, this girl in his
imagination, to allow his male-creature Gus Howkins to be properly obsessed with her. But no further.

Abruptly, explosively, the image of Harriet came thrusting between him and everything else. Her dark-red hair fell like a curtain
in front of his work, his life, his moving about and his standing still.
Her rich low voice drowned all other sounds in the universe. Stung
by the sudden pain, Giles dropped his pen and stood up, as if to
ward off an actual physical attack. It was an attack, certainly; an
attack of pure, gratuitous, useless pain. But how to beat it off?

Deliberately, with therapeutic intent, he summoned before his
mind's eye the image of a pale, intelligent face with parsley-green
eyes, framed in glossy brown hair: of an inquisitively tip-tilted nose:
of a slender boy-woman's body. He listened to a light, quick,
interested voice, saw the smile of a mobile mouth.

Oh, the hell with it! Was there no way to drive out one woman
without invoking another? Giles shook his head and laughed
grimly, laughed aloud in the silence of the room. Endless, rami-
fying farce, the unremitting sexual-go-round! He almost began to
wish that Mrs Pimlott were coming. At least she represented
femininity so diluted with verbosity and absence of physical charm
that he could drink it down like milk.

And yet milk, when one came to think of it, was another life-giving feminine contribution. Was there no escaping? Did all roads lead only to Woman? Cursing quietly through set teeth, Giles moved away from his desk. No use – he could not work this morning. No doubt the effort of the previous evening, when he had forced himself to carry out his resolve of abolishing all relics of Harriet, had left him in this churned-up state. Certainly his agitation was unusual, even by the standards of the agonised past few weeks. Well, of course it had churned him up. He had clawed through pockets, cupboards, drawers, and thrown all Harriet-detritus into a carrier-bag. When at last he went down to the dustbin, his hands were shaking as he lifted the lid and dumped the bag inside. It takes an effort to throw away one's whole life: or even the last fragments of what should have been one's life.

As usual, a walk was the answer. Get some fresh air in his lungs, some movement in his limbs, and imaginative potency might return. He could try again this afternoon, after seeing Helen Chichester-Redfern. Unless that drained him too. . . . Ah, the difficulties of life. How did anyone ever write a novel, compose a symphony, establish a scientific theory, do anything that called for emotional continuity?

He opened the window to test the air temperature. A soft April morning: no need for an overcoat. For the first time since last autumn it was probably warmer out than in. He wondered what the weather was like in Australia that morning. It depended on what part of Australia, of course. But it would be autumn.

He went out into the peaceful town. God bless provincial life. If this calm must be called smug and complacent, then smugness and complacency are good things. Neat houses, neat gardens, a row of shops, a greengrocer's with attractive produce piled outside: cabbages, onions, avocado pears, oranges, carrots of an unreal plumpness and carrot-colour. He stopped to look at them, enjoying his idleness. A card said: 'Cambridge carrots.' Was this merely a neutral description, or a claim to merit? Was Cambridge famous for its carrots?

'I see you looking at the carrots Mr Hermitage it wouldn't surprise me to see you buy a pound you could grate them it makes a nice little salad my Stan's wife saw it in a magazine specially if they're fresh it said in the magazine put a few drops of lemon juice on them but if you ask me ordinary malt vinegar's just as good brings out the flavour not too much of course and you've got a bottle in the kitchen cupboard on the left-hand side.'

Mrs Pimlott. Escape. But how? Standing firmly in front of him, shopping-bag full of potatoes caught in her thick right hand, she barred his way. A good woman. But he feared her. At any moment she would begin telling him about her husband's craze for Turkish baths. He went for a Turkish bath regularly every week and it was not natural, we were not meant to sweat like that.

At such times Giles had a vision of Mr Pimlott, whom he had never met, hurrying off to the Turkish baths to sweat out all the moist, heavy words his wife had injected into his system, through the ears, during the past week. Mrs Pimlott had a round, good-natured face. Giles imagined her inclining it towards Mr Pimlott, at the table, in their sitting-room, in bed, in their bathroom, in the garden, in the street. Her words would slop about inside him, and he would long to sweat, sweat, sweat to desiccate himself.

Standing there in front of a display of spring greens, Giles saw in his mind's eye the towelled figure of Mr Pimlott, lying on a table in the Turkish baths on gentlemen's night, with sweat coursing down his face and neck.

At the exact moment when he saw this sight with the eyes of the mind, with the eyes of the body he saw Diana Chichester-Redfern coming out of the shop. She was wearing a mackintosh of some silvery material – plastic, he supposed – and a rain-hat that followed the outline of her head and framed her face deliciously. Her shoes were the same shiny black ones she had been wearing in the house, when he first saw her. She threw him a look and a smile of recognition, then turned to walk away, heavily laden with bags and bundles.

'Oh, excuse me,' said Giles hurriedly to Mrs Pimlott, breaking necessarily into mid-sentence as she discoursed about her husband's unnatural form of recreation. 'I've just remembered – I'm overdue at my—'

Leaving the statement incomplete, licensing her to wonder whether he was on his way to a lawyer, a chiropodist or a money-lender, he sprinted after Miss Chichester-Redfern, who, moving with light, fast steps in spite of the amount she was carrying , had already almost disappeared in the morning bustle of shoppers. Determinedly, he caught her.

'Good morning.'

'Oh, hello.' He was beginning to know her keen, darting glance, and the smile which lurked perpetually at the corners of her mouth so that even when she was not actually smiling she was ready to do so at any moment. The whole effect was of a question: what possibilities of fun and excitement are there in the person I am now looking at? Her quick, challenging femininity was a stimulus to every male hormone in his body.

'You've got a terrible lot to carry – may I help you?'

'It's all right, thanks – I've got a system.' Of course she would have a system; she was so decided, so full of controlled, flashing energy. 'I go round certain shops, in a definite order, and get the heaviest things at the shop nearest home. But there's an extra dimension today because it's one of my twice-a-week washing days. I start out at the launderette, get the machine loaded and start it off, and then finish up there and get a taxi home. It's expensive, but I can't give all my time and energy to lugging things about – I have to practise every day.'

'May I,' he said carefully, really wanting to prolong this chance companionship with her, 'save a bit more of your energy by carrying some of that stuff for you?'

'But I haven't finished going into shops and I'd have to keep you waiting. Wasting the time of a creative man.'

'But if you lug it yourself you're wasting the energy of a creative woman.'

She laughed. 'Oh, I'm not creative. I'm an executant. Just a channel between the composer and the audience. Like being a critic, really, or a translator.'

'Well, translators have to live. Critics I'm not so sure about. I'm not working this morning, so do let me take a bag. The heaviest one.'

He held out his hand; she smiled and gave a graceful nod of acquiescence, and handed him a bag of tinned food that nearly pulled his arm out of the socket.

'Another,' he said.

'No, I'm balanced now.'

He saw immediately that no power on earth would make her hand over another bag. She had a fairly light one in each hand now, and she was a girl who habitually did things in her way, not anyone else's.

They moved along the pavement in tenuous contact; now side by side and able to exchange remarks, now sundered by lumbering women looking anxiously into shop-windows as they walked along, by prams, by straying toddlers, by an old man standing on the pavement as motionless as a statue.

But she did manage to ask him, 'When shall we see you next at the house?' And he did manage to reply, 'Today, if it's not inconvenient.'

Pedestrians bumped between them; when she could, she looked at him enquiringly and said, 'That's two visits in two days. I don't think we ought to take up such a lot of your time.'

'It's all right. I'm getting a lot out of it.'

'I can't think what. I expect you're just being kind.'

'Your mother's a very interesting woman.'

'Yes, I suppose she is.'

A bus-queue separated them; when he had traversed it, she said, 'Here's the launderette,' and they turned into it. Diana walked over to one of the machines. Its swirling port-hole showed sudden vivid glimpses of this or that garment in between equally sudden dashes of soapy rain. Giles looked at it with a flash of interest. In there, rotating and plunging in the warm, detergent tide, were the clothes she wore next to her skin. And also, the chilling thought came, the nightdresses that hid the dying woman's tormented frame from his pitying sight.

'It should be just about finishing,' she said and put down her shopping bags on a plastic chair. He followed suit. Now, for a few minutes, they were free to talk. The launderette was quiet except for the whirr of the machines; the few customers were mostly slumped in tired attitudes on the chairs, reading newspapers or just staring in front of them.

'What impression did you get of Mother yesterday?' she asked. 'I'm sorry I didn't see you before you went.'

'I told you. Very interesting.'

'Did she keep awake the whole time?'

'She sank back once or twice as if she was so exhausted as to be nearly unconscious. But she always rallied.'

'I'm glad to hear it. She rallies when there's something important to rally for. She's still got that much in reserve, though I don't know how long it'll be there. Some days, when there's nothing to interest her and she's just left alone with her thoughts, she hardly moves from morning till night, and only says yes and no if I say anything to her. I can always tell when I go in in the

— 113 —

morning if it's going to be one of those days. Her colour is different.'

'Different, how?'

'When you saw her yesterday she was pale grey. But on her bad days, she's yellow.'

'How awful,' he said, feeling sorry for her though her tone was matter-of-fact, with no appeal for sympathy. 'It must be . . . it must all take a heavy toll of you.'

'It was worse at first. I've been with her three months now, ever since they first told her she had cancer and they couldn't treat it. In the early days she was always trying to get out of bed and go on with life. And she'd ask my advice about buying a new dress, that kind of thing, when of course I knew she'd never put a dress on again. That was awful. It made me feel so sorry for her. Then, after a month or so, she seemed to enter a different phase where she accepted it. She stopped talking about what she was going to do. Gave all her thoughts to just . . . dying.'

'And you find that easier?'

'Well, it doesn't churn me up so much. When she was being so pathetically eager to live a little longer and do a few more things, I felt so sorry for her. But now, well, everybody's got to die some time. if you went round feeling sorry for everyone who's going to die, you'd just feel sorry for the whole human race, and in the end that would cancel out. I mean if you're sorry for *everybody* you're not individually sorry for anybody.'

He saw her clearly in that moment. Hers was not one of those natures to which compassion comes naturally. She would feel uncomfortable, resentful even, in the presence of someone whose sufferings aroused her pity. Her preference was for the sunshine of life: she felt cold in the shadows. But let that sun shine on her, and how she responded! How she threw back its lustre in vivid reflection!

Suddenly knowing this, he knew in the same instant that he needed her, if it were only as an example to be followed. Her strong drive towards enjoyment, her impatience with anything glutinous or soggy, would show him how to break out of the melancholy into which Harriet had plunged him.

The washing-machine switched itself off, and the clothes inside sank unwillingly into repose. Diana clicked open the door and took them out, then with deft, practised movements stowed them in the nearest drier, spread out to get the full benefit of the heat.

'There. A half hour to go. I'll go and ring for my taxi.'

'Let me do it.'

'Heavens, why should you? You can look after my shopping while I go to the kiosk. It's a very efficient taxi firm – they have their own free telephone.'

'They'd need to be efficient,' he said admiringly, 'to match you.'

She gave him that challenging, disturbing smile, and for an instant her eyes held his. 'After three months,' she said, 'I've got my routines.'

Then she was gone. He mounted guard over her purchases, thinking as he did so what a strange vortex life had flung him into, between the dying woman and the fast-stepping, impatient girl: and how much he welcomed it. Already, absorbed in the challenge of impending death and challenge of sparkling life, he felt himself moving away from the devouring presence-in-absence of Harriet. It was still agony to think directly of her; but when his attention was elsewhere, she seemed to recede into the category of things that had happened in the past. Slowly, perhaps, perhaps, he was beginning to fight back to life; and if that were true, the mother and the daughter had each made a contribution to it.

Diana reappeared, and we waited till the drier stopped. She took the clothes out of it, then began briskly gathering up her belongings.

'They only take about two minutes to arrive. They're getting very used to my ways. All the drivers know me, and they flirt with me like mad, it's great fun.'

Yes, he thought, you would like to be flirted with.

'I'll see you off anyway,' he said, moving with her to the door. Outside, she peered down the street for the taxi. He stood beside her, holding the bag of tinned food, looking forward to seeing her again that afternoon. At that moment a tall, thin clergyman came by. Seeing Diana, he stopped. A smile of glad recognition lit up his cavernous face.

'Diana, how nice to see you.'

'You too, father.' She smiled back.

'How is your mother?'

'No change.'

'You know I'm ready to come and see her at any time if she . . . changes her mind.'

— 115 —

'Yes. She knows that. Thank you very much, father.' Then, as if becoming aware of Giles standing in awkward silence beside her, she said, 'This is Giles Hermitage. Father Roughton.'

The cleric gave Giles an uninterested but slightly suspicious look, muttered a perfunctory salutation, and turned his attention back to Diana.

'I didn't see you at Eucharist on Sunday, dear child.'

'Didn't I tell you, father? I always go to the Cathedral on Low Sunday. The Bishop preaches.'

Was she having him on? Giles wondered. To the Cathedral? Low Sunday, what on earth was that? She went to hear the Bishop preach? *She* did? But the clergyman was listening gravely and nodding, and whatever else he was he was not a simpleton; he had the face of a clever man.

'Well, well, we can't deny the Cathedral its share in your devotions, Diana. But come to us when you can.'

He pressed her hand, nodded to Giles, and strode on.

'Who on earth was that?' he could not help asking.

'I introduced him, didn't I?' she replied with a hint of asperity. 'Father Roughton. He's the Vicar of St Simeon's.'

'Father? Is he a Catholic?'

'No, he's a high Anglo-Catholic, which is what I am. I go to the Cathedral quite often, because it's so beautiful and the singing's so lovely. But St Simeon's is the church I like best. It's marvellously high and traditional. If I go to an ordinary Church of England service nowadays I feel I might as well be with Methodists in a tin chapel.'

She spoke as if it were important to her. Giles nodded seriously, as if he understood. But he felt that some essential clue was eluding him. He could not fit in a habit of piety, an interest in church-going and ritual, to the picture of her that he was beginning to form in his mind – but which was still, he acknowledged, as crude as an Identikit.

'Well, here's my taxi. Thanks so much for helping. I'll see you this afternoon, if you're really going to be so kind as to call. Mother's really thrilled about it.'

She was gone. He went to his local pub for a thoughtful beer, then home for an even more thoughtful lunch.

'And what happens then?' asked Helen Chichester-Redfern, looking eagerly into Giles's face.

'That's as far as I've got. When this seedy, obviously untrustworthy little man suddenly says he knows where Julia is, the story halts to let the reader get his breath and wonder what's going to happen next.'

'But *you* must know what's going to happen next.'

'I do, but if you don't mind I'd rather not talk about the parts of the story that aren't written yet. The writing seems to go very slack if one does that.'

Obviously disappointed, she lay back on the pillow. Her rimless glasses seemed like dead discs in the afternoon light.

'It won't be long,' he reassured her. 'I'm working on it every day, and I'll fill you in on each bit as I do it. It'll be like following a serial.'

'I may not have time,' she said quietly.

That stung him with pity and guilt. 'I feel a cad. If I know how the story's going to go on, why don't I tell you, since you're so interested? It's just that experience has taught me—'

She lifted a hand to stop him. 'Please don't go on. It's I who am ashamed. Yes, I am. Really ashamed. To ask something of you that would make your work more difficult, when it must be quite difficult enough already. Besides. . . .'

He waited.

'Besides, I was being less than honest.'

'How so?'

'I was putting things in an order that isn't their real one. You see . . . how can I put this?'

'Take all the time you need. Only don't exhaust yourself.'

'I do need to know about the book you're working on,' she said slowly, 'but it isn't absolutely my prime need.'

'And what is your prime need?'

'For your help,' she said flatly.

'Of course I'll give you any help I can.'

'You may not have quite understood yet. I don't need help in getting through the process of dying. All that growing weaker and more vague, all the pain and the loss of physical control and dignity, Diana will take care of. Not because she loves me – we've never been close – but because she's a girl who sticks to a bargain when she's made one. She helps me to die, and she inherits what

— 117 —

money and property I have. I know she won't neglect her side of it, however cool she is, and uninvolved.'

'I see that. Then what is the help you still need, Helen?'

'Your mind,' she said with a sudden fierce energy. 'Contact with your mind.'

'Why *my* mind, especially?'

'Because it's creative. You can make things happen. And you have vision. There are so many unsolved questions in my life. I'm dying, the sun for me is going behind a thicker and thicker cloud, and I still don't understand the things that have happened to me.'

'Nobody can settle all the questions that life brings up.'

'But I *must* find some map to it all – something that will help to make sense of it. I *must* – I can't die in this fog. Perhaps any person with your kind of gift could help me, but you're the only one I know . . . and I only know you because I threw myself on your mercy. Please. Think what an effort that must have been for me. And say you'll help me.'

The intensity of her need was hypnotic. Giles had felt it, flooding the house, as soon as he came through the front door. Incredibly, considering the rate at which his interest in her was mounting, he had hardly noticed Diana. She had let him in, and twenty minutes later had come in with the tea-tray; but beyond noticing that she was wearing a plain grey dress and that sandals had replaced her polished black shoes, he had scarcely registered her, so fierce had been the pull of her mother's need. Like a furnace creating a draught, it had almost physically pulled him upstairs and to her bedside.

Yet what was the need? What could he do to satisfy it?

'Helen,' he said gently. 'Speak of anything. Ask me anything.'

She was silent for a moment, then said, 'Why have you never married?'

He stirred uneasily. 'I believe I told you that, last time.'

'You said you'd been put off by the unhappy marriages of your brother and your sister. Forgive me, but I don't find that explanation quite satisfying. Everyone who marries has disastrous examples in front of them – if not among their family, then among their friends. So what other reason? I know from your work that you're not indifferent to women.'

'No. They're important to me,' he said, suddenly seeing Diana's little black shoes.

'Something made you decide not to enter that particular relationship. And it must be connected with the number of unhappy marriages you write about. It's an obsessive theme with you. The different ways that marriage can wreck people's lives.'

'Yes.'

'Yet it's something so central. Don't you feel that for good or ill it makes a life? That an unmarried person, after youth has gone, is somehow incomplete?'

'I'd be prepared to concede that. I feel incomplete myself. But to be incomplete isn't necessarily a disadvantage, for an artist.'

'You mean. . . ?'

'I mean that a building that's half-finished is more open to the winds of heaven than one with all its doors and windows in place and all tight shut, with the electric lights on and no feeling for the twilight or the dawn outside.'

'And that's marriage to you? A building with shut doors and windows?'

Giles felt he could either reply at enormous length or very shortly. He chose to reply shortly, and said, 'Yes.'

'And yet you return to the theme over and over again. You must think of marriage as the centre of personal life. Strange that you should have felt able to do without that centre.'

'How can I reply,' he said, 'except to say again that the artist can function very well out of an incomplete personality? Or perhaps I should say a personality that, because it's open on so many sides, has so many possibilities for expansion, often looks incomplete to people who view it from outside?'

There was another silence, and when at last she spoke, her voice was scarcely more than a whisper.

'These are deep mysteries. What makes relationships succeed or fail, what brings happiness. You speak from the point of view of one who never felt able to commit himself to marriage.'

'Yes. I told you about that last time, too. And how I finally met a woman I'd have been proud and glad to marry and she said it wasn't necessary and now she's left me.'

'I remember that of course. And I'm sorry for the pain you're in. But our points of view are still very different. You could at least choose whether to marry or not. I had the kind of conventional middle-class upbringing that meant that when I grew to marriageable age I would become some man's wife more or less automatically, because people couldn't think of anything else for girls to do.'

'Well, I realised that Diana must have had a father. And since I don't see any sign of him I just assumed you must be a widow.'

From the still figure on the bed came a voice of sudden hardness.

'I am not a widow. I am a deserted wife.'

'Oh.'

There seemed to be nothing to say. He waited. She gathered her strength in a long pause, then spoke.

'Giles, I won't shilly-shally. The gap in the middle of my life, the gap that's filled up with questions that I'm desperate now to get answered, is the gap of my marriage to Diana's father.'

'I think I knew that,' he said, though the knowledge seemed to course through his veins at that moment as a perfect novelty.

She was silent again. Waiting, he noticed that while they talked the weather had turned cold. The thick white sky was besieging the window-panes in a hostile way. He got up, drew the curtains, and sat down again in the Windsor chair.

At last the dying woman spoke: at first in a voice that struggled to push its way through a veil of fatigue, then with gathering strength and animation.

'My husband is a scientist. Research has been his life. For years he was a professor and had to teach, but he always hated that. His work seemed to him a joyful adventure only when he was probing for new knowledge, exploring this avenue and that, not caring how many blind alleys he had to go down if only he could find the occasional one that led somewhere. What he hated was to have to turn aside from his enquiries and give time and energy to inform-ing other people, explaining to them routine matters that had ceased to interest him. He was a thruster forward, Giles. Never an explainer or a sharer.'

'I see,' he said.

'I know nothing about science, and it never worried me that he made no attempt to tell me anything about his work. He simply went to the laboratory in the morning and came back in the evening. Sometimes very late. He expected me, even as a young bride, to put up with irregular hours. He said his work was very claiming and he just couldn't be bothered with things like meal-times.'

'I suppose you adjusted, though I can see it must have been trying.'

'I adjusted. And I enjoyed his company when he gave it to me. He was always quite pleasant. When he'd worked until he could work no more, he'd take a day off and we'd go walking in the country, or drive to the sea. And sometimes we went to concerts together. He was very musical.'

'Scientists often are.'

'As you say. It all seemed to be going along quite easily. I was content, though looking back I can see that I led a dull and eventless life by the standards of today. People *fill* their lives so much more now than we did. I was childless, and it never occurred either to Richard or myself that I might get a job.'

'Richard being your husband.'

'Richard Chichester-Redfern being my husband. I just stayed at home and made the house pleasant and cheerful and became expert in cooking the sort of food that can be kept hot for hours in a casserole without drying up. And I read a lot, and listened to music, and developed my mind so that I could be a companion to him. I never minded not having a child. And of course wives didn't have jobs in those days. It was always thought that being a wife *was* a job.'

She paused. Her breathing had become harsh. He waited.

'I was twenty-four when we got married. That was in nineteen thirty-two. Oh, the world was very different in those days! You can hardly imagine how different it was!'

'I was on this earth. But of course I didn't know yet what kind of place it was.'

She sat up straighter: another wave of strength.

'After seven years of our marriage, the war came. Richard left the university and did some sort of government work. He wasn't supposed to talk about it to anyone, but that was no change because he never did anyway. All I knew was that it was research, research, always research.'

'That must have suited him.'

'It did. He was quite happy all through the war. That's why I could never pin down the exact moment when his life took on a new interest. He didn't seem to be unhappy, lacking something, and then happy because he'd found it. He seemed about the same all the time.'

— 121 —

'A new interest?'

'A mistress.'

Something in Giles's mind started like a wildebeest. Was this the point at which the confidences began? Was she, under so elaborate a covering, playing no more than the familiar game of Telling Him Her Troubles?

But her face was as composed as ever, she shot him no glance of appeal for sympathy, there was no syrup of self-pity in her voice, and she went on in a strong, matter-of-fact vein.

'It happened, as I believe is very often the case, in connection with his work. He was engaged on a piece of research – that eternal research! – with a woman scientist younger than himself. They shared the excitement, they shared the fatigue and discouragement, they shared the final triumph when they found what they were looking for. Meanwhile, I shared nothing but his home, his table, his bed.'

She paused. In the short silence, Giles heard the sound of music from downstairs. Yes, it was a guitar. Diana was at her practising.

'I have no idea whether Richard made the slightest attempt to resist falling in love with his colleague. After our very early days, I was never really in his confidence. Not only did I know nothing of his work, I was held at a distance from all his innermost thoughts. His relationship with me was, in a curious way, social. He sat down with me at the table as if he were a guest who had come to lunch. Even in our intimate life, he was like a visitor who expects to go back afterwards to his own place and his own habits. I see that now. I didn't see it then. Or not clearly. What is a young woman to see, when she has no experience and no standard of comparison? No one but Richard had ever made love to me. I wondered if all men had his attitude, his inner barrier that kept his emotions from flowing towards me. Or whether it was a peculiarity of our relationship. But I only wondered fleetingly, and not very often. I didn't know there was any reason for me to be anxious. And all the time he was giving more and more of his life, more and more of his thoughts and feelings, to this woman. She was five years younger than I, which made her nine years younger than Richard. A good ratio. And she had the key to his real love, that research, research that was the breath of his lungs.'

Giles waited for the outburst of bitterness that seemed heralded by her words. But it did not come. The topic of her grievance was touched lightly, and put aside.

'At last, he began to give her so much of his time that I hardly ever saw him even during his brief leisure. What must have started as an emotional comradeship between a man and woman working together had evidently turned into a real infatuation. When he was not at the laboratory with her he was spending evenings at her flat or going away for weekends. He never made much attempt to cover it up, though on the other hand he never came to me with a statement of how things stood. He just let matters drag along until I found out.'

'I don't need three guesses as to how you found out,' said Giles. 'A helpful friend. Someone who claimed to be trying to warn you and save your marriage, and actually just wanted the fun of throwing the fat on the fire.'

'Precisely so. I had very few friends; I was never the kind of woman who has long, intimate hours of gossip with other women. I was told of my husband's infidelity by a servant. A trusted daily help who had been coming to me for years. She told me she felt it her duty to break the news to me because it was the talk of the neighbourhood. That was needless cruelty: the neighbourhood knew nothing of it. But she had a son who worked at the laboratory in some menial capacity, and was always seeing them together. Of course she saw to it that the neighbourhood got its pound of flesh just as she had.'

'I'm sorry,' he said gently.

'Oh, it's all so long ago, there are times when it seems to have happened to another person. And of course I *was* another person in those days. I was very innocent and foolish. So what, using your novelist's imagination, do you think was my first reaction to hearing the news?'

Giles had already been thinking. 'I don't need imagination to answer that. I only need arithmetic.'

'Arithmetic?'

'All this must have happened about the end of the war, or within a year or two afterwards.'

'It did.'

'Well, your daughter must be in her late twenties. That means she was conceived about the time all this happened.'

'She was conceived in nineteen forty-seven.'

'So you have my answer. Your immediate reaction to finding out that your husband had a mistress was to become pregnant.'

She breathed out: a sigh, it seemed, of gratitude. 'How deeply you understand, Giles. How much painful exposition you spare me.' Downstairs, the softly plangent notes of Diana's guitar stopped, then began again.

'It was not a conscious decision, of course. We had never used any form of contraception. When it became clear that one or other of us must be infertile, I had simply accepted that as part of the ordained nature of things, and Richard as usual took only a polite interest. He had no hunger to become a father – no hunger, as I thought, for anything but scientific knowledge. I suddenly realised, now, that he hungered for *her*. So he must be capable of desire. He would never have gone to her merely for comfort, for shelter and reassurance. He had all those from me. It must have been real need, real appetite. And I suppose the knowledge that he could feel those things made me long for him, now that I was losing him, more deeply than I had before. He still made love to me, in the polite and absent-minded fashion that was all I had ever known. But now the cells of my body were mounting a furious campaign to win him back, to grapple him close to me and hold him.'

She stopped. Her breath was coming unevenly and her face had taken on that terrible shade of grey.

'Helen, don't exhaust yourself.'

'It is not I who am exhausting myself. It is death. What should I save my energy for?'

'To talk more to me. Later, at another time. To help me to understand.'

She took several deep, effortful breaths, then looked at him with all her habitual keen intensity. 'What do you not understand? Have I told the story incompletely? I'm exhausted, and muddled. Have I left anything out?'

He collected himself, trying to speak slowly and impressively, to get through to her.

'You've left nothing out. The story is entirely clear. But I still need help. I need to know the nature of the problem you bring to me. You see your own life so clearly. What can you need to learn from me? Yet you spoke of illumination, of helping you to understand and find calm.'

She answered slowly, with long pauses, her voice coming from far away.

'You're right. Evidently right. We've gone as far as we can go today. Not only because I am exhausted, as you can see. But for your sake. Even with your powers of intuition, some things are too complex, too deeply hidden, for you to see into straight away. Time is needed. To perceive them to their depths.'

'Of course. I'll go now and leave you to rest. I'll come again soon.'

She did not seem to hear, but went on as if talking to herself as much as to him.

'My life is over. Only my death is to come. And when I look back over it, what I see most is this great black shadow in the middle. The sun going behind thick clouds. Then emerging into only a smoky light. I have never been happy since my husband took his love away. And gave it to another woman. Diana has no love for me. When I conceived her. It was the effort of my whole body and soul. To keep him near me. I failed. She was born into a life from which love. Had been stolen. There was nothing. She has. Nothing.'

Helen Chichester-Redfern slumped forward, her head over her drawn-up knees, in a sudden sleep so total that it was like a swoon. Giles rose from his chair and gently, taking her by the armpits, settled her back among the pillows. Her body seemed as weightless as that of a dead heron he had once found on a river bank. It was no more than a frail cage for suffering. As he drew up the duvet around her shoulders she lay without waking, the discs of her glasses pointing meaninglessly at the ceiling.

He stood for a moment looking down at her, with compassion for her, compassion for himself, compassion for all life that must go out into the darkness through the stiff gate of death.

Down the stairs he went, slowly. His body felt heavy with sadness. Pausing in the hallway, he could hear the guitar being played determinedly behind that closed door. Yes, it was real professional playing: the notes were picked out so cleanly, yet with such a lyrical resonance. For a moment he stood enchanted by the sound. Then it stopped and he decided to leave without drawing attention to himself, as he had done the day before. Obviously the musician on the other side of that door was concentrating fiercely and devotedly. When they chatted that morning, she had seemed ready to while away an hour with him after his visit to her mother; but that willingness must have been swamped in the fierce need to work at her art. No, he must go, and rely on seeing her some other time.

Then the door opened and she was there, in stockinged feet and grey dress.

'Oh, you're there. I'm glad you haven't gone. I was practising and I didn't notice the time.'

'Yes, I heard you practising. I was just about to tip-toe out. It sounded too good to interrupt.'

She laughed gently. 'It's nice of you to say it sounded good. It was very rough, actually. I was trying a new piece. I've finished now, anyway. One gets to the end of practising – the edge goes off and then you need a drink and some human company.'

'Oh. Well, in that case. . . .'

'Go in. I'll join you.'

She moved towards the kitchen, and Giles entered her sitting-room and looked about him curiously. It was neat and elegant; he had expected that. The colour scheme was all green and white – green carpet, green covering on armchair and divan, white walls and ceiling. Was that her mother's taste, or hers? (But she would hardly have had time, in three months, to order up a new colour scheme, with all that she had to do.) It was effective, certainly, and restful. A large standard lamp, with a green shade, threw a soft, pale light. Her guitar was lying on the divan. There was a small but crowded bookcase, a wardrobe, a piano, and a large, elaborate machine for playing tapes and records. A musician's work-room. But it was a girl's room too; there were concessions to pure decoration – a screen on which she had pasted reproductions of paintings that took her fancy; a sumptuously coloured rug. And one thing that seemed both an ornament and not an ornament: a small, silver crucifix, hanging by a long chain, beside the divan where she slept.

As he stood taking it all in, she reappeared with a bottle of whisky, half full, and two glasses, on a tray.

'I was just going to have a drink. I've been longing for one, but I can't drink while I'm practising. It makes me play brilliantly for a quarter of an hour or so, and then I start losing precision. It's a pity, but the only way to do it is cold sober.'

She set down the tray, fished under the wardrobe for her shiny black shoes ('I always take my shoes off when I practise. Helps the

— 126 —

blood-flow to the brain') and motioned him towards the armchair. 'Anything in your whisky,' she said, pouring, 'or straight?'

'Straight.' An excitement was mounting in him that needed to be matched by the impact of raw spirit on his stomach. She affected him powerfully; he admitted it, at last.

'Well, cheers. How did you find Mother?'

'She talked a great deal, I'm afraid, and exhausted herself. I've left her sleeping.'

'I'll go and see to her when I've had this drink. Do wait around if you've nothing better to do.'

'Thank you, I will.'

'You say she talked a lot. About anything special?'

'Yes. She told me the story of her life.'

Diana took a calm sip at her glass. 'Nothing much in the way of a story, is it? Only one thing happened to her – being left by my father.'

'Well, I suppose you could say two things. First getting married to him, then being left by him.'

She shook her head. 'I don't think getting married to him was much of a happening. As far as I can tell he hardly noticed her.'

'Why did he marry her, do you think, if he hardly noticed her?'

She shrugged. 'Oh, people in those days got married just because it was the thing to do. Once a man got to a certain position and had an income, it never occurred to him *not* to get married, unless he was queer or something. That's how I imagine it, anyway. And people in those days were prepared to settle for such boredom. A woman would go through the whole of her life and only have one man ever, and that was her husband. And she'd think of herself as lucky.'

Giles stirred uneasily in his armchair. 'Speaking as one who's always avoided marriage' (but Harriet!) 'I ought to agree with you. But surely it wasn't as simple as that. People must have wanted children.'

'Yes, they wanted children and they didn't want to have them without getting married and then they were stuck with it.'

Her tone was different from what it had been in the morning. The sparkle, the edge of banter and challenge, had gone: her voice was flatter, her manner more off-hand. Perhaps she was tired. Or perhaps the thought of her mother's wasted life depressed her, as it well might.

Abruptly, she now rose and said, 'I must see to Mother. I'll settle her down for the night. It takes me about half-an-hour to forty minutes. Do stay if you'd like to. There's plenty to keep you occupied: play some music if you can work out how to operate the machine, or read a book. Or there's the wireless. Or perhaps you play the piano? Not the guitar, please, even if you do play.' As she threw the cascade of suggestions at him, something of her dancing brightness came back. But her tone was still brisk and business-like; her mind was on what had to be done.

She went out, and he waited. At first he sat quietly with his thoughts, but became restive and needed occupation. Obviously, his trade being what it was, her bookcase demanded investigation. Some novels – *Lotte in Weimar*, *The Group*, *The Black Prince*, *Zen and the Art of Motorcycle Maintenance* (pressed on her, he decided, by an admirer); memoirs of musicians, Mozart's letters, a stray volume of Ernest Newman's life of Wagner; Robert Craft on Stravinsky. Auden, yes; the only other book of poetry was an orange-coloured edition of Rochester's *Poems on Several Occasions*, 1680. Why would she be interested in a seventeenth-century poet? He took out the book and leafed through it. Oh, of course. Very witty, very well-turned, and very, very dirty. Obviously this was a modern reprint to catch the permissive eye; not being a connoisseur of such things, he had never gone behind the usual tidied-up versions to what Rochester actually wrote, and now read for the first time the raw version of 'The Imperfect Enjoyment.' Good God, was this the kind of thing she read, in between saying her prayers before the crucifix on the wall and trotting off to the Cathedral with her prayer-book? The sharply etched, corrosively lustful couplets flicked his mind: perhaps it was true and sex, sex, sex was the answer to all emotional problems, as Rochester had believed. (But it killed him in his thirties.)

Time had gone fast. Half an hour, forty minutes: she was back, her duties accomplished.

'I see you've found my Rochester. Good, isn't it?'

'In its own way, startlingly good. He writes well.'

'I'd never have known about it, not being literary,' she said. 'But someone gave it to me. He had his reasons, of course.'

Who the hell was it? The Bishop?

Diana went over to the whisky-bottle and poured herself another shot. She still seemed tense, restless: no welcoming vibrations

— 128 —

came from her. Giles wondered whether he ought to withdraw. But he wanted to stay: and he rationalised his wish with the thought that if the task of looking after her mother depressed her – and it was a heavy task, for a young person not trained to the work – then he ought to stay and try to cheer her. As she sat down on the divan, whisky-glass in hand, her green eyes were lack-lustre and unseeing, her face closed, and suddenly he felt sorry for her.

'This business of nursing your mother . . . it must be frightful. All alone with such a responsibility.'

'I'm not all alone with it. There's a nurse who comes for two hours every morning. She cleans her up and gives her all her injections and things. And Dr Bowen quite often comes in the afternoon.'

'Still, it can't be easy.'

'No, it's not easy but I don't want to talk about it.'

He felt nonplussed. It was hard to have one's offer of sympathy rejected so abruptly.

Diana moved over to the music-making apparatus (it was far too ambitious for any simpler designation) and started it going. He recognised the music as Handel. Without asking whether he wanted any more whisky, she gave him some, and herself too. Standing in the middle of the room, she bent down and pulled off her shoes, and, glass in hand, did a few dance-steps about the carpet.

'Ah, that's better – the music's relaxing me. And not just the music. The whisky. And having you here.'

Bells shrilled in his skull. What was she doing? Complimenting him?

'I'm glad you like having me here,' he ventured.

'Of course. I like men.'

The come-down from 'you', which was individual, to 'men', which was not, jolted him, but he tried not to let his face show it. A fiery swig of whisky, that was the answer. He took one, and sat back as it burnt its way down.

'I ought to get some food, I suppose,' she said. 'I had no lunch.'

'None at all?'

'Well, I had a glass of orange juice with some ice in it. There was no food in the house that I wanted to eat.'

'No food? But I helped you carry about a ton of it.'

'Mostly tinned stuff. I never eat that. I get it so that I can offer something to people who come, and because Mother sometimes takes a little chicken soup or something. I can't bear tinned food.'

'I don't see the logic of your scheme,' he admitted.

'The logic is that I try to avoid being within reach of food, otherwise I'll eat it.'

'But isn't that what food's for?'

'Not for me. I'm a foodoholic. If I'm sitting in the house and there's a larder full of food I'll eat my way through it. Once I get started I can't stop, like an alcoholic with a bottle. I'll even sit in an armchair with a whole loaf and tear it to pieces and stuff it down. So I don't keep any. In my flat in London, that is. I just go out and buy the amount I need and bring it back and eat it. But here, I have to keep some things in stock, so I get tins. There, now you have your answer.'

'Thank you very much.'

She gave that glinting, amused smile. Then, without warning, she got up from the divan and came and sat on the floor beside his armchair. Drawing up her knees and clasping her hands round them, she leaned her back against his legs.

His heart began beating like a machine-gun.

Carefully, he set down his whisky-glass, and with the hand thus liberated he began gently stroking her hair.

'Go on doing that,' she said dreamily.

'Your hair's chestnut.'

'Not really. But it's got chestnut lights in it. This lamp brings them out.'

After a few minutes she turned to face him, laid her arm across his thighs, and lifted her face to be kissed. The first kiss was long and expressive; the second, longer and more expressive.

With a sudden lithe movement she was on her feet, then she was across the room, lying on the divan – which was, he realised, her bed – holding out one arm towards him.

'Come here,' she breathed.

He joined her: they kissed again, more comfortably now and more at leisure, and her hands moved about his back.

'Wait,' she said and stood up. 'I'll be back in a minute. Get into bed if you like.'

Then she was gone, no doubt to the bathroom. Giles rolled over on to his back, staring dazedly at the ceiling. The pace of events had left him literally breathless. But this, he was beginning to understand, was her way. Once she had decided that she wanted something, she drove straight towards it.

He rolled off the bed and turned back the counterpane. The sight of sheets and pillow-cases suddenly made the situation seem real. It was her bed, she slept in it, she made it every morning and changed the linen every week, and she had invited him to get into it and she would join him 'in a minute.' He tore off his clothes, threw them over the armchair, and dived between the sheets. There was plenty of room: it was rather a large bed for one young lady's room, what he believed was known as a three-quarter bed. No doubt she needed it.

She came in, naked, carrying her clothes, her delectable little breasts jogging as she walked towards him. Knowing that in a moment it would be too late for coherent speech, he managed to stammer out a question: 'Is there anything we need to do about . . . precautions?'

She laughed softly, laying her clothes down on top of his. 'Oh, you don't need to worry. Girls like me are on the pill.'

Then she was beside him and everything was happening. Her love-making was as direct and as fiercely concentrated as everything else she did. She was silent, except that when he first entered her she groaned in pleasure, 'You're good . . . oh, you're so good,' and when she came to her orgasm she gave a series of quick little cries, *oh-oh-oh-oh*, almost like a laugh.

She was quite different from Harriet. But every bit as wonderful.

Lying close together in the soft lamplight, blissfully exhausted, they talked like old friends.

'Why do you live on your own?' she asked him.

'Why do you, if it comes to that?'

'Oh, I like it. I couldn't bear the thought of not being alone, and free.'

Giles knew that this ought to have made him think of Harriet, ought to have started his wounds bleeding again; but the nearness of Diana's smooth, lithe body made him so replete and so content that pain could find no way in. Rather than launching into any details of his life, he turned the question aside with, 'I live on my own because I'm not married.'

'What d'you do for sex?'

'Oh, I just take it where I can find it.'

She gave that soft laugh. 'So do I. Fun, isn't it?'

'Mostly. But sometimes you get hurt.'

'Well, it's quite easy to live so that you never get hurt and it's just deadly boring.' She was silent for a moment, then went on, 'Actually, I make a distinction between serious love-affairs, where you really get hooked on someone, and fucking-for-fun.'

'Do the two run concurrently, or is the f.-f.-f. just to fill gaps?'

'Either could happen. Sometimes if you have an intense affair, you're so taken up with the man and you see him every night, or move in and live with him, that you simply haven't any time left for the blokes you just have fun with. It depends, I suppose, whether the man you're mad about is mad about you. Not long ago I got it really badly for a man who simply didn't care about me. It was a real unrequited. He *enjoyed* me all right, he used to ring up when he'd nothing better to do and come round and fuck me, but as far as he was concerned that was the end of it. But I couldn't be casual about him – I really *languished*. I used to sit by the telephone day and night, just praying that I'd hear his voice, though of course he only rang up for one thing. I didn't care what he wanted me for, just as long as he wanted me for something.'

'The whole business,' said Giles, gently kissing her forehead, 'sounds altogether unedifying.'

'Oh, it wasn't the lack of edification that bothered me. It was the smallness of my share in his attention. In between ringing up and coming round for a fuck, he simply never bothered with me. I couldn't tie his letters up in pink ribbon and moon over them for the simple reason that I never had even a short note from him. He used to go away for long trips and not even tell me he was going. On the other hand if he felt like taking me somewhere, he'd ring up and invite me at short notice. And of course I'd drop everything and go. He took me to Toronto once.'

'What was he doing there?'

'What he did everywhere – play music. He's an organist – gives recitals. He's very well known.'

There was a short silence and then Giles said, 'You put all this in the past tense. Is it a closed chapter?'

'I haven't heard from him for ages. At first I thought he'd just gone off on a trip, or was busy and couldn't be bothered. But finally I decided he'd dropped me. So I adjusted. And of course I'd had plenty of fucking-for-fun during the time I was pining for him. In fact he once rang up and said he was coming round, and I had a chap with me and we were all ready to go to bed. I told him I had a headache and got him out of the place so fast he nearly died of surprise.' She laughed merrily. 'Fucking often has its funny side, doesn't it?'

'Yes, the sexual life is a great source of comedy.' He felt impelled, for some reason, to restate that truth in his own idiom.

Turning slightly to relieve a cramped arm, Giles found himself looking up at the silver crucifix.

'You're a Christian, aren't you, Diana?'

'Dinah, please. It's only Mother who calles me Diana. And I think double-barrelled names are silly so I call myself Redfern. Dinah Redfern, that's my name.'

'Dinah Redfern. You're a Christian.'

'Yes, I am. I need a framework and that gives me one.'

'Doesn't it . . . well, conflict with the fucking-for-fun and all the rest of it?'

'Of course not. God made us into sexual beings, it's His doing if we're randy. I never feel the slightest guilt about that – never have since I started. I had a fool of a tutor at College who fancied he ought to take a high moral line: he asked me once if my conscience didn't accuse me. I told him no, not at all, and he went back to minding his own business.'

Giles pondered. 'All the same, I expect you don't report it all to people like Father Roughton.'

'Why should I? I'm not a Catholic. It's not obligatory to go to confession. I believe in God and I go to church, so what I do with my cunt is no business of Father Roughton's, bless him.'

As he pondered this she suddenly said, 'I'm hungry,' and slid nimbly out of bed. He watched while she put on some clothes with those quick, precise movements, marvelling at the slender grace of her nakedness as it disappeared from him section by section. Then she vanished in the direction of the kitchen.

Left alone, Giles made an effort to study the situation dispassionately, to see it from outside like a picture. But the joy that kept welling up out of the depths of his being, and the deep, gratified languor that still possessed his body, made the attempt impossible. Whatever it was that was happening to him, he was content, and more than content, to let it happen.

She reappeared, in too short a time for him to believe it possible, with a dining-room trolley on which she had set out plates, knives,

— 133 —

butter, cheese, a loaf, radishes, a wine-bottle and glasses.

'Here you are. I didn't ask you whether you wanted any food because that's an unnecessary question. A man's always hungry after a fuck.'

'Don't you approve of unnecessary questions?' he asked, sitting up.

'I hate them. It's all right, you needn't get dressed. You can just sit up in bed and eat if you like. But don't make crumbs. I can't stand them next to my skin.'

Not feeling able to guarantee to drop no crumbs, he pulled on shirt and trousers and sat up to the trolley. They ate close together, as in an intimate restaurant.

'This is stone-ground wholemeal bread. I like integral food. There's no point in not being healthy if you can. What do you feed yourself on?'

'Oh, this and that. Sometimes I go out. If I buy bread and take it home I quite often get wholemeal.'

Harriet had been a good cook, always whipping up delicious little dishes. So what. Go away, Harriet, I'm busy. Dematerialise.

'Most people don't know anything about nutrition,' said Dinah, biting into a radish. 'These aren't very good but then they're imported. You can't get decent radishes at this time of year. But I wanted something crisp with the bread and cheese. I love crisp food – if I roast a chicken I eat all the crackly skin myself, and if I make stuffing balls I make them really crunchy.'

Her remark about nutrition had reminded him that her father was a scientist. He wondered if it would be permissible to bring up that subject, and decided to risk it. After all, his interest in this girl – to put it no higher – was vivid enough to make him hungry for any information about her.

'Where does your father live, Dinah?'

'In Canada. Have some wine?'

'I've got some. Do you ever see him?'

'Yes, he sometimes comes over. And I went to see him when Mark took me to Toronto.'

'He's working, then? He's not retired?'

'He's retired from teaching, and when that happened you could hear his three hearty cheers right across the Atlantic. But he keeps on burrowing away like mad. If he stopped finding things out he'd die.'

'Does his woman help him?'

'Yes, they work together. She likes messing about with computers and he doesn't know anything about them, they came along after he'd formed his methods of work. So she's very useful to him.'

'Is he fond of her?'

'I think so. He's stuck to her, anyway. She was quite pretty when they first got going – very tall, much taller than he is, and willowy. Now she's dried up and she just looks like a bean-pole, with glasses. But Daddy's an old man, I don't suppose it matters much any more.'

'Has he . . . been to see your mother since she became ill?'

'No. And he isn't going to. She's just going to have to die without him.'

The answer was dismissive, final. He could probe no further. He looked across at her face, but there was no particular expression in those parsley-green eyes, and the mobile lips were as composed as usual.

'Had enough to eat? Right, then I'll play you some music. That's if you're not in a hurry to go.'

'Good God, no. I'm in Wonderland. I could stay for ever.'

She moved the trolley to one side, its dishes neatly stacked. 'That's good,' she said. Then, with one of her sudden lithe movements, she was sitting beside him on the bed and kissing him. Her voice sounded in his ear with tenderness, or as close as she ever came to tenderness. 'It's good because I've decided to like you. I think you're someone worth liking a lot.'

'Thank you,' he said humbly.

'How funny you are,' she said, standing up and looking down at him with cool amusement. 'Fancy thanking me for that.'

'Why shouldn't I? You mean there's no volition in it?'

'I mean that where sex is concerned, you don't do things because you want to, you do them because you have to.'

'One has no choice?'

'Of course not. We're all helpless in the grip of sex. Once you're really hooked on somebody, you don't ask questions or raise objections. You just put up with anything they do to you, the way I did with Mark.'

Or as I shall with you, his prophetic soul suddenly whispered in the silence behind his forehead bone.

She picked up her guitar. 'I'll play to you. We've eaten, it's not time for you to go home, and it's too soon for another fuck. So what better than a little music?'

It occurred to him that that probably was a fair summary of her attitude to music, though she was so wedded to an ideal of professional competence in it.

He watched as she took the instrument in a light but cradling grip. Her hands, he noticed, were rather large for a woman's; elegant enough, but square-cut and capable. He did not wish them different. He did not wish anything about her different. He was falling in love.

'I'll play a little party piece.'

She worked soberly, bending over the guitar, her agile body tense with concentration. The music played in the soft air like an intangible fountain, building towers and cubes and arches, dismantling and re-building. He did not know the piece, but it was evidently a set of variations. As he listened Giles thought, Harriet educated me about art. Dinah will educate me about music. Have I anything to teach anyone? Do I leave on their minds any mark of my passing?

The last variation of all seemed to grow in the air like an orange-tree with shining fruit. She ended, and spoke.

'That's the Britten Nocturne. I expect you noticed how the Purcell theme comes at the end instead of the beginning where you'd expect. But perhaps you know it.' She laid down the guitar and picked up her glass.

'It must be marvellous to be able to play like that,' he said.

'I don't know whether it's all that marvellous. But it's something I need. It holds me together.'

'You need a lot of holding together? You seem to me a very coherent, one-piece young lady.'

'That's the impression I make because I work at it. I'm a very motivated person – I like to drive towards an objective. I can't just live along from day to day and let life happen to me. I need to make progress towards something. All these years, studying music, practising the guitar and playing it a little better month by month, it's been the second of the two things that held me together. The first is my faith, of course.'

'Oh, yes, of course.' He glanced across at the silver crucifix.

'That's just a fact, take it or leave it, it doesn't matter to me whether you understand it or not.'

'But I like to understand things about people. It's such a big part of my job.'

'Well, when you get to know me better you'll understand the two things that keep me together, my faith and my music.'

As she spoke, she put down her glass and came and sat next to him on the bed.

'I certainly look forward to that,' he said, putting his arm round her waist. 'To getting to know you better, I mean.'

'Well, you can make a start on that straight away,' she said. 'You must have had enough rest by now.'

He watched while she slid out of her clothes. Then she came and leaned her weight against him, pressing harder and harder until he sank back among the pillows.

5

THE DRIVE UP WAS, AS THEY SAY, UNEVENTFUL; I JUST FELT LIKE A piece of dead flesh sitting in a car, a zombie steering a machine through the darkness. It was about two in the morning when I thankfully turned off the main road and threaded my way along the valley, sheep staring with gold eyes into the headlights, and pulled up beside the stone wall and the stile. As I switched the engine off, the intense silence of the mountains closed in, and in it my battered mind seemed to relax and expand, becoming itself again.

I got my bag, locked the car and went towards the cottage. I had no torch to help me in picking my way among the rocks and ferns, but at that moment a fitful moonlight broke from among the clouds, and I decided that nature was welcoming me. Here I was, back among this silence and peace, to finish my rest. The word 'rest' seemed to float before me like a banner: it was what I was living for, the only thing I wanted, the only good in the world, rest, rest, rest.

The canoe was still leaning up against the wall. Nobody had pinched that, anyway. I unlocked the door, switched the light on, took one quick look to see that the place hadn't been broken into (but who would do it? Squatters? Vagabond lovers? Badgers? The Welsh Language Society?), and then went straight up the ladder to the only thing in the house that was real to me at that moment: bed.

It was rumpled, it probably still smelt faintly of her as well as of me, it was slightly dank with the cold moist air of the unoccupied house, but I dived into it and pulled the top sheet and the blankets up round me and burrowed my head into the pillow and then all of us together, the sheets, the blankets, the pillow, me, the bed, the cottage, the valley, the sheep, the mountains, the sea, the cities and all the people in them, the whole world, slept.

When I woke up next morning it was about eleven. A beautiful late-summer day, very still and complete, was just coming up to its full height. I lay on my back a bit and then got out of bed and looked through the window. The sun was bringing out the colour of everything, not a leaf stirred on the mountain ash that stood near my window, the smooth grey skin of the canoe spoke to me of lapping water. It was a perfect day. And I was on holiday.

Going down the ladder, I realised that I ought to be feeling happy. Or, failing that, reasonably content. How absurd I was, to feel empty and let down! How illogical, in a sober and practical-minded man at my time of life, to have that slight ache in the centre of my being, as if something had been pulled out and the cavity had not quite healed yet!

It was ridiculous and I should feel ashamed of myself. I filled the kettle and put it on the electric stove and stood beside it, facing the situation, accepting and assessing the ache inside me. All right, she came into my life. And she stayed in it for a whole night. And, all right, she left again. I couldn't expect to keep her, could I? Not a girl like that.

Then I caught sight of myself in the mirror over the sink, the one I used for shaving in, and thought: Nor any kind of girl, mate.

I was middle-aged, my face was a series of deep, downward creases, I had a knob-nose and a receding hairline. None of this could I do anything about. But I could at least shave off the thick, greying stubble that covered my jowls like detergent foam on the surface of a canal.

Obsessed with the idea of making myself presentable (but to what end? For whom?) I tipped the hot water from the kettle into my shaving bowl. For once, shaving should come before even that sacred first cup of tea. I grabbed my shaving-brush and started lathering, unbuttoning my pyjama jacket so that I could get the foam well down under my chin.

Scrape. Ouch. The razor needed a new blade. The blades were not in my shaving-bag. I remembered. They were in the sitting-room (or whatever the main ground-floor room of the cottage was called). I had bought a new packet of blades a day or two before, and left them in there, on the window-sill or the mantelpiece or somewhere. . . . Lathered, unbuttoned, I stepped across into the sitting-room to look for the blades.

This brought me in front of the window that faced the road.

Automatically, without particularly looking at anything, my eyes took in the scene outside. For an instant. Then suddenly I was standing absolutely still and staring with strained, incredulous attention. Julia was outside.

She was standing beside an old stone gatepost. There had once been a gate there but it had been done away with. Only the post remained, about half-way between the cottage and the road. She was standing by the gatepost, doing something. Hanging something on it. Hanging my old anorak on it. Now she was turning away. Now she was walking back towards the road.

I ran after her. All I had on was my pyjamas and an old pair of slippers. On the left-hand one, the sole had pulled away from the upper part and I stung my bare toes on a clump of nettles. My face was covered with congealing lather. I didn't care.

'Julia,' I called, panting.

At the sound of her name she stopped and turned round. When she saw me running towards her she looked amazed for a second, opening her eyes very wide so that I saw their lovely brown irises. Then her whole face collapsed into laughter.

'Julia,' I said, going up to her.

Her body swayed and her mouth opened. She laughed quite silently, but it shook her. I suppose I did look pretty funny.

'I – I'm sorry,' she managed to get out at last. 'I shouldn't laugh. There isn't really anything to laugh about. But you look so – you're—' She went into another spasm.

'Laugh away,' I said. I felt so glad to see her I nearly started laughing myself. 'The main thing is, don't go.' My stung toes were hurting, and three or four sheep nearby were looking at me nervously, as if my strange behaviour had suddenly made their familiar valley a dangerous place. I finished in a burst: 'I ran after you because I was afraid you'd go and I wouldn't be able to trace you and I'd never see you again.'

She nodded without speaking. Obviously that had been the idea. The gravity and stillness had come back into her face. But she looked better than when I had first seen her, as if she had slept.

'I brought your coat back,' she said. 'I didn't want to disturb you but I didn't see why I should rob you of it, after you'd been so kind.'

'I wasn't kind. I was just doing what I couldn't help doing.'

'You couldn't help being kind, then. And I did appreciate it.'

'Did?'

'I did,' she said, 'and I do still. But there's no point in dragging you into my mess.'

I was about to protest violently against this, to tell her that I wanted nothing so much as to be dragged into any situation, mess or not, so long as it would involve being with her. But there are some speeches you can't make when you're standing out in the open air in your pyjamas, with thick white foam all over the lower half of your face, stinging your feet on nettles.

'Come into the house,' I said. 'Please. Just while I finish shaving and get dressed.'

She hesitated.

'What's the odds?' I said. 'You can surely spare a few minutes.'

After another short pause she said, 'All right,' and began walking back with me to the cottage. I picked my old anorak off the gatepost as we went by.

Once we got into the house she sat down to wait for me, and I went on into the kitchen to shave. But once I got there I panicked. I didn't know what I was going to say to her when I went back in there. I had to shave and get my clothes on, but what then? When I was no longer a grotesque clown, making her laugh: when we were just a couple of normally dressed, washed, organised people, looking at each other across a million miles of empty air?

The lather clung to my face like chilled goose-grease. I seized a flannel and wiped it off, angrily. Then my mocking stubble confronted me again. What kind of a ditherer are you? – can't even get shaved.

I re-heated the water and slopped some into the basin. I was beginning to wish I'd had that cup of tea. I felt empty and powerless. Once again I lathered my face, once again I started to drag the blunt, used-up razor-blade across it, and stopped with an exclamation of pain. Here we go again. Back into the other room to look for the new packet of blades.

Julia was sitting in the armchair with her hands in her lap. She was one of those people who have the knack of sitting still without seeming inert: her stillness seemed to concentrate her energies. I walked past her without saying anything, not because I wanted to ignore her but because I couldn't think of anything to say. I felt such a damned fool. And the worst of it was, I couldn't find those blades anywhere. I looked in all the likely places, while she sat still in her armchair. Silently I vowed that if I didn't find them in the next thirty seconds I would grow a beard.

'Have you lost something?' she finally asked me.

'Razor-blades.'

She twisted round in her seat, looking.

'There's something down here.' She was feeling on the floor beside her chair. 'These are they, aren't they?'

'Oh. Yes.'

As I took them from her my fingers touched hers. My whole body shivered as if I had stumbled against an electric fence.

'What's the matter?' she said, startled.

'I love you.'

Might as well say it now, looking ridiculous like this, and let her blow me away in a puff of laughter and get it over. Might as well be a complete bloody fool.

She put her hand on mine. Her eyes were very gentle. 'You're a nice person,' she said.

'No, I'm not. I'm bad-tempered and futile and I lack moral fibre and my life's in a pretty awful mess, and now I've completed the performance by falling in love at an age when I ought to be putting all that sort of thing behind me.'

'Why ought you?'

'Because it leads to heartbreak. Any middle-aged man ought to stop falling in love because the kind of women he falls in love with are further and further out of reach. He ought to settle for something plain and comfortable.'

'That sounds awfully boring.'

I was still touching her hand. 'A life of awful boredom is almost certainly what I deserve,' I said. But something was kicking and jumping inside me that didn't believe it.

She smiled and said, 'Go and shave.'

I went back into the kitchen with my heart knocking at my ribs. I shaved in jig time, then went over it again slowly because I had made a mess of it, leaving great rough patches. Then I bounded up the ladder to the half-bedroom and found a clean shirt and underwear and socks, and came down dressed. Now what?

'If you need some breakfast,' she said, 'do have it. I shan't run away.'

'I don't need breakfast. But I'll make some coffee.'

I did and we drank it.

— 142 —

Panic threatened to seize me again as the level slowly went down in my cup. Making coffee and serving it had given me something to do with my hands, and enabled me to postpone the urgent questions beating in my mind, but the show-down was coming again.

Yet she had said, 'I shan't run away.'

'You're very quiet,' she said.

'I can't think of anything to say. I've just told you I love you – it's difficult to follow that.'

She looked down at the floor. 'I know I ought to say something, but I'm like you, I can't think what. You've made your move, you've told me what you feel. I can't say anything one way or the other because I don't feel anything. I don't know what I'm going to do and I don't know what I'll feel when I come out of this numbness. Everything's all smashed up for me and I don't know what it'll look like when I put it together again.'

'I understand,' I said.

'I don't know whether you do. I suppose I ought to be sorry about what happened when we first met. It may have given you the idea that I'm . . . well, available.'

'I never thought of it that way.'

'I'm not even saying I'm not available. I just don't feel able to say *anything*. One way or the other.'

'I really do understand, Julia.'

She looked at me with a sudden fixity. 'Yes, that's another thing. How do you know my name? Did I tell it to you that night?'

'No.'

'How do you know it, then?'

I drew a deep breath. 'I've been checking up on you,' I said.

'Checking up on me? How could you? There's nobody round here who knows me.'

'Not round here. In London.'

'You've been to *London*?'

I nodded. 'I went the night before last and came back last night. So much has happened that it seems a lifetime, but I suppose it's only forty-eight hours since you were' – I hesitated – 'here before.'

'And you've been checking up on me in London? What are you, a detective?'

I looked into the depths of my coffee cup. It was empty now. 'I'm not a detective. For a living I run a press-cutting agency, but that's nothing to do with it either. I found your address in the documents on your car.'

'So that's where they went.'

'And I went to London to try to find you because I didn't want you to disappear out of my life and leave absolutely no trace. I mean, I expect you're going to do that anyway but I just couldn't bear the thought that I. . . . Oh, I don't know. That there was anything at all I might have done to prevent your going or slow it down, and I didn't do it.'

I felt I wasn't making much sense. But all of a sudden I had the feeling that I didn't have to. I was getting something over to her. I could see it in her face.

'Look,' she said, getting up from her chair. 'It's a lovely day. Let's stop talking. Take me for a walk. Show me something beautiful.'

We walked straight out of the door and up the hillside. Everything was green and golden and purple. There were some black cattle grazing in the field below us on the right, and their solid flanks glowed like roughened ebony. Everything I could see was beautiful, including Julia, and everything I could see I loved.

We climbed up and up, winding, using our hands to get up on steep rocks. Then we were on top of a long spur, looking down the length of the valley. The purple mountains seemed close by: the blue of the sky was hardening under the heat. You could see for miles. Gulls idling in the sky seemed unbearably white.

We settled our backs against a smooth rock and did nothing. For quite a long time, neither of us spoke; it was enough to be there, to look at what was all round us and let the load slip from our shoulders.

Then she said, placidly, 'What's this about tracking me all round London?'

'Look,' I said, 'you might as well understand the situation. I'm not the only one who's tracking you.'

'You mean Jake?' she asked with a sudden quick frown.

'If Jake isn't looking for you he soon will be. And if he isn't doing it himself, the police'll be doing it for him.'

'The *police?*'

'Haven't you heard?' I said. 'You're supposed to be kidnapped.'

Her face became very still; only her eyes opened more widely.

This, I was learning, was how she looked when something surprised her. She said, 'Kidnapped?'

So I went ahead and told her all the stuff her crackpot brother had handed me. About the Crystal Palace Organisation, and the twenty thousand pounds and how he'd been trying to involve me in it all.

As she listened she shook her head once or twice. When I had finished, she said, quietly, 'Poor Cliff. I must ring him up.'

'He's in a mess, isn't he,' I said.

'He's never been out of one. I was always so sorry for him, all the time we were growing up. He could never get things straight. Perhaps there's something wrong with his brain – perhaps it's malformed in some way. He isn't the sort of abnormal person you could put away in a madhouse – he's competent in all the ordinary ways and he can pass intelligence tests and all that sort of thing. But he simply has no idea how to cope with life. I don't think he's ever made a right decision since he was born, not one single one.'

'It can't have made things easy for you,' I said, 'growing up in the backwash of somebody like that.'

'It wasn't all that hard on me. Not more than on anybody else. But it disturbed the peace all right – he was always having terrible rows with my father, and leaving home and then sneaking in through my window at three in the morning when he was too cold and hungry to stand it any longer. I used to creep down and get food from the larder and make him hot milk and take it up to him, all without waking Daddy. Every time the two of them tried to talk to each other, there'd be a flaming row. I used to think Daddy could have been more reasonable and forgiving, but I dare say any father would have been the same. Cliff was absolutely impossible to deal with. He wouldn't accept any kind of authority and he wouldn't fit in with *anybody*.'

'Has he been a nuisance to you all the time? Since you grew up?'

She was silent for a moment. 'He was in prison from when I was sixteen to when I was twenty. He got in with a really hard gang and they did an armed robbery. He wasn't one of the chief people, he was just a tool that they used, so he got one of the lightest sentences. But he was still in for four years.'

So it wasn't all fantasy about being in touch with criminals. Aloud I said, 'And when he came out?'

'When he came out I was married to Jake. We were poor at

first – poor and happy. We both got work from time to time.'

She fell silent again and I knew her mind was sinking down into thoughts of her ruined marriage; I could feel that cloud of depression coming over her.

So I said, 'And Cliff left you alone? As long as there weren't any pickings?'

She nodded. 'Then when Jake became a star, he bobbed up again and somehow managed to get Jake to buy that flat across the hall for him to live in. God knows why Jake went along with it. But Cliff can be very persuasive. Sometimes he seems almost able to . . . well, to hypnotise people.' She gave a short laugh. 'It sounds ridiculous, but the things he's talked people into. . . . Some of them are just incredible, unless you know Cliff.'

'Yes,' I said. 'I know Cliff.'

A young ewe came tripping by on dainty hoofs. I saw a horny old ram eyeing her from behind a rock.

'Cliff,' I said, 'is probably at this moment delivering a ransom note to Jake, demanding twenty thousand pounds in used notes to be left in a hollow tree on Clapham Common or somewhere. And of course Jake won't take the slightest notice. He'll see at once that the letter must come from some nut. Probably he'll go straight to Cliff and confront him with it. He'll shake him like a dog shaking a rat and Cliff'll break down and confess. That's hypothesis one. Here's hypothesis two. Jake doesn't know where you are and he's worried. He did something that made it impossible for you to stay close to him and you lit out. Come tonight, it'll be four days since you left and haven't communicated since. Four days is quite a long time. Then comes the note – you've been kidnapped. People know he's a rich man. Also, if he makes no attempt to get you back, it looks bad. There could be damaging publicity in it. Jake may be tired of your marriage, he may be hoping you'll go away quietly, but he can't want you to go and be murdered by a gang of criminals. So he's going to try to get you back. What I imagine he'll do, on hypothesis two, is this. First he'll go and ask Cliff what he knows about it. Cliff'll look him in the face and say he knows nothing. If it comes to a punch-up, Cliff's quite fit and he's quite likely to draw first claret. Jake won't get anything out of him that way. So his next move will be to go to the police. He'll pretend to go along with the ransom note and the various telephone calls he'll get in disguised voices and the rest of it, and he'll pass all information on to the police. They'll take it seriously – they'll have to, since you've disappeared.'

'I can't believe it,' she said slowly. 'I'm dreaming.'

'I know. I feel the same. But it might just happen. At this exact moment, every policeman in the country may have been given your description and told to look out.'

'What shall I do?'

'Ring Jake and tell him you're all right.'

She looked away into the distance. Nearby, the randy old ram got to his feet and ambled away after the ewe.

'I suppose I'll have to,' she said.

Suddenly the brightness of the day seemed to have faded. The air was warm and insects were buzzing joyfully in the rays of the sun, but I felt clammy and I could tell Julia did too. It was the prospect that faced us: going into a telephone-box, plugging ourselves in to the world that was the opposite of everything we were enjoying here, making her talk to Jake. . . . She had come a long way to get away from Jake, to leave thoughts of him behind and breathe a neutral air. Obviously to talk to him would stir it all up again, whatever 'it' might consist of. But there was no other way.

'Look, you'll have to do it,' I said. 'Otherwise your brother might be putting his head into a noose that'll draw him back into prison. If Jake gets the police on to him, he'll have started something he can't stop.'

'I don't want to talk to Jake,' she said.

'Of course you don't, but I can't do it for you – he's got to hear your voice.'

She stood up. 'I'll ring in working hours. Then probably Penny'll answer. She knows my voice. And I can write a card and post it this evening.'

There seemed to be nothing more to say. We started going down the slope again. I felt my brain whirling with anxieties. What would she do, once she had got in touch with Jake? How could I hope to hang on to her a little longer?

If she just melted away and left me alone in that half-bedroom, alone in the desolate beauty of the valley which needed her presence to make it lyrical . . . because not even the most piercing beauty could bring you to life if you were dying of loneliness and of missing someone . . . my ears buzzed, I felt desperate, I knew it was all taken out of my hands and I couldn't cope. Suddenly I thought of Daphne getting to the flat and ringing and no one being there. Oh, God, the world was so full of emptiness and aching and sorrow and losing.

When we got to the bottom and came up to the stile, I remembered that I had not bestowed a thought on the logistics of her life during that last forty-eight hours. How had she got here? And, for that matter, where from?

Julia seemed to be pretty well attuned to me because she answered my questions before they were spoken.

'I couldn't think where to go that morning, so I just booked into an hotel at Pwllheli. And I hired a car.'

'You must be solvent, then,' I blurted out.

'I've got a credit card. The bill goes to Jake. That'll all come to an end as soon as we get things straightened out, but till then I don't see why I shouldn't oil the wheels a bit.'

I didn't see why either. She had a nice little Austin Allegro waiting by the stile. And the hotel at Pwllheli wouldn't be a bed-and-breakfast place, either. Why should it? Jake Driver could afford it all right. We were just about to save him twenty thousand pounds, anyway, by making a telephone call.

I hoped Penny would be on duty.

'Where's the nearest telephone-box?' Julia asked me, looking pale, composed and determined.

'Up towards the head of the valley. I'll show you. There's a cross-roads where the village school used to be, and a few houses scattered about.' I had a quick vision of people standing in the box, ringing the doctor on some snowy night in February. A life-line. That's what it would be for us, too. No, not us. Cliff.

I navigated and Julia drove. We got to the telephone-box and stopped.

'Shall I come in with you?' I asked.

'No, thanks.'

I waited in the car while she went into the box. While I sat there I looked round at the valley, the level calm of its floor and the stately authority of its heights, and I thought of Western Approaches Avenue with its traffic and semis and green-roofed pubs, and of Windermere Gardens with its magic-eye doors and Dennis with his epaulets, all the mess and the mistakes. And what was it that Jake had done that was so horrible as to make her turn tail and move away into loneliness? 'Not four of them in there,' she had said. Something she just couldn't take. I didn't know what, but I supposed I could guess.

Then she was out of the box and taking hold of the door-handle and getting into the car.

'What. . . ?'

'It's out of order,' she said.

Most of the telephone-boxes in rural North Wales are out of order ninety per cent of the time. When it isn't the weather it's the vandals. They must have a special Flying Squad of vandals who go round making sure people don't get complacent about being able to telephone.

Julia sat behind the driving wheel, very pale and still.

'I'm going to confess to you, Gus,' she said. My heart gave a great lurch as she uttered my name. 'I'm frightened. As long as I could telephone London without leaving this valley, I felt safe. It seems . . . such a haven. It's been a haven to me once already. I feel I can trust it.'

'And you can trust me,' I said, 'because I'm part of the valley.'

'Put it like that. I haven't sorted out my feelings about you because I haven't sorted out my feelings about anything, yet. But it's true that I do feel safe here, and I feel safe in your little house, and I don't know if I can force myself to leave and face the world. Just think, if the police are looking for me! All the questions and the. . . .'

This was my chance, and I had enough sense to take it, thank God.

'You're going nowhere,' I said. 'You're going to hole up in the cottage and this valley will be your home until it all blows over.' To myself I thought: The rent's paid for another week. Nobody can get in. After that I suppose there's another tenant. But it'll be long enough. 'I'll take care of the telephoning,' I said. 'You can scribble a note saying you're all right, and I'll ring up and tell them it's in the post. That'll hold them from taking any action till it gets to them.'

'But it all involves *you*,' she said. 'Jake and Penny both know your voice, so whoever answers the phone will know you're mixed up in it, and they'll ask you where I am—'

'And I'll hang up on them,' I said. All at once I realised that I was entering one of my Augustus Caesar phases. Those are the days

— 149 —

when I get to the office full of nervous vitality, new ideas for streamlining procedures and drumming up more business. It doesn't last long – five or six hours, usually – but while it does I give everybody hell, including myself. Miss Sarson and Daisy, in those cosy talks they have behind my back, say. 'He's Augustus Caesar this morning,' or, 'It happened last time he was Augustus Caesar.' All right, I was Augustus Caesar now, and I would take care of Julia and lift all problems off her pretty shoulders.

She sat looking through the windscreen in a way that suddenly, chillingly, reminded me of how she had looked when I first saw her. No. *No*. She was not going back into *that*.

I got out of the car and walked round to her side and opened the door. 'I want you to sit in the passenger's seat,' I said. 'Literally and metaphorically. I want to take charge.'

'But it's so *feeble*,' she said. 'I ought to be able to cope with my own problems.'

'Everybody has to let go some of the time,' I said. 'Now do as I say and get out.'

'It's like when you made me get into that silly little boat,' she said and laughed.

That laugh was a sign of release. I had broken the chains of tension and melancholy that were binding her. Augustus Caesar. Suddenly it was a beautiful, still, warm sunny day again, and the valley was lyrical. She got out and went round to the other side, I got behind the wheel, and we started.

'Now, here's what we're going to do,' I said. 'First. Get that letter off saying you're all right. That'll mean going to the Post Office. Not to post the letter, just to get an envelope and a stamp. On second thoughts, a letter-card. You can write that at once. But I shan't post it round here. I shall drive over to Pwllheli, and collect your stuff from the hotel, and post it there.'

'You'll do nothing of the kind,' she said, looking alarmed. 'If there's a police hunt out for me, and you show up wanting to get into my room and pack up my things. . . . Anyway, there's hardly anything. I left London with nothing, and I just went out yesterday and picked up a few things like a toothbrush and a cheap night-dress. I'll post them enough cash to cover the bill. Don't go *near* the hotel, that's all I ask.'

'All right, I won't.'

'Thanks,' she said. 'I couldn't bear it if you set off and didn't come back. I just wouldn't know what to do.' Inwardly I gave a great shout of joy. 'I take it you're going to leave me in the cottage while you go and telephone and post the letter.'

'Yes. I shall drive to Bangor. That's the biggest town in the district, and if they start doing anything silly like tracing the call, it's a big enough place to give them nothing much in the way of a lead. It'll take me a couple of hours, all told.'

'Oh, damn it. What am I going to do for two whole hours?'

'Cook a meal,' I said promptly. (Augustus Caesar is coming!)

'What a good idea. It always takes me ages to cook anything worth eating, and I get very absorbed and forget everything else. . . . You are clever.'

'Yes, I am.'

We had reached a village with a Post Office by this time. I went in, got a letter-card, and stood by while Julia wrote a few lines, using the roof of the car for a desk. She handed it to me.

'It's not sealed,' I said.

'I want you to read it.'

I read: *Jake, I am all right. Don't believe any silly stories about things happening to me. I am not coming back for a while, and then only to settle things, but I am not in any trouble. Enjoy yourself. J.*

'That should stop him worrying,' I said.

'I wanted to put that I was being looked after,' she said. 'But just as I was going to write it I thought he might worry in case it was a code or something. But I *am* being looked after, and I know it. All I don't know is why you're doing it.'

'You know that damned well,' I said. I had a sudden impulse to kiss her, standing there beside the car and with the postmistress looking at us through the window. But I didn't. I just said, 'Let's go and buy some food. What are you going to give us for our celebration meal?'

She thought for a moment. 'Something elaborate. Something that'll make me work and keep me out of mischief.' She deliberated a bit more. 'What kind of stove have you got?'

'Electric. Four rings. Quite a big oven.'

'D'you like Cornish pasties?'

'When I can get them home-made.'

'I can do them very nicely. And they'll be good because they take a long time to prepare and not very long to cook. Is there anywhere you can buy the food before you take me back to the cottage?'

'Yes. We can go to Portmadoc.'

'Is it safe for me to go? If the police. . . .'

'We'll take a calculated risk.'

We drove to Portmadoc and parked in the main street. Then I went shopping while Julia sat in the car and spread out a road map that hid most of her face. The perfect tourist. Before I got out she wrote down what we needed: raw steak, kidney, potatoes, turnips, onions, flour, baking powder, salt, cooking foil, butter. She was going to be busy, all right. Busy feeding Augustus Caesar. I felt very happy.

The shopping didn't take long. When I got back to the car she looked up from the map with the exact expression of a touring wife who has worked out the next bit of the route. I remembered that she was an actress. I named the items as I put them on the back seat of the car, to make sure I had it all. Then we were climbing out of the town, back towards the valley and safety.

I carried the stuff in for her and introduced her to the kitchen. She tut-tutted a bit at the sketchy equipment ('Not one really sharp knife') but seemed content to get stuck in, and I left her and drove over to Bangor. First the letter went off; it was easier, standing outside that big, ugly General Post Office with people scurrying in and out, to believe in the existence of Windermere Gardens; next stop, a telephone-box.

By now it was after one o'clock. Had Penny gone out for lunch? Or was she having a cocktail with Jake? Did Jake really have enough business to keep Penny going all the time? I thought of her orange hair, white dress and gold belt. Did he ever chase her round the desk? Or did he just use her to organise his seamy private life, doing things like ringing up what was that girl's name? Eunice? No, Janice, that was it.

As I thought all this, the telephone in Delmore's flat was ringing away. It rang about eight times and then it stopped and Delmore's voice said impatiently, 'Yes?'

Penny must have been out to lunch. I took a deep breath to lower my tension and said, 'Mr Delmore, I have a message for you.'

'Are you one of those damned—' He stopped short as if trying to hold himself back, to avoid enraging someone who had power.

'Look,' I said. 'I don't care what kind of messages you've been getting. If anybody has told you that your wife's in trouble and you've got to do something about it, they're lying. Forget it. She's all right. There's a letter on its way.'

'Who are you? It seems to me I've heard your —'

'Wait for the letter. It's posted,' I said, and hung up.

As I stepped out of the box it occurred to me that I might, just possibly, have started a lot of trouble rolling towards me. After a few minutes' thought he would probably connect my voice with my face. And if I knew he'd been getting ransom demands, I must be involved in it somehow. And he knew my name, my right name.

What the hell. It was a small enough risk, and even if it had been a big risk I'd have taken it for the sake of helping Julia. And not just helping her. Getting her to myself for several days. Perhaps the whole week, if I played my cards right. Augustus Caesar. Master strategist, potentate, ruler of men, commander of women.

So there I was, standing beside the scurrying A5 at Bangor, suddenly gulping down the knowledge that a few miles away was the most beautiful valley in the world, and in the middle of the valley was a cottage that was mine for another week, and in the kitchen a girl with a pale, beautiful face topped by a helmet of shining black hair who was, with any luck, making a delicious Cornish pasty for me to eat, and under the rafters of the cottage was a half-bedroom with a bed in it where, with any more luck. . . . At that point my imagination switched off. But it switched off not into darkness but into a rose-coloured glow.

Before driving back I went and spent just about all the money I had left at a wine-shop. Bottle after bottle of good red wine to wash down the Cornish pasties and contribute to the honeymoon atmosphere.

Then I drove back, parked her neat little rented car next to my splattered old one, and went down the path to the cottage. Julia was in the kitchen. I went straight through. She had all the ingredients for the pasties spread out on the table, chopped up and ready, and was just about to fold the first one over. She was putting a knob of butter in each corner first, naturally.

When she saw me she straightened up and stood still with a buttery knife in her hand and said, 'Who did you speak to?'

'Jake,' I said.

'You told him I was all right?'

'I said you were all right and he was to do nothing till he got your

— 153 —

note. Which I posted.' I put the wine bottles down on the dresser and began looking for a corkscrew.

She folded the pastry over and then said, 'How did he sound?'

'Cross,' I said.

'Had Cliff started on him?'

'Yes. We weren't in time to prevent that. At least, that's how I interpret what he said when he first picked up the phone. He said, "Are you one of those damned—" and then he pulled himself up.'

'Oh,' she said. 'I see.'

'Of course it's just possible he might have been going to say one of those damned autograph hunters or journalists or something.'

'But why should journalists be pestering him?'

'I imagine they do most of the time, don't they?'

She shook her head and said, 'Not enough to worry him. They ring up with inane questions now and then, but he'd be more worried if they didn't.'

'Oh, well,' I said. 'We may not have been in time to save Cliff from starting a lot of trouble for himself. But at least we've stopped Jake from thrashing about and starting an enormous hunt.'

'I suppose so,' she said dully.

I got the cork out of the first bottle of wine and poured out two glasses. There weren't any wine-glasses in the cottage, so I used beer-glasses. It was better. They held more.

'Drink this, Julia,' I said. 'And put those pasties in the oven. And for the rest, let it all go. You're here and you can't be dislodged till you want to go. Let the place work its magic.'

'How right you are,' she said and gave me that sudden warm, overflowing smile. We clinked glasses and drank.

'The pasties will have to cook for two hours at least,' she said, working briskly on the second one. They were enormous. 'We must go out and not waste this lovely sunshine.'

She shut the oven door and we went out. It was mid-afternoon. The sun was rich and high, just beginning to slope westwards. We climbed up the nearby lump of rock, not very high but enough to gives us a good view of the hills, and the floor of the valley, and the little river that flowed along it.

Now that the telephoning and letter-writing and fretting had all been given their due, we were free to feel easy and carefree. And we did, what's more. The happiness that I had uneasily reached out

— 154 —

for when I got up in the morning, and uneasily missed, was now mine, and hers too.

For a long time we just sat there. I felt so joyful at just being with her that I decided to give no thought to the question of what might, or might not, develop. Just let it all happen. Anything or nothing, I was happy with the whole package.

In the warm hush towards five o'clock, some children came trailing along the valley below us. They had towels but no costumes. When they got to the point not far beneath us, where the river filled out into two or three deep pools, with smooth rocks ideal for getting in and out from, they chased each other into the water and played and laughed, with their little dark raggedy heads bobbing up and down in the clean, flowing water. Julia watched them, first amused, then envious.

'I'd like to be doing that,' she said.

I got up. 'There are towels in the cottage.'

We went down. The children ran away when they saw us coming. I was sorry they went – I liked the thought of being a porpoise among water-babies. But being alone with Julia was just as good.

'Why did they run away?'

'Children like that always run away when they see a grown-up,' I said. 'Anything they're doing is always wrong by the standards of the grown-up world.'

She took her clothes off and sat on one of the big, smooth rocks with her legs splashing in the water. That was wrong by the standards of the grown-up world. So much the worse for the g.-u. w.

The sight of her lovely pointed breasts gave me an erection, so I had to get into the river quickly, to hide it. Once the water came up to waist-height I forgot everything except how cold it was. By the time I got used to the temperature and started remembering her breasts again, the camouflage was well in place.

She sat on the rock, watching me swim clumsily about.

'Is it cold?'

'No,' I lied.

She suddenly slid in and went right under. When she came up, her hair was plastered down with the water and her head seemed as sleek as a seal's. She was a beautiful animal. I was a thick, ungainly, strong animal. At that moment, feeling a surge of

— 155 —

physical vitality, getting real power from my muscles, my spirit kindled by the beauty of the place and her beauty, I didn't see — God forgive me! — why I should not deserve her as well as any man in the world.

We swam for a long time. Then some trippers came and stood on the bridge and stared at us. I thought they would just have a bit of a stare and go away again, but they stood there stolidly, as if waiting for some performance they had paid for and been promised, and finally they were joined by more trippers, until there were seven or eight of them, all staring.

Julia blew some water out and said, 'We're making a public show of ourselves.'

'So it seems.'

'Is there anything we ought to do about it?'

'Yes,' I said and climbed up on to the rock and stood facing the audience. After a brief inspection they melted rapidly away. It was as if a view of my *membrum virile* was what they had come there for, and now that they had had it there was no point in hanging about.

Julia laughed until she swallowed some water and had to climb out on to the rock, coughing. 'The *haste*,' she said. 'Really it isn't as frightening as that,' and she laughed and coughed again.

We were feeling very happy as we got dried and put on our clothes and went back to eat the pasties. Happy, and hungry, and thirsty: and, in my case at any rate, randy.

Still, there was no point in rushing it. We had to eat, whatever we did. The pasties were ready and they were delicious.

'You're a marvellous cook,' I said.

'I got used to making these,' she said. 'Living in theatrical lodgings, I could put them in a low oven before we went off to do the show, and they'd be about ready by the time. . . .'

She was going to say, 'we came back,' but the brightness was already draining out of her face as she thought of the good days with Jake, working like hell and being half-starved and staying in shabby digs or renting poky little flats by the week, working in draughty theatres and living on hope and keeping each other warm in bed and being happy. I could see it all, churning around in her mind. And of course I knew that if I didn't dispel it immediately, it would drag her down into melancholy. So I jumped up with a sudden show of activity, opened another bottle of wine, filled her tumbler, roared out some inanities, and managed – I hoped – to skitter past that dangerous spot.

It seemed to work all right. We ate slowly and the lingering meal wasn't over till dusk had begun to creep along the valley. It was still just as warm outside as in, so we took two chairs out into the garden, or what would have been the garden if anybody had kept it up. With the fragrance of the ferns and the gently ripening black-berries and the harebells in every sheltered spot and the daisies just beginning to close in the field across the wall, where the cattle chewed steadily and peacefully and the river poured on, it was as good as any tidy garden. We took some wine out, of course, and because neither of us smoked I lazily waved a large frond of bracken to keep the gnats away. I didn't keep them all away, but our mood was so benign that we didn't grudge them a bite or two. I felt I had so much blood, so much life, so much warmth, that they were welcome to have a nibble if they cared to.

At last the deep shadows had stolen right along the valley and the evening star had appeared. The moon would rise soon. Romance, romance. And since I have always interpreted 'romance' as a seven-letter word meaning 'bed', my thoughts began to turn in that direction. But I thought I would let Julia make the first move.

At last she finished her glass of wine and said, 'It must be time for bed.'

'Yes,' I said.

We went into the house. The dishes from supper were still on the table. Suddenly I thought how beautiful domesticity was. To live with someone. To eat together and sleep together and wake up together. . . . No wonder marriage is popular.

I sat in the living-room while Julia went and splashed about in the kitchen. Once again we went through that fandango about her using my toothbrush and giving it a wash on the soap. (How many centuries ago had that happened before?) Then she came through and went up the ladder. I could hear her moving about; for that matter, so little distance separated us that I could hear her breath-ing, though I couldn't see her. I could hear her clothes coming off, and the gentle swishing sounds began to heat my imagination. I became very, very restless. Presently the noises stopped. She must have come to rest.

It was now or never, so I went up the ladder. My pyjamas were up in the half-bedroom, so there was no question of getting them on before I went up, like a husband going to his expected bed. I just had my shirt and trousers on.

The moon had come up now, a big clear September moon, and it was shining in through the little window. By its light I saw that Julia was sitting on the bed, stark naked, just sitting there with her knees drawn up to her chin and her hands clasped just above her feet, the way you sometimes see children sitting. She was absolutely motionless, and didn't seem to be aware that I had joined her.

'Julia,' I said softly.

After a long pause she said, 'Yes.'

'Is anything the matter?'

She didn't answer. I stood there for a moment, irresolute, and then I thought, well, if she's lost in some private world of sorrow I might as well be ignored in bed as ignored standing here. So I threw my clothes off and got into bed. It seemed more companionable, if she was naked, that I should be. She was sitting on top of the bed; I was between the sheets, lying on my back with my head on my hands. The moon shone in on us both.

For a long time she just sat there. Then suddenly she said, quite loudly: 'I'm cold.'

'Come into bed,' I said.

'That won't warm me. I'm cold inside. My mind's cold.'

I didn't know what to say to that, so I said nothing. She started clasping and unclasping her hands, nervously. I could feel the tension building up inside her.

'I can't sort it out. I don't understand it, any of it. Two men. Two men in my life that I've been close to. Leaving aside my father when I was a little girl, and a few lovers I had when I was growing up, to learn on . . . once or twice, I thought this was the real thing and I was in love but really I was just learning about it all. Only two men in all my twenty-eight years who mattered very deeply. Cliff and Jake. Cliff from the beginning, and then Jake.'

I kept on lying still and waiting. It seemed to be working well enough.

'And now look at them. Both smashed, both gone rotten. Not that Cliff was ever any different. He always was a loser. I just felt very sorry for him and very close to him. Perhaps being brother and sister we have some central thing in us that's very similar. I always felt close to him, and what did that do for me? Just made me suffer

— 158 —

when he did terrible, foolish, rotten things. And then Jake. Oh, you can't think how I admired him when we first met. When we worked together. He was so talented and so hard-working, and never put out. An actor's life can be hell. But he never had any self-pity, he just picked himself up when anything knocked him down, and got on with whatever there was to do, and if he was out of work and there was nothing to get on with, he'd study. He'd go to the public library and get books, and he read a play every day just so that he knew all about every kind of job he'd ever be asked to do, and he used to exercise. He did his voice and body exercises every single day of his life. I was so happy just to know him, and when he said would I come and live with him I was round there like a shot. And after twelve months of that he woke me up early one morning and told me he'd been thinking in the night and would I like to get married? Would I *like* it? I was delirious. I suppose I'm old-fashioned at heart. They talk about women being liberated and their lives not revolving round men, and for all I know that's true of them but it's not true of me. My life always has revolved round men. I've been happy when some man was making me happy and unhappy when some man was making me unhappy. And now this is where I've ended up. Cliff's gone right off his head. He's lost any touch with reality he might have had. He's a criminal, he's lost in dreams, silly, cheap little dreams of making people do what he wants and getting money and being important. I could die when I think of him.'

She was silent again, so long that I felt impelled to nudge her forward into utterance. Otherwise all this poison would just get stuck in her throat and never come out.

So I said, 'And Jake?'

'Oh, *Jake*,' she said, 'I can't even bear to think about him. I'd rather pretend to myself that I never knew any such person.'

'What changed him?' I said, gently but remorselessly prodding her.

'He could stand trouble and failure. He could stand the bad times. It was the good times that wrecked him. When he started to get everything he wanted and then he discovered that there was no limit to what he wanted, no sense, no realism, no generosity, no sharing, just take, take, take from everybody and in every way. I waited for him to come out of it. I've waited two years and three months. And it's over. I realised that night that this was a different

— 159 —

man. Somebody I just don't know any more. He's a stranger. It would be wrong, immoral, disgusting, for me to live with a man I don't know.'

I couldn't help wondering where, in that case, I came in. But only for a fleeting second. I hadn't really any attention to spare for my own problems. Julia's suffering was too pressing, too awesome. She had started to shake now. I wished she would cry.

'Come into bed,' I pleaded, holding the bedclothes open for her. 'Tell me about it in bed.'

She didn't get into bed. Instead, she turned slowly and faced me, staring into my face with an intensity that was almost ferocious. She might have been getting ready to tell me she was going to kill me. Her eyes glittered in the moonlight. I stared back, hypnotised.

'I'm going to tell you about it,' she said. 'I've got to tell someone. I'll die if I don't. I'm going to tell you exactly what he did that made me walk out.'

She shivered, but not with cold. I lay quite still.

'I opened the door and saw them. That's what I've been seeing ever since. I was seeing it when I was sitting in the car with the tide coming in, and you came and called out to me. I see it when I close my eyes and try to sleep. I see it when I look at the sky. When I try to read a book. If I don't stop seeing it I'll go mad. So I'm going to tell you and then you'll see it too. With two of us. . . .' She left the sentence unfinished, but I knew she meant I could share the horror and help her. So I listened.

'I'd been to the theatre. There was a play I wanted to see because there was some talk that I might get a part in it when it went on tour. The producer had asked me to go and sent me a ticket. He took me out to supper afterwards, to discuss things, and I got back about midnight. I went up in the lift and let myself in with my key.'

Pause. Her breath seemed to be labouring. I could sense her terrible tension. Her breasts were moving fast as she breathed, and although I was so responsive to her physical beauty I found I could contemplate them without any desire. My whole attention was taken up by the need to help her, help her, help her.

'He was with a friend of his called Thomas. I don't know if Thomas is his surname or his Christian name. I can't stand the man. A horrible, greasy little lecher. Always boasting about the girls he has. Jake's only got to know him since he started moving in . . . those circles. I've always thought he probably brought out

— 160 —

the worst side of Jake, getting him into situations where he loses control of himself. He'd like that. He'd like to see everybody brought down to his own level.'

The moon shone calmly on her milky skin.

'All right, I'll tell you what I saw when I opened the door. They had two girls in there and they were in mid-fuck. All four of them. Jake had one of the girls on her hands and knees, giving it to her from behind, and horrible little Thomas was lying on his back with his girl on top of him. One of the girls turned and looked at me when I opened the door, but her expression didn't change. I suppose she was used to doing it in public. I just shut the door again and went away.'

Then she started crying and said, 'I went away, I went away, I went away, I went away, I went away,' and her voice became strangled in sobs and a long, choking groan, and I flung the bedclothes back and pulled her in beside me, and held her tight, and she sobbed for a long time until finally her breathing calmed and she fell asleep, and I lay thinking how much I loved her and looking at the patch of moonlight on the wall, and at last I, too, was released into sleep.

We slept for a long time. The sun was high in the sky when she stirred softly and got out of bed. I was just coming awake, and the gentle movement of the bed-springs rocked me into consciousness. I opened my eyes in time to see Julia get on to the ladder and climb down, disappearing from my view from the feet up. As her face went down below floor-level I came awake sufficiently to take a good look at it. Immediately I saw that she was different. The lines of her expression were more relaxed, her eyes softer.

I rolled on to my back and lay there thinking. The shock of what Jake had done to her, the agony of an involvement with him that was more and more defiling, all that was clear to me now, and I saw that she had been right to force herself to verbalise it, however painful it must have been. And I tried not to be too complacent about my role in the matter. It wasn't because I was particularly important to her that she had told me about it in such detail. Perhaps it was even the fact that I *wasn't* important that had made it possible, as one tells intimate secrets to a stranger on a train whose name one will never know and whom one will never see again. I tried to be realistic and grim. But it wouldn't work. Everything inside me was singing. Whatever the reason, it was me she had told. Whatever the reason, it was my bed she had slept in, close to me with her lovely, defenceless nakedness.

I could hear from the tap-running and splashing sounds that Julia was washing. I thought of what she must look like and began to feel terribly randy. Well, that could wait. But it had better not wait for long, by God. I tried to get my mind off it, but presently she came up the ladder again, glowing with the washing and the towelling, her nipples standing straight out, and I nearly went insane. She must have caught sight of the expression on my face, because she paused with the dress in her hand that she was just about to slip on, and said in an amused way. 'What's the matter?'

I told her.

'Oh, you poor thing,' she said, ' we must do something about it, mustn't we?' And she put her dress back over the chair and slid into bed.

What happened next is not for publication. Imagine it for yourself. But by the time we sat down to breakfast I was good and hungry. And that's how it went on during our week's holiday. I got to know Julia, in her mind and in her body, through and through. It was an experience unlike any I've ever had or shall ever have again. When I first met her she was in that shocked state, withdrawn into her own being and watching the world outside it through those dead, blank eyes. Then, when she realised she was safe with me, she clutched at me for comfort and for the physical relief of her tensions. I suppose, if I'm to bring myself to face it, she enjoyed making love with me because it helped to drive away the memory of Jake. During that phase she was still reacting negatively, as it were – doing things because they *weren't* other things. But very soon, starting from the morning after she forced herself to plumb the depths of what Jake had done to her, she reached equilibrium and from then on she began to reassume layer after layer of her normal personality. It had a richness that even I, who loved her, wasn't prepared for.

To begin with, her physical energy was tremendous. Every morning she sprang out of bed ready to swim in the river and then go for a long, high, clambering walk, with another plunge in the river to cool off when she got back. In between, she sent me shopping in the car to keep up an endless supply of good food and drink. Every kind of enjoyment broke over us in waves, and the weather co-operated with warm, still sunshine. In the evenings, we would sit outside, finishing up the wine, until it began to get chilly about eight o'clock; then we would either come in and light a fire of the wood we had gathered during the day (Julia could gather a hundred sticks while I gathered twenty), or just go straight to bed.

Just about the only hard-headed, practical thing we did was to take Julia's hired car back. She had taken it from a garage in Pwllheli, without specifying how long she wanted it for; they were quite willing, at that stage in the season, to let her drive off in it (having paid the usual thundering deposit) and pay when it suited her to bring it back. We toyed with the idea of just leaving it parked where it was when we returned to London, but obviously that wouldn't do; it must go back or they would start enquiries; or an abandoned car would be reported to the police, which would come to the same thing. So we had to bite the bullet and take the blasted thing back. Julia was afraid to do it herself, in case a description of her had been circulated; I realised that if this were so, they would have circulated the name as well. But it was a risk we would have to take.

'Couldn't you have given a false name?' I grumbled.

'I had to use my credit card,' she pointed out.

There was no arguing with that, so I nerved myself and drove over with the car. Julia followed in my old heap, and parked it round the corner to wait for me. I was sweating as I nonchalantly handed the keys over, saying Mrs Delmore had been called back to town and asked me to bring the car in and settle up. Fortunately the half-asleep young clerk who signed it in had either received no message to look out for Julia, or had forgotten it. I walked away, keeping my walk slow and casual though I wanted to break into a run, and found her giggling at the wheel as she saw my tense appearance.

'You wouldn't do as a criminal,' she said as I got in beside her.

'You're damn right I wouldn't,' I assured her. 'This is as close to crime as I ever want to get.' And to emphasise that we were fellow-conspirators I kissed her for a long minute.

We drove back, and after that one tremor the perfect emotional weather set in again.

'It's the best holiday I've ever had,' she told me several times, and certainly as it went on the graph of her exuberance mounted. Not that she became fidgety in any way, or lost that gift of stillness, that power to absorb the person she was with into a pool of deep, concentrated attention. I suppose the art of keeping still without being inert is one of the things they teach actresses, though I'm convinced Julia had it by nature. But when she wasn't exercising it, her vitality came out not only in that physical tirelessness but in song and laughter. She had a beautiful voice – as I said, not high but very pure and sweet – and as she rattled about in the kitchen, or washed, or pottered about upstairs, she sang bits and pieces of just about everything, though I noticed her favourites seemed to be Gershwin (especially *Porgy and Bess*) and Mozart opera. And then, she was so *funny*. This was something I had been completely unprepared for: seeing that sad, bleak little face with those hurt brown eyes, one couldn't have imagined a laugh or a joke spilling out of her. Wrong, quite wrong. Under her demureness she had a robust, bizarre, almost knockabout humour: she must have enjoyed playing funny parts, and in fact had often got herself cast as comic charwomen or vicars' wives or toothless beldams unable to stop talking – all of which she doubtless made much funnier than they originally were in the script. Now and then she would break into a snatch of one of these roles, as it happened by chance to come to her memory, and it never failed to put me on the floor with laughter. She could reproduce an accent with perfect precision, while giving it just that touch of heightening that made the performance comic rather than realistic. Her cockney was marvellous – it was the one nearest to her own natural speech – but so were her Irish, Scottish and American: the latter broken up into three or four main regions, for she had been on a fairly extensive American tour with Jake and kept her ears open all the way.

'What made you decide to be an actress in the first place?' I asked her one evening as we sat in the gentle, slanting light and drank red wine.

'I wanted to be involved with people. To go out to them.'

'Did that seem a difficult ambition? Something you had to work towards?'

She considered. 'Not difficult. But real. The people I knew when I was growing up, they didn't get involved very much. My father was in a City firm – he wasn't very high up in it, I suppose you'd have called him not much more than a glorified head clerk, but anyway his business was with figures rather than with people. He and Mummy were very nice and they gave us a kind upbringing – my sister and me. Cliff was always another matter. Mummy just didn't know how to cope with him at all – she seemed bewildered by this creature who'd come out of her, he didn't seem to have any relationship to her or her husband. As for Daddy, he just hadn't any way of dealing with Cliff except fighting him, having rows and scenes all the time. He called it giving him more discipline, but when I heard them at it I used to think, God, if that's discipline, give me freedom. Daddy never seemed to try to get to know Cliff. They'd sit down for a heart-to-heart, what Daddy used to call an air-clearing discussion. And within ten minutes Daddy'd be yelling at Cliff and Cliff'd be sitting there quite silent. Just letting it break over him. I was never there, of course, I was just hearing it from another room – you couldn't *help* hearing it, once they got going. But I could imagine Cliff's face. Expressionless, with absolutely blank eyes.'

I could imagine it too. Suddenly I saw Cliff's face, that unpleasant masculine (or indeterminate?) parody of Julia's: the same oval and slightly prognathous shape, the same colouring. But in his case the brown eyes were too far apart, the expression watchful and insecure instead of calm and accepting.

She was still talking it out: I listened, gratefully.

'So that was it, with my parents. The one person they ought to have touched and involved, they couldn't reach. And with everybody else I used to feel that they were just playing a nice polite game. They had friends, quite as many as they needed, and they belonged to clubs and choirs and things, but I could never believe that their friendships were very close. It was difficult to imagine them telling their friends anything really important, about their beliefs or their emotions or anything. I felt that nobody really *touched* anybody.'

'What about your parents themselves? Did they reach out and touch each other deeply?'

She thought for a moment. 'It's hard to tell. I'm sure if they did it was quite wordless. They just shared life with one another, and life to them was habits and possessions. I think they were quite in tune with each other – they argued a bit, mostly about things like moth-balls – but I never knew them to quarrel. It was all very low-key.'

I knew exactly what she meant.

'Any sexual life?' I asked.

'You can never be sure, of course, but I always had the impression that neither of them was very highly sexed and they'd given the whole shooting-match up by the time they were about forty-five.'

'Some people are lucky,' I said. But I didn't really mean it.

'Why lucky?'

'They get peace. From forty-five on.'

Julia sprang out of her chair. 'Come on. We'll go for a really long walk, right along the top of the ridge, and if we find a nice stream or a little lake we'll go swimming, and when we get back I'll cook an enormous meal' – she moved her hands about as if making an immense pie – 'and after all that you'll be so sleepy you'll go out like a light, without even getting up the ladder. If it's *peace* you want, I'll see you get it.'

'Your forecast is wrong in one particular,' I told her. 'With you up there, I'd climb up the ladder even in my sleep.'

She grinned, and led the way into the sunshine.

That's how it was on our week of honeymoon, and that's why, whatever happens to me, I shall always be grateful.

6

Giles Hermitage's next visit to Helen Chichester-Redfern was a sad fiasco. He went to the house at what had become his usual time, about half-past three, and rang the bell, to be met by a pale, set-faced Dinah. Behind her, the large fleshy figure of Dr Bowen could be seen moving about.

'No use trying to see Mother today. It's one of her bad days. Just about the worst she's had, in fact.'

She seemed so totally unwelcoming that he retreated several paces.

'I'm sorry . . . of course I shan't hang about and be a nuisance. I'll come some other—'

'You might as well come in for a couple of minutes. We can arrange when we're going to see each other.'

So that was still in place, thank God. The mother's worsening state did not necessarily mean the end of his dealings with the daughter.

He came in and followed her into her sitting-room. He could hear the doctor running taps in the kitchen.

'Is she unconscious?' he asked.

'It would be better if she were. The nurse is with her. She'll probably stay all day.'

'I'm so *sorry*,' he said, meaning sorry for the two of them. Dinah looked tired, her eyes lack-lustre and her face closed. Even that long, downward-sweeping nose, with its inquisitive outward tilt, had lost its jauntiness. Only her hair shone as bright and brushed as ever.

'It's the first time she's had real pain. Secondaries, the doctor says, beginning to get active. She can't last much longer.'

Dr Bowen now appeared, carrying a glass jug. Framed in the

doorway, which he filled with his strong, bulky body, he ignored Giles and looked straight at Dinah.

'We're going to put her out. I've told the nurse she can go home for a rest and come back in about three hours.'

'All right. I shan't go out.'

'There shouldn't be much for you to do,' he said. 'She's not likely to go off tonight. In fact she may have months of life in her. But these attacks won't let up much, I'm afraid.'

'All right,' she said again. 'Would you like me to make you some tea?'

'Just a cup,' he said offhandedly. 'I have other calls to make.' Then he was gone upstairs.

Now that Giles was left alone with Dinah – even so momentarily, so precariously – he longed to take her in his arms. But her whole demeanour seemed a warning against it. He could hardly believe that fifteen hours ago they had been whole-heartedly making love.

'When can I see you?' he asked.

'You can take me out to dinner. I feel like a meal in a good restaurant. With wine.'

'You shall have the best wine,' he said, 'of the best restaurant in this place. The Belfry, or the Coq au Vin – they're both good. When?'

'Tomorrow night. I've arranged for the nurse to be here with Mother. She'll come for five hours. Six to eleven.'

'Oh, good. I'll book a table for—'

'What I'm going to do,' she interrupted, 'is come round to your place and start from there.'

'Certainly, if you'd rather. It's quite easy to—'

'Don't book the table till about half-past eight. Once I get my legs under a table, and good food and drink, I want to enjoy myself and not have to keep looking at the time. So anything else we're going to do, we'll get done before we go out.'

'Anything. . . ?'

'If you want me to spell it out,' she said coolly, 'instead of taking me to a restaurant and filling me with food and wine and then taking me back home and fucking me, which is standard male practice, you can fuck me first and then take me out to a restaurant and fill me with food and wine.'

'Oh. I see. Well, of course.'

— 168 —

'I take it you've no objection?'

'Objection, my God, it's the one thing in the world I most want to—'

'Well, that's all right, then. Tomorrow night. How far is it to your place?'

'About a mile.'

'I'll come in a taxi. I feel like spoiling myself, life's so bloody awful at the moment.'

'What time?'

'Just after six.'

'I'll be looking through the window. When I see your taxi draw up, I'll rush down and pay the driver.'

'You'd better. I'm not earning any money.'

She showed him out. As he went through the front door he heard the heavy creak of the doctor's feet on the stairs.

When she arrived the next evening, Giles saw at once that the grim mood had lifted and she was back to her normal vivacity. She skipped out of the taxi wearing her silvery plastic raincoat and delicious little hat.

'You're in time,' she said as he paid the driver. 'You must really have been looking out of the window.'

'I was. And what's more I nearly sprained an ankle running down the stairs to pay the fare before you could.'

'You needn't have worried. I'd have hung about, rummaging in my handbag. I'm very good at making people wait.'

They went up to his flat. She hung up her coat and looked round with qualified approval.

'Hm, you're quite snug here. And not as squalid as a bachelor's quarters usually are. Do I detect the hand of a woman?'

'Yes. I had a girl-friend called Harriet who helped me to choose things and told me where to put them.' He felt able to talk about Harriet calmly; not even a tremor in the pit of his stomach; that was what Dinah had done for him already.

'She had pretty fair taste, your Harriet.'

'She taught at an art college. She was paid to have good taste.'

'What happened to her?' Dinah asked, sitting down.

Giles said carefully, 'She fell through a hole in the universe.'

Goodbye, Harriet.

'Aren't you going to offer me a drink?' she asked. It was true, he had been day-dreaming.

'Oh, of course. We're going to live it up.'

'Have you got sherry? That's the correct thing before a dinner-party.'

'I'm sorry, I don't like sherry and I don't keep it. But I've got some dry white wine that's perfect before a meal.'

He poured a large glass for each of them. 'Cheers.'

'Cheers.' Her parsley eyes were full of a provocative light: the corners of her mouth had their lurking smile: her supple, narrow body, as she bent forward to take her glass, seemed an invitation to tumultuous pleasure.

She drank deeply and said, 'Where's your bed?'

He pointed. 'Through that door.'

She put down her glass and went in. He heard the springs murmur as she bounced softly up and down. Then she returned.

'It's a nice mattress.'

'I chose it carefully,' he said. 'I believe in being miserable in comfort.'

She emptied her glass. 'Let's put it to good use. What time did you book the table for?'

'Half-past eight, as you said.'

She stood up and kicked off her shoes. 'Then we've just got enough time.'

Before his riveted gaze, she took off her clothes. In the bathroom doorway, she paused and looked back at him.

'Well, get on with it. I shan't be a minute and I expect to find you in bed.'

'Is that an order?' he asked.

'That's an order.'

When they emerged into the street two and a half hours later, Dinah was in her cheerful, talkative mood ('I'm a compulsive communicator'), and Giles was happy to be carried along by her high spirits. He was dressed with unaccustomed formality, in his one and only suit, with a neat shirt and tie; and this, too, was her doing. When they finally rolled out of bed to get washed and dressed she had asked him if he had any more presentable clothes than the baggy tweeds and corduroys he generally wore, and on his confessing that he had a dark suit of good quality that he kept in

— 170 —

reserve for weddings and funerals, she asked him to put it on.

'Hm, not bad,' was the verdict. 'Turn round . . . your trousers are too slack round the waist. Haven't you got a better tie? And that shirt ought to be ironed.'

'This is the only tie I have. And if my trousers are slack that means I've lost weight round the middle, which is a good thing.'

'Yes, but you'll have to get them altered. You mustn't let your appearance go. I like men to dress up posh when they take me out. Can't you polish your shoes? And you've spilt something on your tie. I shall have to get you a new one if I'm going to be seen about with you.'

So there he was, walking into the discreetly lit restaurant with the red check table-cloths, in a thoroughly unreal state. His mood was a combination of bliss, exhaustion (his bones were full of honey) and sheer hallucination. Surely it was all a dream that this elegantly serpentine girl had just spent two hours in ferociously inventive love-making with him? – a dream that he was wearing his suit and a tie, an outfit he normally associated only with boredom and inconvenience?

The restaurant was a small family business, open only in the evening. The food was like the most delicious home cooking, and the waitresses, who seemed to change every few days, were young ladies with well-educated voices who were obviously doing the job for pocket-money. Giles liked these young ladies; he found them more hard-working, more willing to oblige, more involved in making it a pleasant experience to dine there, than the professional waitress with her fallen arches and sense of grievance.

One of these demoiselles showed them to a table and produced the menu. Dinah looked through it rapidly and expertly.

'I'm hungry. I shall have *bisque d'homard* and then the beef casserole. It's got a fancy name, but that's what it is, beef casserole.'

'You're interested in food, aren't you?' he asked after the waitress had gone, pouring red wine into her glass as he spoke.

'Not at home, as I told you. When I eat a good meal, it's a treat. And I live on treats – it's what keeps me going through life.'

'You just live from one treat to the next?'

'Why not? Have you a better system?'

He pondered. 'I never think about it, I suppose. I mean I haven't a plan for getting through life. I just breathe in and out and things happen to me.'

'Well, does it work? Are you happy?'

'Sometimes I am, sometimes not. I don't think about that much either.'

She attacked her newly arrived lobster soup. 'That wouldn't do for me. I'm very conscious of whether I'm happy or not, and if I'm not I do something about it.'

'Yes,' he said. 'I can see that compared with you, people like me just drift through life. Of course a good deal of my life is lived imaginatively. I mean, in a way it's my job to spend a lot of time day-dreaming, and when you do that you don't notice what's happening to you.'

'I never day-dream,' Dinah said, spreading butter on a piece of bread. 'My life is planned. I work out what I'm going to do and do it. I'm a great one for making lists and writing notes to myself. I like to be in *control*.'

'Except when you're in love, I suppose,' he could not help interjecting. 'I mean, the man you were so mad about that you sat by the telephone day and night. Not much planning about that, I'd say.'

'You'd be wrong. In a sort of way it was all part of my general plan. I mean I *allow* for it. I know my needs are going to drive me into relationships with men and I know those relationships won't always be controllable. But in the overall plan of my life I budget for that.'

'I see.'

She drank thoughtfully, set down her glass and said, 'Does it bore you if I talk about myself?'

'You can't think it does. I'm interested in everything you say, particularly anything you tell me about yourself. You fascinate me.'

'Well, don't get too carried away.'

'It's too late to tell me that, Dinah. I'm in love with you.'

'That's a very silly expression.'

'D'you really think so?'

The Roedean waitress brought their main course: conversation halted while dishes were set out and appreciative sounds made. When they were left alone, he pressed on.

'Don't you think people fall in love?'

'I think when people say they're in love they just mean that they *want* the other person very much.'

— 172 —

'There's a difference between wanting and loving?'

'Of course there is, haven't you noticed?'

'Well, I know that loving someone isn't the same thing as liking them.'

'Look, you can *need* somebody like hell. You get obsessed with them and you long for them all the time. That's how I was with Mark. But when people use the word *love* to describe that – well, it's just covering a hole. I mean they use the word love because they don't know what other word to use. And because they hope it'll give them some sort of leverage with the other person. If you say "I love you" it's more likely to make an impression than if you just say "I need you."'

'Did you tell this organ player' (he did not want to speak the name Mark) 'that you loved him?'

'Of course. All the time.'

'But what you meant was just that you wanted him.'

'I said *need*. That's stronger than want. It's the strongest thing there is.'

'Stronger than love?'

'I've told you, they're the same thing.'

'So love is a strong thing, after all?'

She speared a succulent piece of beef. 'Whatever name you give to it, this thing that grips us and moves us along whether we want to be moved or not, it's the strongest thing there is. It's no use fighting against it, I found that out a long time ago. So now instead of trying to fight it I just build my life so as to leave room for it.'

Giles concentrated for a few moments on his food. Dinah, he noticed, ate rapidly and with relish. A natural enjoyer, she made the simple act of eating a meal into something genuinely festive.

'You've certainly got the emotional life all worked out,' he said reflectively.

'I've got everything worked out. I don't like loose ends. That's why I'm religious, I suppose. I must have a framework and that gives me one.'

'Yes,' he said, remembering how the silver crucifix had looked down on her sensual virtuosities.

'As a matter of fact, I can sum up my attitude to life quite simply, if you're interested.'

'Of course I'm interested.'

'Well, it's got three pillars. First, my faith. I'm an Anglican

— 173 —

Christian. That gives me my bearing and takes care of all the serious side of life, all the moral issues and everything.'

'How d'you mean, takes care of them?'

'Gives me answers.'

There were a number of things Giles might have said, but he kept silent and let her go on.

'Next, men. Would you believe it, I never had sex till I was twenty-four.'

'Well, I might. It doesn't seem to me incredible.'

'I was a good girl at school. It was the line of least resistance. And that's where my third pillar comes in. I like proficiency. I need to be good at everything I do. If there's something I'm not skilful at, I either don't do it at all, or I practise by myself until I can do it without looking a fool in front of other people. That's just the way I am. I chose to be a musician because I had a good ear, inherited from my father, and I knew I could become an instrumentalist if I worked hard. I'm not afraid of hard work, in fact I enjoy it if I can see some return for it. So I worked hard at school, and did what everybody told me, and went to College and studied music, and practised the guitar eight hours a day, and I was quite happy. I got along all right with Mother because I never answered her back. She was always very intense, and of course she wasn't happy – she never adjusted to doing without Daddy.'

'I picture you,' he said. 'A very serious, very charming girl student, winning awards and diplomas.'

'I wasn't a bit charming. And I must have looked a fright. I had a crew-cut and glasses. So I finished at College, and it was time to launch out into life. I came back home for a bit but I soon realised it was a waste of time. I decided to start living, and that meant two things – finding a place to be on my own, and getting the man business organised. So I tackled it one, two, three. First I found a flat. Then I bought a book called *Sex for Girls* or something like that. I read it very carefully and at the same time I got contact lenses and worked over my appearance till I knew I looked pretty. I made up my mind that the first man who took me out, if I found him half-way attractive, I was going to let him initiate me.'

'Lucky man.'

'It was a chap who was doing a thesis on musicology. I'd known him since College. Bill, his name was. He took me to a pub one Sunday lunch-time and gave me beer and bread and cheese and started kissing me. I responded – in fact we started necking so hard that the regulars complained and the landlord asked us to leave. So there seemed nothing else to do except go back to his place and let him get it over. I remember he put a jazz record on. Somebody called Jimmy Noone. He gave it to me afterwards, as a souvenir. He started it playing, it was a twelve-inch L.P., and by the time it stopped he'd seduced me.'

'And since then you've never looked back.'

'I wouldn't expect to look back,' she said, picking up the menu to choose a pudding.

Waking the next morning, Giles could not at first remember why he felt so happy. Then the glad news struck him again with all its force and freshness. He was the accepted lover of that slender, light-footed, parsley-eyed girl! Springing from bed, he washed and dressed hurriedly and tore into his work with demoniac energy. He felt released, vital; ideas flowed; the story of Gus Howkins seemed to come towards him fully shaped instead of having to be quarried out with frightful labour from cold and reluctant stone.

In the afternoon, he called at 2 Princess Terrace and sat for a while with Helen Chichester-Redfern. She seemed tranquil and rather preoccupied. They talked, at her wish, about his work, tracing its graph, comparing this book with that, testing the short stories against the novels, till he felt he could have written a thesis on himself. They had, in fact, very much the kind of conversation he had anticipated before he met her for the first time. But, again as he had anticipated, her physical slope towards extinction seemed to have drained her of vitality; she spoke slowly and faintly, with long silences; he sensed in her the calm of final resignation, as if her mind and body were saying softly, 'If this is death, let it be, let it be.'

Dinah let him into the house, gave him one long kiss which sent him up the stairs with his pulse fluttering, then waited quietly as he brought comfort to her mother. She appeared with the tea-tray, ministered, and withdrew discreetly. During the five minutes in which she was in the room, he felt his body respond to her nearness so exultantly that he felt surprised that the woman in the bed showed no sign of noticing it: surely the singing and shouting of his blood, the hammering of his heart, must be issuing in sound-waves or in nervous vibrations so strong that they would turn any head

— 175 —

towards him? But she was lost in the grey calm of her acceptance.

After an hour he rose, promised to come the next day (it was doubly easy, now, to give this promise), and went down the stairs. The door of Dinah's sitting-room was ajar; he knocked softly and she said, 'Come in.' Entering, he found her standing by the piano, tidying some sheets of music.

'Darling,' he murmured and went across to take her in his arms. She permitted it, but without any yielding movement of her body, and pointed with a warning expression in the general direction of the kitchen.

'Is there something. . . .'

'We're not alone,' she said softly. 'The doctor's here.'

He let his arms fall. In the instant of relinquishing him she drew her hand down the front of his body in a caress, and slid her tongue briefly into his mouth. His physical reaction was immediate and crashingly violent. Then the doctor was in the room, buttoning up the jacket he had doubtless taken off to wash his hands.

'How did you find her?' he asked Giles, his voice off-hand but not unfriendly.

'Rather lack-lustre.'

'A good way of putting it,' said Dr Bowen, pulling down his jacket at the sides and looking at himself in Dinah's long mirror. 'Whether she ever has lustre again, we'll have to see. She's living on borrowed time, but there may still be quite a lot of it. Every case is different.'

'It would be a shame to hurry her,' said Dinah. 'She still gets quite a lot out of life, on her good days. That's something I don't understand. If I knew I was going I'd want to go and get it over.'

Yes, you would, bright voracious mammal, darting through life like a lithe, quick weasel.

'You'd probably want to hang on as long as you could, when it came to it,' the doctor said to her, turning his eyes watchfully in her direction.

'I don't want to talk about it,' she said in her dismissive tone.

Dr Bowen shrugged; Giles took his leave. Dinah came with him to the front door and gave his hand a quick, stealthy squeeze.

'I'll ring you,' he said.

She shook her head. 'I'll be practising. Ring in the morning if you like.'

He felt slightly dashed, but as she turned away she gave him a warm, conspiratorial smile that set him up again. Of course the girl had to practise, and to use all her concentration on it. She was a professional musician. He of all men, struggling himself with the problems of the artist, should try not to be selfish and claiming . . . especially when she gave so much.

After getting home, he worked again – there seemed no limit, now, to his creative energy – then ate a meal and went out to the cinema. Returning at about half-past ten, he read for a while and then went drowsily, happily, to bed. Plenty of sleep on the nights when he was not with Dinah, then he would need less on the nights when he was with her. . . . He chuckled to himself with sheer contentment as sleep sucked him gently down.

In his first deep sleep he had no sense of the passage of time; it was, in fact, barely an hour later when his unconsciousness began to be pierced, more and more insistently, by the shrilling of the telephone. At first his mind refused to wake; when it did, his body refused to move; finally, as the instrument nagged on and on, he dragged himself out of his warm nest and padded across to it, moaning softly with vexation.

'Hello?'

'This is Dr Bowen here.'

'Dr Who? What kind of a time is this to—'

'I'm sorry. But you're needed round here.'

'Round where? Look, I don't—'

'Helen Chichester-Redfern keeps asking for you. She's in a crisis.'

Giles was silent for a moment. His mind, drenched with sleep, could not come up with any reaction. A crisis?

Then Dinah's voice came on, cold and imperative.

'Look, you'd better do as the man says. Get over here as soon as you can. She needs you.'

'Oh. Well, in that case, I—'

'You accepted that you were going to help her. You're not going to let her down, I suppose.'

'No. No. I'll come. Of course I'll come.'

'Good, well, be as quick as you can.'

She rang off. Suddenly wide awake, he put on the main light and started to dress.

Walking quickly through the pitch-dark streets, Giles felt dire premonitions. Something strongly negative was happening. It was more than the woman's death: the sinking to rest of a tortured organism is not negative, or need not be. The vibrations he was receiving came from something worse.

When Dinah let him in he could see at once that she was unhappy. Her face had that tense, closed look he had learnt to recognise, and her voice was lifeless.

'You'd better go straight up. You seem to be all she wants.'

'What is it?' he asked, but she merely motioned her head towards the staircase. Behind her, Dr Bowen lurked silently.

Giles felt weak, shiftless, unprepared for the vast unknown effort that was going to be demanded from him. One hand on the stair-rail, he paused and looked at their two faces.

'Can't you give me any idea what it is she wants of me?'

Dr Bowen said heavily, 'What is it she's wanted from you all along?'

'Oh, I don't know. . . . Some sort of contact, some sort of relationship of minds.'

'Well,' said the doctor, 'whatever it is, this is the last instalment of it. As for mind, she may not have much of one left. It's unpredictable. Consciousness is coming and going.'

'Is she doped?'

'To some extent. But short of giving her a dose so massive that it would put her out altogether and probably put her into a final sleep, it's not possible to control her state any longer. Some kind of consciousness keeps breaking through.'

Dinah looked at him with what seemed to be cold dislike and said, 'Why don't you just go up and be with her? There may not be much time, why hang about asking us to explain everything?'

For an instant he held her eyes steadily. 'I'm hanging about because I'm afraid. It seems to me what I'm here for is to help her to die. I've never done it before. I'm not a doctor or a priest, and I'm afraid of what I'll find when I get up these stairs.'

'If you're afraid, don't do it,' she said, turning away into the room.

Alone, his mouth dry, Giles went up the stairs. The bedroom door was ajar. As he approached he heard the dying woman's voice at normal conversational pitch. He halted: was there someone in there with her?

'Very well, stand in the corner. It won't help you now. You can't look at me, can you? You want to hide your face. You don't want to see the truth, the truth of what you've done to me, and you'd have to see it if you looked at me. Now you're shrinking – that won't help you either. You can be as small as a beetle, but I'll find you. I've got you now. I've got you now.'

Giles's blood ran cold. He had always felt an irrational fear of people who were mad, or drunk, or delirious. If he had lived before the scientific age, he could easily have believed in demoniac possession. People who were demented, for whatever reason, struck him with a clammy terror.

'You thought you could forget.' There was a terrible, calm vengefulness in her voice. 'Get away. To another country. Another woman. Make yourself a new life. Now you're here, trying to shrink in that corner. And he's coming – the man who'll make you sorry. He'll make everyone look at you. All those eyes. They'll all know. Oh. Oh. Stop twisting it. Stop twisting it round and round. But I don't care. You can hurt me. But I'll hurt you more. The eyes will follow you everywhere. So now you're big. Filling the room. I hear you, knock, knock, head on the ceiling. You think I'm frightened of you but I'm not, it's too late for that. Yes, twist it if you like. A harpoon. Just what you would use. But now they see it. They see you twist it in my chest. All those years no one ever saw it. Oh. Oh. Oh.' She was grunting in pain now, and her breath was coming in great gasps.

Desperately, Giles pushed open the door. At once he stopped, appalled by the terrible change that had come over her. In her stretched face and wasted body, what he had seen hitherto was illness. Now it was death. Her eyes were wide open, trained with avid concentration on nothing. Or rather on the shapes clustering about the fog besieging her brain.

'Helen,' he said.

She showed no sign of hearing. Her head, rolling from side to side on the pillow, swivelled towards him and then away.

'He's coming. I heard his voice. You can't run away, Richard. He'll find you wherever you are, and you know why? Because it isn't himself he'll chase you with, it's his words and thoughts. They'll never leave you alone. And the eyes that will look at you. And the knowledge. They've seen the harpoon. And the nails you're putting into my shoulders. You're hurting me but carry on. I'll hurt you worse. I'll hurt you worse, I swear it to God.'

'Helen.'

When she still did not answer, Giles moved swiftly across the room and fell on his knees beside her. Feverishly, he seized her hand and spoke with his mouth close to her ear.

'Helen, it's me, Giles. I want to help you. Giles. Giles.'

Her fingers closed round his hand. He felt the coldness of her flesh against the warmth of his own. He was hot-blooded, vigorous: the eroding years had still not made his body cold and brittle. But this is what the years would ultimately do, this would be the end of it.

'Helen, if you know me, speak to me. Tell me anything. Ask me anything. I shan't go away unless you want me to. It's me, Giles.'

'You hear that, Richard?' she said with sudden loudness. 'He's here! You can't escape now!' Then she grasped his hand with a tightness he would not have believed possible, and with a convulsive effort half reared up. 'Watch him! Don't take your eyes off him! The harpoon!'

As abruptly as it had come, the fit subsided and she sank into sleep. Numbed by horror and pity, he stayed where he was until the pain in his knee-caps forced him to move to the wooden armchair. But he kept the cold, dry hand in his. It was like the claw of a bird that had died of cold.

How long she slept he did not know. An hour, two hours, three? He kept still, determined to be near her until she had no more need of him. There was no sound from downstairs: he might have been alone in the house, or for that matter in the universe, with this fellow human being whose time was so nearly over. Sitting beside her, holding that pitiful hand in his own, Giles knew for the first time what life is, how sacred and how frail, this rich, precarious gift for which we do not know whom to thank, this flame lit by we do not know whom, so easy to tread out that the first of all the commandments must always be 'Thou shalt not kill'. Only Time has a licence to kill, and he needs no encouragement.

At long last she stirred, woke, and looked at him. The lines of strain had gone from her face; she must have entered a phase of relief, a patch of calm. Her eyes focused: she knew him at once.

'Giles. You've come.'

'Yes.'

'I knew you would come before it was too late. My time is very short.'

He sat down. 'I'm here. Say anything you want to say.'

'I may die tonight. I feel death inside my body. Deeply inside: taking command. I see nothing ahead but weakness and delirium. This may be my last clarity. I had to call you. I had to have you near me. There's no one else.'

'I know,' he said gently.

'I may die tonight. I don't believe in an after life. At least, I don't think I believe. Survival of identity after death of the body. It's never been a real idea to me. I think you have your life and then it's over. Mine's over. And there's nothing I can feel except despair. It hasn't been worth it.'

'No, surely you've—'

'Not worth it. Not worth it. All the struggle and the suffering. What have I to show? I produced Diana. A child born out of desperation. A wordless cry for help. Trying to bridge a gulf of darkness and silence between myself and the man I loved. He never wanted to hear me. Now it's all over and I'm dying in desperation.'

'You mustn't talk like this! You mustn't!'

'You know it's true. You can't stand it any more than he could. You want a silver lining. Rose-coloured sky at sunset. Well, it's black, black, black.' Her voice was hoarse with intensity, her breath coming in sobbing gasps.

Giles took her hand. 'You haven't always felt the same. You've had some joy in living. This despair is your mood *now*.'

'It's been my mood for years. Under the cheerfulness I've tried to pretend. It's been my mood ever since my happiness was taken away.'

He sat silent. Her tormented breathing sounded through the room. A car, going by in the rainy night, hooted incongruously.

'I don't believe in a future life. But I still don't want to die in a state of mortal sin.'

'Mortal sin?'

'Lying. Deception. Falsehood.'

He bent close to her and said, with all the softness and compassion he could put into his voice, 'What falsehood have you been guilty of, Helen?'

She was silent, then spoke more slowly, with more of an effort. 'Fundamental. Complete. A lie at the centre of everything.' He waited again. 'I showed you a false face. I hid my real motive. In seeking your acquaintance . . . in telling you I needed your help.

— 181 —

That was true. But I never said what for. I talked about knowing and understanding. I said that before I died I needed to make sense of life. To understand the things that had happened to me. That was all lies. I understood, all right. There's no mystery. Richard spoilt my life. I was a young untried girl. No experience of life, no wisdom, no skills, no profession, no property. All I had to give was my love and I gave him that. He took it casually. Laid it aside and forgot where he had put it. When something he thought better came along, he walked away from my love and forgot it without a qualm. Without a single backward look.'

'You don't know that. It may have cost him an effort.'

'I don't believe it. Men can always justify themselves.'

'All men?'

'I'm not sure. But in any case I'm not concerned with all men. It was only one man who injured me – because I only had to do with one man in my life. He took my love and gave me nothing in return. Except unhappiness. I never did anything wrong. I was a good wife to him, loyal, loving, young enough to be attractive.'

'I'm sure you were all those things. But who knows, ever, how a marriage will turn out?'

She glared at him fiercely out of those dim, deeply recessed eyes. 'My marriage did not turn out. It was turned out. Like an un-wanted domestic animal shut out of doors and left to starve.'

'None of this is news to me. I knew your husband had left you. I knew he was living in another country with another woman, and never communicated with you. So where is the falsehood, Helen? How have you deceived me?'

'My motives,' she said in a slow, drained voice. One of her waves of exhaustion was coming over her, and he sensed that she was fighting against it with every bodily fibre that would still obey her mind. 'I hate him. I'm dying with my soul full of hate. That's all he left me with. And why I got in touch with you. You . . . have . . . power.' Her head sank back; he could actually feel death coming down upon her.

'Helen. . . .' Giles bent forward to see if her heart was still beating. But before he could touch her wrist she stirred, and spoke.

'Richard. Richard.'

Giles waited.

'Tell Diana not to make the tea so strong. She makes the tea too strong, I don't like it.'

Again.

'She won't listen to me. She's yours. I made her for you. Tell her, Richard – the tea! *Please*, Richard!'

Once more she slept. For a long time – ten minutes, twenty, half an hour – Giles sat still in his chair. There seemed to be no point in calling Dinah; no point in doing anything. She would either die, or wake up for another brief struggle, or fall into an indefinite, comatose sleep. All he could do, for the present, was wait: in other words, do nothing.

Finally she opened her eyes and seemed to know at once that he was there, and that they had been talking, and on what subject.

'I want him to suffer. It's right that he should have some pain. In return for what he made me go through.'

'Helen, are you sure you believe that?'

She lifted a hand from the counterpane and let it drop back. 'How could I not be sure? For years, for years it's all I've wanted. Why should he spoil everything for me and walk away scot-free into happiness? Let him suffer, let him know pain and then there will be that much justice done in the world. One tiny piece of justice against all the wrong and unfairness.'

Giles said carefully, 'And is this the frame of mind you intend to die in?'

'Dying or living makes no difference. My thoughts now are no different from my thoughts for thirty years. Only one difference: now I'm dying you might take some notice of me. Because the dying have authority. Tell me it's true. Tell me the wishes of dying people are attended to.'

'Death gives great authority. Everyone remembers a person's last words.'

She seemed to be trying to sit up, but the task was beyond her vanishing strength. He could see how her body clenched itself in effort under the bedclothes.

'Ever since Richard spoilt my life I've been trying to think of some way of hurting him. But I've always been so powerless. He was completely safe from me. In another country, with another woman. Among people I never met. Nobody I could influence against him. There was no point at which I could touch him. So the poison stayed with me. Going round and round in my bloodstream. The poison I longed to inject into him with a sting.'

She was silent. Finally he said, 'Well?'

'You are the answer.'

'Me?'

'You have a sting. A long, sharp, polished sting that would pierce anything.'

'I don't understand you, Helen.'

'Yes, you do. Your sting is your art. You can tell the story so that it becomes real to people, goes home to their feelings. You can make them my suffering and loneliness. You can make them understand what his betrayal did to me. And they will say, "Surely this is not an imagined story. It must have happened to actual people, it has such a ring of reality." And then . . . you can tell them.'

'Tell them?'

'Yes, yes, when they ask you, as they surely will. You can say, "This was Richard Chichester-Redfern, who deserted his wife and broke her heart. He went away with his mistress, leaving her with a broken life full of sorrows." '

Giles swallowed. 'Let me get this straight, Helen. You want me to write a story about you and your husband and his leaving you, and then go on record as saying that it refers to real people, and name names?'

She nodded. 'That is what I want.'

'And that's why you got in touch with me in the first place?'

'That is why.'

Giles said bitterly, 'All that stuff about how you'd always admired my writing—'

'Was perfectly genuine. Reading has been my great consolation. Reading good books by thoughtful authors who had won through to an understanding of life. Its triumphs and miseries. I read you for years and I looked at you with awe as you walked past this house day after day. But it was not until recently, not until I became ill and started to die, that I suddenly realised that you were a source of strength I could tap.'

'Helen, I have to say this. I think the reason you thought of this scheme, this revenge, after you became ill was because your illness interfered with your judgement. Made you more prone to fantasy.'

'Nothing of the kind. All my illness did was to force me to be still. To stop fidgeting about with one anodyne, one palliative, after another. It drove me back on my thoughts and memories.'

'I'm sorry to hear it.'

'Why should you be? If you want to be sorry about anything, be sorry for the lonely agony I have suffered for thirty years. Be sorry that I am dying in the company of a daughter who does not love me.'

'Are you sure she doesn't love you?'

'I am sure for the best of reasons. I do not love her. There has never been any feeling between us.'

Her breathing became harsh, irregular, laboured. She closed her eyes and screwed them up.

'Helen, what's the matter? Are you in pain?'

'Yes.' She was uttering short grunting sounds now, with every exhalation. 'My body is a mass of pain.'

'Would you like the doctor? He's downstairs.'

'He can do nothing . . . for me. If he gave . . . me something for the pain in my body . . . who can relieve the pain in my mind? You. Only you.'

She opened her eyes again and stared into his face with an intensity that scorched him. A fleck of foam had gathered at one corner of her mouth and her eyes seemed to be glazing over. In her agony she had thrust herself sideways, and now lay diagonally across the bed; thinking to render her what service he could, Giles pulled back the duvet and took hold of her, to move her into a central position. But she struck at him wildly. She seemed terrified.

'Leave me alone. Keep off me. You've left me. You went away. You mustn't touch me.' Then she gave a long groan and cried out despairingly, 'Help! Help! It's Richard – he wants to kill me. . . .' Her voice died away into a sigh. Consciousness was leaving her again. He laid her down and pulled the duvet over her up to the neck. She seemed to be asleep or in a coma, but presently the deep, hoarse cries of pain began. He could bear no more: it was impossible to be in a room with such a degree of suffering and not seek for help. He ran downstairs, pursued by those rhythmic grunts of anguish.

Pushing open the door of Dinah's sitting-room, Giles burst into an atmosphere of illusory calm. Dinah was lying asleep on her divan, fully clothed but with a coat lightly thrown over her. Perhaps the doctor had put it there after she fell into an exhausted slumber, or perhaps she had covered herself over and consciously set out to go to sleep, while he sat nearby and watched. Dr Bowen himself was sitting in the armchair with his hands folded in his lap, not reading, not occupying his mind with anything but the vigil itself. He looked up, but without haste, as Giles entered.

'Is she worse?' he asked.

'Can't you hear her?'

The groans from above sounded clearly in the still room.

'It won't last,' said the doctor. 'She'll go back into unconsciousness in a few minutes.'

'For God's sake, can't you give her anything?'

'I could. But it's unlikely that her heart would stand it.'

'If you mean another dose would kill her, then why not? She'd be better dead than going through this.'

Without answering, Dr Bowen rose from his chair and picked up a small bag that evidently contained his equipment. With Giles following, he went out of the room and up the stairs. As they climbed, they heard a long, mumbling groan and then silence. When they got to Helen Chichester-Redfern's bedside, she was silent, with closed eyes. The doctor touched her pulse briefly, then said, 'She's asleep.'

'I wouldn't have believed it. You heard what she was like only a moment ago.'

'Her hold on consciousness is very weak,' said the doctor. 'That's the only shred of comfort in her situation.' He looked down at the waxen figure on the bed. 'She may never wake up again, or she may wake in five minutes and start going through hell again. Or she may even be lucid. What are you going to do?'

'What ought I to do?'

'I can't tell you what you ought to do. I shall stay on, downstairs, until the nurse comes in the morning.'

'I shall stay here,' said Giles. He sank down wearily into the Windsor chair. 'It's probably not much good to her – her mind's wandering and she keeps thinking I'm her husband. But then again, even when I'm not here she still sees him, standing in the corner.'

'Perhaps he is standing in the corner,' said Dr Bowen. He took his bag and went out.

Some twenty minutes went by in complete stillness. Helen was breathing so quietly that several times he bent over to hear whether or not the faint respiration had stopped. But it always sighed on, and finally she opened her eyes and looked straight at him. He knew at once that she recognised him and that her mind had come into one of its patches of clarity.

'Give me your promise,' she said faintly.

'Helen, how can I?'

'You can write that story. It's a story like any other. You have handled similar ones.'

'Yes, but. . . .'

'What are you afraid of? That he'll retaliate? Take legal action? You can easily avoid that. Tell a few people who'll be proud of having inside information. You need never put it in writing, except in a statement to be opened after your death.'

'You've got it all worked out.'

'It's so little I'm asking you. You can do it so easily. A lifetime of telling stories that grew out of your experience. Well, so has this one. It's a story like any other. Tell it. Tell it and bring peace to my tormented spirit.'

He was silent. He could not refuse or acquiesce.

'Why, why do you hesitate? Can you watch me die in this desperation?'

Suddenly, as if a weight had rolled away, Giles heard his own voice say, 'I'll do it, Helen.'

'You'll write my story? In all its pain?'

'I'll write it.'

'You'll remember that you're avenging a great wrong? Make it blistering? Condemning?'

'I'll hit it hard.'

As Giles spoke, he had no idea at all whether he was telling the truth. The thought flashed through his mind: a writer's thought-processes are unpredictable anyway. How could he give an undertaking *not* to use the story of Helen Chichester-Redfern and her husband Richard?

And if he could not promise *not* to use it, why not bring comfort to a dying woman by turning that uncertainty inside out, and allowing her to feel sure that he *would* use it?

She was breathing harshly again, racked by that terrible searching pain. But she managed to croak out, 'You promise . . . you *promise?*'

He said, 'I promise.'

And if that commits me, he thought, it commits me.

She looked at him with steady eyes. In that moment, it seemed

— 187 —

that her agony had fallen away. Her voice was calm when she spoke.

'That's good. You see, it's important.'

'Yes.'

'She's out there.'

'Who is?' He was startled.

'That woman. I can't say her name. But you know. My husband's mistress. It's dark, so you wouldn't see her even if you looked out of the window, but she's on the path outside. She's always there. I lie here and hear her. Especially in the afternoons. She keeps Diana out in all weathers, even when it's cold and raining. Even in the fog she keeps her out.'

'I see,' he said gravely.

'She wants to take Diana away from me, because she can't have a child of her own. So she pretends to be kind to her. Wraps her up in her little red cloak and takes her out in the pram. But I know why she does it, Giles. She wants to keep her from coming inside and getting her meals. She's trying to kill her with hunger. And Diana doesn't mind, she likes it.'

'Oh.'

'Yes, Diana's told her father she wants to die. Then I'll be left alone and they can all say it's my fault.'

'I'm sure it's not your fault.'

'No, but you can see why it's important that you write the book. She'll have to come indoors then, to read it. She can't read a book out in the garden, walking up and down that path. Especially not at night.' A shadow of anxiety passed across her face. 'It won't be a *lit-up* book, will it, Giles?'

'You mean with luminous pages?'

She nodded.

'No,' he said. 'I never write that kind of book. She'll have to come indoors to read it.'

Helen Chichester-Redfern smiled and closed her eyes.

Going quietly downstairs, leaving Helen sleeping or perhaps dying, Giles felt drained, unmanned, close to tears. To stand so close to the invisible vortex of death, even for a few minutes, is to feel the marrow sucked from one's bones.

Suddenly he felt an intense longing for Dinah. Her warmth and femaleness and vitality, and perhaps above all her emotional invulnerability, came to his mind as infinitely desirable. She at least would never give hostages; she would never allow any one man to wreck her life and die miserably cursing him.

The kitchen light was out; the hallway was lit but silent. The doctor must have gone. The door of Dinah's room was closed. He went up to it and tapped gently.

Silence.

He tapped again. He needed her so much, and surely as her lover he had some rights?

She must be sleeping. But surely she would forgive him if he woke her. Or slipped in beside her sleeping body and put his arms gently round her and waited for her to come alive to his presence.

He gently turned the handle and pushed the door ajar. Then, startling him, her voice: cool and wide-awake.

'Don't come in.'

He stood motionless.

'Don't come in,' she said again. 'I don't want visitors. Ring me tomorrow.'

Giles closed the door softly. As he did so his mind registered that her room was not in darkness. There was a soft light in it that must come from her bedside lamp. Perhaps she was reading.

He opened the front door and went out into the silent street. Nothing stirred. The lamp-posts threw circles of light but there was no one to see them. There was no wind. Dr Bowen's car stood parked a few yards away.

Without thinking, without remembering, without hesitating, without comparing, without feeling, Giles began to walk through the darkness in the direction of his dwelling.

7

S O IT WAS ALL SETTLED THAT ON THE SATURDAY MORNING WE
were to break cover, Julia and I, leave our refuge and go
and confront the big world, bristling with problems. We were
going to question Jake, do what we could to rescue Cliff from his
stupid mess, and, in my case, get ready for the next knee-jerk from
Daphne.

Now our sacred week was drawing to a close. On Friday afternoon the landlord, a tall thin Englishman with a long nose and
watchful, suspicious eyes, came in to check that the place was all
ready for the next tenant waiting to be fleeced. He moseyed about
with a list in his hand, checking on whether I had broken anything
or subjected the place to undue wear and tear. Julia was sitting
outside, having a cup of tea in the sunshine, and I noticed him
looking at her suspiciously; I wondered if he was toying with the
idea of charging me extra for having an extra person there, but then
I remembered that I had rented the cottage, *tout court*, with no
strings and no specifying whether it was to be occupied by one
person or twenty. I felt bolder then, and even considered suggest-
ing that he roll about on the bed a bit, to see if the springs were
sagging at all. In the end he consulted his list and said I must have
broken two tea-cups which I knew damn well weren't there when I
arrived. I paid up, of course.

After he had gone, the whole thing entered a mood of coda. It
had been the best time of my life, the only few days of perfect,
unclouded happiness, and these were the last hours. We were so
tranquil together that I might have allowed myself to hope for some
sort of future with Julia, but when it came to the point I simply
didn't dare. I knew that if I started building real hopes, imagining a
future together in any sort of realistic detail, and then if it just didn't
happen, my world would crumble into dust and I should crumble

with it. So I lived in the present instead. We went for a last walk on the hills, and saw a perfect late sunset over the distant sea, and then came back and made a fire and ate and drank beside its lovely glow. And then we went up to the half-bedroom and made love and fell asleep. She seemed utterly relaxed: everything she did seemed to come to her naturally, without complication or afterthought. So I allowed myself to be happy, one more time.

Waking in the morning was different, though. There was that big patch of sunlight on the wall, just as there had been every morning when we woke. But now it seemed empty, antiseptic; it seemed to be saying to me, 'Stop dreaming, stop living in a world of vague promises, face your situation, get up and cope.'

Julia was sleeping gently beside me. Her rich black hair was spread out on the pillow and one creamy shoulder was exposed. I looked at her, feeling the breath blowing gently out of her nostrils, watching the delicate throb of the pulse in her throat and the occasional slight movement of the eyes behind those closed lids with their faint tracery of little veins. How beautiful she was, and how gentle; completely a woman and a mature human being, yet at the centre of her nature as innocent as a child. I tried to feel gratitude that life had brought me the privilege of being close to her for a while, but I could only feel sadness. Because now I felt sure it must be the end. She had accepted me because I was part of a necessary withdrawal from life, a brief escape that had saved her from breaking; I went with the valley, with the cottage, with the beef stew and red wine and firelight. When she got back into the main current of life she would have to resume her normal personality, coping with problems and resisting impact from many directions, and inevitably I would come to seem peripheral, unimportant. For a moment I felt intense sadness: no, call it by its right name, self-pity: a lump formed in my throat. Why pretend? I would go on playing my part, but it was inevitably doomed to be a part of diminishing scope. Julia would go out of my life, probably very soon, and when she did, a whole chapter would be ended. Sexual love, with all that it means in one's life, would be over for me. Life would never again float towards me a woman who would rouse all my passion, all my tenderness, all my strength, as she had done. It was over.

I got up and went downstairs. Working mechanically, I filled the kettle and made tea. I cursed myself for a weakling and a coward.

Surely a real man would snap out of it? Surely he would rejoice at the unexpected bounty he had enjoyed, rather than shrink in dread from the emptiness that was coming?

Desperate, I splashed myself fiercely with icy water. Be clean at least, and healthy, and strong. Because from now on there will be no room for weakness: it must be all strength, and endurance. I drank a mug of tea outside the back door. The air was crisp and pure, brightened but not yet warmed by the strong sun. The world was a beautiful place, whatever happened to the individual souls who had to live in it.

That was my last moment for reflection. Julia came down, and washed and dressed, and I made breakfast and we ate it, and she cleared and washed the dishes while I went round and made a last check that everything was ready for the next person to invest a slab of his or her existence in this place. Who would it be? Someone just enjoying a rest from the struggle of life? Or someone at the end of an epoch, like me; or at the beginning of one? But I had no time for such speculations. The place was in apple-pie order, the landlord had already relieved me of the key, and all I had to do was walk out, slam the door behind me, and drive away towards the smoke.

Standing in the living-room for the last time, I took Julia in my arms. I wanted to say something, but what? So I just kissed her and said, 'Thank you.'

'No, no,' she said, 'thank *you*.'

And she smiled at me: a smile of real tenderness and gratitude: was it just my fearfulness that saw in it, also, the sunset gleam of a goodbye?

Then we were in the car, driving, the narrow road snaking away under our wheels, the sheep looking up momentarily from their ceaseless cropping, the mountains shining purple in the sun, and then it was the main road, and traffic, and villages and towns, and before long it was the drab slog of the motorway, and Julia was sitting very still in her seat, staring out of the windscreen in a way that reminded me, suddenly, of the fixed gaze she had worn when I first set eyes on her: back in another existence, otherwise known as ten days ago. I was another man now, a different I, but I guessed that she was the same she.

About tea-time, London groped out to meet us. I drove straight to my horrible little pad, and we let ourselves in and washed and attended to nature and freshened up generally, and drank some bitter black tea. It was time, now, for action. And action could take only one form, to begin with: to be in touch with Jake. I dialled his number, and when his voice, tinged with the usual impatience, said 'Hello?' I silently passed the telephone to Julia.

Just for an instant, she made no move to take it from me, keeping her arms down by her sides. Then, quite slowly, she brought her right hand up, took the receiver, and lifted it – slowly, as if it were heavy – to her ear. I felt ashamed. Why had I been such a crass fool as not to see that the first words she exchanged with Jake on the telephone would be an effort for her, and a pain? Why was I so self-absorbed?

She was speaking, and keeping it very crisp.

'Jake, I'm coming round to see you. Gus Howkins will be with me. You've seen him before. We're coming to find out what's been happening over this kidnap nonsense. I don't want to discuss anything else.' A pause. 'That's understood then. We'll be round straight away.' Pause again. 'I don't care whether you're free or not. Send her away.' She rang off.

'What did he say?' I asked, not wanting to know but needing to cover the silence.

'He said he was glad I didn't want to discuss anything beyond that one thing because he's been rehearsing all day and he's tired. And then he said we ought to keep the visit quite short because it wasn't a free evening for him.'

In other words, the bastard had been on his usual form.

Julia stood quite still beside the silent telephone. Her face had lost the relaxed, shining, welcoming look it had worn at the cottage and become more still, more inward-looking, tinged with a deep sadness. All at once I felt an impulse to seize her in my arms, to swear I would fight all her battles for her, all of them: to protect her from life and be damned to what happened to me.

Actually all I did was to say, 'Why don't you just stay here and I'll go and talk to him?'

Even as I spoke I knew it was a fool suggestion. Sit in my scrubby flat, feeling more suicidal by the minute, wondering what he was saying to me?

She gave that quick, flashing smile and shook her head. 'I'd better come. It's not that I don't trust you to ask the right questions. But if Jake's trying to cover anything up, I'll be more able to get it out of him. Simply because of the length of time I've known him.

I've had plenty of chance to get to know the look that comes into his eyes when he's lying. I don't want any more chances, come to that, in fact I don't *want* to see him again at all, but I'll have to, so let's go round now.'

Wise, considerate, cautious, protective, looking-after Gus Howkins, that's me, folks, said, 'It's coming up to dinner-time and we haven't had anything since breakfast. Shall we go and eat something first?'

As I heard myself utter the words I thought, W., c., c., p., l.-a. G.H. is a pathetic old nanny-goat.

Julia said, as I knew she would, 'No. Let's go now.'

We went out and got into the car again. I thought to myself that if I ever got out of all this alive, I'd sell the car and never get another. We drove round to Windermere Gardens, found a space in the car-park, and crossed a trim lawn to the front door. A thick, close night was coming in; the air swirled about us as slowly as water. The building streamed with sharp electric light.

And there was Dennis with his epaulets. Good God, did the man never go off duty? Wasn't there a sub-Dennis who took over in the evenings? Or was this an identical twin? In any event I hated him just as much. He gave me his usual narrow-eyed glare, rang up from the corner of the lobby, watched us get into the lift, and there we were, standing together like strangers in the smoothly climbing box of steel and expensive woodwork.

Julia had gone inside herself, gathering strength for the shock of confronting Jake. She didn't meet my eyes. I wondered what I was doing in the situation at all. It was all so clearly between the two of them.

We got to the right floor and I rang the bell. In the moments that followed, I wondered if Driver would come to the door himself, or whether Penny was there even at weekends, coping with everything. In any case, would he be alone? What was the reason why, after a hard day's rehearsing, he was not free in the evening? Some girl, doubtless. Would it be the Janice he had been fretting about when I called the other time?

I glanced quickly across at Julia. She was looking straight in front of her, her face expressionless. But as I watched, she blinked rapidly four or five times. I had never seen her do that before. It was the only outward sign of the agitation that must have been burning her up.

Then the door opened and it was the same old Jake Driver, familiar to millions of viewers, shock of hair, broad shoulders, angry-bull eyes, the husband of this woman whom I loved and who had briefly been mine.

'Julia,' he said and it was obvious that the tone was rehearsed: it was so light and non-committal. Then his gaze wandered to me. 'You'd better come in,' he said. It was a good performance, but I was in a mood to want something more than good performances.

We went in. No sign of Penny, or for that matter of a girl, Janice or otherwise. The long black leather sofa, the low table with drinks, the enigmatic picture on the staring white wall – they were all ready for us.

Jake led the way in, leaving me to shut the door. In the middle of the room he turned to face us. He used the space theatrically: this is my area, what do you want of me?

Standing beside Julia, I felt the nervous power flowing through her body. She was young, restive, full of pain. She wanted to be rid of this man, but first there was the question of her brother. Umbilical links. Unfinished business. When it was finished, she would be over the horizon like a flash, looking for new worlds, burying memories.

'Sit down,' said Jake Driver, 'and have a drink.'

'No,' Julia's voice was cool and steady. 'Don't bother to be a good host or any of that stuff. I want some information and that's all I want.'

'And what does Gus want?' he asked, looking at me dangerously from under lowered brows.

'Gus doesn't want anything,' I told him. 'Except to help Julia through a bad time, if it lies in his power.'

Ignoring my answer, he turned his eyes back to Julia. 'D'you feel like telling me where you've been for the last ten days or so?'

She said coolly, 'I don't think you've got a right to know.'

'Whereas you, of course, have a perfect right to disappear into the blue, causing anxiety right and left, and giving twisted little blackmailers an opportunity that they weren't slow to use.'

There was only a tiny pause before she answered, 'If you don't think I ought to have disappeared into the blue, perhaps you'll tell me what you think I ought to have done instead. Under the circumstances.'

He shrugged. 'You might at least have kept in touch.'

'In touch? With *you*?'

Whether he would have said anything in response to this I don't know, but Julia took up the slack without waiting.

'You've been having ransom demands about me. All right, here I am. You knew all along I hadn't been kidnapped, because Gus rang you up. And I wrote a note. So you must have known it was all a crazy scheme on somebody's part.'

'Not just somebody. Your loving brother.'

She blinked again, hard and rapidly. I felt the anguish that was running like a tide through her veins, and I wished my worthless body could have been thrown into that flood, if it would have halted the fierceness of the tide for a moment.

'What did Cliff do?' she asked, though of course she knew what Cliff had done.

'What didn't he do. First, he got hold of the information, from somewhere, that you'd gone off into the unknown.'

'Well put. That's just what I had done.'

'So Cliff, always racing his little mind towards the next corner, comes up with the idea that if I know you've cut out, I'll be worried.'

'Which of course was a mistake.'

'Not altogether. The situation did have its worrying sides.'

I put in, 'Like, what would happen to your public image?'

He gave me a cold, hard look. And no words.

'Where is Cliff now?' Julia threw the question at him.

'In prison.'

There was a silence, then she asked: 'What prison?'

'I don't know. Probably Pentonville.'

'Why there?'

He shrugged. 'Nearest prison to where the arrest happened.'

Julia sat down, very carefully, on the black leather sofa. I stood in the middle of the floor and said, 'Will you give us the details? Or shall we have to get them from somewhere else?'

'Oh, there's no need to go sleuthing around,' Jake said, his voice grimly casual. 'I'll give you all the information, for what it's worth. First of all, read this.' He passed over to her a sheet of type-writing.

She read it, frowning, and then handed it to me. I read: *The twenty thousand pounds must be in used fives. They must be in this bag. No other will be excepted. On Monday, 12 September, take*

*the train at 11.21 at night (23.21) from Lewisham to London
Bridge. Get into the furthest-back carriage and choose a
non-smoking compartment. That train still has compartmented
carriages not the newer coach type. Put this bag on the rack with the
twenty thousand in it. Then get behind a newspaper to hide your
face. There will be very few people on the train. When it gets to
London Bridge, pretend to be very intrested in the paper and sit
there finishing the column your reading. Everyone else will get out
of the compartment. When they have all gone, you get out. Leave
the bag behind on the rack. It will be picked up.*

*You will be temted to try something on. So we tell you now. If the
man we send to pick up the bag does not get back in forty minutes
(normal journey time would fifteen) Julia's throat will be cut and
her body dumped on waist ground outside the city, IMEDIATELY.*

I put the paper down on the table. 'Nice typewriter Cliff uses,' I
said.

'The letter as I actually received it was in disguised handwriting.
The police have got that, of course. I got Penny to take a copy
before it went. Not that I mind. But I knew Julia would be round
sooner or later, wanting the story.'

'You knew that, did you?' she said coolly.

'Of course. You're very fond of Cliff.'

She stood up. 'Yes, I'm very fond of Cliff and I'm going to go and
see him in prison and give him every possible help I can.'

'You won't find it easy to see him. They make a lot of difficulties,
unless you're a lawyer.'

'I'm a close relative. And I'll have a lawyer with me.'

'All right, but let me tell you you won't have Frank Hopper
because he's working for me and he won't do anything that
damages my interests.'

Frank Hopper must have been their usual solicitor.

She demanded, 'How the hell can it damage your interests if I try
to help my brother?'

'Your brother has been a bloody nuisance to me and now he's
overstepped himself. I'd like to see him put away for a good long
spell.'

She stood staring at him. Every line of her body was rigid. 'Jake,
I'm not here to discuss things with you because as far as I'm
concerned we've got absolutely nothing to discuss. I just came to
find out about Cliff. But now that I'm here you can just tell me one

— 197 —

thing. What is all this babble you're giving me about Cliff over-stepping himself and you getting him put away? He'll leave you alone when I'm gone and he can't claim to be one of the family any more. You won't be troubled with him, why can't you just forget him? Unless, of course, you're going to tell me that you did give him twenty thousand pounds.'

'Of course not,' he said contemptuously. 'If you want proof that Cliff's brain is undeveloped, look at the utterly screwball way he tried to set the thing up. He actually was on that train. So was I. The ransom note was left here inside a cheap brief-case, the one that had to be used, so I did just as I was told. I took the right train and got in at the end carriage and sat in a non-smoker and read the paper, the whole business. Except that the brief-case was full of newspaper and there were half-a-dozen plain-clothes men on the train. When I got out at London Bridge, leaving the brief-case up on the rack, Cliff came along and tried to pick it up.'

'Was he really that foolish?' I couldn't help asking.

Delmore didn't look at me as he answered. 'He only did one thing that showed even the ordinary criminal degree of cunning. He had with him a brief-case identical with the one he'd left here. So that if he was picked up he could have some cock-and-bull story about mixing up the two. Taking the twenty thousand pounds by mistake.'

'Instead of which,' I said, 'all the police will be able to prove is that he took a brief-case full of newspaper by mistake.'

This time he did look at me, a brief, incredulous glare, as if the furniture had started answering back. 'They know he wrote that note. They know he tried to get twenty thousand out of me by blackmail. With threats of murder.'

'They've proved it? He's written a signed confession?'

'They're sure enough of it to keep him locked up till the whole story's sorted out. And don't tell me he'll get away with anything short of a stiff sentence. With his previous convictions, they'll lock him up and throw away the key.'

In the dead white of Julia's face, her eyes were brown pools of pain. She said, 'Jake, you wouldn't. You wouldn't do it to him. You know he's ill.'

'Nothing to do with me. It's the police who are prosecuting him. Why don't you go round and talk to them? Get them to drop their case?'

'I might,' she said desperately. 'At least I can hire a good lawyer. I'll find one from somewhere.'

'Julia, darling,' he said wearily, 'good lawyers cost money. You're going to divorce me, which means that except for what you can screw out of me for maintenance you won't have any money.'

Julia turned to leave. 'Congratulations,' she said over her shoulder. 'At least you've still got enough mental clarity to know what the situation is. Naturally I'm going to divorce you. Or leave you, at any rate. The details can come later. I don't want your money. Those two whores can have it.'

'Oh, they weren't professionals,' he said calmly. 'No one was working. Just a little evening party.'

At that, I knew I must get Julia out of there. If the bastard was going to torment her like that, flicking a cool whip at her face, the faster and further she got away from him, the better. I wasn't going to let this interview go on for one more moment. Quickly, I stepped in between them and said to Delmore, 'Julia's got rather a busy evening. I think I'll take her away now.'

'Oh, you'll take her away, will you?' he said nastily, coming up close. 'Suppose I want to talk to her?'

'You have no rights in the matter,' I said. If he wants to attack me and break my bones, I thought, let him do it. I haven't much more use for them.

But instead of hitting me – perhaps that bulk, and that dangerous look, went with physical cowardice, or perhaps he simply didn't care enough – he just said, 'She happens to be my wife.'

'Not any more,' I said.

Julia was at the door now. She opened it and said, 'Gus, come on.'

I turned my back on Delmore and walked out. As I did so I felt all my muscles tighten up, and I had to resist a nervous desire to spin round and face him. I didn't want him on my back in a flying charge, or landing his fist on the back of my head and stunning me. But he just stood there, and I followed Julia out of the flat.

Going down in the lift she didn't say anything. When we got outside the building she walked by my side to the car, mechanically, looking straight ahead. We got in, and I didn't ask her where she wanted to go. There was only one place we *could* go: my pad. I wished I had had a cheerful, pleasant place to take her to, where she could relax and forget her troubles. Nobody ever forgot their troubles in a place like the one I was renting.

Anyway, we went there. And she sat in a stiff, uncomfortable armchair and I poured her a drink and she still sat looking straight in front of her. I cursed the idea, then, of ever taking her round to see Jake. It had plunged her right back into depression: worse than depression, a state bordering on the shock she had been in when I first met her.

Since she was obviously not going to talk, I tried to fill in the time constructively by thinking. We needed a plan of campaign. Obviously the first priority was to help Julia to get into contact with her brother. She would never rest till she had seen him and heard all about this crazy pathetic escapade from his own lips – lies, evasions and delusions included. Probably the first step would be to get a lawyer – Frank Hopper or another, it hardly mattered. In all this, she would need help, and this (I reflected with a touch of opportunism born of my love) meant in turn that she would need me, that I still had some sort of role that I could play in her life.

Not that I hadn't enough work of my own to do: my well-earned holiday was over and I was due in the office on Monday morning. Miss Sarson would have a lot of work ready on my desk, and Daisy would be clacking restlessly about. But I could telephone and say I'd be in as soon as I could, and give the morning to helping Julia to get in touch with Cliff.

I even picked up the telephone and rang Pentonville prison, more for something to do than because I expected any results. Obviously they weren't going to tell any stray person who telephoned whether they had, or had not, a man named Cliff Sanders among their inmates. The warder, or whoever it was, who answered the phone could hardly be polite to me. He just told me to ring on Monday morning when the lady Welfare Officer would be on duty. She wouldn't give me any information either, but she might at least tell me where I could start asking.

'It's no good starting operations now,' I said to Julia. 'There's just nothing doing till Monday.'

She nodded bleakly. Then we just sat looking at one another. I wanted to lie down and howl like a dog. Were we the same two people who had been so happy, and so close together, in the cottage? Did the cottage really exist, and that lost, dreaming, green and purple valley, or had I just hallucinated it all?

Then Julia spoke.

'Gus, I'm sorry.'

'Sorry what about?'

'Oh, you know, don't pretend. I can see it all from your point of view. I was nice to you in Wales, we had fun together, you seemed terribly happy and much younger. Now it's all fallen to pieces, not because you've changed, you're just as nice, but because I'm too unhappy and lost to be nice to anybody. I just want to crawl away and hide. I don't like my own company, and I certainly don't expect anybody else to like it.'

'I understand about all that,' I said. 'You don't have to project towards me. I just want to help you, that's all.'

'Yes, but why do you want to help me? It's because you're in love with me, isn't it? I mean, you're a kind sort of person who'd probably be glad enough to help anybody, but you've got a special set of reasons for helping me, haven't you?'

'Yes. I can't bear the thought of not being with you.'

'That's just what worries me. I'm so far down that I just can't think of responding to you. Or to anybody.'

'Then don't. Just let me help you and don't try to respond.'

She shook her head. 'I can't live like that. I can't just take from someone all the time and not give. If I'm going to be alone in my mind I ought not to be with anyone. It's so cheapening for them.'

'Listen,' I said, 'don't worry about cheapening me. Life has gone pretty solidly wrong for me and there isn't much in the way of disappointment and frustration and loneliness that I haven't tasted since I turned forty. And I've reacted pretty badly, I've been selfish and frivolous. So if it's unselfish to try to help you even if you don't notice whether I'm there or not, well, I'm quite prepared to be unselfish for a bit. Just don't worry about it. Have another drink. Or some food. I've nothing in, but we can go out for something.'

'No, thanks. I just don't want food, or a drink.'

'What do you want?'

'I don't know,' she said.

'Well,' I said briskly, 'we might as well be practical. You'll be staying here tonight. Oh, no strings attached, I understand that. I know well enough that that side of our relationship is over unless and until you choose to restore it. But I don't see where you'll go, at this time of night, if you don't stay here. And I don't like the idea of taking you round to an hotel, dumping you there, and leaving you

— 201 —

on your own – not in your present state. So you'll stay here.'

She nodded unenthusiastically.

I thought fast. In the poky little bedroom I had a double bed. When I furnished the place I'd chosen a double bed in a fleeting mood of optimism, in case one day I found someone to share it with. In the eight months I'd been there it hadn't happened yet – and wasn't likely to, unless Miss Sarson happened to have a glass of vermouth too many at the office party one Christmas and decided to take a leaf out of Daisy's book. Obviously I couldn't expect Julia to climb into that bed with me: it was one thing at the cottage, but here the vibrations were all wrong. No, Julia must have the bed, and I would doss down on the sofa in the living-room, where I was sitting at that moment.

I was just about to start explaining this to Julia when she began speaking. I couldn't tell whether she was talking to me or to herself, but I listened anyway.

'I feel so lost. So lost. I don't know what my life was given me for or what use I'm supposed to make of it.'

Who knows that? I thought.

'Two weeks ago I had two men in my life. Now I look for those two relationships and what do I find? One of them has just simply crumbled into pain. The other – well, where is Cliff? How can I find him, how can I bring him any comfort? I can't sit him down in a chair, and cook him a meal, and be his sister and his friend and his mother all in one, not if he's going to be shut away from me.' Now the tears began to overflow. 'I'm useless, I can't mean anything to either of them, and they're all I've got. . . .'

Her voice choked off into sobs. As for me, I felt that a mountain of cold grey ash was settling down on me. In the candid honesty forced out of her by pain, she had completely forgotten that I existed. Gentle and giving as she was, she could not even discern my existence as a loving, needing person.

Well, might as well get that learnt. I remembered, in some cold pocket of my mind, that the bed had not been changed lately. I went and got out clean sheets and pillow-cases and stripped the bed and made it completely over. Everything was in perfect order. My limbs moved efficiently, my mind was cool and ordered, and I was all alone and dying.

When Julia finally stopped crying she got into bed and went to sleep. Her weeping did not subside gradually; it stopped as if switched off. She was utterly silent, drained, inert. For some curious reason it suddenly came to my mind that this was how she would be if, in her professional work as an actress, she was required to portray someone who had suffered emotionally till they could suffer no more. A deep, unfeigned sleep came to her quickly.

I shut the bedroom door and lay down on the sofa. There was no sound in the room except the traffic in the street outside, and no sound in me except the faint creak of my heart, withering away inside my chest like a dead grasshopper in the desert.

In the morning I made a pot of tea and took a cup to her in bed, just as I used to do at the cottage; and then we had breakfast together, just as we did there, and took it in turns to wash and dress, and it was all just the same as during our honeymoon, except that it wasn't, that there was a pall of depression and indecision hanging over everything, a feeling that life wasn't beginning anew but slumping back into its old, tired shape. But of course it was! My London flat wasn't a cottage in a Welsh valley. If you looked out of the window you didn't see the purple of the mountains, and the rowan-tree, and the bright, clear water of the stream hurrying over the rocks; what you saw was a featureless main road, shaken with incessant traffic. It wasn't very noisy at the moment, being Sunday, but that didn't make it any better. The depressed lull of an urban Sunday isn't peace, it's just emptiness. It was all different, and it was the reality; our honeymoon had been the dream, and my saving her life, and her clinging to me in bed, and laughing and singing in the kitchen, and drinking wine in the evening sun. All that was then, all this was now, and I had the dead valley of Sunday to get through before I could even have the anodyne of going to the office and sorting out Miss Sarson and Daisy.

Thoughts of the same kind were obviously going on in Julia's mind. She looked abstracted and rather depressed. While I was splashing about in the bathroom I heard her telephoning, though I didn't hear what she said, and when I came out she told me what was going on.

'I've just rung Judy. She's a friend of mine I used to work with. She's in a group that does children's theatre – it's mostly improvisatory, with the accent on getting the kids to join in. I've known her for years.'

'Yes?' I said.

'She's got a big flat. Normally her chap's there, but he's away in Canada or somewhere for a couple of months, so there's some spare room.'

'Yes?'

'She says I can move in for a bit. It'll be a place to go while I get straightened out. I mean, I can't stay here, under your feet.'

I was silent, too depressed to speak. She didn't need that little bit of polite evasion. Of course it wasn't a question of her being under my feet. It was that the situation we were in was a false one, full of unsolved and insoluble questions, and every hour she lived in my flat made things more uncomfortable.

She moved about, gathering up her bits and pieces, and when she was about ready to go she moved over to me and looked straight into my face.

'I'm not just walking out of your life, Gus. I want to be in touch with you. I mean, I'd miss you if I didn't see you.'

'Well, keep in touch,' I said, but the words came out flatly.

'You've been very good to me and I know you love me.'

'Yes, I do.'

'And I care about you. I really do. We've been very happy together and you've been wonderfully good and protecting and I like you very, very much. If I were in a different mood and it was evening and not morning and if we were drinking wine and sitting in front of a fire, I might even say I love you. I think with parts of me I do.'

'I know how it feels,' I said.

'And although I'm sure it's the best thing for me to go and move in with Judy, I'm not just going to walk out and leave you flat. Let's make a date. Let's go out to dinner together, *soon*.'

'All right. I'm free any time.'

'Well, it's Sunday now, let's have dinner on Wednesday evening. I'll ring and suggest somewhere to meet.'

So we agreed on that and she left.

How I got through the rest of that day I'll never know. After the door closed behind her I stood in the middle of the horrible little living-room and looked at my watch. It was ten past nine, and I had the whole day to get through. A light, gritty rain was falling outside. My soul was coming apart at the seams.

Suddenly the telephone rang, making me jump. I reached out for the receiver with a purely mechanical reflex. To hear the telephone ring and not answer it you've got to be on your guard, and I wasn't on my guard, and at once I realised that I'd bought it again, because it was Daphne, who else?

'Gus, why are you hiding from me?'

'I happen to have been away.'

'That's what I mean, running away, not facing up to anything.'

'It was my annual holiday and I was in North Wales. I've done all the facing up to things that I intend—'

'What about me? It must be very nice to go off and treat yourself to a holiday. Nobody thinks of offering me a break, stuck here at Hilda's, worrying my heart out, waiting for you to make up your mind.'

I took a deep breath. 'What d'you mean, make up my mind? I *have* made up my mind, months ago. We're getting divorced.'

'Gus, I'm coming round to see you.'

'I shan't be here.'

'I've been patient all this time, waiting for you to see reason. April's coming down soon, what am I going to say to her?'

'Well, what d'you usually say to her?'

'I've told her we're going back together.'

'You've told her *what*?'

'Well, Gus, we *are*, aren't we? You can't go on being so ridiculous. Or have you got someone else?'

'No,' I said.

'It would be just like you to get involved with some foolish little—'

'Look, Daphne,' I said, 'I'm living here on my own and that's how it's going to stay.' It probably is, too, I thought. 'And don't waste your time coming round here because I shan't be in.' Then I rang off quickly.

After that, I knew I had to go out. And the only place to go was the office. I couldn't stand the thought of walking about in the rain by myself, and besides there was the anaesthetic of work, never to be under-estimated. Of course there was always the element of risk, since Daphne, obviously, knew where the office was and might come looking for me there. But I could always lock myself in, and keep the light off, and just hold my breath if there was a knock on the door. God, how humiliating.

So I went round to the Howkins Press-Cutting Agency, silent and deserted in a silent and deserted building. There was a heap of letters waiting to be attended to – things that Miss Sarson and Daisy hadn't been able to cope with by themselves. Complaints, of course. Dear Sir, I pay good money to your press-cutting agency to supply me with every printed mention of my name. And behold, when I bought some celery at Frinton-on-Sea last week, wrapped round it was a copy of the *Churnet Valley Advertiser and Stock-breeder's Gazette* in which I am distinctly mentioned by name as having passed a vote of thanks to the Mayor. That kind of thing, plus my usual stint of reading. Back numbers of all the principal daily, weekly and monthly papers, London and provincial. My personal share of the work is a list of two hundred and forty names, all beginning with letters L through P. I have to keep all those names in my head and speed-read the complete range of papers, looking for them to jump off the page at me. It's soul-destroying work. Sometimes I wonder why I ever set up the agency. I must have had dreams of growing rich. Why else would one pour out the years of one's life like dishwater? I sat there in the heavy silence, answering angry letters and reading newspapers, till seven o'clock in the evening when the Sunday pubs opened. The office was two miles from where I lived and I decided to have a drink in every pub that lay directly on my route. I didn't cheat by going down any side streets or visiting pubs I could see in the distance; I had to pass the actual door, or, rather, not pass it. Even so, I went into fourteen pubs and had a drink in each. I wanted to smooth the rough edges off reality. All right, I know that's how people become drunks. This evening it struck me as quite a good idea, being a drunk.

So I was staggering a bit when I got back to the flat about a quarter to ten. Not much, because I have a strong head, but a bit. And my diction was a bit slurred when the telephone rang and I answered it.

'Howkins here,' I said, resisting a temptation to say 'Herekins how.'

'Gus, it's me, Julia.' She sounded agitated.

'Whass matter?' I asked keenly.

'I'm ringing up to alert you. The police are on to us.'

'Pleesh? On to us? Wha' for?'

'A policewoman came round to see me and get a statement. She's only just left.'

'They acted . . . pretty quickly,' I said, sobering up.

'I'd told Jake where I was, so that if he wanted to be in touch over

— 206 —

any legal business to do with our separating. . . . Anyway, the police asked him where I was and he told them here, and they've been on to me and I'm sure it won't be any time at all before they're on to you too.'

'On to me? What for?'

'Oh, it's all awful. Apparently we were breaking the law like *mad* when you kept me hidden away in the cottage while all that kidnap scare was going on. She practically told me we were accessories or something. Fellow-conspirators.'

'But that's ridiculous. You were in a state of shock and I kept you out of harm's way while this ineffectual lunatic was scooped up.' I was quite sober now, uttering long sentences.

'That's not how they see it. They say we knew about Cliff and we ought to have come forward.'

'It didn't make any difference. He'd already committed the crime – demanding money with menaces. And it didn't stop his being arrested – in fact the arrest probably wouldn't have happened if we'd been there, trumpeting that you were safe and well.'

She gave a sound like a sob, quickly caught and held back. 'Don't say that. It makes me think it's all my fault that Cliff's in prison.'

I said, 'It's Cliff's fault that Cliff's in prison. You were driven wild with unhappiness and had to run away from your life, and he tried to snatch a mean little advantage out of that, by screwing money out of your husband.'

'All right, you needn't start being hard and cruel about Cliff.'

'I'm not, for God's sake. I've got every sympathy with Cliff and I know he can't help what he does. But to say that you and I helped him is just—'

'Well, get your story straight in your mind, because I'm sure it won't be long before they come to you. This evening, I dare say.'

'You told them you were with me, of course?'

'I told the woman everything just as it happened.'

Everything? Just as it happened? Did you tell her we were happy? Did you tell her about the rowan tree and about the way the dawn light shone on the wall of the half-bedroom?

I said, 'You wouldn't want to try to deceive them. And they'd only find out anyway.'

'That's what I thought. So I coughed it all up. I'm sorry, Gus – I've got you into a bad situation.'

'Listen,' I said. My brain was cold and clear, though the whisky and beer I had had were still burning around in my veins. 'Get one thing straight. You were the best thing that ever happened to me. I'm not sorry I kept you in that cottage for a week, it was the only week of my life in which I was totally happy and that's worth all of it. If I go to prison for helping Cliff to blackmail Jake, I don't care, I don't care, *I don't care.*'

'When I was a child', she said in a small, sad voice, 'my old granny had a saying, "Don't care was made to care." '

'This don't care won't be,' I said. And at that moment the doorbell rang. 'I'll have to go,' I told Julia. 'Someone's at the door.'

'Oh, Gus, it's probably them. Oh, I'm so sorry, Gus.'

'Don't be. And remember our dinner date on Wednesday.'

'Oh, I will,' she said, but with a kind of undertone that suggested doubt as to whether we should be at liberty to do normal things like going out to a restaurant.

'I love you, Julia,' I said. 'Goodbye. I'll ring when I have anything to tell you. What's your number?'

As she gave it to me and I wrote it down, the doorbell rang again, imperiously this time.

I finished writing down Julia's number, told her not to worry, said goodbye, and took my time getting across to the door. It was a Jehovah's Witness, trying to sell me *The WatchTower* and a shiny book on bible prophecies. After I got rid of him it struck me that I ought to have bought the book. I could have used a few prophecies.

Then I told myself to be calm and do ordinary things, and above all have something to eat. Quite probably the police would be content with Julia's statement. After all, she was the wife, and once they had the husband's side and the wife's side. . . . I opened a tin of sardines and started to grill them. I had no bread, but there was a packet of pumpernickel in the cupboard. Grilled sardines and pumpernickel aren't my idea of a four-star meal, but I needed something to put down on top of the drink. The shock of Julia's message had sobered me momentarily, but I could feel drunkenness gathering for another assault.

The sardines were nearly ready when the doorbell rang again.

Detective-Sergeant Ambrose was a quiet man. He had a quiet voice and slow, deliberate movements. He introduced himself, and made quite certain that he was addressing Augustus Robert

Howkins, before informing me that he had come to take a statement. He waited to be invited before walking slowly into the flat and waited to be invited to sit down before settling his solid frame into a chair. Then he looked carefully at me and I looked carefully at him.

He had a broad face, on a thick pillar of a neck, and below that his shoulders were very wide and I could tell even through his jacket that his arms were muscular because the muscles obviously wanted to burst out of it. His hands were square, with short, clean nails. He wore very thick glasses and behind them his eyes peered myopically, giving a quizzical impression as if he were always on the point of saying something funny and rather ironical. His hair was brown, cut very short, and just beginning to go thin at the crown. He wore a heather-mixture tweed jacket and his tie was a smoky blue. He looked about forty-five.

'I have to caution you, Mr Howkins,' he said in his quiet, calm way, 'that you may be in trouble. Fairly serious trouble. I'm sure you know what I'm referring to.'

'Yes,' I said. 'You're referring to the fact that when Mr Clifford Sanders pretended to Mr Jake Delmore that his wife Mrs Julia Delmore had been kidnapped by an outfit called the Queen's Park Rangers or something—'

'The Crystal Palace Organisation.'

'– the said Mrs Julia Delmore was taking refuge in a cottage rented by me, Gus Howkins, the party of the first part, in Caernarvonshire, and that neither she nor I told anybody where she was until a week had gone by.'

He stirred his heavy shoulders slightly, looked at me with immense calm and patience through those pebble lenses, and said, 'That is just about the position, sir. I'm glad you're clear about it in your mind.'

I must have been slightly drunk still, because I came on more aggressively than I normally would, to a policeman. Policemen frighten me, as a rule. But something, either the drink inside me or the deep wish to be a big strong champion for Julia, made me give him a straight look and say, 'What I'm not clear about is why it was wrong to give shelter and rest to a woman on the point of breakdown.'

'Could you swear in a court of law that she was on the point of breakdown?' said his patient voice.

'I could if it would do any good.'

'Did you take her to a doctor?'

'No.'

'Have you any other person's word that she was in danger of a breakdown?'

'Well, she'll tell you the same herself.'

He sighed. 'You must see, sir, that that won't meet the needs of a defence in court.'

'I thought the law considered people innocent until they were proved guilty.'

'That is so, Mr Howkins, but people who are under suspicion don't cease to be under suspicion simply because they can produce an account of their motives that satisfies themselves and no one else.'

He had me over a barrel, and he knew it. But I wasn't going to give up straight away.

'Look,' I said. 'The girl was under extreme stress. She'd walked into her home to find two men, one of whom was her husband, conducting a sexual orgy with two girls. It shook her so much that she couldn't just sit down on the sofa and say, "Darling, isn't it time your guests went home and we had a drink and talked this over sensibly?" She was shocked, shattered, bitterly hurt, robbed, wounded, scalded. She couldn't sit still and she didn't know what to do. So she got into her little car and just drove and drove and drove until she got to the sea and couldn't drive any further.'

Detective-Sergeant Ambrose made no attempt to interrupt me as I poured all this out. Only when I paused for breath did he say, 'We know all this, sir. It's in Mrs Delmore's statement.'

'Forgive me if I tell you things you know already. But I suppose the reason you came round here was to find out how it looks to *me* – why *I* behaved as I did.'

'Very well, sir, go on.'

'I was on holiday in the neighbourhood. I was canoeing in the estuary and that was the only reason I happened to go by within a few yards of her and saw her face as she sat in the car with the water already swirling round the tyres.'

I stared at him and he said with that immovable patience, 'Well, sir, what was the face like?'

'You know what I'm going to say. It was the face of someone in a state of shock. Very pale, expressionless . . . *withdrawn*. I thought at first that she'd been taking drugs. But there wasn't time to speculate. Those tides come in very fast. If she'd stayed where she was, the car would have been under water in less than half an hour. In ten minutes it would have been in enough depth of water to make it difficult for her to get out, even if she'd had her wits fully about her, and when she did get out she'd have been a long way from dry land and with an eight-knot tide trying to push her off her legs. She might just have made it, but quite possibly she wouldn't. So I saved her life, you might plausibly say.'

He took out a little notebook and consulted it. 'That was ten days before you and Mrs Delmore appeared in London together, at Mr Delmore's home. It must have been very trying for her to be first upset and then in danger of losing her life. But did it take her ten days to get over it?'

'Nobody said it did. She came back to my cottage and stayed one night. Then she disappeared, early in the morning before I was awake.' Imagine the rest for yourself, Mister Detective. 'I went back to the wreck of her car, found some documents that enabled me to trace her, and went to London to see what was happening to her. I was in London all day and then I drove back at night. The next morning she turned up at the cottage again. But you know all that.'

'Yes,' he said, peering at the notebook in his ironic way. 'In between, she'd booked in at the Prince Llewelyn Hotel, Pwllheli.' He made quite a good job of pronouncing 'Pwllheli.' Somebody must have been coaching him. 'She booked for three nights but only stayed one. When she didn't come back and they found she'd left articles of personal attire in her room, the management informed the police as a matter of course.'

I liked the way he said 'articles of personal attire.' It was the first thing he said that made him sound like a policeman on the beat, which was probably where he'd started. I thought of her buying things in Pwllheli – toothpaste at the chemist's, a nightdress; perhaps some of those knickers made of paper, that you throw away the next day. Her few odds and ends. And then leaving them behind, rather than come out from the haven where I was hiding her. A great surge of grief washed through my heart. Why couldn't time stand still, and life be always as it had been during that week of happiness?

Detective-Sergeant Ambrose was moving his shoulders about,

settling his bulky body in his chair, in a way that I recognised as the preamble to an utterance.

'Mr Howkins, the object of this visit is to obtain a detailed statement from you, in writing and signed, about your part in the pretended kidnapping of Mrs Delmore and the blackmail demand by her brother. You'll appreciate that the law has to approach all these matters with an absolutely open mind.' He had a trick of clicking with his tongue before a sentence that was going to be important: not exactly sucking his teeth, but moving his tongue against the front of his palate in a way that made a little sound like *tsk*. He did it now. 'Clifford and Julia Sanders are brother and sister. She marries Delmore. The marriage turns out to be unhappy and becomes more and more so. I gather she's now left him altogether. But before taking that step, she disappears into a remote valley in North Wales, and her brother demands a large ransom from the husband, claiming to be the mouthpiece of a gang of expert kidnappers.'

'Yes, but surely you can see—'

'Wait a minute, please. *Tsk*. The law has to be open-minded. It has to start from the facts as they can be established, and to look at them objectively. Mr Delmore is a successful actor who makes a lot of money. His marriage to Mrs Delmore dates from before that success, when they were both struggling. Isn't it a probable hypothesis that she feels jealous of that success and money, and, since she isn't happy with him, wants to prise him loose from a good solid sum before she goes? And gets her brother to help her?'

'No,' I said. 'It isn't probable and you as a detective must know it. You must be saying it as a test, to see how I'll react.'

'Why isn't it probable?'

'Because her brother has a criminal record. He's always been unstable and anti-social, and she's always been worried about him and tried to help him where she could. If she were going to get up to any such absurd business as you describe, she'd never choose to work with her brother. Apart from being known to the police already, he's an obvious figure of suspicion because he's been sitting on the sidelines of their marriage for some time, trying to get Delmore to take him on as his manager or something equally crackpot. Of course as soon as there's any hint of trouble it's Cliff who's going to get investigated. In the event, he makes such a childish farce of it that he's arrested before there's any need for an investigation. It's an open and shut case – a nut behaves in a nutty way and is caught. What he needs is psychiatric treatment.'

'*Tsk*. That's what all criminals need. But there aren't enough psychiatric hospitals to put them in, or enough doctors to attend to them, so we have to put them in prison. They probably wouldn't have responded to psychiatry anyway. Prison makes them worse, so they come out and do the same kind of thing again, and they go back into prison and it makes them worse still, and so it all goes on.'

'And you spend your life,' I said, 'hunting down these people so that they can be put in prison and come out years later more twisted than ever?'

He looked at me through those thick glasses and said, 'What d'you want us to do? Leave them running loose in society? All the thugs and the thieves and the arsonists and rapists and the men who beat old ladies with iron bars to get their handbags off them and steal their Old Age Pension?'

'I take your point,' I said, 'and I'll admit that I find those questions too difficult to solve. So let's get back to my own predicament. Julia Delmore goes off on her own, her brother brings out this cock-and-bull story of a kidnap, and I find her and give her house-room for a week. So that makes me an accessory before the fact or whatever you call it.'

'She was away and nobody knew where she was.' Detective-Sergeant Ambrose ticked off the points on the fingers of his right hand. 'Her brother was playing on her husband's natural anxiety by demanding money. So, he was committing a crime. So, anybody who helped him, who furthered his cause in any way, was also committing a crime. As an accessory. To get out of it, you'd have to prove that you knew nothing about the ransom demand at all – that you just treated her as a person who needed help and you gave her what help you could.'

He stopped and gave me a look that made me feel there was something else in his mind. Something that he was wondering whether to put into words, or not. But all he actually said was, 'But you did know. You telephoned to say she was all right.'

'Does *that* look as if I were helping Cliff?'

'Anybody was helping him,' he said, 'who kept Mrs Delmore hidden where she wouldn't be found.'

I thought I had better go back to an area where I felt reasonably safe, so I said, 'You must have done enough background enquiry to know that Mrs Delmore and I had never met until that afternoon on the shoreline. Until I saw her sitting there, I didn't know of her existence.'

'Tsk. That fits in with her statement.'

'Since it happens to be the truth, I'm not surprised that it does.'

He looked down at his hands as they lay calmly in his lap, then quickly up at me. 'I take it from that, sir, that you consider yourself and Mrs Delmore to be two completely truthful people?'

'I didn't say that. I know that completely truthful people are very rare. Perhaps they don't even exist at all, because when people aren't consciously deceiving others they're probably doing it unconsciously. But I'm perfectly certain that neither Julia nor I would be the type to make up any lies in a situation like this. She, because she's too sensible. I, because I'm too frightened.'

'May I ask what you're frightened of, sir? Have you ever been in trouble with the police?'

'Never in my life. I'm law-abiding because the whole business of the law brings me out in a cold sweat. I'm frightened of policemen because I'm frightened of handcuffs, and cells, and stone corridors, and little high-up windows with gratings, and warders with bunches of keys, and the thought of sitting in a cell with two other men and a chamber-pot with a wooden lid.'

'You've got an active imagination, Mr. Howkins.'

'I know I have. It's supposed to be a good thing.'

'What puzzles me,' said Detective-Sergeant Ambrose, 'is why, if you have such a distaste for crossing paths with the police, you should have acted in a way that you knew was an obstruction of justice.'

I opened my mouth to say I didn't know it, and then I shut it again. Of course I knew the reason why I had kept Julia in the cottage, but it wasn't one I could tell to him, or to anyone in an official position. In the eyes of the law, in the perspective of the whole cool, decision-making, punitive world, it was a non-reason. 'I did it because I was in love with her, your honour. She was making me happy, and I haven't been happy for so many years that I couldn't bear to bring it to an end.'

How could I say that to Detective-Sergeant Ambrose?

He probably knew it already, anyway. From the look he gave me when he said 'You gave her what help you could,' I could tell the whole thing was clear enough to him.

— 214 —

So I gave up arguing. I got the typewriter out and wrote a statement, telling him before each sentence what I was going to put in it. I set out all the facts. When I had finished he read it through in his slow and careful way, got me to sign it and put it in his pocket.

'Thank you, Mr Howkins,' he said, getting to his feet. 'We shan't need to trouble you any more tonight. One thing I must ask you, though quite unofficially. You're back from your holiday now. You'll be dividing your time between this flat and your office mostly.'

'Yes. My office is at—'

'We know where it is,' he said quietly. 'All I wanted to say was, quite unofficially, that we'd prefer it if you'd stay at home for a few weeks now. Don't be tempted to take any more holidays in remote cottages. We shall need to be in touch with you.'

'And it'll look bad if I don't co-operate?'

'It looks bad already, sir. At the moment, we don't propose to take you into custody—'

'My God! I should hope not!'

' – but if you start getting dodgy, we may have to.'

'You needn't worry,' I said feebly. 'I'm not a dodgy person.'

'Thank you, sir. Good night.'

I went back from the office early the next evening; as soon as we closed, in fact. I was too frightened to do anything else. I had the feeling that even if I went and sat in a cinema Detective-Sergeant Amrose would come and sit in the next seat, quizzing me rather than looking at the screen. So I bought some food and went home, through the rainy streets, to cook it.

Home! I thought, as I let myself in and switched on the light. What a place to be calling home, at my time of life! The only thing that cheered me up was the sight of the canoe, stowed away in its two big green bags, lying in a corner. It reminded me that there were other things in the world besides my worries – that there were rivers, and fish, and flowers growing on the banks, and harmless fun in the open air, and feeling well.

I had some food and tried to settle down with a book, but I was so unsettled that I kept reading the same sentence over and over again. When the doorbell rang, I was positively relieved, even though I was convinced it was Detective-Sergeant Ambrose coming to take me away in a Black Maria.

As a matter of fact, it was Julia.

'Come in, come in,' I panted. 'My God, I've never been so glad to see anybody in my life.'

Even as she stood there on the landing I could see that she was tense and anxious. She was blinking rapidly, as she had done when we were just going in to see Jake.

'Did the police come round?' she asked me straight away.

'Take your raincoat off, at least,' I said. 'Here, let me hang it up. Yes, a Detective-Sergeant came round and took a statement.'

'It looks bad, doesn't it?'

'It might be worse. At least we're not locked up.'

'That could still happen,' she said, and shivered. 'I couldn't stand that. My marriage to Jake was a kind of prison, during the last months. And just when I'd got out of it and was starting to breathe the free air. . . . I tell you, I'll *die* if they lock me up.'

'Now listen, Julia,' I said. 'Nobody's going to lock you up. Cliff's in trouble, and possibly I am too, but you – you're just the innocent victim of all this.'

'They don't think so. You should have seen how that police-woman treated me. She was all motherly and protective, probably it's a standard manner they learn for dealing with delinquent girls of sixteen who run away from home and hang about bus shelters, but behind it I could feel she was cold and accusing. I'm sure she thought I was a criminal.'

'It doesn't matter what she thinks. If it comes to a trial, it'll be a matter for the judge and jury. And you'll have a defending counsel. I'm sure you've got nothing to worry about.'

She sat down and stared at the electric fire. 'I believe you're right, Gus. And of course I came round here to get comfort, to have you say exactly that kind of thing to me. But I only believe it with my brain. With my body, I can't feel anything but fear. My blood's afraid and my bones are afraid and my belly's afraid.'

I knew how she felt, because I felt just the same myself.

'And another thing,' she said, almost crying now. 'I went to see Cliff this afternoon. It was awful. I just couldn't get through to him. He's gone into a world of his own – he's reverted to what he must have been like all those years in prison. I wanted to discuss plans with him, to work out a strategy. And d'you know the only thing he'd talk about?'

'What?' I said.

'A five-pound note,' she said through set teeth. 'He kept asking me to bring a five-pound note and slip it to him. He says he needs money to buy his way into the prison barter system. I kept trying to get him to talk about the situation generally, and what chance he had if he pleaded not guilty, and I kept telling him I'd get him a lawyer and he must talk to him and tell him everything, and try and grow up and act responsibly, and he just didn't seem to *hear* me. Every time I stopped talking he started going on about how he needed a fiver. It was *horrible* . . . I felt I'd lost touch with him already. Towards the end, he wasn't listening to me and I wasn't listening to him. Communication had broken down. And that's before he's even convicted! What's it going to be like when he's been locked up for ten years or however long it's going to be?'

'You think he's certain to be found guilty?' I asked.

'Well, wouldn't you find him guilty if you were a judge and jury?'

'No,' I said. 'I'd refer him for psychiatric treatment. He's just inadequate.'

'That's the awful thing, he's ill, but not in a way that anybody can help him with. If he had bad lungs or was paralysed or something, he'd go to a nice comfortable hospital and everybody'd be sorry for him and be as nice to him as they possibly could, but because it's his mind that's ill, they lock him up, and what else can they do? If they don't lock him up he goes about being a nuisance, and telling lies to people, and working out little schemes for getting the better of everybody, and it's all so pitiful, pitiful!'

And now at last the tears came. I took her in my arms and she sobbed and sobbed and drenched my shirt-front. Broken half-sentences and strangled words kept coming out, mingled with snorting and sobs. I had never known a woman cry so tempestuously, and it went on and on. I was deeply moved to pity, and yet I was not so frightened on her behalf as I had been during those earlier times when she had been in stunned, frozen despair. The very violence of this grief seemed to me to have something healing in it.

She shook, and sobbed, and mumbled, and grasped at me, and gradually our two bodies seemed to become one. How long we half-lay, half-sat, slumped in that armchair I don't know, but long before we straightened up I knew how it was going to end. I knew we were not going to disentangle, and stand up, and groom ourselves, I straightening my tie, she wiping her face and combing her hair, and then start making cool, responsible, ordinary conversation, looking at our watches and planning this and arranging that. I knew that, having clung to me in that spasm of demented grief, she was going to cling to me for the rest of the night, in bed.

And so it turned out.

8

As Giles Hermitage arrived home and opened the front door of his flat he looked at his watch. Almost three-thirty. Might as well go back to bed for what was left of the night. Might as well get some rest. Might as well this, might as well that.

He undressed and lay down in bed, staring up at the dark ceiling. No thoughts came. He preferred it this way. It was as if his mind had been dowsed under an enormous extinguisher, the size of a meat-cover. Lying perfectly still, thinking of nothing, he had only one impression: that it was essential to keep still. Somewhere in the room, it seemed, there was an enormous and very sharp two-handed sabre, ready to sweep across and decapitate him if he sat up. The only way to be safe was to lie motionless and supine.

Dawn crept up outside the windows. A weak light spilt into the room. Briefly, Giles slid below the level of consciousness. For an hour or so he was neither asleep nor properly awake. When he came back to full wakefulness, he did so in slow, gradual stages, his body waking before his mind.

As soon as he was up and had drunk some tea, he went straight to his desk. His mind gratefully accepted the obligation to think about Gus Howkins and Julia Delmore, to observe Jake in his gilded setting, to stand about warily like Dennis, to gaze calmly at human folly through the thick lenses of Detective-Sergeant Ambrose: even, if necessary, to posture and dodge and evade like Cliff. What he could not do was face, for a single instant, his own experience as it built up outside the charmed circle of his desk. He did not know what to do about Helen Chichester-Redfern, or what to feel about Dinah, or what kind of life to plan for himself; he did not know how, or even whether, he was going to survive.

Sitting down, he stared heavily at the last sheet he had written, reading over and over again the words, 'she was going to cling to me for the rest of the night, in bed.' That was it, she was going to cling to him, she was torn with grief and he was going to lie close to her, bringing her comfort with the warmth and strength of his body and the solidity of his love for her. That was the nature of love – it was warmth, it was shelter against the bitter winds of life. He knew all about love, he had had it with Harriet *you're boringly secure* with Harriet *you're boringly secure* Harriet Harriet gone Australia gone married and now he was having it was going to have it had had it with Dinah. *When you get to know me better. Why I have to have things to hold me together. My faith of course. My music. I shall go to early Mass, Father. I like to be good at things.* And those deep burning eyes in that wasted face. *It's right that he should have some pain. Bring peace to my tormented spirit.*

Shut the door on it. Shut tight. He could not deal with it, any of it. Never mind it. Ask nothing. Why was the doctor still there no no. Why did she not want visitors no no. Ask nothing. Do nothing. Think nothing. *Ring me tomorrow* no no. Leave it all. No need to go there again. Princess Terrace, no. 2. You must know the house. You so often go past it. Not again.

Gus, Julia, Jake, Penny, how cosy. A world where he could call the tune, shape events. If I wanted to make Detective-Sergeant Ambrose retire from criminal investigation and open a little sweet-shop. If I wanted to make Dennis get into the lift with Penny and flash his wang at her as they glided upwards. If I wanted. If I wanted. They would have to:

All day he worked, ignoring Mrs Pimlott, pausing in mid-afternoon to gulp down a few mouthfuls of the lunch he neglected at midday. Towards evening he was in such a trance of fatigue that he could drive his pen onward only by paying obsessional attention to calligraphy, forming each letter as if making an illuminated manuscript. Rapid scribbling was for those times when he felt the surge of energy: when that energy was spent, he wrote with the deliberation of a craftsman, obsessionally.

At last he stood up from his desk, moved across to his bed and lay down on it without undressing. The scimitar was in the room again. He had to lie still, as the darkness deepened and became total. As he lay there, covered lightly with one blanket, a voice boomed in his head the lines he had known for so many years and never understood till now:

But that two-handed engine at the door
Stands ready to smite once, and smite no more.

Once more he lay awake most of the night and at last sank into a state more like an uneasy trance than a sleep. But as the sun came up he rolled on to his back and went to sleep in good earnest. He was woken by the insistent ring of the doorbell.

Who could be calling on him at this hour? Dragging himself back to consciousness, he looked at his watch. Eight-twenty. Who on earth. . . ? Smoothing down his rumpled clothes, he went to the door, deciding *en route* that it must be the postman with something that needed to be signed for.

It was Dinah in her silvery raincoat and hat, smiling at him.

'Hello, aren't you up yet? I thought you were a morning person.'

'I am as a rule.'

'Well, I seem to have woken you up this morning. D'you mind very much?'

'I don't mind at all.'

He held the door open and she came in.

'I thought you'd be having breakfast and I suddenly imagined the smell of fresh hot coffee. I've been to early Mass. They call it Communion but I call it Mass. The Catholic names are the right ones. Of course I didn't have anything before I went. I came out feeling terribly empty.'

Giles muttered something about putting the kettle on and made for the kitchen. He felt terribly unprepared. Having lain all night in his clothes (why? why had he done that?) he seemed to himself a foul object, crumpled and haggard. He felt sure his body must be giving off a sour reek. Why did she always put him at a disadvantage? Not only physically but mentally, spiritually, she was neat and fresh and organised, he was seedy and sagging. Yet he knew that, at the core of his being, he had a strength that was greater than hers. It was just that she was so continually alert, so unremittingly *ready* for life.

He started the kettle boiling, and returned to find that Dinah had taken off her hat and coat, hung them up neatly, and had lit the gas fire and was sitting on the floor beside it, warming her hands. All in the time it had taken to fill the kettle. She had on the dark-brown dress with the bright check pattern in the V at the top. She looked, as he had seen her look before, at once demure enough for a church and lascivious enough for a bordello. Lying on a small table near the door, he noticed her handbag and, neatly placed beside it, a small volume bound in morocco leather and marked with a gold cross. Of course! Her prayer-book!

'Where did you go to this Mass?'

'At the Cathedral. And don't call it "this Mass." It sounds disparaging somehow.'

The Cathedral, he reflected, was about equidistant from here and from Princess Terrace. If her thoughts on emerging were occupied with hot coffee and only hot coffee, she might just as well have gone home. So she must have had some kind of impulse to see him.

But was it on, or off? Were they lovers or had he been displaced, already, by the ginger-haired doctor? Or was he – shudderingly – supposed to share her with the g.-h. d., and with anyone else who caught her fancy?

What went on?

'D'you mind if I make the coffee?' Dinah asked, getting to her feet. 'I'll probably do it more quickly than you and I'm particular about how it tastes.'

'Go ahead.'

'Is everything where I can find it?'

'If it isn't I'll help you,' he said, sinking into a chair and staring at the gas fire.

She went into the kitchen and he heard clinking and pouring.

'White or black?' she called.

'White. The milk's in the fridge.'

'I knew it would be, silly.'

Incredibly quickly, she was beside him with two large cups of coffee, and had sat down on the floor again with hers. She enjoyed her coffee as she enjoyed everything, devouringly, savouring the steam in her nostrils as well as the liquid on her palate and the warmth in her throat.

'Mm. That's better.'

'D'you want some breakfast? You must be hungry.'

'I never eat breakfast. I have coffee and have a bath, and then I have some more coffee and do the crossword. Then I'm ready for the day.'

'But of course today you had your bath first, then went to the Cathedral, and you're having your coffee now.'

'Yes.' She smiled.

'What about the crossword?'

'I'll do it after lunch.'

'Which is it, *The Times?*'

'Of course.'

They were talking like two people who had just met at a party.

'Well,' he said, setting down the empty cup and rising from his chair, 'I'll shave and have a bath. I must be a disgusting object.'

'Why are you dressed? Did you sleep in your clothes?'

'Yes.'

'Why?'

'Oh, because,' he said, and went into the bathroom. There, he started the bath-water running, and while it filled he cleaned his teeth and shaved. Then he rummaged in the linen-cupboard for a clean towel (remembering suddenly but painlessly how this particular towel had been bought for him by Harriet), and with sigh of contentment got into the bath. Life might be too much to cope with, but there were still hot water and soap.

Pleasure and drowsiness engulfed him. Lazily, he soaked his forearms, the part of his body that probably least needed washing but was accessible with the least effort. Then the door was gently opened and Dinah came in. Sitting down on the most convenient place, which happened to be the lid of the lavatory bowl, she surveyed him calmly.

'I like looking at men in the bath. They're like great smug animals, lying there.'

'I'm not men, I'm me.'

'I know you're you. But you're men as well, or I wouldn't like you so much.'

She was rolling up her sleeves.

'What are you going to do?' he asked.

'Soap you, of course.'

Kneeling on the bath-mat, she bent over him with the calm concentration of a nurse. Taking the soap, she methodically worked up a rich lather, while her eyes brushed over his body as if selecting at what point to begin. With a sigh, Giles abandoned himself completely to her spell. She could do what she liked, be what she liked: he loved her.

She soaped his chest, then his thighs. He knew that sooner or later her hands would arrive at his phallus. They did. Her pale, alert face gazed down at the effect she was producing.

'It's getting bigger all the time.'

— 223 —

'What did you expect?' he moaned.

'I can't stand much more of this,' she said softly. Then, abruptly, she got to her feet.

'You're not going to stop there!'

'Of course not.'

She disappeared into the living-room, and reappeared naked. 'This is a morning when I'm going to have two baths.'

Giles had a sudden, appalled vision of Mrs Pimlott letting herself in. In the same instant, he remembered that it was not one of her mornings. But even if it had been, this would just go ahead and to hell with all the Mrs Pimlotts in the world

Dinah stepped into the bath and submerged opposite him. The water-level rose to within an inch of the top. He reached down past her to the plug and let some out.

The next hour rendered out-of-date Giles's sexual fantasies of thirty years. When it ended, they were lying side by side on his rumpled bed, and Dinah was looking at her watch.

'I must get back. The nurse goes off duty at ten.'

Good God, he had entirely forgotten about her mother. The poor dying woman might never have existed. But he could not feel guilty. He could not feel anything but happy.

'Has the nurse been there all night?'

'Yes. Ten till ten.'

Dinah was dressing.

'May I see you home?'

'Of course.'

The nurse opened the door to them. She was wearing the complete outfit, starched cap, starched apron, right down to the rubber-soled black shoes. This slightly surprised Giles, who had vaguely imagined that nurses dressed up like this only when they worked in hospitals.

She was a quick, strong, lively little woman, but when she saw Dinah her face became expressionless.

'Oh. Thank goodness you're back at last.'

'Of course I'm back. Has something happened?'

'Everything's happened. I've called Dr. Bowen. He's upstairs with her now.'

Dinah went straight up the stairs, leaving Giles standing just inside the front door, feeling in the way. The nurse, having admitted them, shut the door again, and Giles's first instinct was to open it and leave at once. If, as was clear, Helen Chichester-Redfern had become even worse than when he last saw her, there was nothing he could do, and some things he could hinder, by hanging about. He was turning to go when the nurse said, 'I've just made some tea, if you'd like a cup.'

He did not need tea, but he interpreted something in her voice as a request for him to stay. Perhaps there were things she wanted to tell him. Thanking her, he followed her into the kitchen and sat down on a wooden chair. His legs ached and his pulse was irregular; he had not slept adequately for two nights, it was barely ten o'clock in the morning and already he had scaled a sexual Everest. A voice inside his head asked coldly, 'How much longer can you go on living like this?'

The nurse gave him his tea and sat down on the other chair, looking at him appraisingly across the table.

'Did you meet Diana in church?'

'No. She called on me after the service.' Suddenly he saw in his mind's eye her morocco-red prayer-book with its gold cross, lying within earshot of the rapid *oh-oh-oh* of her orgasm.

The nurse stirred her tea in an irritated manner. She had a strong, bony face that had once been handsome. Her hair was very fair, and now that it was beginning to go grey, the grey and the gold caught the light in the same way and it was difficult to know which was which.

'I suppose it's important to go to church. Or the Cathedral or whatever it is. I don't bother with all that myself. But I do see it's not the sort of thing you can object to. So when she said she was off there, I couldn't very well ask her to stay. But her mother's been bad all night.'

'Bad?'

'In pain, and very exhausted. Getting worse all the time. You never know how long people will hang on, but in the light of my experience I'd say she won't see tonight.'

Abruptly changing the subject, she said, 'You live near the Cathedral?'

'Not very far.'

Her normal human curiosity was engaged, even at a time like this. (But then she was very inured to death.) She wanted to know why Dinah had called on this man, why she had spent over an hour with him while the last grains of her mother's life were running out. (But if he told her, detail by detail, she would never believe it.) And why he had escorted her home.

'We haven't been introduced,' he said, 'but perhaps you know me?'

'Yes, you're that writer man she admires so much. She's got all your books up there. I've been looking into them now and then when I've been here at nights. Very interesting.'

She said 'Very interesting' in the way people say it when they are shown the traces of a Stone Age village, or the lay-out of a South-East Asian catamaran, when they happen not to want to know about these things.

'Did you get to know the mother first, or the daughter?'

'Both on the same day.' He was giving nothing away. Yet he felt that his adventures of that morning must be written on his face.

'Well, pretty soon there won't be a mother to know.'

'Did Dinah,' he forced himself to ask, 'did she know when she went out this morning that her mother was so bad?'

The nurse considered. 'Basically, yes. I tried not to be alarmist of course. I just told her I'd been busy with her most of the night. If she'd gone in and seen her she'd have noticed a change for the worse, but she didn't. I just heard her getting ready to go out and then I heard her going down the stairs. So I called to say her mother was having a bad spell, and she called back that she'd be home before I went off duty.'

'Just that?'

'Just that. "I'll be back by ten," those were her words.'

Giles drank some tea, thoughtfully. What he deduced from those words was not Dinah's heartlessness – he had already identified her as a person to whom compassion did not come easily, perhaps did not come at all – but the fact that she must have planned ahead to come and visit him. If she had intended originally to go to Mass and come straight back, she would have said 'I'll be back by half-past eight.' So she must have formed her intention before going to worship. Getting up, having a bath, dressing, gathering up her prayer-book, she must have been thinking ahead to those savage ecstasies they had enjoyed. He had a quick vision of that pale, lascivious face composed in prayer.

'I've seen 'em all,' said the nurse. 'A death takes people in a lot of different ways. If they love the person who's dying very much and

— 226 —

don't know how they'll get on without them, they sometimes go to pieces. Men more often than women. But you can never tell ahead of time. With some, it brings out the best in them.'

'I suppose so.'

'But one thing I am sure of,' said the nurse. 'I never saw one as cool as this one. Not a close relative, that is. Housekeepers are different. Unless they're looking to inherit – they make a big fuss then, to convince you it isn't the money that's in their thoughts.'

A heavy tread on the staircase: Dr Bowen was coming down. Giles stiffened. He did not want contact with this man. If there was any point in it, he would go through with a meeting: but was there any point? Ought he not to cut out now, and keep in touch by telephone?

His escape-route was blocked. The bulky form of the doctor filled the kitchen doorway as he came in.

'Go off duty, nurse,' he said.

'Yes,' she said submissively. 'I'm off as soon as I've drunk this tea.'

The doctor put a small case on the kitchen table and started rummaging through the contents. He ignored Giles.

'You'll be coming back tonight?'

'Ten till ten again. Or shall I be needed before that?'

He shook his head. 'Heavy sedation. She may never need anything again. Except laying-out and burial.'

The nurse said timidly, 'You're leaving her here? There's no point in getting her to hospital?'

'The hospital's too full already. You know that. There's no point in letting her lie in a hospital bed just to die.'

'No. I just thought. . . .'

'Don't think, nurse. Go home and get some sleep.'

'If the kids next door will let me,' she said, reaching for her overcoat.

'D'you want a soporific?'

'I've got all that. But when they play cowboys and Indians under my window, nothing works.'

He nodded soberly. 'Well, get as much rest as you can and don't come back till ten tonight. I dare say there'll be plenty to do then.'

'Will Miss Chichester-Redfern be able to manage till then?'

'If she needs any help I'll give it to her.'

The nurse departed. Dr Bowen snapped the case shut, then sat

— 227 —

down at the table and began writing on a slip of paper. Giles sat still, determined to say nothing until he was spoken to – which, he realised, might not happen at all. There was a newspaper on the table; he was sitting on the wrong side of it, but began reading it upside down. He had just spelt out

SOVIET REPLY TO WESTERN NOTE

when he became aware that Dr Bowen had raised his head and was staring at him coldly.

'Are you likely to be here this morning?'

'Well, I'm here now. I could stay on if there was anything I could do to help.'

The doctor stood up. 'The woman's dying. I've put her into deep sedation. I have some other calls to make but I'll be back this afternoon. You'd better stay till then, if you can. The girl oughtn't to be left alone with a dying mother. I know she's been dying for months but there ought to be someone supporting her when she actually goes.'

Giles nodded. So he and the doctor were to share that supporting duty. All other thoughts banished. Well, it was fitting.

'And if you want something to do for the next few minutes, till I leave,' the doctor said, 'you can go and collect this prescription.'

He held out the slip of paper covered with cryptic medical handwriting. As he did so his grave, impersonal expression subtly changed. With the minimum alteration in the lines of his face, it became the exact expression of a prefect giving an order to a fag. The switch from a gruff, off-hand, just-within-politeness manner to an unspoken insolence was skilfully managed: Giles had to admit it. If this was the calibre of the modern physician, the nation's health was in safe hands.

He made no move to take the prescription from Dr Bowen's hand. After the barest hesitation the doctor laid it down on the table before him, and with no further words strode briskly out of the room. Giles heard his strong, assured tread going up the stairs. Sitting by himself, he tried hard to focus and control his emotions, but they kept slipping away into a blur of contradictions. Then he had recourse to an old device, stepping back into the protecting circle of art. Supposing he were writing this story instead of living it, how would he rough out a possible conversation, the plot having got to this point, between the novelist and the doctor? Tapping his fingers lightly on the table, Giles tried out a few possible ideas.

Dialogue 1.

GILES   A couple of nights ago I came to the door of Dinah's room and pushed it slightly open. I could see she had the light on in there but she wouldn't let me come in. When I went into the street I saw your car.

DR BOWEN   How did you know it was my car?

GILES   It's a Rover, in a distinctive shade of dark red.

DR BOWEN   There are a lot of those about.

GILES   All the same, I have an idea that it was you she had with her. Am I right, by any chance?

DR BOWEN   That's a professional secret, Jack.

Giles got up and refilled his tea-cup. The dark brown liquid was cold and stewed, but he sat down and sipped it while he tried another variant.

Dialogue 2.

DR BOWEN   I'm glad you're here, Hermitage. I've been wanting a word with you.

GILES   Yes, I'm here. What is it?

DR BOWEN   I ask you as man to man, do you think it's decent to try to come between me and Dinah?

GILES   I might ask you the same question.

DR BOWEN   Don't equivocate, man. I was in the middle of an affair with her when you came on the scene. I know it can't last, but I had looked forward to receiving her undivided attention until all this is over and she goes back to London.

GILES   Who ever had her undivided attention?

DR BOWEN   Some people must have. Did she ever tell you about this organ player, Mark?

GILES   You're damn right she did. She can't go many minutes without talking about him.

DR BOWEN   He really had her where he wanted her. A free whore who wouldn't give him any diseases.

GILES   Well, it seems to be all over now.

DR BOWEN   I wouldn't bank on it. He'd only have to snap his fingers and she'd come running. But meanwhile it's

	between you and me, and I'm asking you to do the decent thing. First come, first served. I had her going very nicely and I don't relish competition.
GILES	What are you going to do about it?
DR BOWEN	(darkly) I expect I'll be able to think of something.
GILES	Look, you must know that in this field of illicit sex there aren't any moral imperatives. It's a jungle – you just take what you're powerful enough to get.
DR BOWEN	All right, if there are no moral imperatives, what's to stop me waiting for you on a dark night and bashing your face flat with half a brick?
GILES	Nothing, except that your hands are probably tied like most people's. I bet you've got a wife and family. You look the type who would. They'd be hurt by the scandal.
DR BOWEN	Certainly I've got a wife and family. And a beautiful home. My family life means a great deal to me. My children are doing well at school and my wife does the flower arranging for the Harvest Festival. What's more, this year she was the runner-up in the Inter-Women's-Guild Treacle Tart Shield. I tell you, my home life is a dream of happiness.
GILES	Then why do you go about having sordid promiscuous affairs with young women?
DR BOWEN	That's what makes my home life a dream of happiness.

No, no, he thought, setting down his empty tea-cup. None of this had the ring of truth. He was indulging in the mental equivalent of doodling; if these dialogues had been written down, he would have crumpled them up straight away. Why could he not focus the doctor? Why could he, an experienced professional writer, not think of an exchange between them that might actually have taken place?

He tried one more time.

Dialogue 3.

GILES	Shall we be frank with each other?
DR BOWEN	Convince me first that there's something to be gained.
GILES	I can't do that. Clear-sightedness, truthfulness, are

— 230 —

distasteful to many people and you might be one of them.

DR BOWEN You must know that when you put the matter like that, you turn it into a challenge I can't refuse without feeling inferior.

GILES Very well, accept it. Are you in love with Dinah?

DR BOWEN I'm very attracted to her. I suppose she's just amusing herself with me, but it's an amusement I'm very willing to share. 'In love' is a vague term.

GILES To you it may be. To me, it's precise. It indicates a degree of emotional need. Related to pleasure but not identified with it.

DR BOWEN Are you asking me to state the degree of my emotional need for this girl? Surely you can see that's impossible.

GILES Impossible or not, all the indications are that someone is going to get very badly hurt in this situation, and soon. If she makes a choice of one of us and drops the other, the dropped one will be hurt. If she carries on playing us off against each other, we'll both be hurt. But you, I suspect, less than I. You have a wife and family – some of your emotional needs must be catered for in that quarter.

DR BOWEN I'd rather not discuss that.

GILES It comes down to this – we're both helpless in her hands. And she's without compassion: it was left out of her make-up. She keeps up the charade of being a Christian, but the chief moral virtue of Christianity, charity, is scarcely even a word to her.

DR BOWEN That's all right with me. If she hurts me, she doesn't have to feel sorry for me. I'll go it alone.

GILES I envy you that stoicism, and I pray that I may never need to emulate it.

Giles had barely finished sketching out this hardly more credible scenario when he heard the doctor coming down the stairs and, immediately afterwards, the closing of the front door. He was gone. Now the house was shared between Giles, the young woman he loved, and the old woman who had drawn him into this situation and who still, from her deathbed, continued to exercise an inexplicable magnetic pull at his emotions.

— 231 —

Everything was silent. What was Dinah doing? Some pitiful service for her mother? Or, if the mother was sedated almost to the point of non-existence and needed nothing, was the daughter sitting by her bedside in quiet contemplation? At all events, it was unthinkable to go up and disturb them. He would wait down here. Better still, he would go out to the chemist's and get this prescription made up.

Putting on his coat, he went out. There had been a slight shower of rain, and now the fresh April sunlight was covering everything with sheets and lines of gold. The world seemed a strange, dreamlike place, where anything could happen: very beautiful, very lyrical, and very dangerous.

The pharmacist told him Mrs Chichester-Redfern's prescription would take twenty minutes to prepare. Rather than go back to the house, he spent the time pacing about in the only green space in the neighbourhood, which happened to be a churchyard. It was old, no one had been buried there for over a hundred years, and the tombstones were being sucked relentlessly into the soil, canting over, as they went, at various drunken angles. It was as if the occupants of the graves had joined some endless subterranean Bacchanal among the earth-spirits. Giles's sense of unreality increased. He could easily be dreaming the whole thing. But he went back to the chemist's and there was a neat little parcel of white paper with two strips of Scotch tape. As he took it in his hand, he came back to the world of the concrete and the expected.

Dinah was downstairs when he got back. She was in the kitchen.

'Hello.'

'Hello,' she said shortly, not looking at him.

'Any change in your mother?'

She shook her head. 'There won't be, now. She's in the last stages. At least I hope so, for everybody's sake.'

She poured some coffee, and without asking set a cup in front of Giles. They sat at the table and drank in silence. At last he said, 'D'you want me to go?'

'No.'

He waited to see if she would add anything to this bare negative, but nothing came.

'D'you mind if I sit in your room?' he asked at last.

'No.'

Setting down his empty coffee-cup, Giles went into Dinah's

sitting-room and settled himself in the armchair with *Lotte in Weimar*. After three or four pages, he discovered that he was reading the same sentence over and over again. Giving way to his fatigue, he closed his eyes. When he opened them, Dinah was in the room. She had changed from her Cathedral-going dress and was in a white shirt and jeans. He had not known she ever wore jeans. He followed her with his eyes as she moved about the room, tidying it. Her waist was incredibly slender and supple; the jeans followed the outlines of her crotch as if they had been sprayed on; as she moved about she wriggled her hips, unconsciously and ever so slightly. A wave of sleep-tinged concupiscence washed through Giles's body.

'Dinah,' he said.

'Yes?'

'I love you.'

What he had meant originally was 'I lust for you,' but the words modified themselves as they came out, and the second statement was truer than the first; it included it, moulded it, lifted it up.

'I'm pretty pro you too,' she said. 'I like having you about.'

'Is that as far as it goes?'

'How far d'you want it to go? To tell someone you can stand having them about is high praise as far as I'm concerned. It's as far as I ever go, anyway.'

'I'll settle for it.'

'Would you like a drink?' she asked. 'It's time you started waking up for lunch. You've been snoring for hours.'

'Oh! Not *hours!*'

'Well, a hell of a long time, anyway. You must have been tired. I suppose you're getting a bit old for the sort of thing we were doing earlier on.'

'Most men, of whatever age,' said Giles with dignity, 'feel exhausted after making love at breakfast-time. And yes, I will have a drink, thanks. Anything you've got in the house.'

She gave him sherry. While they sipped, she came and perched on the arm of his chair.

'Stay here today. You're a help.'

'All right, I will. Thanks.'

She ruffled his hair gently. 'I know I don't seem to be taking much notice of you. But you understand, don't you? Most of me is away somewhere. But it's nice to have you here.'

— 233 —

'I'll stay,' he said.

They kissed. Then she said, 'I'll look at Mother and then get us a bite to eat. I'm *starved*. That's what fucking always does to me.'

He wished she had not added those last words.

She slid off the arm of his chair and vanished. He heard her light, rapid tread going up the stairs. Then silence. Then his name called from the bedroom.

'Giles.' Her voice was dead, flat, drained of resonance.

He went to the foot of the stairs and called up, 'What is it?' When she did not answer, he went up and through the open door of the bedroom.

Helen Chichester-Redfern lay rigid on her back, her nose pointing up at the ceiling, her eyes not quite closed so that a tiny half-moon of white was visible in each of them. Her hands lay in stiff attitudes on the counterpane. Dinah stood absolutely still, looking fixedly down at her.

'What's happened?' he asked.

'I can't feel any heartbeat.'

Giles moved forward and took up one wasted wrist. The cold, reptilian feel of it immediately told him he was touching dead flesh. There was no heartbeat, and no breathing.

'Well, it's happened,' he said.

'She's dead?' Dinah asked quietly.

He nodded. 'She just went off while nobody was looking. That last big shot of sedative must have finished her.'

'Well,' Dinah said in that flat voice, so different from her normal interested liveliness, 'there's no point in pretending we're sorry. It was what everybody was hoping for.'

'Including her,' he said.

'Including her.'

Dinah went out of the room. Giles lingered a moment, looking down at the dead woman's face. He felt a sense of anti-climax. Was this all? The heart quietly gave up, the breath stopped moving in and out, and all that remained were a few formalities, a form to be signed, and a lump of refuse to be shovelled into the earth. He felt that some farewell should be uttered, some concluding words found, but what? The woman on the bed had struggled seventy years for happiness and fulfilment, and lost: and now it was all history, trivial anonymous history, the history of nine-tenths of humanity.

He went down the stairs. Dinah was at the telephone.

'Well, when he does come in,' she was saying, 'just tell him that my mother died this morning, a couple of hours after he left. We shall need him to sign the death certificate. Thank you: good-bye.'

She put the telephone down and said, 'Dr Bowen's wife doesn't like me.'

'Has she ever met you?'

'No.'

'Well, that's why she doesn't like you then.'

She sank down on the divan and said, 'I ought to send a wire to my father.'

'I'll do that. Just give me his address.'

Sending off a transatlantic cable occupied Giles for the next ten minutes. When he returned, Dinah had taken up her guitar and was picking at the strings. 'All done,' he said with an effort at cheerful matter-of-factness, but she seemed not to hear him.

Inclining her head over the instrument as if it were imparting confidences to her, she fingered and plucked and at last went into a rapid pattern of notes that sounded, or at any rate sounded to Giles, like Bach. He sat and listened. The music, beautiful and intricate, made a circle round her from which he felt excluded, but this did not distress him; it was impossible to be jealous of something so delicate and so generous.

Still she played on as the afternoon light crept across the floor: if she had any thought for the dead woman upstairs, or for that matter for the food she had offered him, she did not show it. In these first hours of the new freedom and new desolation of having no mother, she was alone with her music.

Only once, in what must have been more than two hours of playing, did she pause and look across at him.

'You're still there. I'm glad. D'you know what that piece was?'

'No.'

'It was by Smith Brindle.'

'I never heard of him.'

'Well, you have now,' she said and moved straight into another piece, this time tempestuously Latin, with thundering chords and high, plangent flights. In the middle of it, there was a knock on the door.

Giles answered it: he expected Dr Bowen, but it was the nurse.

— 235 —

The doctor had telephoned her, she said, to come round and see if there was anything she could do.

'Well,' he said, 'there's nothing you can do for the mother any more, and as for the daughter, she's getting help that neither of us could give her, from her music.'

'So I hear,' said the nurse disapprovingly, as inside the room Dinah's music started up again. 'But there is something I can do for the mother. I can get ready to lay her out.' And she went upstairs.

Giles went back into Dinah's room; she was playing again, but fitfully; the spell was broken. As he entered she stopped and said, 'What's that woman doing?'

'Just the routine things.'

She put down the guitar, moodily. 'D'you think it's awful of me not to be up there with her?'

'If you want to know what I think,' he said, 'I think you've done as much for your mother as anyone could possibly expect of you. Now she's dead and you're off the hook.'

'You say that because you want to please me. I expect underneath it you think I'm pretty awful. I bet you think it was wicked of me to be fucking with you this morning when my mother had only a few hours to live.'

'You weren't to know that. She's been officially dying for months, you couldn't have known that this was to be the day. And I don't see why you shouldn't get your needs satisfied.'

'Especially if it happens to satisfy *your* needs at the same time.'

'All right, be nasty to me if it helps you. I'm in love with you, I can't help it, you're the most attractive girl I've ever met, and I'd rather go to bed with you than do anything else in the world. Meeting you was a better piece of luck for me than getting the Nobel Prize for Literature would have been. So naturally I'm pleased if you get into my bed. And the fact that your mother was about to depart this life seems to me nothing much more than a coincidence. She might have died while you were receiving the sacrament, if it comes to that.'

'Yes,' she said, expressionless. 'I made my peace with God first, and with your prick afterwards. That's the life of a religious woman.'

'If anyone else said that, I'd assume they were being satirical. But I'm getting used to the way your mind works.'

— 236 —

'And how does it work? Tell me, I'm interested.'

There were a number of things Giles could have said in answer to this, and he rapidly surveyed them in his mind. He could have said, for instance, 'I've now realised that your religion is a purely liturgical exercise, undertaken for your emotional comfort, and involves not even the beginnings of an effort to bring your behaviour into line with the teachings of the sage whom you describe as your Saviour.' Alternatively, he might have said, 'Totally selfish people, who live entirely for their own pleasure and convenience, always exercise a certain fascination over ordinary, mixed-up people. Their purity of motivation is hypnotic to the rest of us, who are never certain from moment to moment whether we are living for others or living for ourselves.' Or he might have said. . . . But at that moment there was an imperious ring at the front door and he rose to admit Dr Bowen.

It would not be quite true to say that the doctor pushed past Giles without taking any notice of him; he took as much notice as a preoccupied Edwardian businessman would have taken of a housemaid. Putting his head in through the door of Dinah's sitting-room, he asked shortly, 'It's all over, then?'

'Yes,' Giles heard her answer.

'Has the nurse come?'

'Yes,' again.

'I'll go up,' he said.

Once more he came past Giles with the barest glance in his direction. Giles was interested to see how completely the doctor in him had driven out the man. He heard a low-voiced colloquy between doctor and nurse upstairs, without being able to make out any words, then went and joined Dinah.

'D'you want me to go, now the doctor's here?' he asked.

'I don't want you to go at all. I want you to stay here all day and all evening. You're a free agent, but if you want to please me that's what you'll do.'

'That's what I'll do,' he assured her, and sat in a corner of the room to wait.

Presently the doctor came down. Standing in the centre of the room, filling it with his presence, he looked down impartially at the two seated figures, but his words were only for Dinah.

'I've signed the death certificate. Natural causes. The nurse is laying her out. Have you an undertaker in mind?'

— 237 —

She shook her head.

'The nurse will handle all that if you want her to. There really isn't much else for you to concern yourself with. You'd better get some rest. There's bound to be some nervous reaction, probably more than you quite realise yet. I'll prescribe you a sedative.'

'I don't want one,' she said.

'I'll prescribe it all the same.' He scribbled something. Giles suddenly thought of that neat white package he had fetched, only this morning, from the chemist. Medicine for a woman who would not live to take it. Care, love, skill, wasted on the dying. It happened every day. And was it any less wasted on the living?

Dr Bowen stood looking down at the slender girl who had solaced herself, these past weeks, with his body. She lifted her green eyes and returned his gaze absent-mindedly, as if he were a stranger sitting opposite her in the train.

'Let me know if there's anything you need,' he said. 'You're not registered as my patient, but for the time being I regard you as being under my care.'

'That's good of you,' she said indifferently.

Suddenly Giles remembered the third of his fantasy-dialogues, and the last line he had thought of for the doctor to say. 'If she hurts me, she doesn't have to feel sorry for me. I'll go it alone.' In the silence of the room he could almost hear the man's voice saying those words. And he remembered also: *She is without compassion: it was left out of her make-up.*

Dr Bowen picked up his little case and moved towards the door. His leave was wordless. No one said 'Good afternoon.' The little politenesses had crumbled like discarded plastic toys.

The door closed behind him, and Giles knew that he had won a victory, though how much meaning there was in it he dared not speculate. Let it suffice that he was here, alone with her. Oh, no, not alone: there was the dead woman on the bed upstairs, and the living woman busily making her presentable for the grave.

They sat silent. Presently the nurse came down, discussed a few matters with Dinah, and took her bleak leave. Now they were alone. The daylight was sinking. Dinah switched on a small lamp. Its pool of light seemed to draw them together, isolated in an uncomprehending world.

Then, abruptly, she said, 'I'm hungry. I want a steak smothered in onions. And a baked potato in its jacket. And a big salad.'

'There are restaurants that serve all that,' he said. 'Get your coat.'

He telephoned; a suitable restaurant would be open in half an hour.

'That gives us just time to get ready,' he said, taking charge.

'I don't need to get ready,' she said. 'I'll just walk out as I am.'

'Well, I'll wash and comb my hair. I feel dishevelled.'

He went upstairs and splashed about in the wash-basin. It was a strange thought that the room next to the bathroom, so lately the scene of all that intensity of need, was now nothing more than a store-room for a dead body.

Giles looked in the mirror. He saw a man tired, ageing, but alive; still in business with life, still taking, still giving. He pulled down his jacket to take some of the creases out of it, re-tied his tie, combed his hair and went down. A steak smothered in onions, a bottle of wine, the frank talk of lovers.

Dinah was lying face down on the divan and he saw at once that they were not going anywhere. Her shoulders were shaking. He sat beside her and tried, gently, to pull her over so that he could see her face, but she buried it fiercely in the cushions while the storm of weeping swept through her.

'Dinah, darling, darling,' he said gently, 'I understand.'

'No, you don't,' her muffled voice came through snorts and sobs.

'I do, yes, I do.'

She suddenly snapped upright and stared into his face with eyes still brimming.

'You think I'm crying because I loved my mother and I've lost her. Well, I'm not. That's just what you would think, you're stupid, you've got a big pulpy heart and you think that makes you holy.'

'I don't – I—'

'You're too stupid and sentimental to know what I'm feeling. I'm crying because I *didn't* love my mother and I *shan't* miss her. I can't love anybody, I can have good times with them but I can't love them, now do you see why I'm crying, damn you?'

He saw. And he held her close to him in a compassion deeper than any need he had ever known.

9

THE NEXT MORNING JULIA WOKE UP IN A POSITIVE FRAME OF mind, full of resolve. She was no longer afflicted with that rapid blinking, a small fact on which I silently decided to congratulate myself.

'Are you very busy today?' she asked me, leaning up on one elbow.

'I suppose the straight answer is that I'm always busy, but never too busy to do things with you.'

'Can you get an hour off this afternoon? To come with me to see Cliff?'

'Certainly,' I said. 'But are we sure I'll be allowed to? Isn't there some law against fellow-suspects getting together?'

'We'll see,' she said. 'I'll ask Frank Hopper.' So she had decided to consult this Hopper after all, in spite of Jake.

She did ask him and, rather to my surprise, it turned out to be all right. Prisoners on remand are allowed visitors at the discretion of the authorities, and I could pass muster, even though I was involved, because I hadn't actually been charged with a specific offence. They were just keeping me under observation, like a duodenal ulcer.

We had lunch together and went to the prison at two-thirty. Never mind if I don't specify which prison it was. They're all much of a muchness, except the psychiatric and top-security ones. Those are ante-chambers to hell, the rest are ante-chambers to ante-chambers to hell.

Frank Hopper met us outside the big oak doors. He was standing under a framed notice that listed all the things it was forbidden to bring to prisoners. He was a tall, youngish man whose hair was thinning in an exaggerated V. It was quite thick in a stripe down the middle of his head, but the sides were going. His brow was very

lined, as if he spent a lot of time worrying, either about his clients'
troubles or his own.

'You'll have to wait while I sort it out,' he admonished us at
once. 'I've cleared it formally but we still have to get straight with
the warders who actually do the supervising.'

'Shall we wait out here?' Julia asked. He gave her a suspicious
look and said, 'No, no, you have to be in the waiting-room.' He
made it all sound like some obsessional game that had to be played
by the rules. Quite right, I suppose.

The waiting-room had the usual stink of human misery. There
were wives and kids and old mothers and skulking chaps who might
have been anything. Since Cliff was on remand and therefore
entitled in theory to some little comforts, I had taken a box of
cigarettes for him. A warder came round and collected it and gave
me a signed receipt. So far so good.

We waited a long time. The waiting-room had some more
notices up about what you could and couldn't do. One of the
women was crying, steadily, and a boy of about fourteen, who was
with her, stared at her in frozen embarrassment.

At last we were cleared. Frank Hopper came in briefly and said,
'It's all right to go in. He's allowed two visitors. Just one thing – are
you free this evening?'

Julia looked at me and I said, 'Yes.'

'I thought it might be useful to have a conference,' he said. 'At
Jake's place.' He looked more worried than ever, but added, 'It'll be
a help if we all get together and straighten out the position.'

Julia said, 'Does it have to be at Jake's place?'

'He won't agree to it otherwise,' said Frank Hopper, 'and he's in
a position of strength because he's the only person who's done
nothing illegal.'

'No,' she said reflectively, 'I suppose driving your wife out of her
mind isn't illegal.'

'Don't let's get into all that, Julia,' he said quickly. 'You know
the worst crimes aren't always the punishable ones. I'm only a
lawyer. See you at eight o'clock.' And he ducked out.

Then a warder came and beckoned us to go into the visiting-
room. It was a long, narrow room with little tables down the sides. I
had vaguely expected to sit behind a partition and talk to Cliff
through wire mesh. Not that I'd ever visited anyone in prison
before; I must have seen it on the films or something. But it was

more humane than that. You just sat at these tables, as if in a café, and a warder sat high up at the end, where he could see what everybody was doing. Humane. Except that the place had the sour reek of captivity that no antiseptic can ever scrub out. The walls were dark-green up to shoulder height, and above that they were custard-yellow. I shall never see dark-green and custard-yellow together, for the rest of my life, without wanting to lie down and howl.

Cliff was sitting at one of the tables, waiting for us. He had his grey suit on. His pathetic little smart business suit, rather square-cut on the shoulders. It made him look like an insurance salesman, which is, I suppose, what he ought to have been. He smiled at the sight of Julia, but when he saw that I was with her his smile vanished.

'What's the idea, bringing him?' he asked as we went to sit down.

'You're allowed two visitors. I suppose I can bring Gus if I like. He's deep enough into it all, surely.'

He shrugged, impatiently, and said, 'Have you got it?'

'Cliff,' she implored, 'for God's sake talk about something else. I'm here to help you to plan, to see if we can get you out of this mess, even now, and all you can talk about is—'

He motioned her brusquely to silence, though her voice was too low to be heard by the warder on his platform.

'You mean you haven't got it?' Cliff scowled.

'I never said I would. I don't think you ought to start breaking rules and trying to buck the system at this stage. Can't you just be patient and wait and see what can be done?'

'Patient!' He almost spat the word at her. 'Have you any idea what it's like in here?'

'Well then, let me try to get you out.'

He glanced round, as if checking whether the warder was looking at him, then said, 'All right, let's be realistic. Nobody's going to get me out. They've got hold of me and they're going to get a conviction. It saves them trouble. Once they've convicted me they can leave me to rot in here and wash their hands of the whole business.'

'Besides,' I couldn't help putting in, 'you *are* guilty, aren't you?'

Cliff stared at me uncomprehendingly, and I was dismayed to see that even Julia shot me an injured look. After a pause Cliff said, 'Guilty?'

'Well, yes. You did cook up that story about a kidnapping, and try to sell it first to me and then to Jake Delmore, didn't you?'

'You ought to grow up,' said Cliff, pitying and contemptuous. 'Nobody cares about guilty and not guilty. They're just words. It's a machine, that's all – it draws you in and it chops you up.'

'That's what we're still hoping to stop, Cliff,' said Julia.

'Give up hoping,' he said. 'They've got me and they'll keep me. My only way now is to make the adjustment back to prison life. I had long enough outside to start looking at life differently. For the next stretch of years I've got to get back my prison psychology. Well, I've started. I know the ropes, I'm up to all the dodges that make life in the nick just that little bit more comfortable so you can stand it and not be broken. I can keep fit, I can do press-ups in my cell, I can talk to people and give them the benefit of my experience, I know how to deal with the hard boys, I know the right approach to the screws and the doctor and the chaplain and the governor. I've got it all doped out and from now on that's all there is for me. But one thing I need. A lousy five-pound note. And you, my own sister, won't bring it to me. How do you like that?'

He almost had me reaching for my wallet to give him a five-pound note there and then. But I knew it was against every conceivable regulation to try to slip money to a prisoner, and involuntarily I stole a glance at the warder on duty, sitting impassively on his perch at the top end of the room. He was very tall and bony and his face was very grim. He looked like the kind of prison officer who would be kept in reserve until the inmates had done something that really called for punitive action. I shuddered. Inwardly I decided that, if I once got out of this situation, I would never again infringe the law in the slightest particular. Not even a parking offence would I commit, if it meant starting on a path at the end of which one met chaps like him.

Despairingly, I took my eyes off the warder and looked sidelong at Cliff and Julia. I had never seen them together before. It was a strange sensation. They were so obviously brother and sister, yet so totally different. They both had these oval faces, brown eyes and black hair, and clearly defined, not to say slightly prognathous, jaw-lines. But he had those impossibly far-apart eyes; and where her face was open his was closed: not just closed, but collapsed somehow, as if it had drawn itself inward in an attempt to hide every thought that was passing through his brain. And where she had that beautiful stillness, he was as restless as a ferret.

'I'm trying to get you a decent lawyer,' she was saying to him. 'Cliff, do pay attention. Frank Hopper's going to put me in touch with a good man. And when he comes to see you you must tell him *everything*. For God's sake don't try to be clever with him or he can't help you – won't even try, if he thinks you're holding out on him.'

'Lawyers can't do me any good,' he said. 'Look, all I need from you is the very simple piece of help I described to you yesterday. Now, I'll give it to you again.'

'I won't listen. I'll walk straight out of here.'

'Tell *me*, Cliff,' I said, just to keep the peace and make her stay in her seat a little longer in spite of the despair I could see on her face.

He gave me a very hostile look, and at first I didn't think he was going to reply, but after looking across at Julia and seeing how stony with refusal her expression was, he thought better of it and turned to me.

'All right, I'll tell you what to do. Come tomorrow and bring a tin of cigarette tobacco and a packet of papers. You're allowed to give me a smoke during visiting time, and I like to roll my own, see? Now, the screw'll be watching, but I can sit well forward and he won't get a clear look. You hand me the packet of fag papers and I'll take out the top one. Only it won't be the top one, it'll be the fiver, rolled up tight. I'll take it and it'll disappear in the palm of my hand – you'll see. Then I take a real cigarette paper and you pass me the tin and I'll roll one. A couple of puffs, my hand goes to my shirt, and the fiver disappears for ever. But once I get back to the lads, I'm in business. With that small amount of money, I can buy myself into the system.'

'You use money to buy tobacco which you then use instead of money?' I asked him.

'Yes, dad,' he said scornfully. 'Try to picture it. You can't pass money around in the cells. Chaps are afraid to handle it. If they're searched and found to have money, they get hell. But snout's all right – they're allowed to have that, and if they have a bit more than they normally would have, who's to keep tabs on it? Now, there are just one or two points at which snout can be bought for money: a bent screw here, a well-organised ring there. I know where to tap them, 'cause I know my way round in clink, see?'

I listened in silent horror. It seemed to me that his voice, and his vocabulary, had become coarser, more proletarian, since he had shed the slight veneer of worldly sophistication that came naturally to him in the outside world. He no longer seemed to say things like 'Let's put it this way.' His persuasive technique had all been dropped, no longer needed. His horizon had diminished, to the corner of a cell, a whispered conversation in a corridor, the furtive handing-over of a twist of paper in the shadows of a wash-room.

And the most dreadful thing of all was that the diminution seemed to make him more comfortable.

Julia made one more attempt to get Cliff to see the situation in its entirety, but nothing could budge him from the five-pound note. It was rather like visiting an eleven-year-old boy at a prep school and trying to talk to him about the overall scope of his education when all he wants is a new cricket bat so that he can improve his game and get into the First Eleven. As I listened to them wrangling in low, urgent voices, it struck me, chillingly, that his grip on the situation was probably, all things considered, as realistic as hers. The hope of getting him out was doubtless a forlorn one. He seemed not even to consider the possibility of avoiding a prison sentence, and of course he was right. Sooner or later, when his trial came up, Julia and I were going to be put in the witness box and asked whether Cliff had, or had not, been responsible for the kidnap story. And of course he had and we would have to say so. I, in particular, would have to recount all that guff he had been giving me in Luigi's Espresso Lounge. I toyed, as I sat there, with the idea of trying to keep it to myself; I had left it out of the statement I had written for Detective-Sergeant Ambrose, merely saying that I had been in contact with Cliff and that he had given it as his opinion that Julia had been kidnapped. But I knew it would come out, under cross-examination from a clever and determined lawyer, within two minutes, and I glanced again at the granite-featured warder. No, no, the thought of laying myself open to the vindictiveness of the law, of entering that world of imprisonment and punishment, was not to be borne, except for some supremely important cause that would allow me to think of myself as saint and hero. And was defending Cliff such a cause? Was it even justifiable at all?

The best place for Cliff, I thought bleakly, was inside, where he could do the least harm. In the end, even Julia would see that.

They had finished their dialogue by this time and lapsed into silence, stubborn on his side, baffled on hers. The last few minutes of visiting time dragged by, and none of us said anything. Then the unsmiling warder got down off his chair and said it was time to go. A few last messages, the odd tear and sniff, a handshake between a prisoner and an old man who looked like his father, and the whole meek flock of us were filing out of the door.

As Julia turned away from Cliff she said, 'I'll come again when I've found a lawyer.'

'When you do,' he said, 'don't forget the errand.'

She shrugged and walked out without looking back at him.

The turnkey let us out into the street, and we stood there feeling empty and deflated. Then Julia said, 'Thanks for coming with me, Gus. Will you be coming to this talk-out at Jake's tonight?'

'Certainly,' I said.

'I'll see you there, then,' she said, and began to move away.

Naturally I was hurt that she didn't suggest having dinner beforehand, or going for a cup of tea now, or doing anything together. Just going separately to Jake's, as if I meant no more to her than Frank Hopper.

'You'll see me at Jake's,' I said. 'Just like that? No contact in the meantime?'

She gave me a wan smile and said, 'Gus, I'm sorry, I know how you must feel. But I've got to crawl away by myself and hide for a few hours. I can't face talking to anyone or being with anyone. I'm in too much of a state.'

At that, of course, I understood and I let her go.

I spent the next four hours working like a madman at the office. I didn't manage to shift the load of work that was waiting for me, but I was, I hoped, enough of a controlling presence (Augustus Caesar) to prevent Miss Sarson and Daisy from actually going on strike. They were beginning to get fed up with having to run the business on their own. So I worked and worked and worked, and for several stretches of a quarter of an hour or so I managed not to think of Cliff or Jake Driver or even of Julia.

At five-thirty I sent the women home; at seven o'clock I closed the office, went to the next-door pub for a sandwich and a glass of beer, and at eight I was at Windermere Gardens. I didn't take the car. It was back at the flat; I use it as little as possible in London and in any case I was so utterly sick of driving that I didn't care if I never saw the damn thing again. I took a bus over to Jake's, and I didn't hurry;

I didn't want to be the first to get there and have to make laboured conversation with Jake – or, more probably, to endure his freezing silence – so I hung about in the street, waiting till someone else arrived. Pretty soon a car drew up and Frank Hopper got out. I was just breathing a sigh of relief – if he was there, the talk would be professional and to the point – when to my surprise the bulky figure of Detective-Sergeant Ambrose hauled itself out from the passenger's seat. After the usual screening by Dennis, the two of them got into the lift. I was speculating on what it meant, that they should have turned up together, when a taxi stopped and Julia was there. She turned to pay the driver, and I came up alongside her.

'Oh, hello,' she said and gave me a warm, responsive smile. Evidently she had licked her wounds and got back to something like normal.

'I think the party's ready to begin,' I said. 'Frank Hopper's just gone in, accompanied by the plain-clothes man who came round to see me. I don't know what that bodes.'

'Nor do I,' she said, 'but we're going to get some progress one way or another. Let's go up.'

She swept past Dennis with the ease of one who was, nominally at least, still a resident of Windermere Gardens, and there we were, ringing the Delmore bell once more.

Penny opened it, her orange hair shining softly in the lamplight. She and Julia exchanged little sounds of hostile politeness, and then we were in the big room with the long black sofa. Jake was standing in the middle of the room; Hopper and Detective-Sergeant Ambrose, who must have just sat down, got up from their armchairs at Julia's entry.

Frank Hopper introduced the detective to Julia and then launched straight into the proceedings.

'Detective-Sergeant Ambrose and I,' he said, 'have just come from a quiet little dinner together. We know each other non-professionally, as it happens. We've been talking over the situation, and I'm going to keep quiet while he tells you the line of thought we've been pursuing.'

Julia sat down on the sofa and I sat beside her. I noticed that she kept her eyes off Jake. She was very still and composed.

Detective-Sergeant Ambrose started by looking at all our faces in turn with that ironic, short-sighted gaze. He had on a dark suit, not the jacket and flannels he had worn on his visit to me, but the muscles of his arms and shoulders pushed against the seams in the same way. He made quite sure he had our attention, and then began speaking in his quiet, even voice.

'What I have to say is strictly off the record. It's entirely unofficial. On the other hand, it wouldn't be quite true to say that it represents my own opinion and nothing but that opinion. I'll tell you straight away that I have been in consultation with officers higher up, and that they know what I think and are prepared to give it some weight.'

He stopped and was silent, looking intently at the doorway. I turned and saw Penny standing there. She looked lovely in her white dress and gold chain, but Detective-Sergeant Ambrose was obviously not impressed.

'This is Penny, my secretary,' Jake Driver explained. 'She's stayed on a bit late, finishing some work on a contract.'

'Will she be going home now, sir? Because if it's all the same to you, my few remarks are meant only for the ears of the people who are primarily concerned in the matter.'

'I've finished anyway, Jake,' she said quickly. 'I'll be off.'

'Thank you, Penny. Same time tomorrow, love.'

She was gone and the door had closed behind her. But Detective-Sergeant Ambrose still wasn't satisfied. He got up from his chair and walked into the room where Penny had been, stayed there for a moment, then came back and sat down again. I conjectured that he had been looking to see if she had left a tape-recorder switched on, or anything of that kind.

'To recommence,' he said, looking round at us all. 'Everyone here has some reason to be concerned in the case of this poor devil Cliff Sanders. Mrs Delmore knows him as a sister, Mr Delmore as an in-law' – *Not for much longer*, said Jake's angry-bull expression – 'and also as a man who has harassed him with threats and tried to extract a large sum of money from him by means of those threats. Mr Howkins knows him as a man who spun him a cock-and-bull story when he was pursuing some private investigations of his own, and who, wittingly or unwittingly, has got him into a very awkward position with the law. And then of course there's us, the police. We know Clifford Sanders as a man with a criminal record, whose slippery ways have landed him in prison once before. So we're all concerned with him.'

We all sat perfectly still. Looking quickly round the circle, I couldn't help being struck by the difference between Jake and Julia, who were trained in controlling their bodies and faces, and the rest of us. Hopper looked as if he were acting, and I felt I probably did too.

'Now, there are two ways of looking at Cliff Sanders and the situation he's brought about. The first is the tough way. He's a nuisance to society, he's been a nuisance before and unless he's watched very carefully, or somehow persuaded to change his ways, he'll be a nuisance again. According to this view, what he wants is a long prison sentence and that's the end of it. He's tried to obtain money with menaces, he's put everybody to a lot of trouble, he's been arrested, which means that a charge will have to be brought against him. You can't just arrest people and let them go as if it was all a game, not in this country anyway. If he's in custody he's got to be brought up for trial. And when he is brought up, it's going to look bad, and the tough view is that it ought to look bad. The worse for him, the better it's going to be for everybody else.'

'Except those who love him, if anyone does,' Julia's voice suddenly spoke beside me. Detective-Sergeant Ambrose acknowledged her intervention with a grave nod, and proceeded.

'The other possible way of looking at it is the lenient way, the way that makes all the allowances. *Tsk.* You could say that he's not a serious criminal, that he's just feeble-minded. Inadequate, if you like, unable to manage life. The crime he committed years ago didn't call for much cleverness, he was just taking orders from somebody else, but if this latest thing is anything to go by, his prison years didn't do anything for his intelligence. He's even less clever now.'

Through the springs of the sofa, I felt the movement of Julia's body as she winced.

'If this is a specimen of the kind of hoax he's going to try on, I should say society has very little to fear from him, except as a fringe nuisance. He could only take in somebody who's as confused as he is. Such people do exist, and they need protection, so we shall have to do *something* about him. But long and harsh prison sentences aren't going to do any good. So the soft view would be this. *Tsk.* He's the weak member of a strong family. He's been trying, in his silly way, to make something out of the fact that his sister's husband has come into fame and money. And within that framework, it shouldn't be impossible to show the whole thing as a psychotic rather than a criminal operation. Trying to make himself important within the family situation. I gather he'd made repeated efforts to get Mr Delmore to take him on as business adviser or something. A position in which, if I'm right, he would have been useless.'

'Much worse than useless.' Jake nodded.

'So the lenient view sets it up this way. He's a misfit, he wants to have power and influence in his immediate circle, but he's getting nowhere. Suddenly he blunders into a situation that he thinks he can exploit. There's an emotional upset between husband and wife. The wife goes off to find calm where nobody can get at her. She's disappeared. Immediately he's on to it – his mind races and comes up with a story. She's been kidnapped, she's going to be murdered, he can claim to be able to put a stop to it if a big chunk of money is handed over. *Tsk.* It's a pathetic story; nobody's taken in; all that happens is that a brief-case full of newspaper is put on the luggage rack in a suburban train and the time of a few police officers is wasted. I believe I'm right, Frank, in saying that a good lawyer could make it look very much like a pathetic attempt to score points within a game of family relationships rather than a criminal action.'

Frank Hopper stirred uneasily and said, 'Except for the previous conviction.'

'The previous conviction makes a difference, of course. He's not going to get off absolutely scot-free. But if a good lawyer got up and put the case for leniency very strongly – made the whole thing out to be trivial – there's a fair chance that he would only get a suspended sentence and be handed over to the probation service. Provided, of course, that there was absolutely full co-operation from the two people most nearly concerned.'

He looked at Jake, then at Julia, and as if in conclusion he gave his tongue-against-palate sound. '*Tsk,*' he said.

'Co-operation?' Jake growled.

'In the witness-box, Mr Delmore.'

'You mean I've got to get up and swear in court that Cliff wouldn't hurt a fly?'

'Not necessarily. Only that it would be a very silly fly that let itself be hurt by him.'

Jake thrust his hands deep into his pockets and hunched his

shoulders. 'That's asking a lot. He's been a bloody nuisance to me for a long time, and I'm not a particularly silly fly.'

Julia said quickly, 'I'd see to it that he didn't bother you, Jake. I'm going and I'll take him with me.'

'It's still a lot to ask. And suppose we do manage to get him off lightly. What's in it for me? Why should I knock myself out for somebody who's never done anything but disturb my peace?'

She forced herself now to look at him intently. 'Oh, you'll get peace, Jake. Neither I, nor anybody to do with me, will ever bother you again, and you'll be able to do just as you like. I only want to say this: I know I don't mean anything to you now, and after what's happened you don't mean much to me, but for the sake of what we used to have I'm asking you to be a human being, just once. Do your best for Cliff and we'll call it quits.'

'That seems to me a fair way of putting it,' said Detective-Sergeant Ambrose. 'What do you say, Mr Delmore?'

Jake stood in the middle of the room, his hands still deep in his pockets, his head on one side. He was turning the matter over in his mind, and not being very used to thinking, he was doing it slowly.

The rest of us just sat there and waited. What else could we do?

10

'Is anyone coming back afterwards?' Giles asked.

'No,' said Dinah. She was looking at her face in a small mirror; after uttering that one word she applied a dark-red cosmetic to her upper lip, and moved her lower lip back and forth across it so that the colour spread evenly. It was only a little more pronounced than the natural red of her mouth. Giles watched, fascinated. Then she added, 'I think she had a few friends, but nobody who was close to her. There were a couple of women who used to visit her when she first fell ill, but after she knew she was dying she seemed to lose interest in them. They stopped coming – sensed that she didn't want them, I suppose. Anyway, I can't start picking up all those threads. All I have to do is tidy up and leave, and I'll never be back. There's nothing for me in this place.' Catching sight of his face, she added cheerfully, 'Except you, of course. But I imagine you're capable of getting on a train to London.'

'I may not want to stay here myself,' he said, 'if there's no chance of seeing you here.'

'Oh, you can put me up for a weekend now and then,' she said. 'Anyway, there'll be time to discuss all that. The main thing now is, are we ready?'

They were ready. It was two-thirty in the afternoon; Helen Chichester-Redfern's body lay in its coffin, with a screwed-down lid, in the small ground-floor room next to the large sunny one which Dinah used; in a moment they would be on their way to St Simeon's church and then to the graveyard.

Giles, dark-suited, was to be the only officially recognised mourner; Dinah was to represent the family; long, thin Father Roughton was to speak the prescribed words and a local firm of undertakers was to do the driving and portage the coffin.

The two shiny black cars, the ration of melancholy and dignity that could be purchased for a reasonable outlay of money, now drew up outside Princess Terrace. Sober-suited men entered, various greetings and instructions were exchanged, and the perishable part of Helen Chichester-Redfern set off on the last stage of its seventy-year journey towards the soil.

Uncomfortable, feeling in a false position, but glad to be near Dinah, Giles sat on the edge of the polished leather seat as the car swayed majestically through the tangle of streets towards the church.

'Was St Simeon's your mother's church?'

'No, it's mine. She had no religion. I think my father brainwashed it out of her in their early years together. It's just a kindness to me that Father Roughton's going to give her the funeral service there.'

Oh yes, of course, he remembered. Dinah liked St Simeon's because it was Anglo-Catholic. 'High.' She would, of course, Giles reflected. Since her Christianity was so purely liturgical, it would please her to have a church that offered the maximum of ritual solemnity without making her take the final step and accept Catholic discipline. He thought briefly about this, then dismissed it. If you took on Dinah, you bought the package, including her self-indulgences, and if one of these indulgences was to play the Christianity-game, why should he, a non-believer, find anything distasteful in that?

They drew up now in front of a Victorian church that looked as if it had originally been put up as a shoe warehouse and then decorated by a team of demented surrealist pastrycooks. Two dark-clad figures were already waiting for them at the lych-gate: Father Roughton and a large young man whom he introduced as his curate. Smoothly, but with surprising speed, the coffin was wheeled into the church on a trolley, and the ceremony began.

Giles and Dinah were alone in the sea of empty pews. He tried to make his mind a blank, mumbling responses when necessary, kneeling and standing as she gave him the example. The atmosphere was familiar enough; it took him straight back to the first twenty years of his life when he had been forced by parental leverage to attend church every Sunday; but his own reaction to it was different from what it would have been then. This insistence on personal immortality, on the survival of identity after physical dissolution, struck him as a tedious fairy-tale constructed to console, and thereby to dominate, people whose lives were too harsh for them to bear undisguised reality. Where was Helen Chichester-Redfern now? Her body was in that box, and her personality, surely, was in the minds of the people who had known her, and in the extent to which her passage through life had made any alteration in the world.

As if to answer these unspoken vibrations of disbelief, Father Roughton halted the service at an appropriate point and, standing tall and solitary as a pine before the empty pews and the two attentive heads, delivered a short address.

'We are here today' (at least he did not say 'gathered here') 'to bid farewell in this life to our departed sister Helen, and to help launch her soul on its journey to God. I do not think Helen believed in God; if she did, she made no outward manifestation of that belief and bore no witness, for I never met her in a place of worship, and only through the devotion and good offices of her dear daughter do I know of her existence on earth, or that that existence has come to an end. That is a matter of regret to me as it must be to all Christians, but it is not fatal. She was a good and patient woman, sorely tried in her life, a good neighbour, a good friend, a good mother, quiet and studious in her habits. And now, whether she believed in Our Lord or not, she stands before him for judgement, and our thoughts and prayers are at her side, for that is the judgement we shall all meet. Indeed, we are meeting it minute by minute, and we need her prayers as she needs ours.'

Dinah's head dropped forward on to her clasped hands, though whether her fervour was a mark of respect for the priest, or an isolated stab of grief at the thought of her mother, Giles would never know. He himself, for all his scepticism, felt a wave of vague, unlocalised emotion. They were, after all, in the presence of death, and in a place set aside for the confrontation of the deepest things.

Then it was all over and the coffin was being wheeled out into the sunshine again on its neat aluminium trolley. Towards the sunshine, and beyond that, the clay and fibres and pebbles and worms.

This time, they were joined in the car by Father Roughton and the young curate. Giles felt uncomfortable and in the way. The younger cleric was shy and anxious to please; the older, though perfectly courteous, seemed to convey in a single penetrating glance that he understood the reason for Giles's being part of the situation at all; a sexual involvement with Dinah; the difficulty of sharing a woman's bed without finding oneself taking some sort of part in her life. He felt unjustly accused. After all, there was the whole involvement with Helen too, the emotional weight he had carried, the thoughts he had shared with her. Was it not Helen's pitiful summons that had brought him into the house, and within Dinah's magnetic sexual pull, in the first place? He defended himself, but only in the silence of his own mind, against an accusation that never got as far as words and so could only be answered by thoughts.

He looked covertly at Dinah. She was at her most demure, eyes downcast and hands in her lap, but that tiny smile played about the corners of her mouth and he saw a glitter in her eyes that he had come to recognise as the sign that she scented a sexual challenge. The two clerics were holy men, but men all the same; Father Roughton with his devouring eyes, deep voice and Torquemada-like features would probably be very attractive to women. As for the young curate, though he had hardly had time to set into a final shape and his face was still a boy's, he was a fine young animal. His body, under the cut-price clerical suit, was broad and strong, with a tapering waist; he looked like a rowing man, the popular young athletics master at public school. He even had the curly chestnut hair of the type. Dinah reined in her sexual magnetism until they had finished the business of lowering her mother into the earth and were coming away from the graveyard; then she unleashed it on the guileless youth until Giles could have sworn he heard the blood boiling over in the victim's veins. Already, she was feeling an access of new energy, that was clear – a liberation from the long duty to her mother, an exhilarating loneliness and unaccountability. She was free to do anything she liked from this moment on, and the first thing she was going to do was expand and bask in the presence of three men at once: one her licensed lover, two who would never be close to her in that way, but who for the moment were within the range of her attention.

At her request, the funeral car took them all back to No 2 Princess Terrace, and all four were provided with a glass of sherry. The young curate, stimulated both by the smoky-golden liquid in his glass and the equally smoky radiance of Dinah's attention, flushed and moved restlessly; the power in his long limbs seemed bursting for expression; Giles sensed that he would have welcomed

— 255 —

a two-mile hurdle race or a swim against a flood-tide.

And what, meanwhile, were his feelings? Jealousy? Oddly, no. The more he felt the waves of her sexuality, whether or not they were directed towards him, the more he rejoiced in the pure flame of her energy. That energy was sexual before it was anything else; he suddenly remembered a remark she had let drop in one of their conversations: 'When people aren't thinking about something else specific, they're thinking about sex.' Whether or not it was true of most people – and by and large he suspected that it was – it was certainly true of her. To accept her at all was to accept that her femininity, and the power it gave her to attract men, was the mainspring of her life. Everything else was more or less ancillary: her art was a channel for her energies, her religion a storage-bin for the deeper moral issues that might otherwise have interfered with her pleasures.

So, accept it! Standing there, watching the light, graceful movements of her body as she moved about the room replenishing sherry-glasses, hearing her quick, interested voice, seeing the smile that played round the slender line of her lips and the light in her eyes, Giles knew that whatever Dinah was and whatever she did, he loved her. Her vitality, however cruel in its demands and caprices, seemed to him logical, a force of nature, and he was content to yield to it like a sand-yacht blown along by the mistral.

Father Roughton was questioning Dinah with a warm yet lofty solicitude. Would she be all right, coping alone with so many things to be settled? Was the house to be sold? And what of – he lowered his voice, as one who approaches a delicate matter – her father?

'There'll be no need to trouble him,' she said lightly, yet with a decided tone that showed she had thought seriously and made up her mind. 'He knew she was ill, of course. But all communication had ceased between them. They communicated through me, or not at all. He's not mentioned in her will. Some of her little income came from him, and that stops now, of course. Everything else, which in fact just means this house and the things in it, goes to me.'

'You sound well in control,' said Father Roughton approvingly.

'Father,' she said, pouring him more sherry, 'as long as I have spiritual guidance from you and from my parish priest in London, I can cope with the things of this world.'

Did Giles detect any note of falsity, any element of polite flattery, in the words? He did not. Evidently, compartment-minded as she was, when she said things like that she fully believed them. And he knew that if the silver crucifix above her bed could tell Father Roughton of the things it had seen, that would make no difference to her; nor, probably, much to him.

The conversation drifted to lighter topics, and when Giles next paid attention the young curate was describing to Dinah, a trifle over-eagerly, the exploits of a dramatic society with which he was embroiled.

'They're prepared to be ambitious,' he told her. 'Not just the usual thrillers and domestic comedies – they're quite willing to have a try at Ionesco or Pinter. I'm sure if you came to one of the productions – or, better still, dropped in on a rehearsal and saw the thing in the making. . . . I mean, of course it's only a leisure activity, and for an artist like you it could never be anything serious, with your – your creative outlet already taken care of . . . but. . . .'

It was obvious that the swain was working himself up to the point of trying to interest Dinah in undertaking a role in one of the productions, was already seeing himself playing opposite her in some stark, meaningful drama in which he would have an innocent and socially acceptable opportunity to set her heart aflame. Dinah, instead of cutting his hopes short by the simple expedient of pointing out that she had no intention of staying in the district, chose rather to involve Giles in the badinage.

'Oh, I've no gift as an actress,' she said, acting to perfect effect. 'Giles here is loaded with histrionic talent – he's the man you should get.'

'Well, of course that would be splendid,' said the curate mechanically, 'but it's leading ladies we're short of.'

'You *must* be short, to ask me.'

'I thought you were saying the other day, Gerald,' said Father Roughton the Torquemada, 'that you had a glut of women members and couldn't persuade enough men to join.'

'Well, women *members*,' said the curate, fencing desperately, 'but talent, talent, is always short. I was hoping to interest Miss Chichest. . . .' His voice trailed off and he buried his innocent nose in his sherry-glass.

'If I were in charge of a dramatic society,' said Giles, rescuing him, 'I'd certainly try to persuade Dinah to join, no matter how many ladies already belonged to it.'

'Premise not accepted,' said Dinah mockingly. 'You wouldn't be in charge of a dramatic society.'

'No, I'm not the organising type, but if I were. . . .'

'If you were,' she said, 'you'd probably make a lot of fatal mistakes and one of them would be getting people like me to act.'

Father Roughton now rose to take his leave, and abducted the young curate with him before the enviably handsome lad could sink even more deeply into infatuation. Giles admired the older man's professionalism, but was glad to see the back of the pair of them. He felt that he had had enough of religion, certainly of Dinah's safety-net kind, to last for a long time.

After they had gone, Giles and Dinah went back into the sitting-room. Suddenly the emptiness of the house asserted itself as an oppression. The dying woman had, after all, been a presence. Even her stilled and silenced body in its screwed-down coffin had, in a sense, shared the house with them. Giles felt, or thought he felt, the force of Dinah's loneliness. He felt an impulse to be helpful; if he gave her some aid in coping with her immediate problems, it would tide her over till she could get back into her normal life.

'Have you made any plans yet?' he asked, by way of moving into the subject.

'I rang up my agent this morning and told him I was available for work. That's more a formality than anything else. He very seldom has any work for me.'

'Well, you'll be busy enough while you wait for it. There'll be probate for the will, and deciding what to do about the house. . . . Will you sell it?'

She looked at him without answering.

'I imagine you'll hardly want to keep it on. And it ought to sell very quickly, a well-kept property near the city cen—'

'*Stop it!*' she suddenly hissed.

He halted, surprised. 'I just thought you'd—'

'I don't care what you just thought. I am a grown-up person and I have perfectly clear ideas about what I intend to do.'

'Well, of course, but I—'

'You thought poor motherless girl, no one to turn to, she must be lonely, I'll put my wise old head at the service of her young one.

— 258 —

Well, forget it. I am not, repeat not, the kind of woman who has to have a man to lean on when there are decisions to be made. To me that's not what men are for, they're for fun, not usefulness. I don't need your help or anybody else's, is that clear?'

'Perfectly. And please forgive me. I'm not a very self-reliant person myself and I don't always recognise self-sufficiency when I see it in other people.'

She smiled, relenting. 'That's all right. Only don't ever do it again. Don't offer help or advice unless I ask you for it.'

'I promise not to.'

She came and sat close to him. 'And now we've got that understood, give me a kiss.' He did so; she reciprocated interestedly, then went on talking. 'You see, it was important for me to stress my independence, because I'm just about to make a suggestion to you.'

'I can't imagine any suggestion you could make that I wouldn't agree to. Except to go away.'

'Quite the contrary. I want you to come and be near me.'

'Willing. More than willingly.'

'I mean actually move in here. Go and get a suitcase and come and be the lodger for a week or two. Till I go back to London, in fact.'

He got to his feet. 'I'm off for that suitcase now.'

'Wait a minute. Don't be in a hurry. I want to talk a bit now that we're alone.'

She poured the remainder of the sherry into two glasses. 'Might as well finish this. Then we'll go on to a real drink. I feel like hitting the bottle tonight. But what I want most is to be close to you.' She kissed him again. 'Not because I need you to hold me up – just because I like you.'

'Thank you.'

'I've decided I like you very, very much. I even know why. I don't know whether anyone's ever told you this before, but you fit into a rather rare category.'

'How do I?'

'Well, on the whole men fall into two types – strong, amusing, sexy men who are *bastards*, and nice men who on the whole tend to be slightly wet. It's never happened to me before to meet a man who's got the best of both. You're sexy and you're fun to be with, and yet you're not a bastard, on the contrary, you're very nice.'

'Thank you. That's the nicest thing anyone's ever said to me.'

'Oh, it can't be.'

'Well, perhaps not, but nobody's ever said anything to me that pleased me so much.'

'Oh, that's nothing,' she said. 'I've decided I'm going to please you a *lot*.'

Later, he went for his suitcase. While he was away she cooked a delicious meal; afterwards, she played her guitar to him in the soft lamplight. Sitting back, listening to the gentle chords, with a glass of whisky beside him, Giles felt that all his life had been a preparation for this one evening, and that he hardly cared if he never saw another day.

Except that, when it came, the next day was just as good, and the next, and the next. . . . There were times when he felt guilty at feeling such strong, settled, unbroken happiness in a house where a woman had just given up her life in suffering and resentment; but then he would reflect that the house deserved to be cleansed and blessed by happiness after such a prolonged exposure to the dark rays of misery.

The days passed with just enough activity to avoid a vacuum; there was a lawyer to see, house-agents to be dealt with, and, once they got going, prospective buyers to be shown round the house.

Giles, now that the sun had come out on his storm-beaten interior landscape, was more contented than he had ever been: not merely contented, but uplifted, irradiated. Dinah was transformed; her impatience and angularity had disappeared, and she gave herself to their relationship with no hint of reserve or constraint. As they lived together day by day and meshed in more and more closely, she evidently took pleasure in sharing all her thoughts and feelings with him, from the most important to the most trivial. Her talking, which was always fairly incessant, became a kind of thinking aloud. It was an amazing guided tour of a woman's being and, as Giles once or twice paused to remind himself, pure gold to a writer.

Since they were together for almost the whole of every twenty-four hours, he was able to watch her during all phases and all moods. The physical actions that punctuated the day – dressing and undressing, preparing food, washing her hands, brushing her hair – seemed to him an avenue of perception to the rhythm of her life. Her contact lenses, for instance; before lying down to sleep or to make love, she would sit at her dressing-table and deftly (she did everything deftly) pull down the lower lid of each eye and slide the little transparent half-walnut-shell from the pupil. Then she would put the pair of them into a little case that lay always in the same exact spot, and, rising, would come towards him ready for action. Next to the contact-lens case lay another little container with seven round spaces marked with the names of the days of the week: her contraceptive pills. She discussed all this, like everything else, freely and copiously.

'It's the nearest to an absolutely effective method. Sometimes it can happen that one can go through you a bit too fast, if you have diarrhoea for instance. But if you just watch for that kind of thing and take one every day, it's really not possible to conceive. Mind you, I think I'd be healthier if I didn't take the pill – it does rather make one a battle-ground of hormones – but there seems to be no alternative. I asked my doctor if I could have my Fallopian tubes tied up, but he said they were sticky about doing that for women who weren't married. Silly, isn't it? I mean I'm damn sure I'll never want a child. Even if I could see myself in the role of a mother, I wouldn't go through the actual process of birth. It's just not on. Everyone who's looked at me with an obstetric eye has said the same thing, that I'm too narrow and I'd have a lot of trouble. So it's just as well that my ambitions don't lie in the direction of the nappy-bucket.'

At other times she would think aloud about her plans. 'When I get this place sold and the money's in the bank, I'll buy a little house in London. I'm sick of flats where you have the neighbours complaining if you play a bit of music at night, and watching to see who goes up and down the stairs. I'll get an end terrace house somewhere, with a little strip of lawn to sit out on in summer. And I'll keep it so neat and clean, everything in its place where I can put my hand on it.'

'Any room for visitors?'

'Oh, there'll be a spare room. And I'll have a double bed, of course. You can come very often. Whenever I'm not too busy, or when I'm resting after a concert. You can have a hook for your coat, and a place to hang your sponge-bag in the bathroom – I'll even find you a bit of permanent space in the wardrobe. You'll be privileged.'

He realised, with awe, that this was as far as she would ever move over for anybody. It was the extreme limit of her toleration of another person, and she was extending it to him. The greatest triumph of his life! The piece of luck he had long given up waiting for!

She even seemed to enjoy ministering to him; she took his clothes to the launderette and brought them back thoroughly dried and neatly folded. He, for his part, devoted himself entirely to pleasing her, and his efforts were rewarded.

On their fifth morning together, an even brighter sunshine came flooding in. They had got up late and eaten a leisurely breakfast; at almost ten o'clock Giles was in the bath when he heard the telephone ring. Evidently Dinah answered it, for the ringing stopped and he heard her voice. A few minutes later the bathroom door opened and she burst in, her eyes shining, her body flushed with such joy and excitement that there was no keeping still. Before he could even ask her what the good news was, she had bent down and showered him with rapturous kisses.

'My agent. That was him on the phone. He's booked me for a recital. In the Purcell Room at the Festival Hall. Three weeks from now.'

'Three weeks?'

'Yes. Someone's fallen ill who was going to do a recital on the harpsichord. Just in time – the publicity's on the point of going to press. So they can substitute my name.'

'Oh, Dinah! How wonderful!'

She looked at herself in the mirror, carefully, as if to see whether she were really the same person to whom this wonderful thing had happened.

'I mean,' he went on, lying back in the soapy water, 'I'm sorry to hear this other musician is ill, but—'

'Oh, she'll get better. She's a very strong girl. I know her, she's called Letitia Letcombe. She's more established than I am, but I'm just as good a guitarist as she is a harpsichordist. And it's the breakthrough at last.'

'Will it be a solo recital?'

'I'm the only instrumentalist. I share it with a couple of singers.'

'Plenty of programme time, eh?'

'He says I'm to be prepared to play forty minutes, in two spots. It's enough to bring me to attention. If it were any more I doubt if I could be properly rehearsed.' The thought of rehearsal seemed to bring her abruptly down to the level of hard work and gravity. 'My God, I must get on with it.'

'I suppose the first thing you'll do,' he said, trying to take an intelligent interest, 'is to work out a programme.'

'Do you imagine, you ass,' she said affectionately, 'that I haven't got a programme in my head already? I've been day-dreaming about this for three years. I know exactly what I'll play. I'll give them the Castelnuovo-Tedesco Sonata in D major, and Falla's piece on Debussy's tomb, and some nice flamboyant Villa-Lobos and a slice of austere Bach and I'll have them just where I want them.'

The next twenty days passed in a happy trance. Giles took all household chores away from Dinah. He, who so habitually faced the lonely toil of creation, felt privileged to protect and serve a fellow-artist. Only when she felt the need to stop thinking about music and do something with her hands, when she positively *wanted* to slice vegetables or stir mixtures, did he stand aside and let her have the run of the kitchen. He also took off her shoulders the business of selling the house, coping with a thin but incessant stream of maniacally suspicious, nose-poking, cupboard-opening, list-ticking-off inquisitors. Since buying and selling property never fails to bring out people's most deep-seated anxieties and shows them in their worst light, the experience would have depressed him had not his happiness with Dinah placed him above the reach of depression. His favourite obsessional was the man who produced from his pocket a large glass marble and put it down on the floor of each room in turn to see if there were any unevenness that would start it rolling. But the insulation-fiends and the plumbing-testers and wall-thickness-knockers were almost as bad. All of them he coped with, imperturbably.

This left him with relatively little uninterrupted time, and under normal circumstances it would have been out of the question to do any work on his novel; but happiness gave him energy and energy made him restless, so one day he telephoned for a taxi, disappeared, and came back twenty minutes later with his typewriter, a supply of paper and the box-file containing his work-in-progress. Thereafter, fitting it round the edges of his other activities, he wrote every day in furious bursts of inspiration. The novel grew and grew; never had he worked so fast. Dinah's mood of liberated optimism flowed into Giles, ridding him of his usual timid, slothful hesitancy. He hurried Gus Howkins through episode after episode, bringing him at last to that safe anchorage in which Julia recognised, reciprocated and rewarded his love. Writing these last pages, his own happiness seemed to flow effortlessly into words.

All this time Dinah practised, both by playing her chosen pieces again and again and by poring silently over the scores, meditating on interpretation. But hard as she drove herself, she never went to the point of an exhaustion that would have taken off her edge. She was aflame with excitement, but controlling it. Her art, Giles realised, was to her a supremely important avenue of life, something that directed and canalised her energies and in doing so intensified them; it did not take primacy over life, it ministered to it. Thinking back over his own exhausting and soul-consuming struggles, over the months and years when the demands of his art had forced him to pour away his actual life like cold soup left untasted on the table, he saw clearly the difference between the primary and the secondary artist, between the originator and the however dedicated interpreter. Since he loved Dinah, he was glad that she was a performer and not a composer; he could not have borne to see her consumed in that fire; he wanted her freshness and vividness, her love of life, preserved alive.

On Sundays she walked demurely off with her prayer-book, returning composed and pleased, to resume her usual pattern of life, sharing her energies between work and pleasure, with, if anything, more conviction than ever. Once, Father Roughton paid a call; Giles was in the middle of showing someone round the house, and he did not disturb the quiet, grave conversation that he knew to be going on in Dinah's room. The young curate never came back; perhaps he had been warned not to. Father Roughton was not the type who would look with approval on the upsetting of apple-carts.

On one of those Sundays, they made love so whole-heartedly after lunch that it was bed-time before they felt like getting up. So they ate some apples that happened to be on a dish on the window-sill, drank a glass of wine, and composed themselves to sleep. As Giles drifted down towards unconsciousness his mind suddenly fished up the lines about Shakespeare's Cleopatra:

                              for vilest things
Become themselves in her, that the holy priests
Bless her when she is riggish.

With the words went an image of Father Roughton bending gravely over Dinah's bed when she was giving herself up to pleasure, and blessing her. The mental picture was so ludicrous that he chuckled out loud.

'What's the joke?' she murmured sleepily.

'Darling,' he said into her ear, 'have you ever heard the word "riggish"?'

'I can't remember ever hearing it.'

'What would you say it meant?'

'Well, if I'm to guess I shall need to know who you're applying it to.'

'I'm applying it to you, my love.'

'Oh, then,' she said, settling herself more comfortably, 'I suppose it means randy.'

Near enough, he thought, sloping downwards into peaceful unconsciousness, near enough. And the holy priests bless her. When she is riggish. And I bless her too. For the sake of what we have known together. Always, always, I bless her.

11

N O ACTOR EVER HAD SUCH AN AUDIENCE. WE SAT ROUND IN A ragged circle, determined not to miss a syllable, hardly daring to listen to our own breathing.

Jake Delmore, actor – Jake Driver, television star and idol of millions – stood looking at us for a long time. I could see the second-hand of Detective-Sergeant Ambrose's watch sweeping round. He had a large, clearly marked watch – he would, of course – and because the sleeves of his jacket stopped rather high up on his powerful wrists, you could see the watch at all times. I wasn't counting, but I thought that second-hand went right round the dial before Jake broke his silence. But when he did, speech came to him readily.

'All right, that was enough time for reflection. My mind's made up. I'm going to bat on your side. Any help Cliff wants from me, in court or out of it, he can have.'

I heard Julia catch her breath. Detective-Sergeant Ambrose stirred in his chair, as if all the muscles in his body were changing position in response to this new situation. Only Frank Hopper seemed exactly the same. I supposed that as a lawyer he was in work whichever way the mop flopped.

'If we all make light of it,' Jake went on, 'and say we were never worried and never took it seriously, the heart'll go out of the case against him.'

'If we weren't worried,' said Frank Hopper, 'why did we get the police to help us?'

'To pull him in for his own good,' said Jake easily. 'In his own interests he couldn't be left to wander about and play fantasy-jokes on people. So now he's safely out of circulation, we thank the police gracefully for their help, and apologies all round, and please be nice to the poor lad.'

Julia said, 'That's pretty nice of you, Jake. I wasn't expecting you to be so nice, and I'm sorry I misjudged you.'

For a moment Delmore looked at her, steadily. Then he shook his head. His face was very composed, and very cold.

'No,' he said. 'I must put you right about that. For some reason it's important to me not to have you misunderstanding me, getting the wrong impression of my motives. And when I say "you" I mean not just Julia but all of you here.' His eyes flicked over our faces, contemptuously; it was not venomous contempt, but the kind that is nine-tenths indifference. 'I don't want any of you going out of here with the idea that I'm a nicer person than I actually am, or that I'm doing this out of kindness for that little squirt Cliff.'

We waited while he poured himself a drink, and said, 'There's whisky here if anybody wants it – help yourselves.' Nobody moved. 'I'm going to help to get Cliff off the hook, or as far off it as we can. Not because I like him, or because I care what happens to him. Least of all to earn good opinions from anybody here. My motive is quite simple. I want him off my back. My one requirement from Master Cliff is that he should turn his face away from me and march off by the left, at the double. I want to forget his existence. Not just because he's a horrible little rat-like creature, though he is that, of course, but because he's part of a whole world, and a whole chapter of my life, that I want to bring to an end and forget about.'

He looked round at us again. He certainly had us listening, and all at once I understood how much he was enjoying it. Having an audience in the hollow of his hand – as an actor, it was the breath of life to him; and, since what he was telling us was important to him personally, it was a breath full of oxygen.

'I want to be done with the past.' He spoke quietly and savagely. 'I don't suppose any of you understand that feeling. You all live lives that change very slowly if they change at all. It's never happened to you to wake up one morning and find everything totally different, and it never will happen. For you, today always has to be built on yesterday. But the change that happens when an unsuccessful actor becomes successful – not just successful, a star, with people running after him waving cheque-books – that's something you just couldn't see, unless you've got more imagination than I give you credit for. He quite literally wakes up in a new world. Everything that used to be impossible – all the things he saw when he pressed his nose to the glass – well, now they come dropping into his lap. Not just satisfactions – not just money and good clothes and women and travel – but his higher ambitions too. He can play good parts, he can measure himself against the world's great drama, if he's got the guts to do it – play with people who'll force him to get up on tiptoe and grow till he's as big as they are. To do that, you've got to be new. You can't go into it with the rags of your old shabby life flapping about you. All the stewed prunes in chilly little boarding-houses and wearing the linoleum off agents' stairs. Playing Shakespeare to parties of school kids who're doing it for "O" level, with whole schools coming in ten minutes late and kids going to the lavatory at the beginning of the big soliloquy and banging the seats. You need to forget all that when your world changes. Otherwise you take it all with you and it weighs you down.'

He paused, and in that pause Julia said in a cool, precise voice, 'That goes for people, too, doesn't it?'

Jake looked at her without expression. 'In most cases, yes. If they were close – if they were really part of your life in the time you want to forget about. I'm making an effort to be honest, Julia. I'm saying exactly what's in my mind, because I've got a pain inside me that I think might go away if I told the truth and lived the truth.'

'Go away to someone else, I suppose you mean,' she said.

'If I met you for the first time today,' he continued, ignoring the interruption and still with his eyes directly on hers, 'I'd find you very attractive. In fact, I'd come after you with bared teeth.'

'Thanks for nothing. Now that I've taken a look at the kind of girl you find attractive—'

'You've done nothing of the sort. All you did was catch a glimpse of a couple of dames who were just making us a little sport. As I say, I'd come after you if I met you now for the first time. But it isn't the first time. You're sentimental about the days when we lived on curry and chips and worked for starvation wages. The comradeship, the struggle. Well, you can take it away and bury it.'

'That's what I'm going to do,' she said quietly.

'Right, that's understood and agreed, and as far as Cliff's

concerned he's part of that disposal operation. I just don't want to know about him.' He drained his whisky-glass with the air of a man bringing something to a close. 'If Cliff goes to prison for seven years or whatever it'd be, he'd be sending waves of resentment at me all the time, and so'd Julia. Nobody's ever going to let me forget it, even after he comes out. But if I help him to get a light sentence or even avoid prison altogether, he can clear off and be a nuisance to somebody else and I'm free to forget him.'

There was a silence and then Julia said quietly, 'Well, that seems to wrap it up.'

Jake said nothing: Detective-Sergeant Ambrose filled in the silence. 'That seems as complete a statement as we need at the moment. Thank you, Mr Delmore.'

Frank Hopper said quickly, 'Will you be taking a formal statement?'

'Some time in the next few days,' said Detective-Sergeant Ambrose. 'At Mr Delmore's convenience. He's a busy man and we don't want to rush him, when he's being so co-operative.'

I looked at the man with real interest. Suddenly I saw him as a human being. I would have liked to talk to him, to question him about his feelings, but it was out of the question in that company.

'We'd all better be going, I suppose,' said Frank Hopper. He looked across at Jake to see if he was going to invite anyone to stay on, but Jake wasn't.

'Go if you like,' he said, to everyone in general and no one in particular.

We all got up and reached for our coats. Detective-Sergeant Ambrose opened the door and stood aside for Julia to leave first. She did so without looking back at Jake. I knew they had exchanged their last words, that I was witnessing something final – the parting of husband and wife.

I followed her out. Frank Hopper came next, ducking out thankfully. He looked furtive, like someone in a club that has been raided by the police and is glad to dodge out by a side door, hoping not to be recognised. Just why he found the whole thing so painful I knew I'd never find out, but obviously he loathed it. Was he in love with Julia? Or with Jake? Speculation, speculation.

Detective-Sergeant Ambrose stayed behind for a moment to have a quiet word with Jake; fixing up, doubtless, when they could send someone round for a statement; then he joined the rest of us on the landing. Julia had already pressed the button for the lift, and at that moment it arrived.

We all got in. I hardly dared look at Julia, though my face was not a yard from hers. When I did see it, I was glad to see that its outlines had softened: she looked reprieved; not yet joyful, but alive to the possibility of joy.

Suddenly freed from shyness, I turned to Detective-Sergeant Ambrose. He was standing in the corner of the lift as it floated down, as contained as ever, his big hands hanging loosely, his easy-to-read watch gleaming on the wrist.

'Tell me one thing,' I said.

'Yes,' he said, turning his pebble lenses patiently in my direction.

'You sounded really glad,' I said, 'when Delmore decided to go easy on Cliff. You sounded as if it really mattered to you.'

'It does matter to me.'

'That's what I don't quite understand. As a detective you work to apprehend people who've offended against society. Once they come to court, does it matter much to you what happens to them? Whether, for instance, Cliff Sanders goes to prison or not?'

Detective-Sergeant Ambrose looked across at me with that immense, weary patience.

'Have you ever been round one of Her Majesty's prisons?' he asked me.

'No. The nearest I got was in the visiting-room yesterday. That was enough for me. I don't like those places.'

'Nobody likes them,' said Detective-Sergeant Ambrose. The lift slowed, and stopped. The doors slid open. Still he stood there, looking at me. 'They weren't built to be liked. But at least when they were built, they were calculated on a certain number of inmates. That number has been swamped. The prisons are overcrowded. Every time a new convict goes in, the others have to squash up and exist in a bit less room.' The lift doors started to shut. He reached out a hand and pressed the button to open them again. 'Less room in the cells. Less room in the exercise yard. Less room in the lavatories. Less room in the workshops.'

He let his hand drop. 'Any time I can keep a man out of prison, or even shorten his sentence, I'm doing a good turn to a lot of poor devils who are at breaking point. And who know that, if and when they do break, no one will care.'

I nodded. I felt no impulse to speak. Julia moved out of the lift and I followed. We all said our brief, quiet valedictions in the hall, under the cold eye of Dennis.

After we got outside, Julia turned to me on the pavement. 'Are you free for the rest of the evening?' she demanded. I have to use that last word instead of just 'asked'. There was a decisiveness, a thrust, a crackle of energy, in her voice.

'What d'you mean?' I said. 'I'm free for the rest of my *life*.'

She said, 'I want a change of atmosphere, and I know just where I can get one. Come on.

We walked quickly along the glistening pavement. It was a rainy autumn evening, but we happened to be between showers, and the air was soft. I asked no questions. Julia marched us to a bus stop and we waited a few minutes. As we stood there, I said nothing. I had decided that my function was just to be with her as long as she needed me, and to breathe in and out.

We had to wait about five minutes for the bus. Only once did Julia break her silence, and that was to say, in a conversational, almost casual tone, 'Jake isn't the only one who wants a change.' She caught hold of my arm, and pressed her cheek against my shoulder, like a cat rubbing itself against someome. Then she let go of my arm and stood there as if nothing had happened. Her eyes were shining in the gleam of the street lamp. I thought how much I loved her. As the bus came towards us, a huge swaying lighted box, I knew that if I could ensure her happiness by throwing myself under it instead of getting on as a passenger, I would be honestly glad to do it.

Still, I was even gladder that I seemed to be able to contribute something to her happiness by being alive and beside her rather than lying squashed in the road. Long may it stay like that, I thought as I paid the fare.

She had told me where to book to, but the destination didn't mean anything to me. And when we got out, at one end of a long, wet street in north London somewhere, I still didn't connect with anything. Without explaining, she walked me a few yards and we went into the public bar of a big, impersonal pub, one of those barn-like places you'd pass by without a glance and certainly never go into: just another outlet for the mass sale of somebody's standardised beer.

The place was almost empty. Two youths were playing that hand-operated football game, with the little doll-players on steel rods and wooden handles to twirl them with, and an old man with rheumy eyes and a greasy cap was sitting in a corner with a pint. There was a faint smell of antiseptic.

'Have we come all this way to visit this place?' I couldn't help asking.

Julia smiled. 'Let me buy you a drink.'

I let her buy me a pint of the bright, fizzy stuff that squirted out of the gas-pump, and she got herself one too, and we went and sat down. The clock said five to ten.

I drank some and put my mug down and said, 'Well?'

'Not long now,' she said. 'It comes down about ten.'

Comes down? What does, the ceiling?

She evidently wasn't in the mood for explanations, and I didn't blame her. In any case I was quite content just to sit next to her. We leaned back peacefully, taking a pull at our beer now and then, and after a while she held my arm again, and leaned up against me. I could feel the warmth and firmness of her body, and my mind went back to the half-bedroom in a certain cottage in a certain valley, a certain number of light-years away.

So we sat, in an inoffensive dream, till about seven minutes past ten. Then the door opened and three or four young people came in, talking and laughing. Another minute and the door opened again: a chap and a girl. Then again. And again. In ones and twos, in clusters, they kept coming. There was an air about all of them which somehow gave them a common denominator, though they were of all shapes and sizes and physical types. Near me, at the bar, stood a frail-looking lad with soft fair hair and a sensitive face, drinking with a big, strong youth with a humorous, ugly face and enormous hands and feet. A solidly built girl, just short of fat, with a chubby face made beautiful by big dark eyes, was talking and laughing clear above the din. Oh, yes, the din: the place was getting noisier and noisier, they were three deep round the bar, and the landlord and two hefty barmaids were pouring out drinks as fast as their hands could move, exchanging quips and comic insults, all the time, with

— 272 —

this sudden wave of eager, vivacious customers.

I looked at Julia. Her eyes were going from face to face: she was searching for somebody. By this time, of course, I had it. I catch on slow but I catch on good.

'What theatre are they from?' I asked.

She told me. One of those little progressive outfits that never achieve a permanent home, and divide their time between playing in the upstairs rooms of pubs and fitting up deserted warehouses and garages.

The door opened again and a girl came in by herself. She was about five feet three or four and had a rich cascade of golden hair. When she saw Julia making signs at her she stopped on her way to the bar and came straight over to join us.

'I wondered if you'd be here,' she said. 'I went to bed last night without waiting up. I thought you were probably all right somewhere.' She had enormous blue eyes and opened them very wide when she spoke to you.

'I was with Gus,' said Julia, indicating me. 'Gus, this is Judy.'

It was at Judy's flat that she had taken refuge, I remembered. I said hello and went over to get a round of drinks, leaving the two girls to talk and catch up with things.

I had to wait a fair time to get served, but I didn't mind. I enjoyed standing among the crowd of young players. Most of them were joking and camping around, telling stories that involved a lot of mimicry and were punctuated with explosions of laughter. But some were far from laughter. One couple, jammed up against the bar by the crowd and against each other by their own wish, were looking with total fascination into each other's eyes. Their faces were grave, absorbed, racked with the intensity of their consciousness of each other. Was I watching the beginning of a great love, or a tidal wave of passion that would sweep through some basement flat for six hours and leave them just good friends when they turned up for rehearsal in the morning?

And in one corner a tall, spectacled young man in a woollen cap was arguing about (I felt certain) Stanislavsky with a tubby chap in a jersey. Great questions about the future of theatre were being settled, even if nobody could remember afterwards quite what had been said.

I felt a wave of affection and trust for this mob of drinking, laughing, chattering, feeling and reacting people. At least they

— 273 —

weren't playing the game of life cannily with cards held close to the chest, training for some safe profession and keeping their heads down. They were blazing into life, nursing great ambitions over their gas-rings, scattering colour and vitality wherever they went.

I got served in the end and took the drinks over to where Julia sat with Judy, dark head with gleaming fair head. They made a wonderful picture. I was in love with Julia, but I could see that Judy had her field of force. Those headlamp eyes!

'It's a smashing bit of luck,' she was saying animatedly.

'I should think so. . . . How much rehearsal, did you say?'

'Just three weeks. Then straight into the tour. North-east of England, then Holland and Germany. We'll be away two months.'

'It sounds fantastic!'

I listened, waiting patiently to be filled in and not much caring if I wasn't. It obviously concerned some job that Judy had landed. They discussed it exhaustively, naming a lot of names that meant nothing to me, and I found that some of their high spirits came over to me as I sat quietly there, drinking.

At half-past ten the landlord called time and the place emptied as quickly as it had filled. Nobody argued, nobody needed to be dusted out, they just drank up and went. I remarked on this to Julia.

'Oh, nobody stays up late in this end of the profession,' she said. 'After the show they get in here for a fast two or three drinks and then it's home to bed, by yourself or with someone, but bed in any case. They're in the theatre again at nine-thirty.'

Judy was getting into her coat and looking at us enquiringly. 'Are you. . . ?' she said, and left the sentence unfinished.

Julia turned to me. 'Gus, d'you mind coming back to Judy's with me tonight? I'm in the spare room but there's a place for you.'

I didn't know whether she meant a place for me in her bed, or on the floor outside the door, but whatever it was I was willing to settle for it. I could see that she didn't want to let go of Judy. She wanted to go on with their happy, sharing talk, and she wanted to stay a little longer in that atmosphere of a common dedication and comradeship, battling on and taking the hard knocks and the good times together. How much more attractive it all seemed than my lonely, dreary flat with only me to talk to and only her troubles to think about!

And yet, and this is what made my heart sing, she didn't turn me away and go off with Judy. She invited me along, and Judy was quite happy with an extra person.

It was some distance to Judy's flat. Luckily a taxi was just going by. We all sat together in the back seat, Julia in the middle, and as the taxi accelerated away we sank gently back against the cushion. We were all relaxed, completely at ease with one another, and in that moment I heard Judy say, gently, 'Did you go to see Cliff?'

'I went to see Cliff and I went to see Jake.'

'How's it all going to be?'

'All right. Jake's going to do his best to clamp things down, so Cliff'll get off fairly lightly.'

I saw Judy's flashing smile. 'Isn't that marvellous?'

'Yes, Jake's done the decent thing. End on a good note.'

'Is that it? A clean break and no hard feelings?'

'That's it.'

When we got to Judy's little flat I expected to start feeling awkward, an intruder, odd man out. But I didn't. Both the girls took me so completely for granted, made me feel that my presence there was something natural that didn't have to be adjusted to. I reflected, as I helped to slice bread and set out a few things for a meal, that my generation had made such a heavy business of the forming of pairing relationships, whereas theirs, growing up in the sixties, had never seen it as anything to get steamed up over. If one girl went to see another she took a bloke with her or she didn't, and nobody was counting. I don't mean that Judy treated me like a piece of wallpaper, in fact she talked to me quite a lot, but she made me feel that I had as much right to be there as to be anywhere else.

She made me laugh when I questioned her about the work she had been doing with theatre-for-children. She described it all so vividly: the whole trick was to get the kids involved with imaginative play, help them to feel their way into a situation. They would go out into a playground and get them together and start with a thing everyone had to pretend, such as, for instance, that they were afraid of the colour red. They hated and retreated from anything that was red: if someone had a red coat on, or a red tie, they shuddered away. Then, gradually, they mimed getting their courage back bit by bit, forcing themselves to touch the red coat or tie, until finally they were chasing red things all over the place. Judy described it to me with so much involvement and passion, and what made me laugh came right at the end.

'You must like children very much,' I said, 'to share an experience with them like that.'

'Like children?' she said, opening her eyes very wide. 'You must be joking. I can't stand the little buggers.'

'There's no business like show business,' Julia called from the kitchen, through my laughter.

That's how it was that night, so warm and friendly and safe, it gave me the feeling that as long as I wasn't false, as long as what I was feeling was genuine affection, genuine happiness, I couldn't put a foot wrong.

When it came to bedtime, I just had to bunk in with Julia, because there wasn't anywhere else to lie down, unless I had gone in with Judy. So we lay in that narrow bed together and giggled a bit and made a few jokes and kissed and fell asleep. I didn't feel any particular need to fuck her. I just felt so happy to be close to her, and sharing each breath we took, and I felt as if it had always been so.

In the morning I got up before the others and made some tea and then went to work. When I got to the office Miss Sarson had a surprise for me, not an altogether joyful one. My daughter, April, had been trying to telephone me.

I say 'not altogether pleasant' because I was rather afraid of the meeting with April that I knew would have to take place sooner or later. I love April very much, and always have, but that didn't help me at the moment. I wasn't sure what attitude she was going to take over this business of my splitting up with her mother, whether she was going to take sides and be disapproving, and just because I adored her so much I couldn't bear the thought of alienating her.

She had left a number which couldn't, I decided, be Hilda's; it must be somewhere in a different part of town. Where was she staying? What was she doing? I hadn't seen her at all since the break-up, though I knew she had been to see Daphne: we had exchanged a few letters, but hers had been pretty uncommunicative. She was not much of a letter-writer and anyway her life was too busy. She'd gone into nursing and her training, which was evidently going quite well, was taking place at some big teaching hospital in the north.

I rang the number, and got her, and arranged to see her back at the flat as soon as I finished the day's work. As soon as I hung up I started worrying about it. Why did she want to see me? To twist my arm to go back to Daphne? To have a flaming row? Her voice on the telephone had been friendly enough, but terse. Not that she's ever anything else. She doesn't like the telephone and always keeps her conversations very short.

I left the office sharp at five-thirty (black looks from Miss Sarson and Daisy, who were still finishing up, putting the covers on typewriters, etc.) and got home in time to have another good worry before six, the time when April was due to come. Prompt at six the door-bell rang. I let her in, and she gave me a daughterly kiss.

So far, so good. Then I backed off and looked at her as she removed her coat. I have never really got used to the fact that April is a grown woman. I loved her so much when she was a little moppet, and her image in those years is stamped so indelibly on my mind, that I always see her in double focus. And then, she matured so quickly. Even as a sixth-former she had a level head on her shoulders – plenty of fun, of course, and sparkle, but so balanced. Where on earth she got all that sanity from, I don't know. It must have skipped a generation in both Daphne and me, and all landed on her.

So, as I say, I looked at her. Nineteen years old, already familiar with pain and death – and, unless my intuition was all wrong, with love. She looked back at me, calmly, and smiled. I thought how beautiful she looked. She has Daphne's red hair but her features are more like mine, or what mine would be like if they weren't middle-aged and squashy. She was wearing jeans, which I regretted, but you can't stop them doing it, and a sort of coarse-knit thing like a tabard, which I didn't regret. I don't know what the right word for it would be. It was like a jersey, but not form-fitting; like a jacket, but with no buttons; it had wide, but not flowing, sleeves; it said, and was meant to say, 'I am free, and unceremonious, and' – since there was a kind of folk-design worked on it – 'in sympathy with hand-industries and poor people.' I really liked the look of her. My daughter! I thought. Well, not just mine. One thing she's certainly inherited from Daphne: her strong body. Graceful, feminine, but tireless. All right, I'm singing her praises. Knock thirty per cent off because I'm her father. But with the seventy that are left she's still a wonderful girl.

Now she gave me that clear-eyed look that had me shaking in my shoes. Heavens, I used to change her nappies, but this can't be the same person as that little helpless lump of humanity.

'Well, Dad,' she said gently, 'how's it all going?'

'I'm alive,' I said guardedly.

'Just that? Nothing better?'

'I think it'll be better when things shake down into their final shape. If they ever do.'

'You mean, I suppose,' she said, sitting down, 'when Mummy gives up trying to get you back.'

'Well, look,' I said, 'it's going to come to that sooner or later. She'll have to find someone else, or get used to being alone. It's just no good. We'd only drag each other down and in the end no good would come of it.'

'I've been saying that to her. I've been telling her she might have to get used to that idea.'

'I'm sure you're a great help to her,' I said gratefully.

'Oh, she doesn't need all that much help. Mummy's stronger than you think. Of course to you she shows her weakness because she needs your sympathy.'

'Well, she's got that,' I said. 'Unless you think it's a contradiction in terms, giving someone your sympathy from a distance.'

'Sometimes it's the only thing you can do. Anyway, I didn't come to see you to lay the law down. You're both grown-up people and you'll have to live your lives.'

'Yes, April,' I said humbly.

She looked at me suspiciously, to see if I was putting on an act. But I swear to God I wasn't. I really did feel humble in her presence, because she was young, and uncluttered, and had the world at her feet, and yet was kind and had patience with me.

Now she stood up and started wandering about the flat, looking at the different rooms. 'May I explore?' she asked.

'Of course. Not that there's much to see.'

— 278 —

She looked all round and then came back with her verdict. 'No, you're right, there isn't much to see, but you could make it better if you had the slightest idea how to set about making a home.'

'Well, I haven't.'

'I know that, silly. Some time I'll come and stay a weekend with you and we'll go shopping on the Saturday and pick up some things to brighten the place. But there are some ideas I can give you straight away. For instance, this room would look much bigger if you put the chairs *this* way round and then pushed that sideboard thing round *there*. . . . Come and help me.'

Obediently, I sweated and grunted and pushed. Sure enough, the room did look bigger.

'Are you going to stay here long?' she asked, still looking round.

'It depends whether I can find something better. I just took the place because it was any port in a storm. Perhaps one day I'll have the energy and positiveness to tackle the problem freshly.'

'Oh, don't start having energy and purposiveness. It wouldn't be like you.'

'I said positiveness, not purposiveness.'

'No matter. That wouldn't be like you either.'

I decided to fight back. 'I see you've kept up that bad habit of wearing jeans. Haven't you got a skirt?'

'I wear a skirt all the time when I'm working, and a starched white cap, and low-heeled, sensible shoes. That ought to please you.'

'Are you going to stay a nurse for ever?' I asked, trying to trap her by suddenly coming at her from a different angle.

'Who knows what I'm going to do *for ever*?' she asked absent-mindedly, her eyes travelling over my furnishings. I could feel them wilting under her appraisal. 'Why d'you have to keep those two huge bags in your bedroom?'

'Where else would I put them? And you know what's in them, don't you?'

'Yes, your awful old canoe.'

'It's not awful, it's what keeps me sane.'

'That's a matter of opinion,' she said. 'Anyway, who's sane?'

'You are, April,' I said, meaning it.

— 279 —

'Not all the time. Last week I bought a car that had no reverse gear.'

'You did *what*? Did you know it had no reverse gear when you—'

'Yes, I did. The bloke who sold it to me said he was knocking ten per cent off the price because it only goes backwards if you push it.'

'But you can't get out and push every time you want to go backwards.'

'Yes, I can. It's a tiny little foreign car.'

'What kind is it?'

'It's registered as something called an Amilcar.'

'An *Amilcar*? But they went out of business years ago. You've been swindled.'

'No, I haven't. Every car has to be registered as something. The chap was explaining to me. So he put "Amilcar" on the licence sticker because some of the parts are that. The chassis, I think he said.'

'And the lousy gearbox that doesn't work. It must be radically unsafe. It'll let you down going along the motorway and you'll break your neck.'

'It's very safe, actually. And I never have to bother pushing it backwards because the bloke who sold it to me's usually along too. He does the pushing.'

'You bought the car off him and he goes everywhere in it with you?'

'Not *everywhere*. I bought it because he was flat broke and now he isn't flat broke but he still needs the car more than I need it.'

'Who is this con man?'

'He's an immunologist,' she said, giving me a straight, I-dare-you-to-say-anything look.

I said bitterly, 'Well, I always knew doctors took advantage of nurses.'

'Look,' she said, 'this chap is tall and strong and has very nice eyes and a nice voice and is very, very nice altogether, and if he wants to take advantage that – is – all – right – with – me.' She spaced the last words out and spoke them very distinctly.

'All right, but you don't have to buy his crummy—'

'What about you?' she interrupted. 'You're very censorious, but how can you guarantee that you won't make a fool of yourself some day and be happy doing it? Just because you're senile, that's no guarantee that you'll always live in an emotional vacuum. You may meet somebody.'

That was my cue to tell her what I'd been up to. Ought I to mention Julia? But then, what to say? I didn't know how long Julia would be staying in my life, so how could I tell April? And that was what she would want to know. If I said, 'I've been having a whirlwind affair with a pretty actress,' that would be like telling her I had eaten three cream buns in a tea-shop. She would want to know how it was going to affect the shape of my life, and how could I tell her that?

So I stood looking at her, not knowing what to say, and in that silence, so help me God, the door-bell rang. And I opened it and Julia was standing there. I had the uncanny sense, for a moment, that I had pulled her towards me by thinking about her. But it turned out to be just coincidence.

She was carrying a soft leather grip in her hand, bulging with what I supposed were her clothes, and as she came over the threshold she said, 'New developments. We can't stay at Judy's, not at present, anyway. So I hope it's all right if I—'

Then she saw April and stopped and said, 'Oh, you've got company.'

'My daughter, April,' I said. 'April, this is Julia. I haven't mentioned her yet, but I was going to get round to it.'

Liar, I said to myself.

The two girls looked at each other. I could almost hear each one's brain racing away like mad. But April's was racing the faster.

Julia put down her grip and walked over to a chair. 'Let me sit down, at least,' she said. I didn't like the sound of that 'at least'. Where was the sense in giving her the impression that she wasn't welcome? Perhaps she wasn't getting that impression, but April was taking her in very interestedly, and it can be slightly disconcerting to be the target of that kind of keen scrutiny, when you hadn't expected anything of the kind.

So I had recourse to the good old remedy. I had a bottle of wine in the cupboard, and faster than the hand could follow the eye I had dragged it out, and a corkscrew, and three glasses.

'Let's have a drink,' I said, 'and get to know each other.'

With a glass of wine in their hands, they both relaxed and

smiled at each other. Then Julia told me what had happened at Judy's. Apparently her chap, who had been away in Canada, had turned up on the doorstep, just after lunch, without any kind of warning.

'It seems he makes a habit of doing that. He never, never gives her any advance notice when he's coming back. If she makes any protest, he says he expects her to be glad to see him whenever and wherever he turns up. And if she isn't, that shows there's something wrong with their relationship.'

'If she's expected to hold herself in readiness to jump for joy whenever he appears,' I said, 'and he's free to come and go as casually as that, without consulting her, then in my opinion there's something wrong with their relationship already.'

'That's what I think. I've thought it for some time, and today I had the impression that Judy was starting to think it too. She was pretty fed up. If he was expecting a big welcome, she certainly didn't switch it on for him. The temperature started to drop, and every time either one of them said anything it dropped a few degrees more. So I got out. There's no point in doing anything but leave them to sort it out.'

April, who had been listening silently, asked, 'What does her bloke do, that he goes away so much?'

'Oh, he's an actor,' said Julia. She spoke as if the question had reminded her, rather to her surprise, that there are some people in the world who are not actors.

'You both live in closed worlds,' I said. 'April never meets anyone who isn't medical, and Julia never meets anyone who isn't on the stage. You'll have to communicate through me.'

'A right mess we'd get into if we did that,' April said in a northern accent.

'What's the big variety act?' I asked her.

'That's how the patients talk in the hospital where I work. They say "Bah goom" and things like that, they really do. I thought they were putting it on at first.'

Julia began to intone,

A seaside resort they call Blackpool,
It's famous for fresh air and foon,

and straight away the two of them were at it, bandying jokes and snatches of rhyme and proverbs in heavy dialect. It was fooling

— 282 —

around, a let-down of that slight tension they had felt on meeting one another, but like most play it was very serious: they were sounding each other out, seeing if they had the same sense of humour and saw life in the same way. I refilled their glasses, which in the circumstances was the best contribution I could make.

After a couple of minutes they dropped the north-country clowning and began to talk like people. They discussed me as if I weren't there, but with an affectionate humour that made my heart sing. They dissected my taste in interior decorating (unfairly, since most of the grot was simply stuff I hadn't bothered to change since moving in), then went on to the probable chaos of my domestic arrangements.

'D'you think he's got any food in?' April asked.

'I doubt it. He hasn't been taking meals at home much lately.'

They went into the kitchen and hunted. I sat listening to their voices. 'Here's some bread – a bit stale, but I think it's eatable.' – 'Three eggs! Better than nothing.' – 'Some tomatoes, only one seems actually rotten.' – 'A few tins, here, but no opener. I suppose he uses a rusty penknife.' – 'No, he bashes them in with a canoe paddle.' – 'No butter, of course.'

I appeared in the doorway and said, 'There's a delicatessen on the corner that stays open. I could get anything we needed for a meal.'

'Good,' said April calmly. She came back into the living-room and sat down at the table. 'Let's make a list and send him out, Julia.'

'Suits me,' said Julia, joining her at the table.

'Have you got enough money to do a decent stock-up?' April asked me.

'I've got seven or eight pounds on me,' I said. 'They sell wine too.'

April picked up a pencil from beside the telephone. 'All right,' she said. 'Here goes to make a list of essentials.' Then she raised her head and for an instant looked straight into Julia's brown eyes. 'You'll need to get to know his tastes if you're going to be his girl-friend.'

The words thumped into my mind like falling bricks. My God! I thought. The little fool! How crass can you get?

But it must have been the right thing to say, because to my

amazement Julia just smiled at her with that wonderful serenity and said, 'I'm his girl-friend already.'

For an instant, April looked as if she were about to say something, and something positive. But, always economical with words, she just looked up at me and gave a little nod. That nod said I was in the clear.

They went back to list-making, and soon I was going down the steps and out to the delicatessen, with a big shopping-bag. I still didn't believe it. That the two of them were getting on, after that initial watchfulness, so marvellously – no jealousies, no antagonisms . . . but then, why not? Hadn't it been just my ingrained pessimism that made me fear that they would be cold and hostile to each other?

Look at it this way, I said to myself, neither of them is possessive about you, so they're not trying to cut each other down. They just like you, that's all.

Me? Somebody likes *me*?

Yes, and what's more, here is the friendly neighbourhood delicatessen. Mrs Rattner will tell you all about her chilblains, while you choose some egg noodles.

I got all the stuff and hurried back to the flat. (Never thought I'd hurry to get back *there*.) When I let myself in, Julia was doing something in the kitchen. I went in and put the groceries down and looked round for April. She didn't seem to be there.

'Where's April?' I asked.

'April's gone.'

'Gone? But we were just going to—'

Julia turned round from the stove and looked at me. She had on her serious expression: all her features very still, and only those deep, dark eyes regarding me with that concentrated attention.

'You're not to worry,' she said. 'April told me to say that. "Tell him he's not to worry," she said.'

'All right, I won't worry, but why did she decide not to stay?'

Julia wiped her hands on a kitchen towel, came through into the living-room, and picked up her glass of wine.

'Try to understand, Gus, will you?'

'Go ahead, I said.

'It was very important to April to know . . . what goes on. Whether you and I are close.'

'Well, are we?' I demanded.

'Yes,' she said. 'You heard me tell her that when she forced herself to ask me directly.'

'I wonder why she didn't wait and ask me.'

'I can answer that. Two reasons. One, she couldn't bear to wait, she needed to know *now*. Two, she probably didn't trust you to give her a straight answer.'

'She'd have been right, damn it,' I said. 'You can only give a straight answer if you're clear in your mind. And where you and I are concerned, I'm not clear. I don't know what's going to happen, I just live from day to day.'

'Right, so she didn't ask you. I'll come to you and me in a moment, but first I want to talk about April. What you do is important to her.'

'Not all that important. She's got her own life to—'

'Important, I said. Remember this – she's never seen you happy. Or not for a long time, anyway. I mean, I'm guessing, but if your marriage has been going wrong, it must have taken some time to get to the point of splitting up.'

'Well, yes and no,' I said. 'There was this man with his Flahs.'

'I don't know what you mean and I'm not going to stop while you explain it. Tell me later. The point now is April. She's a very, very good person and she loves you.'

'Still?' I said.

'Still. She's got to adjust to loving you and your wife separately, as two distinct people with distinct lives. That's if you're really not going back to her. You've never talked to me about it.'

'That's because there's nothing to talk about. I'm not going back to her.'

'You seem very sure.'

'I am very sure.'

'Have I made any difference to that?'

'As it happens, no.'

'You see,' she said, looking at her wine-glass and revolving it slowly, 'there are all sorts of adjustments for April to make. But perhaps the biggest one is what I said, that she doesn't remember what you're like when you're happy. You'll become a different person if you're happy, and then she'll have to alter all her feelings. She won't have to feel sorry for you any more, and that's bound to be a big change.'

'She'll weather it,' I said. 'April has a very tender heart, but not the kind of tender heart that goes about being professionally sorry for people's misfortunes, and enjoying it. She's too vital and too in love with life for that. She'd far rather be surrounded by people who are having a good time and feeling good about life.'

'That's all right then,' said Julia.

'Why is it all right?' I asked roughly. 'Come on, girl, talk turkey. You know only one thing will make me happy. Am I going to get it?'

She smiled and twirled the wine-glass a bit faster and said, 'You mean me?'

I nodded, and stared at her.

'Well, you've got what you want,' she said. 'I'm coming to live with you. We'll look round for a nicer and less cramped place than this, but till we find one we'll get along all right here.'

I took hold of her and kissed her. Half-way through, she put her glass down on the table and from then on she gave as good as she got.

After a bit she pushed me away and said, 'Calm down. There are some things I want to say yet.'

'Say them,' I said. 'Tell me how it's going to be.'

'We'll live together,' she said. 'I'll go round and look for jobs. Quite probably I'll get Judy's part in this company she's been with – those people you saw last night. Sometimes I'll be in work, and sometimes I'll be on Social Security.'

'No, you won't,' I said. 'No woman of mine is going to—'

'Oh, shut up and don't be such a Victorian. It's the normal procedure nowadays. There'll be enough calls on your money anyway. So, we'll live together. I'm not going to say how long for, because I don't believe in legislating for the future. But it might perfectly well be for ever, because you suit me. With you, I feel free and secure. I can be myself. And you can be yourself too, and it's a self I like.'

'Only like?' I said.

'All right, if you want a big squashy, seedy marrow of a word,' she said, 'it's a self I love.'

'I'm not going to tell you I love you,' I said, 'because you'd only say I was being squashy and seedy.'

'Be squashy and seedy if you like,' she said and kissed me

again. This time, when she got to the point of no return, she went on harder than ever.

Hours later, I remembered and asked her, 'What happened to April?'

'She left. But very gently. The whole business of making that list was just a device to get you out of the place, so she could talk to me for a few minutes.'

'What did she say?'

'I'm not going to tell you. We both spoke of you with love, let that be enough.'

It's enough, by God, I thought.

'And then she slipped out before you got back. She said she wanted to leave us alone, as we were obviously making each other happy. But I could tell there was something else as well. She needed to get away by herself and think. She wants time to get used to the new you.'

'Bless her,' I said. 'You know, I couldn't possibly say which of you I love most, her or you.'

'Oh, you love her most. You'd be a monster if you didn't. But there's no clash, you love me in a different way.'

'Ways,' I said. 'Plural.' Then I went ahead and demonstrated one of the ways I loved her. Afterwards, I rolled on to my back and lay there, trying to let it all sink in. But it was all so incredibly good, I had to go to sleep with my luck and happiness still floating in a coloured cloud above me.

Julia sat up in bed and said, 'Are you hungry?'

'Starving,' I said. 'And this time I want to do better than tinned Irish stew and whisky.'

'Darling, don't say that,' she said softly. 'It was the best meal in the world.'

So there we are. All these things happened over a year ago, and it's all still true. And still sinking in.

12

Dinah looked round approvingly at the neat, anonymous hotel bedroom.

'I like it. What a good idea you had.'

Giles nodded. 'It's years since I stayed in a London hotel. But when I used to, I usually came here. I remembered it as a comfortable place.' He did not trouble to add that its prices had gone up something like fivefold since those days. This was Dinah's coming-out, and any expense was legitimate. For their first-class train tickets, for their room and bath at a good hotel, for their taxis and conveniences generally, he had drawn from the bank a sum he had vaguely earmarked for next year's summer holiday: but what holiday could equal this, as a magnificent, revelling treat?

Giles carrying two suitcases, and Dinah cradling the case of her guitar, they had taken the train that morning. On getting to London, a couple of hours later, Dinah had hurried away to the concert-hall to get the feel of its acoustics and discuss programme details, while he settled into the hotel and booked a table for lunch. They had just eaten that lunch, and a good one it had been; now they had three or four hours to rest before the recital, and Giles was determined that the rest period should go as smoothly as everything else had. It was a new sensation for him to stage-manage someone else's performance, and he was enjoying it. He had, of course, like all men, some experience of cosseting women at times when they needed to be cosseted; Harriet, now and then, had felt tired or unwell and let him look after her and surround her with small attentions. But Harriet's rhythm of life had been more placid than Dinah's; even if she had been a painter successful enough to occupy the public eye, painters do not give recitals, and there had been, in Harriet's life, no prodigious expenditures of nervous energy such as Dinah was to make that night, and had been winding up to for three weeks.

Dinah slipped off her dress – more, he understood, not to crease it than to give him any ideas of liberty-taking – and lay prone on the bed. In her black nylon slip, with her face hidden in the pillow and her stockinged feet kicking idly, she seemed as innocent as a child; her narrow, sinuous body looked for once playful without sensuality.

'You must relax completely,' he directed, sitting down on the bed beside her.

'I can't. My neck muscles are tense.'

He began gently kneading her upper vertebrae, digging his thumbs firmly into the muscular tissue, going up all the way from just above her shoulder-blades to a point level with her ears.

'Mm. That's working.'

'Of course it's working.'

A moment later: 'It's lovely, but do you have to do it so *hard*?'

'It won't work if I don't put some ginger into it.' But he relaxed some of the pressure.

'Mm. That feels marvellous. I'll always employ you before a recital.'

'In that case I want my name in the programme. Pre-concert massage by Giles Hermitage.'

'Oh, then you'd get requests for other people. And I want you to be just for me.'

'I want you to be just for me, too,' he murmured.

What had he said? How could such a thing be? But he was too happy to police the words that escaped him.

She was happy too, to judge from the smile she gave him as she rolled on to her back.

'My neck's done now. Think of something else.'

He thought of something else.

In those next hours, lying close to Dinah in the large soft bed among furniture they had never seen before, away from troubles and possessions and complications, Giles felt a pure happiness that was, if possible, even greater than the peaks of delight she had already brought him. They seemed entirely at peace with

— 289 —

one another, entirely at one in the things they needed and hoped from life. He even found himself thinking, without urgency and without pain, of the death of her mother and that tortured last request. Should he tell Dinah about it? No, there would be time in the months and years to come. Let her mind be free of all such thoughts now. So, caressing her and revelling in her nearness, he thought about Helen within the solitude of his own skull. Would it, after all, be out of the question to write her story as a novel? To accept the challenge of imagining it, to convey the essence of Helen from his memory of her, and of the other two characters from his imagination, and make it live for the reader who had never met any of them? It would have to have a plot, of course; husband-meets-younger-woman-and-leaves-wife wasn't enough, on its own, for a novel; but the plot need not be a complicated puzzle; it could be a matter of angles and perspectives. Should he tell it from the point of view of the husband? See Helen as he must have seen her, from the outside? But in that case, what would become of Helen's request that he write it as a bitter condemnation of selfishness? Oh, but that objective had never been a real one. Still, the man might have shown a certain ruthlessness that perhaps went with the scientific temperament. There were interesting reaches of characterisation there. . . . So he pondered, in drowsy happiness, till Dinah claimed his attention and art gave place to life.

'My God, don't let me go to sleep and miss the concert!'

'There isn't the slightest possibil'ty of that.'

'Yes, there is. You're awfully sleepy. I shouldn't have got you to perform, I suppose.'

'I tell you, don't worry. I've rung the desk and asked for an alarm call at half-past five.'

'Oh, they'll forget. People like that are always inefficient.'

'Well, I'll stay awake myself, then,' he said.

'That's easier said than done. You've already dropped off about three times.'

'Only for cat-naps. All right, let's talk about something.'

They thought for a moment. Then she began shaking with silent laughter.

'What's the joke, darling?'

'I was just thinking,' she said, 'of the first time I met Dr Bowen.'

'I love the way you always call him "Doctor Bowen". Hasn't he got a first name?'

'Yes, it's Frank, but I don't like the name so I just used to call him You. And I think of him as Dr Bowen. You'll never guess where I first met him.'

'Do I have to guess?'

'No, I'll tell you. It was at the hospital.'

'There's nothing surprising about that.'

'Wait till you hear what *part* of the hospital.' She giggled again. 'It was at the V.D. clinic.'

'The *what?*'

'The V.D. clinic. Haven't you ever been to one?'

'Yes, once. A long time ago.'

'Well, I went to this one, just after I came down here to take care of Mother. I'd been cutting a bit of a swath in London in the last two or three weeks before I came away. I'm sure they were all perfectly reasonable men, but somehow one evening I started worrying. You know a woman can have gonorrhoea without knowing it. She can have no symptoms but all the time it's attacking her kidneys and one thing and another, it's awful. So of course I do something about it.'

'Yes. It wouldn't be like you to sit about and worry.'

'I like certainty. If there's something I *could* know, I want to know. There are enough unanswerable questions in life. It may be something to do with my father being a scientist. And in any case I like to look after myself.'

'Yes, darling. So you went to the clinic.'

'It was terribly funny. I was there with a lot of poor little sluts who just looked *dazed*. The type who get clapped up by men they're never going to see again and they can't even remember which one it was. And some old ones who'd either had it for *years* or must have got it from their husbands. And there was I, aloof and dignified, with my cultural book. I must have looked like one of those people who try to keep it up that they're not really there, that they took a wrong turning when they were looking for the family planning clinic or something.'

Giles had a very clear mental picture of her, sitting upright on a bench, reading George Eliot. Or perhaps *Lotte in Weimar*. And at the same time, taking in, with quick penetrating glances, all the other patients. And, when her number was called, getting

— 291 —

up with a single decisive movement and walking briskly in to see the doctor.

The doctor?

'Are you going to tell me,' he said, 'that Dr Bowen examined you to see if you had anything?'

'Well, no. But he might have. He was there. A lot of doctors work part of the time in these clinics, you know. There's such a lot of sexually transmitted disease about, they can't find enough specialists to man them. It's fairly routine work, just checking up.'

'All the same, it wasn't he who checked you up?'

'No. But as I was coming out, I saw him, in a white coat, leaning against the wall. He noticed me. I felt his eyes on me as I walked past.'

'But look here, let me get this straight. If you were down there to look after your mother, and he was your mother's doctor, you must have met him already.'

'No,' she said. 'That was how I knew he was after me. My mother had the same doctor she'd had for years – a very old man, close to retiring. Then, a couple of days after I saw Dr Bowen at the clinic, he turned up on the doorstep. He's a partner in the same firm as the old man, and he'd persuaded the old man to off-load a few cases in the last months before his retirement, and he'd taken good care that one of them should be Mother.'

'Good God. Is that the sort of thing doctors do?'

'Well, it's the sort of thing *he* does. But I think his reputation's beginning to catch up with him now.' She spoke amusedly. 'He's emigrating. Going to Canada to look after Air Force personnel. He told me about it. He'll be getting the equivalent of eighteen thousand a year.'

Giles whistled. 'He's successful all right.'

'Well,' she said placidly, 'he was certainly successful with me. Till you came along.' She kissed him, lazily.

'Are you glad I came along?'

'Yes. Yes, Giles. I'm glad, I'm glad.'

In the taxi on the way to the recital, Giles found he could not keep his eyes from Dinah; as the lights from outside surged and swam across their shadowy little moving room, her eyes had a brilliance, and her pale face a composed alertness, that hypnotised him. The intensity of his love for her burned in his blood-vessels. Almost, it forced itself into utterance in words, a declaration of passion that would have torn the covering from his heart like the peel from an orange. But he decided this was not the time for emotional speeches, and stopped short of speech.

The taxi set them down near the musicians' entrance, and she gave him his instructions.

'From here on I play it alone. Go and take your place in the hall and wait for me in the foyer when it's over.'

'All right, darling. Good luck.'

'I'll play specially for you.'

'I love you, Dinah.'

'I love you too, Giles.'

She had said it.

Half an hour later the recital had begun. Dinah shared the programme with two singers, a baritone and a soprano. Both performed separately first; their music was pleasing enough, but Giles was living for Dinah to come on for the first of her two appearances. At last, she did so; her slight, tense figure walked quickly out under the lights, she sat down and took hold of her guitar. There was a music-stand near her chair, but she had no need of it; she knew her programme note by note. He knew how her heart must be beating: what fear, and yet what exultation, flooded her veins. He leaned forward, sending vibrations of love and strength towards her. Perhaps, at every recital of music, there is someone in the audience who feels like that.

She touched the strings; obedient, the instrument sang the first few notes. It was beginning. The music woke and stirred into life as she released it from its polished box.

On the brightly lit platform, she played: in the dim, studious hush of the auditorium, he listened: and there stole over him the deep, calm sense that all would surely be well. He had seen her prepare and ponder and rehearse; but only now, for the first time, did she display her artistry in its pure strength. Humbly content to be levelled among the audience, just one in the mass of attentive heads she was addressing, he saw her vocation in its

— 293 —

uncluttered outlines. To be the living channel for all that passion and beauty, some of it created by men who might be in that same room listening to her, some of it by men who had been centuries in their graves, but in either case to interpret, to make her warm, living woman's body the instrument of their driving power, to use her skill of brain and fingers to make the guitar sing and talk and chant *for them*, and beyond them for the listening myriads who, giftless themselves, hungered to share in the gift of the composers – this was a supreme fulfilment of her nature, on a level (almost) with her love of men.

And he, Giles? What was to be his part in all this? Listening in rapture, watching her tense weasel-body bent over in concentration, he knew that there was so much they shared: surely nothing could break the current between them now that it had got into this rhythm. Men she liked, yes: just men, any men, so long as they were personable and potent; sex for her was a wonderful, murmurous jungle where she hunted with feral relish and ferocious satisfaction; but it was clear to him now that, while the Dr Bowens of this world could come and go in her life, she had found a repose, an anchorage, in him, because they had a common language and a common aspiration. And he knew that this was why he, ageing, battered, adrift, a bundle of needs and frustrations, had the right to be important to her.

Happiness, pride, ballooned in him. He felt almost as if his body were weightless, that he would presently rise up to the ceiling. When she finished, he sank back exhausted and blissful as from love-making. She was marvellous, miraculous, one of the immortals already! The applause she earned was brisk, and he helped it along till his palms smarted. Oh Dinah, Dinah.

The soprano and the baritone came together in a duet, Haydn's arrangement of *Schlaf in deiner engen Kammer*, that ravished Giles; he felt he could endure no more beauty, that he would 'die of a rose in aromatic pain,' and, fortunately, at that point it was the interval and he could walk about mindlessly, drink coffee, push through the doors for a few draughts of fresh air to bring him down to normality.

Settling into his seat for the second half of the programme, he found that some of the awe of the occasion was wearing off. That Dinah was there on the platform, performing to an audience, seemed no longer a miracle, but if anything something even better – a deeply satisfying and joyous manifestation of normality. Her dedication and artistry, and the attention it won her, were simply part of the expected order of things: she was being now what she had for so long been becoming. Giles even found himself relaxing sufficiently to wonder whether his own presence played any part in her experience of this triumph. When she looked at the audience and acknowledged their applause with a gracious smile, did she see him there? Once or twice he thought that she looked straight at him; that, though the auditorium was in shadow and the stage strongly lit, her eyes had found him out. Improbable as it was, he clung to the thought and did nothing to discourage it.

After Dinah's performance had ended, there were some forty minutes to go before the end of the programme. He waited, tranquilly, his mind full of glowing images of how they would spend the rest of the evening. Of course she would not be ready to go out straight away; she would want to linger for a while and be sociable with the other musicians; perhaps some of her own musical friends, having the entrée to the dressing-rooms, would go and seek her out and offer their congratulations. He would wait; he must not hog her; he would be calm and benign and supporting. And then again, her agent must surely be here, on this night of nights – doubtless he, at least, would go and visit her backstage and reaffirm his belief in her and outline future plans.

What a fool he had been not to make time to slip away to a florist's and get her a really big bouquet. That was the kind of thing the occasion called for. Armed with it, he might even have the nerve to go backstage himself, though she had not invited him.

Instead, he waited in the foyer. All round him, the audience put on their coats and, released into chatter and sociability, went out in twos and threes into the mild dampness of the night. He remained, in a rapidly emptying space.

For a time, he tried to move the lagging minutes along by concentrating on pleasant thoughts. He counted the money in his wallet; it was enough for an excellent dinner at any restaurant they wanted to go to – surely she must be hungry? – and besides he had a credit card that should be good in most places. They could really live it up.

An attendant came up and said the building must now be locked. Was Giles waiting for someone?

'Yes. Miss Redfern.'

'Miss . . . ?'

'She was performing here tonight. Dinah Redfern.'

'Oh,' said the man indifferently. Obviously musicians to him were anonymous, interchangeable parts of the machinery that kept this place going and provided him with a living. 'She'll have a dressing-room then, sir. They won't be locking up yet. You'd better go round there. She'll be in Four-B, most likely. Outside, turn left and. . . .' He gave directions, waiting to lock the doors and catch his bus home.

Giles followed the directions. Outside, the moist air made a halo round the lamps; he felt as if he were moving through a dream landscape or perhaps taking part in a film.

He found Room 4B. He knocked and a woman's voice said, 'Come in.' Entering, he found that it was a medium-sized *salon* with armchairs and sofas, with small dressing-rooms opening out of it. There were three or four people sitting at one end, talking among themselves, and they did not look up at him. But the one who had said 'Come in' was looking at him enquiringly. She was, he saw, the soprano who had performed.

'Er – Miss Redfern,' Giles said.

'She left about ten minutes ago,' said the soprano. She was, Giles now noticed, a very pretty Jewish girl, fresh and blooming, rather plump, with bright, dark eyes. During the concert he had taken no notice of her appearance, so occupied were his thoughts with love of Dinah. Now, looking at her close to, he saw her clearly. She would make someone happy.

'She left?' Giles repeated. The words seemed like empty sounds. What could they mean, *She left*?

'She went out with a man who came back to see her,' the soprano said.

A man? But I am her man.

'Was she expecting you?' the girl asked. 'You'd better have a drink now you're here, anyway. There's some left.'

'Thank you,' said Giles. 'It's very kind of you . . . but I'd better . . . I mean, I ought to go and . . . see if she's anywhere about.'

The singer wrinkled her creamy, smooth brow and said, 'Oh,

I was forgetting. Silly of me, but so much has been happening. Is your name Giles?'

'Yes.'

'In that case there's a message for you.'

'From Dinah?'

She nodded and went over to a kind of sideboard. 'It's here,' she said, and handed him what he saw to be a programme of the concert. On the outside, Dinah had written his name, *Giles Hermitage*. He opened it. Inside, in the white space across the top, were some words in her clear, well-formed handwriting.

It was so characteristic of Dinah that her writing was as easy to read as print. The letters were perfectly formed and the whole effect was clear and decisive. She hated mess, scribble, indecision. She liked to know where she was and everyone else to know where they were.

She had written, *Sorry, am called away. All a bit unexpected. Don't try to get in touch. D.*

The pretty Jewish girl was watching his face. He swallowed and tried to smile. Then he turned and left the room.

The way back to the outside world was short; the night was still as balmy as when he last saw it, three or four minutes ago in another life. At first he walked without knowing where. Then he saw a car-park. People came and went in cars. They used cars for moving about in. If a man had come and taken her off, about ten minutes ago, he might have come in a car. And be just moving off. If he got there in time, if he intercepted the car, he might, he might what? Well, he might. If he got there. If it was she. And he. He and she, in a car. He might. Leaving the car-park, he just might.

He approached. As he did so, a car started up at the far end and moved smartly down towards the entrance he was aiming for. It was a Porsche. He knew the make because he had once been given a lift in one, by a young director of the firm that published him. It was shiny, and fast, and competent. Like Dinah.

Giles kept walking towards the mouth of the car-park. The Porsche accelerated briskly, reached the exit, hesitated briefly as the driver looked up and down the road, then shot off.

Was it? He was not near enough to see how many people were in the car, let alone to recognise them. He had no means of knowing whether that car was the one that contained Dinah and her man. Or whether they had gone in a car at all. Perhaps he had kept a taxi waiting. Or perhaps they had walked arm in arm, laughing, towards the nearest tube station.

And yet the image of that compact, streamlined car nosing out of the deserted car-park and dwindling into the softness of the night was the one that would stay with Giles as the symbol of Dinah's going.

Standing on the pavement, watching the place where the car had been, he noticed that he still held in his hand the programme the Jewish girl had given him. With Dinah's farewell writing on it. He folded and tore it: into two, into four, then into eight. After that the thickness of the paper resisted the grip of his fingers. It was too tough to tear any more.

13

N O ACTOR EVER HAD SUCH AN AUDIENCE. WE SAT ROUND IN A ragged circle, determined not to miss a syllable, hardly daring to listen to our own breathing.

Jake Delmore, actor – Jake Driver, television star and idol of millions – stood in the middle of the room and tried to begin unburdening himself. Clearly, he wanted to say something that was important to him, but he found it a struggle. His face had lost its professional assurance; he no longer seemed to be selecting one after another from his armoury of expressions and beaming them at us. What I read in his face was nothing professional; it was honest bewilderment. Yet what could he possibly have to be bewildered about? The man who held all the cards, who had every advantage, who was winning in the battle of life in which the rest of us were either losing, like me, or marking time, like Julia, or perhaps just digging away in some underground gallery of their own, like Detective-Sergeant Ambrose?

When at last Jake did speak, the words that came out were so unexpected that at first they struck my ear as meaningless syllables.

' "Ye elves of hills, brooks, standing lakes, and groves;" ' he said gravely, ' "and ye, that on the sands with printless foot do chase the ebbing Neptune and do fly him when he comes back".' He was looking straight at Julia, holding her eyes which had come up to stare into his. 'Where did you last hear those words, doll?' he asked her.

'At Wolverhampton,' she said, sounding almost hypnotised.

'How does it go on?'

'Something about demi-puppets.'

'You remember,' he breathed as if in relief.

'Of course. You had a lot of trouble with that speech.'

'I wasn't right for the part. But we were a very young company, and I was about the only male in it who could make himself sound like an old man.'

She giggled softly. 'You managed to make yourself sound about forty. That seemed old by the side of the rest of them.'

'I had trouble with the beginning and middle of that speech,' he said. 'The end part was all right. "But this rough magic I here abjure." '

He looked round at the rest of us, as if challenging us to crack the code in which he had elected to talk to his wife. Detective-Sergeant Ambrose immediately filled in with 'Shakespeare. *The Tempest.*'

'Act Five,' I said, just so that the policeman shouldn't stand out as the only educated man among Jake's audience.

'We were working with a little fit-up touring company,' said Jake, remembering. 'A pittance had been screwed out of the West Midlands Arts Council and we were doing a Shakespeare for the edification of the good people of Wolverhampton. God knows what kind of a mess we made of it. But Julia was Miranda, and I was jealous of the bloke who played Ferdinand and kissed her on stage, though she was coming home with me every night.'

Julia said, forcing a roughness into her voice, 'What's this got to do with anything?'

'It's got to do with us, darling.'

'Us is finished.'

' "This rough magic I here abjure;" ' he said in a harsher voice, staring round at our faces. ' "I'll break my staff, Bury it certain fathoms in the earth".' His voice became almost a snarl as he ended, ' "And, deeper than did ever plummet sound, I'll drown my book".'

In the short silence that followed, Frank Hopper said wearily, 'D'you mind telling us what this is supposed to convey, Jake?'

'I'll tell you,' Jake Delmore said. 'Yes, I'll tell you.' But he continued for a few moments to look at us without speaking, as if, now that he had moved away from the lines he had been given to learn, he was finding it difficult to come up with any word of his own.

Finally he said, 'Magic spells. That's what I'm talking about. Magic spells.'

If he thought I was in danger of casting him as a Prospero, I couldn't help saying to myself, he had another thing coming.

'Here you are in front of me,' he said, 'four of you. You've each got slightly different motives for coming round here, but at bottom you're all the same – you all want me to do something for you. You've all got problems that I can solve. Good old Jake, the man with the magic wand, he'll solve our problems because he's got none of his own. That's what you think, isn't it? That I've got no problems?'

Nobody spoke, and he went on. 'I've got money, and I've got fame. They've come quite suddenly, but they're solidly here – they won't go away in a hurry. As far as all that goes, I'm on top of the world for a few years yet. I went on the box, I was a success, the series got good ratings, each contract I get is better than the last, they keep offering me more and more money. Jake Driver, king of the world. He has everything he wants – a nice place to live, good meals, good times. All the birds clustering round him. No wonder he thinks marriage a very unnecessary tie. So he behaves wildly, his wife cuts out and leaves him, and he couldn't care less, just snaps his fingers. That's what you all think, isn't it? No problems, no worries, no regrets, because of course there's nobody he loves and so there's nobody he could possibly miss when they go.'

He paused and glared at us. 'So the way you've got it worked out, I've got everything and I can afford to give anything away. When there's a big favour you want me to do, *of course* I'll do it – why not? What can it cost me? I don't need to be helped or reassured, I don't need any support because I get my ego boosted all the time by those millions of satisfied viewers.' He glared round at us again. 'Well, I may have news for you. It may be that I *do* need to build myself up, it may be that there *are* things I'm afraid of, and things I regret, and people I miss. And it may be that I *do* need to get my own back a bit, here and there, and not just take everything with a laugh. So Cliff tried to frighten me and get twenty thousand pounds out of my bank account? Oh, ha-ha, good old Cliff, he doesn't mean any harm, and besides, we're sorry for him, and of course it doesn't matter to Jake.'

Julia said, 'Jake, don't build up a grudge against Cliff. If you want to take out your frustrations, take them out on the rest of us.'

'Oh. At least you acknowledge that I might *have* some frustrations.'

'Everybody has.'

'I don't believe it. I know *you* understand a lot about me, but these' – he waved, dismissively, towards the rest of us – 'just assume that because I've got money, and strangers come up to me in the street, there can't be a cloud in my sky.'

Detective-Sergeant Ambrose shifted his bulk in the armchair and said, 'Do I understand you to say, Mr Delmore, that because of the difficulties of your life you don't feel in a forgiving mood, and because you don't feel in a forgiving mood you're not likely to do anything to soften the blow for Cliff Sanders? Forgive me, sir, but however unofficially, I do represent the police, and we have to know where we stand.'

'Yes,' said Jake Driver. He swayed his head from side to side just like a bull. 'A bit of knowing where we stand wouldn't hurt any of us, I fancy.'

'Well, I know where I stand, Jake,' said Julia. 'I'm cutting out, and if—'

'Ah, but do you?' he interrupted her. 'Do you know where you stand? Are you so sure of that?'

'I know you've made it impossible for me to—'

'Look, Julia, get one thing straight. I love you.'

Oh, come on, I told him silently.

She must have thought the same because she said, 'Jake, if you think I'm going to swallow that after what you—'

'After what I did the other night. After the sight that greeted your eyes when you walked in here from the theatre. Well, if I can't live that down I can't. But you might at least give me a chance to make things clear.'

'*Clear?* How can it be clearer? I saw with my own—'

'You can at least get the background to it.' He stopped. 'Look, I'm not going to spell it all out in front of this crowd. I'm going to send them away and I want you to do one thing for me, if it's the last thing you ever do. Stay behind. Talk to me, listen to me, share my home one more night.'

'No,' she said.

'Yes. Otherwise it's no dice with Cliff. Darling, listen to me. I've got to use what leverage I've got, and your feeling for Cliff is just about all there is. I want to use it to revive some of your feelings for me.'

'Why d'you want to?' she asked indifferently. At least, her voice was indifferent, but I had a horrible feeling that underneath it there was a stir of real curiosity.

We all sat still for a moment. Then Detective-Sergeant Ambrose, with immense deliberation, got to his feet.

'I have the feeling,' he said, 'that the rest of us ought to withdraw. There seems to be nothing left for us to discuss at this stage. The next step must be between Mrs Delmore and her husband.' I hated the way he said 'husband.' 'Whatever is the outcome of any discussion between them, it's going to be the deciding factor.' He looked round at all of us. I expected him to say 'Tsk,' but he didn't. He just started moving towards the door. One by one we got up and followed him.

The door closed behind us and already I felt it was closing on all my hopes. Julia was the other side of it with Jake, the man she had been so young with, who had been through those early years, living on hope and boiled cabbage with her, who had made her love him so much that she had wanted to be his *wife*, for God's sake. And the door was shut and I was outside.

'We'll keep in touch,' said Frank Hopper to me. He seemed in a hurry to get away, as if he couldn't bear the sight of me. I supposed he found the whole situation distasteful and embarrassing. So did I. Detective-Sergeant Ambrose said nothing. He just went quietly to the lift and pressed the button.

I let them go down together, while I went down the stairs. The thought of standing with them in that plushy interior, wafting slowly down to street level while we tried not to look at each other's faces, was enough to give me a haemorrhage. I preferred the clean-swept, lonely steps, one after another, flight after flight of them, down, down.

When I got into the lobby Dennis gave me a sour look. Since I was on the way out rather than in he let me go by unmolested, but he conveyed pretty clearly that he thought I had no right there in the first place. As I came out of the building I was just in time to see Frank Hopper's car driving off. Detective-Sergeant Ambrose was sitting beside him as before.

That left me standing on the pavement, alone. It wasn't raining, but the air was damp and chill with what could have been approaching rain. The summer was good and over. The year's summer, and my summer.

I moved without much purpose in the general direction of my flat. Pretty soon I left the plushy neighbourhood of Windermere Gardens and was threading my way through side streets that had a vaguely sinister air. I took no notice. My head was full of what ought to have been thoughts, except that somehow they wouldn't take shape as thoughts. They just crammed my skull with a kind of stiff, obstinate paste that wouldn't move, or attach itself to words or images. I've come to know that paste since. I think they call it despair.

There was a pub at the end of the street. It didn't look particularly inviting, but I went in anyway. The clientele consisted of two old women drinking Guinness and a cluster of youths round a pin-table machine. I bought a whisky and a half of beer to chase it with, and went over to a corner. The drinks just seemed to disappear, so I went and got the same again. That seemed to disappear too – I didn't remember drinking, but suddenly the glasses were empty. So I got a grip on myself, went over and got a third instalment, and carried it back to my corner with a determination to make it last this time, while I sat and thought things over.

Thought things over? What a mistake! What could thinking do for me now? It wasn't my brain I was registering with – it was my body. I don't know, and I wouldn't expect to know, how human perception is parcelled out as between the mind and the body, but I do know this: when Julia and I were close together, loving each other, it was my body that renewed itself and blossomed, it was my body that learnt a new language, that became a vehicle of joy, that sang and rejoiced and rampaged through the universe. My mind shared in the general benefit, of course, but as a subordinate partner, getting the good news at second-hand. Well, now the opposite was happening. As I sat in the pub, mechanically draining alcoholic liquids into a dead belly, my body was getting the vibrations from that closed room half a mile away. It *knew*, and passed the knowledge on to my mind, that Julia was listening to Jake, feeling close to him, welcoming his thoughts, seeing his point of view, touching him. . . . And I swear to God that my body knew exactly the moment when they went to bed and started fucking. Why not? Why shouldn't it know? The blessing of her love, the joy of her embrace, had irradiated my blood and bones, given life and hope to every atom of my body, and now she was giving all this strength and happiness back to their original owner, and my body could read the bad news just as it had been able to read the good news. As I sat slumped inertly on that torn leather bench, I knew that she was Jake's again. After all, what had he done that a woman could not forgive? I knew already, had known for a long time, that a woman never, in the end, finds sexual misdeeds unforgivable, however monstrous the form they take, because any depth of lechery, any abyss of betrayal, does at least indicate a need for what women have to give, and if he needs what women have to give then sooner or later he will need *her* again – that's how they reason it out, unconsciously, no doubt, but firmly. So Jake had run mad with that horrible slimy friend of his and a couple of girls! What did it matter, so long as he was sorry when it was over and hadn't contracted any diseases? She would take him back, of course she would, they were the same kind of animal. I loved her far, far more than he ever could: but, in the end, what pull was there in that? People don't love the ones who love them most, but the ones who attract them most; in about one case in a hundred thousand, the good Lord steps in and gets the two into line, and then you have one of those marriages that really *are* made in heaven. Well, I hadn't achieved that with Julia, or come anywhere near it, and that was the knowledge I had to face now, the knowledge I had to live with.

Live? Was it really necessary to live? Come to that, was it possible? After all, it's your body that decides whether you live or die. If it doesn't want to carry on the struggle of survival any longer, your body will soon enough produce a cancer, or a wasting disease, or a glandular disorder of some kind; or, simply, guide you towards some fatal self-indulgence.

I didn't know. The future would reveal which way out my body would decide to take. Only one thing I knew for certain, as I sat there in front of two empty glasses, not feeling drunk yet but not able to muster the energy to go up and get more to drink. One thing, but it was enough. He had her back, she was flowing towards him, she had forgiven him and in so doing had cast me off: with no ill-will, just automatically, as a living tree lets fall a dead leaf.

Then the image of Daphne came to me, strongly; all at once I could see her as clearly as if she were sitting opposite me, there in that greasy pub. I saw her as she was when I last talked to her. It was after I had left our house in Western Approaches Avenue, and she had taken refuge with Hilda. It was summer, and we had met one evening in a public park. We sat on a bench and talked. Mostly we were quite unemotional, both of us trying to keep the discussion cool and not make fools of ourselves in public. Just once she put her hand on my arm and left it there for a moment: thinking, perhaps, that if she let it lie there, like some harmless domestic animal curled up before a fire, it would engender some kind of warmth between us. I sat quite still and continued to talk in a calm, uninvolved voice, as if I were oblivious of the touch of her hand, and after a minute or two she took it away again; it joined her other hand and the two of them lay tidily folded in her lap. It seemed a tranquil enough gesture, a signal that she accepted the situation as it was and as it must now be: but in fact that was the moment when she began to lose control. Before long she was weeping and imploring; then she was clenching her jaw and shaking her fist in my face; then she was weeping again, soundlessly, the tears pouring down her face. I could see that face so clearly now, swollen-eyed, the cheeks drenched with the salt flow of her grief, and I could see the hands clasping and unclasping in her lap. Suddenly they seemed to me like the hands of a dying woman, as one might see them, in the afternoon light, lying helpless on the counterpane of a final bed.

Talking to Daphne on that park bench, as the birds carolled on the branches and children played over the fresh grass, had been (I now saw) like sitting by the bed of a dying woman. When the body has decided to die, there is no stopping it; the vital essence drains away, and all an onlooker can do is offer such consolation and such understanding as can be mustered. And perhaps we do these things for our own sakes, to be able to walk away from that bedside and go on living despite the taste of death in our mouths.

My wife Daphne, sitting on that park bench in the mild

summer air, staring at me with those brimming eyes, had been like a dying woman: her eyes had been turned not towards the death of her body but towards the death of her emotions, the fading of her ability to be happy. I could read her thoughts so clearly – she knew that her foolish escapade, trivial enough in itself, had provided the jar that had knocked the lid from the dull, commonplace vessel of our marriage, and once the lid was off the musty reek of failure and boredom reached everyone's nostrils. The Flahs man had meant nothing to her except a little flattery, a few new tricks in bed, a brief respite from the eternal sameness of marriage, and I did not blame her in the least. But the impact had been made, the stone vessel of habit and expectation had lost its lid, and the stench could only be left to clear with time. One thing had been plain to me: I was not willing to pick up the lid and put it back, sealing in all that staleness for another thirty years; and I was the only one who could do it. She felt – I could read it – that her mistake had lost her all love, all security, all possibility of building; so why not simply say that what she was facing was death, and have done with it?

Visualising Daphne, I forgot the lush grass, the whirling children, the evening sunshine, and put her into a bed with her head back among the pillows. I saw her flesh wither away and the bones of her face appear: her hands, lying still, became as chalky as a cadaver's. Such bird-song as I could hear came through the slightly open window from a featureless suburban garden. And I felt afresh her power over me – for she had power to call me to her side, to fix my attention, to rive my spirit with grief and pity at the sight of her sufferings. She was dying, she was sinking into blackness, but as she sank she pulled me forward, pace by pace, into a desert of stone and salt.

Her image blinked out and was replaced by an equally clear picture of Jake and my Julia. They were making love now. I knew it as plainly as if I were watching them on a television screen. I sat there, facing that knowledge, and as I did so the fires inside me, one by one, went out.

Now I knew there was nothing left but age, the slow dying-out of impulse, the cooling of the warm blood in my veins till it became thin, cold soup, pumping wearily round and round my body just because it had nowhere else to go, waiting for release and the end of pain.

Without even bothering to get any more to drink I buttoned my overcoat and walked back to the flat.

14

Giles Hermitage laid down his ball-point writing implement. Though it was barely eight o'clock in the morning, he had been writing for three hours and now the last chapter of his novel was finished – the re-written, realistic last chapter. When he gathered up the manuscript for the typist, he would throw out the happy, euphoric phantasmagoria he had written during that blissful three weeks in Princess Terrace, and substitute the sad, truthful version he had just penned. For of course that was how the story of Gus Howkins and Julia would actually have ended, in the real world. She would have gone back to her egotistic, unscrupulous, successful owner and let her dream-haunted adorer drift away on the tide of his own chaotic thoughts. As he thought over the story, Dinah's voice echoed in his head: 'Strong, amusing, sexy men who are bastards, and nice men who on the whole tend to be slightly wet.' Well, the s., a., s. b.s had always won and always would win.

He stood up from his writing-table and looked out of the window. Early spring had changed to summer since that morning when he had first opened the letter from Helen Chichester-Redfern. Now she was dead and so, in most respects, was he. As the green earth rioted in joy and abundance, as life danced and waved and beckoned from every crevice, Giles faced the knowledge that his own life had come to a halt.

He had known it ever since he stood, frozen into cold, aching stone, in that car-park. How many hours he stood there, or paced back and forth in the nearby streets, he did not know. Somehow, but he had no memory of it, he had got back to the station and, slumped on a bench, waited for a train that clanked through the rainy dawn. Mid-morning found him back in his own flat; at once, without attempting to sleep or eat or even wash, he had thrown himself into the story of Gus Howkins and Julia, clutching at it as the one rope that moored him to anything that could be called sanity. Since then, for three days, he had alternated between fitful snatches of sleep, hasty meals when actual starvation threatened, and long hours at his work-table. During these hours he had sometimes written fast, sometimes slowly and sometimes not at all, staring at the blank paper while patches of light grew and travelled across the wall. When Mrs Pimlott came, he went out for a walk or took a long bath, running more hot water in when it cooled, waiting out the time till he heard the front door slam behind her. He did not dare face her, or, indeed, anybody; he felt his behaviour would be such that they would telephone a doctor and get him taken away to a madhouse. Normal life, normal procedures, were unthinkable. It was not until half-way through his second day at home that he remembered the hotel room where they were to have spent the night. He had left his suitcase there, and so, for that matter, had Dinah. He telephoned, apologised, and enquired the amount of the bill. The receptionist told him that 'Mrs Hermitage' (for of course he had done a routine Mr-and-Mrs signing-in) had come for her case, but that his was still there, and that she had settled the bill. He rang off, nervelessly. He had known it was goodbye, but that cold little fact confirmed it. To take away her suitcase, and leave his to its fate; and to pay the bill for a room she had not occupied – it seemed a gesture of turning-away, a statement that she wanted to be in no debt to him. Perhaps, the thought pressed in through the doors of his mind, she had dropped by for her case in company with the man she had been with all night; celebrating with him: he would be in a generous, victorious mood, and perhaps it was he who had given her the money to settle the bill. Oddly, even these hypodermic thoughts did nothing to stir his emotions. He contemplated the whole shocking mess as if it were a disaster that had happened to someone else who had lived a long time ago.

After the departure of Harriet, he had been a seething mass of agony. Now, he was simply an empty shell, a container in which there had once lived a man. This deadness was terrifying to him, but he was dimly aware that an even greater terror lurked behind it: that when, if ever, the anaesthetic of his stunning wore off, the pain would begin, and it would be like the pain of Harriet, only worse. And if it were worse, he would not be able to stand it. And if he could not stand it, the only alternatives would be suicide or mental disintegration. And since he could not commit suicide, not having the temperament to contemplate it, he would break apart. His mind would fly into fragments and men in white coats would lead him away and lock him up.

So it was better like this, not feeling, not thinking, not living as a man at all. The story had been there to protect him, to draw off the fevered discharge of living into a shaped vessel. But now the story was finished. What now? Start another? No, never. He could not imagine setting his mind to work on a new subject. There were, for him, no new subjects, nor would there ever be. The only reason he had been able to contemplate the story of Gus Howkins was precisely because that story had been his companion through all the recent events in his life. It had gone along with him, step by step, providing an alternative existence that had strangely held to the same contours as his actual one. It had been a life-saving overspill; he had been able to write about the joy and sadness of Gus Howkins because they were closely linked to his own joy and sadness. But a new story, a fresh subject, conjured out of the air – the thought terrified and repelled him. It would have meant a new adventure, and he had not strength enough for a new adventure. He had not even strength enough for a return to his old pattern of monotonous non-event. He had nothing but the husk of a life that had become unlivable.

What should he do? A day stretched ahead in which, though exhausted enough for a hospital, he needed activity of some kind. If he had none, and if he relaxed, the thought of Dinah would come in, the flavour, the presence, the feel of her, and with them the knowledge of all he had lost, and then he would go mad, irretrievably.

As he stood in frozen indecision, he saw the postman approach Sunderland Court with deliberate step and bulging sack. He pictured the man's methodical, unhurried movements as he filled the numbered mail-boxes. Another day's messages: quotidian life rolling on. Well, why not? He would go down and see if there were something to deal with. Bills to pay, circulars to throw away, anything.

As he went towards the door he glanced over at the carton of mouldering letters. Perhaps he ought to clear them all off first, before going down to see what was new today? But at the thought, his stomach tightened into a knot. No, no, let the dead bury their dead. Start looking at today's letters today, tomorrow's letters tomorrow. He could not dredge back into his dead life: better to go forward, even into the living death that awaited him.

He went down. There were four letters. He carried them up the stairs held loosely in his hand, not bothering to look at them until he got back and was once more standing before the window. Now. Look. Number one, a buff envelope. Number two, a circular. Number three. . . .

Number three was an air-letter. From Australia. The writing was Harriet's.

Giles sat down at the table. For a wonder, his paper-knife was lying within reach, looking docile and ready for work. He picked it up, and slit open the letter very slowly and carefully, reading the instructions. First fold here. Slit here. He worked with the deliberation of a man on the edge of a nervous breakdown to whom the simplest movement is a task to be planned like a chess move.

It was done. He had the letter open. The letter from Harriet in Australia.

Giles, Giles, my far-away lost darling,

See how small I'm writing. The plane flies in twenty minutes. You know I usually write big, sprawling words. Now I'm writing so small, so small – because I *am* small, I'm broken and little and ashamed and I want to creep into a crack in the floor but there isn't one, airport floors are made of some awful plastic or rubber. I'm crying Giles, sorry about that smudge. This letter isn't to say anything, I mean, I know you won't ever listen to me again or do anything for me or *love* me, who could, and I'm writing on a horrid little table where people have spilt drinks, and I've spilt a drink on it, and I'm crying and people are looking across at me and the plane goes in 20 min. and I'm going to Hobart. Giles, I'm trying to pull myself together, trying to write to you sensibly even though you won't answer or probably *read* it even, darling, I broke your heart and it was all for nothing, worse than nothing. I thought I knew A. but I hadn't even begun to know him, he's cruel, CRUEL. Look, his first wife divorced him for cruelty, a charming little detail I didn't know till we had an evening with some relatives of his out here and the wife told me while we were in the kitchen making mayonnaise. Yes, mayonnaise for a lobster! I can tell you I was the lobster, I had this thick gooey mess all over me, all over my life, not sperm, I don't mean anything as healthy as that, just *his* CRUELTY. I can't bear to think about him, Giles he's mad, but it must be a catching sort of madness somehow, because he gave it me, I honestly can't think back now to why I ever got close to him, I think he must be a hypnotist or something – O I know you'll just think I'm making excuses Christ the paper's moving, I keep writing crooked oh no it's just that I'm a bit drunk O darling Giles O I miss you and I'll never never see you again O God the plane goes in ten minutes now O Giles I'm crying so hard and I'm drunk well I ran out of the house with just this suitcase while he was away at work I could never tell you I could never tell anybody what he did to me Giles he's ill, he should be in Broadmoor if they have one here but I expect they don't, they're all so damn healthy. I got a cab out here and the next plane going to somewhere he won't find me is Hobart, that's why I'm going there, it isn't that I know anyone or know what to do but I'll get a job there, I'll be a waitress or anything. I can't get out of Australia now, I'm stuck here for the rest of my life, all right I've bought it, I had a happy life and I had you, darling darling Giles, he must be a hypnotist.

Well it's too late. I've finished my drink and I'm going over to a post-box I can see in the corner and I'm going to post this. I know I'll never see you again, Giles, but this is just to say I love you and I'm sorry and if you ever could just write a line to say you don't hate me and you think sometimes of our good days. I expect Poste Restante Hobart will find me and I'd be so grateful. End of space – goodbye – Harriet.

Giles put down the letter, very carefully, as if it would be damaged by abrupt contact with the wood of the table. He had no feelings. The word 'Harriet' was no more than a word to him – an aspirate, an open vowel, and some attractively grouped consonants, ending with a brisk, decisive cut-off on the 'et.' It was a pleasant word, but it brought with it no image, no sound. What he did next was done by his body only, with no detectable signal from the mind. But perhaps the bodily action was enough.

He went over to where the telephone stood on a small table, with the directory under it. He lifted it off, opened the directory with the same slow deliberateness as he had slit the letter, and began leafing through the yellow pages. He found 'Travel Agents' and selected one whose name was familiar. Then he dialled the number.

The telephone rang for a long time. It entered Giles's benumbed mind that he was ringing too early. The office had not opened yet. He was about to replace the receiver, and perhaps never take up the matter again, when someone at the other end picked it up and said with a hint of querulousness, 'Arrow World Travel. Yes, we're open, even *this* early.'

'I'm sorry,' he said. 'I'm sorry to disturb you.'

'You happen to be speaking to the proprietor. Fortunately, I make a habit of getting to the office half-an-hour before my staff to begin the day's decision-making in peace.'

'That's a very good habit.'

'Yes, I have efficient habits.' Suddenly Giles saw his interlocutor as a balding man in horn-rimmed glasses, tanned from judiciously planned visits to sunny places, very keen eyes, a trouble-shooter. 'And like all efficient people I sometimes get impatient. I hope it isn't something trivial you're ringing about?'

'No,' said Giles. He thought he could do business with this man. 'No, I don't think you could call it trivial. I want to go to Australia.'

'Australia? Any special part of the place?'

'Hobart,' said Giles. 'Can you quote me?'